Lost Legend of Vahilele

G.R. Wilson

Copyright © 2017 Georgia Ruth Wilson

All rights reserved. No portion of this publication may be reproduced, stored in any electronic system, copied or transmitted in any form or by any means, electronic, digital, mechanical, photocopy, recording or otherwise without the written permission of the author. This includes any storage of the works on any information storage and retrieval system.

This is historical fiction. Any resemblance to any actual person living or dead is the invention of the author's creative mind. This includes historical events and persons who may have been recreated in a fictional way.

Cover photo by Jennifer Noelle 2017. All rights reserved.

ISBN-10: 1974696251
ISBN-13: 978-1974696253

IN APPRECIATION

I strive to recognize the dedication of archaeologists whose efforts to define ancient history circa 1200 BC engaged my interest in the Lapita people of the South Pacific.

ACKNOWLEDGMENTS

Although this novel is purely imaginative, its foundation is based on months of research on the Fijian islands, her legends, and her people about whom I respectfully depict a fictional narrative. Many thanks to A.B. Bertini on the island of Vatulele for his encouragement. I also recognize the hours of feedback necessitated by the many drafts put before writing partners, but I could not have completed the project without their diverse comments and enthusiastic support.

A glossary of Fijian words as I understand them is located at the back

CHAPTER ONE

1950: The Storyteller

As evening shadows gather on the island of Vahilele, so do barefoot children eager to listen to this aged wise woman with piercing gaze and unruly silver-spun hair. My bronze arm stretches forward to stir the embers in the center of our circle. My tales stretch backward, the oral history of my tribe. Our future depends upon the lessons of the past.

"Deep within the long ago passage of man's turbulent Dark Ages, the gods conspired to bring two worlds together. One world would end. We must never forget this story. It is our past and our present. Listen carefully, my little ones."

They quiet in my presence, watching a tiny flame erupt as I ignite a beacon to guide them back to a crossroads in our history. "While war was waged in faraway lands, Muslims against Persians, Greeks against Romans, Saxons against Welsh, our little Fiji yanuyanu was isolated and unconcerned with worldly events.

"Our ancestors from Vanuatu in the west had braved unknown seas and settled on Vahilele with a desire to live in harmony, but they could not escape the tentacles of other societies that threatened to suffocate our independent culture. Our royalty was held in high esteem because these leaders were thought to have direct contact with the tribal gods that brought the forces of nature together for good.

"Hundreds of years ago in Na Koro, the central village on our island back then, many huts of palm branches and bamboo clustered around a grassy clearing worn down to sand and clay by generations of brown feet imprinting a legacy.

"One day, a trading canoe returned from a neighboring Fiji island. The crew was very weak, and reported that many on nearby Viti Levu were sick and dying. They were thankful to get home. But they had brought smallpox back with them, and within a few weeks, hundreds of their tribe perished, including the King and Queen of Vahilele.

"Their daughter Lapita was known for her beauty and gentle spirit. Her marriage to the High Priest had been broadly celebrated, and the birth of their son was a beacon of nui taka, the future. But the people were resentful that the power of royalty could not convince the gods to spare them in this attack by an unseen foe. They lost faith and hope. Many directed their anger and frustration at their remaining leaders, Lapita and her brother Tavale."

Carefully considering my words, I sip my yaqona, our Fijian coffee, nectar of the gods. I wait for a latecomer to get settled, and then I continue. "One day a worse peril came to our shore. There was a conflict of wisdom. Our island vosa flowed naturally like air and water because we were a peaceable people. Other languages had many words for trouble."

Through dusk and into darkness the youngsters absorb The Story. I weave a tapestry of oral tradition with my words and gestures, striving to vividly portray the personalities of the makawa, the ancient ones. As their mothers and fathers did before them, every child internalizes his own vision.

Each one hears the same words but imagines different faces performing in their own minds as I change my voice for each character. The story never ceases to mesmerize and inspire its listeners. The Story is borne on the wind. Forever.

Back to 650 A.D.

Siga

A deathly stillness surrounded young Siga as she walked the path to the Bure Kalou, the island's temple. No breezes stirred the fragrant hibiscus nor the elegant palm branches. She could not even smell the smoke from the great funeral pyre on the beach. It was as though the gods ceased to breathe upon Vahilele.

The royal family had not the power to save themselves. They had been afflicted with the pox one by one, as had hundreds of others. If the gods showed them no mercy, what chance did her mother have? Yet she had whispered that Siga must take water and comfort to Princess Lapita.

"Her son is the last of the royal family. She must be strong to care for him." Nana struggled with her words, and Siga did not want to cause her mother more anguish. Although she did not understand why a small prince deserved her care when she could be helping her mother whose blood also ran from ancient veins, Siga obeyed.

She saw only one other person roaming in the twilight. Her friend Dede Nikua plodded along in the distance under the weight of two water jugs like those Siga was carrying on a cane pole across her own shoulders. Dede also carried the burden of keeping her little brother alive since their nana had passed away under the last moon. The village had lost hundreds. Every family vale that Siga passed secluded the dead and whispers of those who would soon leave this world and join the makawa. And so she continued her assigned journey to the yanuyanu temple of the High Priest. She longed to talk with Dede and share comfort but their paths would not cross tonight.

Observing privacy and respect for her elders, Siga softly called out, "Adi. Adi. Adi." as she climbed the stone stairs. But there was no answer. She held her breath and nudged aside the white linen in the doorway.

"Princess Lapita?"

The feeble light of a dying sun showed a large area covered with woven mats fringed with shells surrounding a small circle of cold ashes. Siga gasped. The tribal spirit fire had expired! Would the entire island be destroyed? Without a spirit fire, there was no communication with the gods. Without communication, there was no protection against evil.

"Princess?" There was no answer, and Siga feared the worst. With a stick near the fire, she stirred the ashes. One bright ember showed life. She needed directions for this important task. Fearing she would trespass outside her boundary of propriety, Siga nevertheless approached the tapa cloth separating the living quarters from the public meeting room. Her cause was righteous. She peeked around the curtain, dreading what she might see.

Princess Lapita sat near her reclining husband, the High Priest of Vahilele. In her lap was the infant prince, whimpering in the gloom. His fragile body was covered with the pustules that infected his father and Siga's mother and half the tribe. The sign of the pox.

"Princess, the spirit fire is almost out." Siga's urgent whisper seemed to rip through a sacred silence.

Lapita's thin shoulders shuddered. "The gods have left us." Her voice was raspy and weak. Siga stepped closer to catch her words. Lapita's head lolled down toward her son, her bony hand caressed his cheek. The child's eyelids flicked briefly.

Siga hurried to fill a bilo with water and returned to Lapita's side. The Princess dipped her finger into the wai and sprinkled droplets onto the prince's lips. There was no response. She waned next to him and closed her eyes.

Siga took water to the High Priest who lay amid foul-smelling banana tree leaves. Her twelve years had not prepared her for so much agony. She had survived the disease but so many had not. She dampened the end of her skirt and swabbed the runny sores on his face as she did for her mother. There was no response. He was cold. His spirit was gone. She bit back a cry of despair.

A footstep outside and a soft "Adi. Adi. Adi," returned her attention to duty, the importance of keeping the spirit fire alive for others, for the rest of the tribe.

She rounded the curtain and ran into her grandfather, Matai Malolo.

"A storm is coming, child, and your nana needs you."

Faced with a family crisis, she forgot the tribal fire and ran for home.

That night, nature's fury claimed many islanders already weakened by man's disease. Siga's last vigil lasted through the cyclone, through the heavy rain, through the darkness, until her mother's hand fell from her grasp. A roll of thunder moving eastward seemed to accompany the spirit passing from a broken shell.

"She is travelling with the wind now, Siga. Let her go." Grandfather's gentle touch kept the child from embracing her mother's still form. "She is released from pain. She joins the makawa."

Siga could hear all around her the cries of despair amid the ruins left by raging winds.

"Where is Father? I must tell him." Siga rose from her knees.

"Stay here until the storm ends. Coconuts continue to fall." Grandfather embraced her in the faltering light of a torch he protected. "We must wrap your mother in the masi cloth she prepared for this journey."

Siga felt his tears on her cheek. "Do we have to take Nana where the others are laid? To the funeral pyre?" She choked back her tears.

"Yes. We must cleanse the village from the pox." In the wavering light, Grandfather propped up the damaged bamboo wall. A hole in the thatched roof had allowed a torrent of water to invade their hut as though it were at the bottom of the ocean. Blood was washed away and the smell of death replaced by fresh salty air. Their spirit fire was doused.

"But I didn't go with the wind." Siga fingered the sore on her arm.

"You are kaukaua, strong. But you take care. I could not lose you, too."

"You will forever have our beautiful yanuyanu home, Grandfather." She held the corner while he secured it with hibiscus bark rope to the poles that had held it for years until now. Floor mats and pottery were scattered around them like coral on the beach. "I must go back to the Bure Kalou."

"It is too late to help Princess Lapita. The gods allowed a foreign disease to diminish our kai, our beloved people, and Vahilele rulers did not have the wisdom to come against it. Not even our High Priest had the power to keep himself and his son alive." Grandfather tested the security of the temporary repair. "And now this windstorm. We are being punished. We have lost favor with the ancients."

Siga tried to unite the loose papayas and bananas with their baskets as the remnant of the storm moved past them. The darkness limited her efforts to put things back together. Her mother's loss left an empty place, and now her beloved Princess was gone also. Her tears were endless. She felt the hole in her heart would never heal.

"Rest, my little manumanu vuka. At first light, we will have much to do." Grandfather sat cross-legged near the remains of his only child and chanted traditional songs in remembrance of her honorable life.

CHAPTER TWO

650 A.D.

Bahram

Throughout the night, the moaning wind and hissing water issued a malevolent threat to the sailors on board the *Nabataea*. North of Vahilele, the crew barely got her sails reefed and tied before violent shifting wind currents crippled the merchant ship. Waves towered three times the height of the vessel heaving her bow toward an angry sky only to plunge it downward as the stern rose behind. Over a sharp clap of thunder, Bahram heard the hull crack on coral he had glimpsed when lightning illuminated a faint hope of land in the distance. Now the powerful sea raked the *Nabataea* over that Pacific reef, shearing off oars and centerboards. A scrappy rower disappeared into a mighty wave that reared in a flash of light, like a devil's hand rising from the ocean depths to pluck him into eternity.

"Man overboard!" The closest rower shouted an alarm as he clambered to a higher perch. Thirty men fighting to save themselves ignored him.

In the early morning chaos, Bahram attempted to descend the ladder to inspect the bulkhead and was jostled by crew scuttling upward and out. The smell of fear mingled with the odor of sweat and the fragrance of spices.

"We're taking on water!" shouted a sailor.

Bahram recognized Nawfal's coarse voice.

"The hole is too brengsek big!"

Someone below him with feet in swirling water yelled, "Keep moving!"

Over their shoulders, in the flare of a cabin lantern below, Bahram glimpsed the captain's two hounds in the rising water, swimming toward the ladder. The ship listed and the hold went dark. A dog whined. Bahram pulled himself to the deck slipping and sliding in sea foam. He strained to catch sight of the *Nabataea* captain who was obsessed with establishing a new trade route.

Wind and sea now controlled their course. The merchant ship pitched wildly and the flapping of the pilot house door was soundless within the deafening tumult. The storm's full fury was upon them. The next flash of lightning accompanied a sharp downturn of the bow, riding a churning path to a dead end. As the rigging ripped through his fingers, Bahram saw iron rivets snap like reeds, loosening lines fore and aft. The ship was sinking. Only God knew the final cost of this venture.

"Land! South!" Bahram pointed in that direction, an uncertain command. He hugged a cedar mast, squinting for sight of his captain and first mate. Without them, it was the coxswain's job to take the lead, so Bahram shouted the words every seaman dreads. "Abandon ship!" The churlish wind flung his words back to his mouth. "Brengsek!" He turned to the side and screamed. "Now! Abandon ship!"

He glimpsed Ghazi struggling with the rudder.

"Now! Now!" Bahram motioned frantically. "Jump free or she'll take you to hell!"

His friend Abu jumped first, followed by others.

Bahram stumbled to a cracked railing that rose straight up and then bucked forward into the liquid wall that surged to greet him. With mates on either side, he balanced above the foam before flinging himself into a swirling abyss. Downward he sank, kicking and clawing at a voracious ocean that sucked the boots off his feet. He fought to find air, but when he bobbed to the surface, an oak plank slammed into his head. The blow stunned him. Pain on top of cold despair disabled his willpower. Bahram drifted. Bridging the numbness, a strong tug and a taut elbow at his neck lifted him higher. It was Nawfal.

Instinct for self preservation seeped through Bahram in spite of the roar of oceanic force, and he kicked his legs again, making an effort to survive. Together they grabbed the leather straps on a floating sea chest, a temporary oasis. The two held on to a slender hope in the turbulent waves. When they saw the captain's black dog struggling beside them, Nawfal hoisted him to the top of the trunk. Now there were three clinging to a flimsy refuge.

Suddenly an unknown force gripped Bahram's leg, jerking him under black pitch. He reached down to grab long hair and raised Ghazi, who scrabbled close to the others for a hold on life. Now there were four.

Bahram tried to shout "Keep together," to the other dark shadows that surrounded him on the face of the deep, but as soon as he opened his mouth, sea water rushed in to choke him. He had to lead by example. The swarthy Persian released his hold on the trunk and began a measured pace toward the white cliffs he had sighted on the horizon. Reaching out with muscled arms to move himself forward, kicking as hard as he could, and gulping breaths of salty air, he progressed through the inky wilderness. It would be a daunting task, but Captain Koch would expect him to show others the way. He passed survivors holding on to cargo casks, some to planks, anything that floated, and he was dimly aware of shouts muffled by ocean roar, but he did not pause to rescue anyone. *I have to keep moving forward.* One hopeful breath at a time, he strained to reach the island that glittered when a jagged thunderbolt sliced the darkness effortlessly from heaven to earth.

At the barrier reef, the ocean surf clashed against the outgoing tide in a fierce battle, and it seemed to take a lifetime before Bahram was scrubbed across the coral and abandoned on shore amid fossils of shells and jellyfish.

While first light amid rose-tinted clouds revealed the remnants of the assault by surly ocean gods, Bahram dragged himself onto shore. His body had been pummeled by debris, and every bruise was deepened by the pounding breakers. Every muscle throbbed. He was thankful to dig his fingers into the sand before he passed out.

Awakened by the slurp of a ship dog's rough tongue on his cheek, Bahram saw he was not alone. Ghazi sprawled close by. Before a tropical morning sun baked them where they lay, the two mates crawled to shelter near boulders at the base of a cliff where the surf had flung a burnt-out canoe hull. Struggling to sit upright, Bahram turned to look back at the sea, still raging beyond the barrier reef that had snagged their *Nabataea*.

He reached out to pat the whimpering wet dog beside him whose eyes searched the surf. "Dedan, looks like you're with me, now. I don't see our captain."

Bahram took stock of his physical condition. He seemed to be whole and unbroken. The leather pouch containing his monetary worth, coins of copper and Sassanian gold, still hung around his neck.

Ghazi leaned against a boulder nearby, examining one of many bloody cuts. "Ripped the skin, not the bone. I live to fight another day."

Bahram saw the dog's attention shift to the beach where a handful of battered survivors along the water's edge were clustering to face a new peril. From surrounding palm trees, dozens of brown men shuffled toward them with raised spears and shouts. Most were clothed in loincloths, or knee-length fabric secured at their waists. A hunchback with a cane staff wore a headband and patterned sarong draped across one shoulder.

Ghazi pushed himself to his feet. "You have to take charge, mate," he said to Bahram.

The tallest native yelled, "Taro-va!" The islanders stayed at a distance. All of them appeared to be frail, but they had strength in numbers. Their dark eyes stared at the sailors. In silence.

Nawfal picked up a splinter of broken mast and held it high.

"*Tovolea mada*," growled the native leader, hoisting his spear. Nawfal dropped the wooden weapon at his side but flexed his fists.

Bahram scrambled up to make his way toward the conflict.

A ragged shipmate sank to his knees and bowed his forehead on clasped hands. "Mercy. We don't come to harm you. Have mercy." He spoke in Arabic, the language of traders. Another seaman followed his example, bending down until his forehead touched the sand.

The tall leader grunted and lowered his spear. "Vahilele." The islander gestured to the swells that heaved its litter of cargo and bodies upon the beach. "Phoenix *Vanua*." He approached Nawfal, the largest sailor, and put a scarred forearm across his own chest. "Tavale." He stood undaunted and held Nawfal's scowl. Then he swept his arm toward a path through the palm trees. "Na Koro." He motioned with his spear, and the other natives circled the shipwrecked traders to herd them away from the beach.

Abu broke away from the apparent captives to meet Bahram and Ghazi who lurched unsteadily toward him in the sand. "Not to worry, they're harmless. See their sores? Smallpox already has them beaten. The natives have more casualties than we do." He pointed to the edge of a clearing where bundles of wet brown cloth had been placed near a smoldering fire. "What should we do? Some of the men are afraid they'll be infected."

"Nothing much we can do right now. We're exhausted," said Bahram. *And we have no leadership.*

Months ago in a Po-Li bar, his mentor had outlined a new venture. "Simple," said the captain with eyes sparkling. "We can slide east of Sumatra to riches in paradise."

Simple. Bahram snorted at the memory. *And where are we now? Not paradise.*

Their captors led them to a grove of forty-foot sandalwood trees dwarfed by taller vesi trees and gave the parched men a refreshing juice from coconut cups. The sailors seated themselves in a protective cluster and compared wounds.

"*Kura*," said Tavale, rapping his chest. "*Kura*. Mmmmm." He held his drink aloft and drank.

Island women attended to the injuries, washing foreign matter from the wounds of those who did not recoil from the scabs on their thin bodies.

One sailor's broken arm was set by a toothless old woman. Next to him, a weary seaman mumbled, "Do you think she can handle that?"

"She can't make it any worse," said the crippled rower, "but if you hadn't lashed me to that plank, I wouldn't be here to find out."

"That was an unexpected impulse on my part. From now on, I'm going to call you Breaker."

The rower almost smiled, and nodded an acceptance of his new name.

Abu was looking all around, considering options. "We could escape to the forest," he whispered to Bahram. "See how dense it is?"

The sailor seated next to him peered over his shoulder toward the unknown.

On his other side, Bahram glanced at Abu's hawkish nose and black beady eyes. Like a bird ready for flight. "We don't have a choice, mate," he said. "We need their help, and they need ours. I will not leave our men rotting on the beach." He shared his cassava bread and water with his new four-legged friend while Tavale watched them suspiciously.

With rusty voice, Bahram took control. "Nawfal and I had the pox in Muziris. After we rest and take care of our own, we can help the villagers. Ghazi, you and the others recover our supplies. We need to inventory any rescued cargo. After we gather strength."

Sweet kura juice and sleep revived Bahram enough to consider a walk back to the beach to see the remnants of the shipwreck. With gestures, he communicated his intentions and received permission from the tall leader. Accompanied by the humpbacked native flanked by two men with spears, the sailors were taken to an area where corpses from the shipwreck had been placed. Bahram stood in front of each one, saying their names and reflecting on past conversations. He heard other survivors moving behind him, a few curses, a few painful exclamations. Several waded into the lagoon to pull out two more still floating in tidal currents. Tears dampened the faces of wiry mariners.

"If I ever get back to Bali, I have to tell Ahmed's widow," muttered one. "She's expecting their first child soon. Rotten luck."

"Have you seen Derrick, the Australian boy?" Somebody called out.

"Over here," was the answer.

"What about the first mate?"

"I found a shoe that has to be his. It's a big one, scarred by that shark bite near Palembang."

"I remember that. We ate the brengsek man-eater."

"And he was tough as shoe leather. Good trade." The joke was mumbled, and few smiled.

Bahram found the one he searched for and knelt. He bowed his head of tangled black hair to murmur in his childhood language, "Well, Captain, we made it to the end of the world. You were on the right course, but the wrong day. We had one hell of a storm." This was the man who had taught him how to sail, how to barter, how to drink. The man who had taken a chance on an inexperienced Persian youngster and taught him a skill. They were both delinquents from their different religions and found much in common. Bahram realized he had lost his best friend. "It was an honor to know you," he whispered. He removed the heavy pouch from around the Captain's neck to send to his mother.

When tears filled his eyes, he pinched the bridge of his nose and stood erect before he embarrassed himself. Sight of the captain's boots reminded him of his sore bare feet, and he quickly squatted again. *You won't need these, my friend, although I fear I cannot hope to fill them.* Bahram plucked loose a bone fastener from the captain's vest to remind himself that dreams can be deadly. He took the boots under a palm tree to try them on while he gazed over the lagoon and pondered the fate that had spared him but not Captain Koch.

Around him he heard the sounds of sorrow, one man recovering the body of his son. Another sailor wept over his lost brother. The *Nabataea* shipmates now had a stronger bond forged by the raging sea.

When he noticed the cargo floating in the lagoon, Bahram shouted to Ghazi. "Round up the barrels and put them together at the side of the beach. I shall talk to the natives about a final resting place for our men."

The man who grieved over his son approached, his blond hair a contrast to his dark-haired shipmates. "Bahram, I can't throw my son into a fire with those diseased savages."

"I will see what I can do to find a respectful burial place, William. I cannot promise anything. Most likely, foreigners brought the disease, and they might think we have it, too."

Next to him Abu said, "There's no reason to call them savages. So far they have been helpful. Besides, I thought Zoroastrians cremated their dead."

"I'm a Christian."

"I didn't know."

Bahram said, "Abu, find the Chinese trunks packed with cloth so we can properly shroud our mates." Somebody had to lead. Why not him? He saw the hunchback native squatting on the edge of the sand and walked toward him.

That afternoon, with the permission of the villagers and the loan of adzes and Tridacna shell scoops, the shipwrecked sailors scraped a trench in sandy soil. Islanders watched quietly. Abu told Bahram he communicated with one native who said he'd lost his entire family to the pox, and he wanted to stay busy to outpace despair.

"Get his name. We might need his help tomorrow," said Bahram.

The bodies of the *Nabataea* crew were wrapped in silk for perhaps the first time in their lives and laid close to each other like brothers in the womb. Boots were removed for the survivors to make sandals from leather soles. Pouches with valuables were given with the deceased's name to Bahram.

He would send them all to the ship's sponsor for the sailors' families.

The first mate was the only one not recovered, and Nawfal remarked, "He had the burial at sea that all sailors accept when they sign on for a voyage."

When the mass grave was filled in, Jews, Christians, Muslims, Hindus together, the men surrounded their mates. One of them volunteered to scratch their names on a stone to mark the place.

"I want to put a cross over my boy," said the bereaved father.

"Go ahead. It's not how you die that is important," said Bahram. "It is how you live. Good thoughts, good words, good deeds." He patted the man sympathetically on the back. "We will remember his bravery."

The silence surrounding the survivors motivated Bahram to speak out. "We remember all these men, and we give their souls back to their God. We ask mercy on ourselves, and we humbly thank the Creator for another day."

Some of the sailors mumbled, "Amen."

Dedan laid by his master's grave all night and howled, a fitting tribute to their lost companion, in Bahram's mind.

CHAPTER THREE

1950: The Storyteller

Within the circle around the fire, the youngest child's eyes are wide as he listens to the tribal story for the first time. He interrupts me to ask, "But what happened to the little girl? Where is she?"

A brother's elbow in the ribs and a chorus of warnings to be quiet stifle him. "Shhh...that's the best part. You have to wait for it!"

I wet my lips with yaqona and continue the tale.

650 A.D.

Bahram

By a unanimous vote among the sailors while they rested below swaying palm fronds, Bahram was elected to represent them. He enlisted the aid of Abu who understood some parts of several different languages encountered in his travels from Africa to Java. Under perfect blue skies, the two shipwrecked outsiders accompanied the dark-skinned hunchback on a sandy path through a tangle of foliage. Bahram was entranced by the tropical beauty surrounding him. *This must be the paradise the captain was chasing.* Bright colored birds serenaded the way past fragrant bushes.

As they trailed behind the old man, Bahram muttered to Abu. "Can you understand what the chief is saying?"

"I don't know if this fellow is the chief, but his name is Bati," said Abu. "I think he's similar to an elder on a ruling council. Nevertheless, he's somebody of importance. I can pick out familiar words because he uses some merchant Arabic."

Despite the warming soft breezes, the idyllic scene had frayed edges. Bati sat down near a large pavilion where three older women were clearing fallen branches and leaves from the area. They cast wary eyes in the sailors' direction.

Bati gestured down the path and seated himself under a vesi tree.

Abu said, "I think the old man is in pain. Let's continue on and leave him to rest."

When they came to a cluster of huts, Bahram saw the warrior from the beach who had given them kura juice. He was standing with arms crossed over his chest in front of a large dwelling set apart by its surrounding gardens. Bahram nodded at him, the greeting acknowledged by an expressionless tilt of the tall man's head. The rest of the huts looked vacant. Many were badly damaged, and a few totally destroyed. Household goods were strewn among the palm branches on the ground.

Bahram turned to Abu. "Ask that big native where everybody is."

In spite of the use of a few words in Arabic and a few foreign words, Abu had to repeat himself several times and use hand gestures before the golden islander understood and responded. Tavale pointed to the timid smoke plume rising in the distance.

"They are trying to reignite their funeral pyre," Abu told Bahram as they made their way back to the beach.

Closer to the feeble fire that consumed what was not drenched, Bahram and Abu watched as thin brown people struggled to cope with a new reality. Few of them had the energy to pick up the driftwood and drag it off the beach to place on their ineffective pyre. They moved in slow motion.

"Bati said that the European pox was brought to Vahilele by one of their own who traded in Viti Levu, the next island. The villagers are not going to trust us. There are hundreds dead."

"I understand," said Bahram. "But the sooner we help them, the sooner they will change their minds about us."

"And offer some of that island hospitality?" Abu said eagerly.

Bahram snorted. "Not to you. You are too short and too ugly."

Abu cackled.

With the sailors' help in dragging scattered dead limbs to feed the fire, soon the searing flames reached to an apathetic sky. As he worked, Bahram reflected that the fabric of his life had always been drenched with death and destruction. He occasionally had heard the echoes of fear and anguish that his Persian neighbors had cried out when fortifications of their city had crumbled before the advance of the Muslims a few years before. Today it was the impartial onslaught of disease in the South Pacific.

The Persian felt pity for the exhausted natives. They were victims ravaged by an enemy they could not identify. Certainly they were defenseless.

The next morning, Bahram collected his men and gave out assignments to sailors accustomed to grueling labor. Bahram led one group as he assessed the damaged huts in Na Koro, the main village. He methodically entered each native dwelling, searched for injured and ill inhabitants, and then marked huts to be destroyed. He tried to block out the stench of death even as his stomach roiled. Nawfal followed with his group of men, executing Bahram's decision to burn or to spare. With nostrils and mouths masked with strips of their tattered shirts, the death detail burned the first hut along with its dead occupants. The next two huts had smallpox survivors now immune, but the bodies of their loved ones were wrapped in shrouds and carried to the area designated for cremation. Bati was in charge of this last rite.

Fearful islanders came out of hiding and straggled around to watch with somber faces, many covered with runny sores. Some supported themselves with long cane poles, and some leaned into each other.

Bahram approached a dwelling with a high-cone thatched roof, a little different from the neighboring huts. It was slightly elevated on a rock-lined base with a stairway of large flat stones. It was the hut where Tavale had stood the day before.

A sailor came out carrying a small corpse swaddled forever. "Bahram, there's a woman in there, barely alive." He carried his bundle down the steps toward the beach.

An elderly woman in the crowd keened. "*Sega. Sega. Turaga.*" The wail was picked up by others. "*Adi. Turaga.*"

Bahram recognized the pain in the universal expression of grief. He paused to take several breaths of fresh air before he entered.

When he first saw Lapita, she was merely a brittle husk huddled near a cadaver wrapped in fabric charcoal-stenciled with turtles. Incoherent, she clutched reeds in skeletal talons.

"Hindu," Bahram whispered to the sailor coming in behind him. "I saw this in Srivijaya. She expects to be sacrificed upon her husband's funeral pyre. I'll get her out. You take care of him."

"Burn the hut?"

Bahram considered the rolls of parchment standing up in an earthenware vessel. "Not yet." He pointed to the various glass jars stored neatly against one wall, the broken quills, the flint and steel for striking fire. "These furnishings indicate a higher class, a position of importance." He noticed an Indonesian mortar and pestle like one he had seen in Java. "We'll wait. We want to preserve as much as we can."

With fingers shredded by battling sails and coral reef, Bahram gently lifted the emaciated woman from her knees. He pulled aside the white cloth panel that hung from the bamboo framework and shepherded her tiny steps through the doorway. Dried leaf bracelets on the wrist that he supported crumbled and fell into the silent misery surrounding them. The warrior from the beach met him outside and led him to a neighboring hut. With a bow and a slow sweeping gesture that called attention to a jagged scar on his forearm, Tavale invited them in. A pregnant woman helped to settle the patient on a pallet in the corner, and then she left without speaking. Bahram looked around at the orderly contents, sparse but clean.

The tall warrior with scabs on his face and chest caressed the woman's thin shoulder and murmured, "*Moce*, Lapita," before he followed his wife out the door.

Bahram tried to get the attention of one of the natives to help, but they all drifted away. Nobody stepped forward. So over the next few hours, in addition to directing his shipmates, Bahram took on the task of checking on this bird-like creature he had rescued. He encouraged Lapita to swallow as much water as she could handle. In other countries, he had witnessed the devastating toll of the complications from this disease. Because his own life had been recently spared by an omniscient god, Bahram was inspired to nurture another life in distress. *Good thoughts*.

As Bahram came out of the hut, Ghazi grabbed his arm. "Should there be any kind of ceremony? This is a pagan tribe. We found a pit of dead snakes that were left to feed on each other."

"Ceremonies can be later," said Bahram. "And we won't pass judgment on these people because they don't share our Zoroastrian religion. We've experienced that prejudice ourselves. Our role here is to give aid." *Good words*.

In the sun-drenched breezes of paradise, the mariners moved hut to hut attending to the despair of strangers. Cries of mourning mingled with smoke. When Bahram learned that Tavale and his wife had moved to a larger dwelling abandoned by victims of the storm, he and Dedan spent the night close to the glimmer of life in the weakly responsive widow. *Good deeds*.

There was much to do in addition to taking care of smallpox victims. Bahram's crew labored many days clearing away the uprooted trees. They learned how to split bamboo canes, beat them flat, bind and cover them with plaited coconut leaves for roofs. They helped weakened natives replace broken frameworks not only in the central village, but also at the fishing village near the northern beach where the *Nabataea* sailors had been washed ashore. It was several days before Bahram learned of a third village on the southern tip of the island.

"Me and Nawfal followed along the shore to see how big this place is. We came upon flooded fields and then more *vales*," said Abu. He rested his sinewy frame near the shed that the sailors built to store the ship's rescued cargo.

"Another village?" Bahram sagged next to him. "More bodies?"

"We didn't wade through water to count heads but this village is smaller, maybe thirty people moving around."

"What is a *vale*?"

"Hut. Home."

"So they need help, too," said Bahram. He plucked at a sizeable hole in his breeches.

"I sent a couple sailors down there when we got back. I didn't have time to explore," said Abu.

Nawfal sat down beside them. "Looks like we are still in rescue formation. But some of our mates want to leave."

"They will have to exercise patience. The outriggers have to be repaired, and we have to wait for the navigators to recover their strength," said Abu.

"What are you saying? I've been a rower for years." Nawfal's thick eyebrows rose.

"There's a big difference in paddling a smaller craft. You wouldn't last an hour."

Nawfal snorted.

Bahram interrupted. "What was growing in the fields?"

"Taro. The natives call it *dalo*. It's a dry, starchy root that can be used in a variety of dishes. The leaves are also eaten. Right now those fields are under water."

"We'll have to drain them. Tomorrow. Anything else?"

"The cyclone devastated the fruiting breadfruit trees, but on a knoll higher up from the taro, away from the beach, there is another field of yams."

"Good, we need more. We have close to two hundred people to feed, and a diet of fish and bananas will get tiresome."

"Dog stew sounds good," said Abu.

Bahram growled, "No. He earned his freedom. He is a survivor, like us." He rubbed the captain's button that he had attached to his own shirt.

Abu paused before he changed the subject. "I want to see what is on the northwestern side that slopes upward." His dark arms glowed with rivulets of perspiration where he had ripped the sleeves from his tunic.

"Those were the cliffs we saw before the *Nabataea* went down," said Bahram.

"One day I might get inland, but it's rough hacking through the scrub brush."

Bahram clapped his mate on a shoulder. "One day at a time. I don't think we are going anywhere for months. I understand a merchant ship rarely comes past. Maybe once a year."

"I still want to know how big our prison is," grumbled Abu behind his sparse beard.

A clucking commotion behind rustling bushes interrupted their conversation. They heard a loud squawk. Amid a flurry of feathers, Dedan came out of the forest with a large black bird in his mouth. He dropped the load at Bahram's feet and wagged his tail.

"Looks like chicken dinner tonight," said Bahram glancing triumphantly at Abu. He hooted loudly as he roughed up the dog's head. It was a strange sound on this somber shore.

CHAPTER FOUR

Lapita: The Legend

    Lapita lay motionless, with eyes closed and arms at her sides. She breathed in the smell of acrid smoke and putrid sickness that lingered on her sulu and body. Tears still burned and trickled down her temple onto the pillow of banana leaves beneath her head. Alone now, she relived her son's last breath, when she begged the gods to take her instead. She had willed herself to die with him. Before the pox extinguished his thoughts, the High Priest had expected their son would survive to lead their tribe. Her husband's spirit abandoned his body shortly afterwards while she still rocked and wailed over her little one. Their spirits rode the wind together. Even though her beloved husband had counseled her to stand kaukaua, stay alive for the sake of their people, Lapita accepted the fate of a widow in her tokatoka community because she wanted nothing more than to join her family in eternity.
    She felt her shoulders raised slightly, her oily hair gently pushed off her face and her parched tongue tickled by moisture. She couldn't swallow, couldn't struggle. She could do nothing but exist. Wai dribbled down her throat. A deep warm voice breeched the heavy fog around her ears and gently murmured. Moment to moment, she became more

aware of the presence of the strong arm that held her upright, the dark hand that swabbed her fevered skin.

As he bathed the crust from her eyes, light no longer stabbed at her senses, and she could make out a foreigner of robust build with heavy black beard. Her own kai did not have such hairy bodies. This was a stranger who continually spoke words Lapita did not know.

"I am Bahram. Drink."

The second day this Bahram tried to get her to take a few grains of cassava. He said "eat." But she could not. She slept a while, and he was gone when she opened her eyes. He left a bowl of tavioka near her hand, but she had no strength to reach for it. She dozed again. When she awoke, the bowl was broken, the tavioka gone. Lapita understood. She had been judged by the tokatoka and found guilty.

The tribulation started under the last moon. The Vahilele men who had gone to Viti Levu with masi cloth to trade for sugar cane returned with the pox, a death sentence they shared with half the tribe. Too late, their Chief realized the cargo spread disease. Too late came his order to burn the outrigger canoe. Evil had befallen Vahilele. Lapita knew the islanders believed that the royal family was responsible because it did not have the power to protect the island. Her people would believe it was the gods' will. As the daughter of the Chief, and wife of the High Priest, Lapita was part of the failure. She must die. It was required she share her husband's cremation. Lapita did not expect the native women to minister to her in her darkest hours. She expected them to help her into the next world.

Lapita drifted through dreams of past days when she was a youngster ignorant of sickness and sad times. She had often watched her friends, boys who were only a little older than she, push off in their canoes and paddle across the lagoon, through the passage in the reef into the open ocean. Then they had their hands full with the excitement of traveling toward the rising sun's first strands of daylight. Stories returned to Vahilele about the brave navigators who found new islands to settle. Sometimes these friends returned, and she witnessed that in a short time they had grown into wise men.

She often begged to go but her father said her place was in Vahilele. He would tell her stories from his grandfather about their ancestors who settled Samoa and Tonga. Some returned to Vahilele to lead others in a flotilla of double-hulled canoes to a new land. Always they would keep a connection to their past, just as Vahilele kept a tie with Sigatoka and Tikopia which were still connected to Papua and Vanuatu. Lapita heard the stories often, and she remembered the history of her people with their golden skin and raven black hair. Her father commanded her to stay in Vahilele. Until he lay dying, and then, he told her she should seek the will of the Phoenix.

On the fourth day Lapita was more alert. She could hear the morning welcome by the goshawks overhead. She imagined the sun god Tiki rising out of the distant water, pulling his fiery gift of light and warmth. While she recited prayers with eyes closed, imagining a sunrise, she heard a muted footstep and felt the scaly wriggle of a boa constrictor along her leg. *What did it mean? Danger or gift?* The snake could wrap itself around her neck and eventually steal her breath, but she was ready. If her presence was truly ca, if her people thought her evil, she should die. But in her past, priests ate the constrictors and used the vertebrae for royal necklaces. A loyal supporter could be bringing tribute that she was too weak to handle. She felt pressure around her arm. Suddenly running steps and loud curses accompanied a jerk at her side and noisy stomping close to her pallet. Through her eyelashes, she saw the man named Bahram lift a writhing five foot snake of light and dark brown markings and carry it outside. Decades of family tradition created anxiety in the treatment of this snake. *If a sacrifice is rejected, there will be confusion within our kai, an insult to the giver regarding his spiritual intent.* When Bahram reentered the hut and helped her to drink and eat a little tavioka, she asked for her brother. "Tavale? Tavale?" Her voice was a scratchy murmur but she had faith that he was still alive, and she had to talk to him.

Tavale came that night. She heard the shuffle of bare feet beside her.

"Lapita, I am here."

She rolled her head toward him and tried to open her eyes, but they hurt with the bright light of the fire in the center of the vale, shared from his own. She settled for his presence. When she mumbled his name, Tavale placed his big hand over hers and squeezed.

"Vinaka." She tried to smile.

"You must try to get stronger. Our people need guidance."

"You are the first son. You will lead."

"You must help me. You are older and Nana always said you had the favor of the gods."

"Because I look for it, brother." It was the first effort at humor she had attempted in weeks. Their long relationship was a comfort. "We are surrounded by the wisdom of the ages." Her voice was weak and soft. "We cannot see it like we see the sky and the sea, but I can feel the connection when I search. I can breathe it in, and my heart swells when it touches me." She motioned for wai, and he helped her take a sip.

"I remember how you cared for me when I was little. You took me down to the beach and let me play in the lagoon." Tavale's stern mouth almost smiled. "But you thought you were my boso."

"You were a little boy unafraid of the force of the waves crashing on the rocks. I feared you would swim the lagoon. One way." Lapita's words, her vosa, wavered.

"I liked the steady rhythm of the water, even then. It was dependable and the same for everybody. Although I longed to be favored by Dakuwaqa."

"You must have been a favorite. Dakuwaqa could have bitten off your arm," she whispered.

Tavale rubbed the long scar above his wrist and remembered. He grinned.

"When you rode with Uncle Momo the first time, you rejoiced when the spray hit you on the face. He said you were born to be a navigator."

"I learned much while paddling between islands. I saw that the night sky has many paths marked by the stars." He laughed as he reminded her. "You were so jealous. You put a hole in my canoe when I returned."

Her laughter was soundless puffs of air.

The night moved on. Bahram came in and left again without conversation, leaving the royal heirs to whisper their stories. Tavale told Lapita that he was prepared to be the next chief and lead their people in the tradition of generations before him, through the messages that she heard from the makawa.

"Even if you are now too ill to read signs, listen to Bahram. His arrival shows that the gods look favorably over all the kai Vahilele." Tavale's tears glittered in the firelight as he took his sister's hand. "It is my turn to watch over you. Sleep, beautiful sister. Ni mataka will come soon."

The following day, Tavale's wife came to bathe Lapita, rub her skin with fragrant oils and wrap her in fresh masi cloth. Melane's burnished face was marked by the pustule scabs that testified to her own battle with smallpox. Lapita lay on her pallet surrounded only by family who sat with her for two days until she was stronger and could feed herself. As Lapita showed signs of recovery, the elderly women in the tribe showed signs of mercy toward her. They served her offerings of kura juice. There were no more broken bowls or stolen tavioka.

As Melane lovingly washed the thick black hair of her aunt's daughter, thereby a cousin as well as a sister-in-law, Lapita made plans for the ritual to ensure Tavale's baby would be born bulu, healthy. She must do everything possible to keep the royal line connected to their heritage in Viti Levu. This was her most important role.

"Melane. Bring to me my rosemary leaf, cinnamon bark and ginger," she whispered. Hearing her sister-in-law's silent fear, Lapita explained. "The pots with the half moon at the Bure Kalou."

"Do you think my baby will have the pox?" Melane's lip trembled.

"That is not for me to know until it is time to know. Also get the raspberry leaf and the big bilo with the hawk wing on the second pole. Siga knows which ones." Lapita was puzzled by the hesitation. "Did my little Siga recover?"

"Your helper lives. Her mother passed on with the wind of the cyclone, as did two sick children in Na Koro. Many from the fishing village were taken. A hut in the field village collapsed, and three strong tagane are no longer with us." said Melane. She fanned Lapita's damp hair back from her face on the pallet. "I will do as you ask in the morning. Today you need to rest. Vaka malua. Sit in the sun and our koro neighbors can see you are kissed by the gods. All marau, all happy in Vahilele." Her throaty laughter brought a smile to Lapita.

"Melane, I need your help. This is important for your little peipei, our new prince." Lapita reached out with her spindly golden arms which had escaped all scars. She patted Melane's shoulder, darker than her own. "Also I need the ashes from Bete's lovo, his underground oven. Kerekere, help me." Lapita lay back on her pallet. Her soft smile was firm, but she was so tired.

Their village needed a High Priest, a new Bete. Would she be able?

Lapita grew weary of silence. She was alone in the vale, but aware of the activity going on outside around her. She slowly moved herself to a sitting position. *Maybe this will be a good day. I do feel better.* The Persian was nowhere around. She called out softly, "Siga." There was no answer from her caregiver, the granddaughter of an elder council member. Even though Siga was inexperienced at cooking and cleaning, she was a fast learner. Siga's wavy black hair and golden brown skin attested to her ancient bloodline. The Princess regarded her as a younger sister.

Lapita put one foot on the floor and slowly rose, balancing carefully with her hand on a sturdy pole that supported the roof. She hesitated before moving because her head was swirling. She wilted to the matted floor just as her helper came around the curtain.

"Princess, let me help you." Siga put down the water pitcher she carried and hurried to take the arm of her mistress.

"Vinaka. I feel stronger today." Lapita's smile was feeble. "Before I stand."

"Get back, little girl," barked a foreign vosa. Steel arms encircled Lapita and raised her to a sitting position.

Siga cried out, "Saka! Sega! No!"

Lapita looked into an unfamiliar black face. "Who are you? What are you doing in my vale?"

"Sorry to startle you, madam." He used the language of traders.

Lapita did not understand all his Arabic words. He tried speaking in other strange words, but she shook her head.

In the vosa of their yanuyanu, Siga told Lapita, "Saka is a sailor. A friend of Bahram's, the man who lives in this vale with you."

"Abu," said the little man and pointed to himself.

"Abu," repeated Lapita. "Vinaka."

Abu backed away and regarded her with bright eyes making her aware that her twisted sulu revealed her long legs, thin and weak from no exercise. She pulled them under herself and sat back on her heels.

Siga offered cool wai to her mistress and stood at her side.

"That is an unusual design on your pottery," said Abu in Arabic.

"Pottery?"

When he pointed at the cup, she said, "Bilo."

"*Bilo*," he repeated. "And this cloth?" He fingered the sulu that Siga wore.

"Masi sulu."

"*Masi*. It's called tapa elsewhere, but this workmanship is better quality."

"Work?" Lapita regarded the curious little man who was trying to speak to her.

He imitated the pounding of the tree bark that made the masi. "Hard work."

"Cakacaka," she said.

"Much *cakacaka*," he agreed with a smile.

Lapita smiled also. The effort to use her mind was energizing. When Abu left, she lay down again with the sense of improvement. The activity had exhausted her, and she slept under Siga's vigil.

CHAPTER FIVE

Bahram

Bahram sat with some of his shipmates in the shade, their backs against a hut. "We need to organize the three villages on the island with a common purpose," he said. "Now that the natives are recovered from the pox, they are in a position to rebuild." *Good words*.

"The natives rest after the midday meal, and they rest again before their evening meal. After the singing and dancing, they rest again." Breaker gestured at the closest vacant clearing. "They have recovered, but do you see anyone working?"

"I am working on my artistic skills," said Nawfal, whittling a whistle similar to one he had as a boy. "Some of our mates are busily repairing huts for our own *Nabataea* neighborhood up the hill where it's cooler."

"I am busily watching the women walk past," said Abu. His grin gleamed in his thin ebony face. "No complicated plans for me."

"This should be a serious discussion," said Bahram. "Too many native survivors sat down with their grief wrapped around them like cloaks, and they are still sitting. If they had work to do, they would have less time to dwell in misery. Look at our sailors. They could also be grieving and complaining, but they are moving forward." He had given much thought to the benefits of a new agenda. *Good thoughts.* His was a bold plan of communal living where some men fished, and some men grew crops for the island, and some men repaired canoes and fishing nets. "We could help the village leaders plan a course for a new tomorrow."

"Since Tavale was the chief's son, he'd be a natural leader." Abu yawned and stretched.

"Except that he rarely speaks. I think he resents that I'm sharing a bed with Lapita."

"Is that the native *vosa*, 'sharing a bed'?" Nawfal chortled. "I'd be resentful too if it was my sister."

"You are jealous that sister is my friend." Bahram winked at Abu. "I told sister that she should be grateful I kept her people from heaving her into a fire along with her dead husband." He stroked Dedan as the big dog lay against his bare legs stretched out in the sand. "She understands." Tattered trouser edges had been cut off. Now his legs were as dark as his arms and chest. Coral cuts had healed well and were almost invisible. "She is an obedient mate."

Bahram recalled the wilted grace and beauty that aroused his desire to bring Lapita into his bed before the other sailors could persuade her into theirs. Her gentle spirit now reminded him of Shahrbanu, the Persian maiden at home he had once hoped to marry. He had departed his country because he could never be worthy of one in her position. An island princess was a good alternative.

"There are three old men who still have the clan's respect. I think they're the only ones who remain from a ruling council," said Abu, always alert to his surroundings, always clever.

"I've seen them sitting in the same spot every day. They must be the wise men, the thinkers," said Nawfal. He snickered. "But then, I haven't seen any workers."

"No cakacaka here." Abu laughed.

"Caka what?" said Nawfal.

"Cakacaka! Work!"

"Their way of life has been devastated." Bahram was willing to take the high road befitting a future leader.

"Everyone deserves another chance. Have we not been given ours?"

"Why don't we make plans to leave this place? We have the coins to get a ride to Vuda Point harbor." Nawfal looked hopefully toward Bahram. "We could even barter some of the merchandise we rescued from the *Nabataea* cargo for a place to stay. Like the leather and the copper. Although, it might be a nice gesture to leave the silk here for the ladies. They have been hospitable."

"We need to investigate before we load up our comrades and move. We could be stranded there among cannibals."

Abu pointed toward a path at the end of the clearing. "Kai Vahilele must have some kind of industry. Over that way is a large black cauldron sitting on ashes under a shed. Probably related to their tapa cloth." He yawned again. "When I awake from my nap, I'll ask questions." He grinned at two attractive native girls whispering together on their way down the path.

"You are easily converted. And distracted." Bahram shook his head. He needed a dependable first mate. Too many men required detailed instructions.

"Girls are running around half naked. What do you expect? It's hard for a man to think about working," said Breaker, running a stick inside his bandage to scratch his arm.

"Even the ugly women look good without clothes on." Ghazi's heavy jowls were covered by a heavy black beard, like a bear.

"You were on a ship too long," mumbled Nawfal.

"I got off in time, mate."

"Just in time," said Breaker. "I'm looking for happy times now. Excuse me. I think that young lady wants to oblige me."

"She's too old. I like the younger ones," said Abu. "I am an Epicurean," he snickered.

"My religion don't hold with that idea." Breaker left the group.

Ghazi snorted. "He has a religion? I hadn't noticed."

"Life gets hard soon enough." Nawfal stood and stretched his large frame. "Let children be children."

"You take care of your life. I'll take care of mine," Abu snapped.

"Pay attention now," said Bahram. "I am trying to discuss a serious issue. Down by the lagoon, they have several double-hulled canoes with platforms connecting a long side with a short side. Maybe that industry would hold their interest."

"Those are outriggers. And well made," said Nawfal. "Tavale's friends returned yesterday. They left the island in three canoes and came back with only two, loaded with breadfruit."

"So they must have traded an outrigger," said Bahram. "And you say they are well made, in spite of the lack of iron? These people live like their grandparents, with concern only for today's food and entertainment. They don't even have wheels on this island." When Dedan stood up and shook, Bahram rested an elbow on his knee pulled to his chest and stroked his beard. "I still think our late captain had a good idea to develop commerce. It didn't work out for him, but I heard him talk often about the high prices he could command from goods in the Java bazaar in specialty products."

"Don't forget that continental traders take the Silk Road through hostile deserts and have to pay taxes to highway robbers. Kai Vahilele doesn't have wheels, but then they don't have tariffs either," observed Abu with closed eyes.

"Right. And camels need food and rest. Which adds to the cost of doing business," said Nawfal.

"Captain Koch was a wise man with experience on the Silk Road, navigating over the desert by the stars. He expected to use the same stars over the water," said Bahram.

"He was unusually wise," agreed Nawfal. "I never understood how he got around the pirates in the Red Sea."

"His was a good idea to go further east, but his timing was bad." Bahram spoke reverently. "He didn't respect the seasonal winds that carried us miles past our destination, and it was a fatal mistake for him. It's a wonder that eleven of us made it to shore." Unconsciously, he rubbed the captain's button on his shirt.

"The question is how long will eleven of us stay here?" Nawfal cast a sidelong look at Abu.

CHAPTER SIX

Lapita

Lapita awoke to a peace that told her Bahram had left their bure, their sleeping room, which was smaller than what she was accustomed as wife of the High Priest. The night before, he had shared his plan to go to the field village, the last area that needed repair from the storm two moons past. Lapita rose, leisurely enjoying her privacy.

The laughter of children at play gave Lapita's heart a pleasant nudge that reality shattered when she abruptly recalled that smallpox had taken most of the children. So who would be scuffling in the forest? She raised her bamboo blinds but saw no one. The occasional hoots that she had identified as children were getting further away.

Since she needed water that her young helper had failed to provide for her bath, she would seek her own. She felt kaukaua, her legs stronger than the week before. When she was first married she could do everything by herself even though she always had the assistance of servants as daughter of the king. She picked up a pitcher and stepped into the sunlight. Immediately she felt chastened. Her first duty was to be thankful for what was freely given to her. *All knowing Degei, how generous you are. Give me strength through your Phoenix spirit.*

Lapita walked the path into the forest where early

morning shadows still held the evening's cool air. A short walk from Na Koro brought her to the tumbling brook where two youngsters frolicked under their mothers' close supervision. She had often brought her son here, a time of simple pleasure that in retrospect she valued more.

An old memory guided her. She put aside her pitcher to get wai later, and she climbed the path that ran alongside the freshwater stream flowing from a higher origin. She no longer heard the squeals of happy toddlers downhill. There was only the brook gurgling over rocks gradually flowing south, like a determined child seeking its way to the mother ocean. How strange the quiet where there was once continual joy. The pox had reshaped her island culture.

Shortly before the path curved around the boulders forming the virgin pool, Lapita heard rustling leaves and snickering within the foliage. She suspected the ages-old spy game. *Some things do not change.* She quietly made her way around thick undergrowth to a grove of tropical chestnuts. Two boys perched in a tall tree whose secondary branches made a dense hideout close to the pool where four naked girls chattered, oblivious to the presence of male observation. Lapita approached the base of the tree, eye level with another youth who had just started his climb amid the multiple trunks.

"Young tagane!" She spoke with authority. "What do your friends look for? There is no fruit in that tree."

The startled boy jumped down at her feet. "Princess! Ahhh... we are playing a game of war." His dark eyes were stretched wide, his feet rooted but inching away as though disconnected from the rest of his body, with an urgent mission to flee.

"The only war around here is on the ground, not at such heights." It was all Lapita could do to keep from bursting into laughter. "I know you are too thoughtful to spy on young girls in the bathing pool. Do you know these girls? Are they playing this game also?"

"No, Princess." The boy's mouth dropped open in horror. "They do not know we are here." Lapita could feel the youngster's fear, and she felt compassion. She called up to the boys higher in the tree. "Young tagane, come down." They obeyed and stood before her, trembling.

"You are the son of Rangi, the navigator?" She addressed the last one to stand before her.

"Yes, Princess," came the bleak response. His brown skin lost a shade of color.

"I think he could use your assistance. It is more wise to learn what he can teach you than to steal secrets." She looked at the others. "Nothing good hides in shadows."

"Yes, Princess," they chorused.

"You may go."

The boys' feet turned to run before their shoulders did, and they collided, fell, scrambled up as one, and scampered away. Lapita had to cover her mouth to contain the merriment. How much joy her people brought her.

A sharp pang of sorrow reminded her that her own young son would never pass through this stage of burning curiosity. But there were many sons who were lost too early, and she must take pleasure in the few who survived.

Lapita returned to the path that carried her around rocks to the virgin pool. And there was Siga, laughing with three friends, her lower half submerged in water, elbows anchoring her to the rock where her friend Dede Nikua perched, knees to her chin, arms around her legs. None of the girls had on sulus, innocent as the young sea turtles who instinctively made their way to life-giving food though danger was all around. Before the pox, dozens of youngsters convened here.

This was the virgin pool for girls over ten years old, where the secrets of womanhood were shared by older teens. This was the school of life where girls learned that the responsibility to tribal survival flowed between their legs. Here they learned the cycle of life requires blood, the hope of the future.

Lapita paused at the edge of the stream. When Siga waved at her, Lapita motioned the child to her side.

"Do you need me, Princess?"

Siga broke away from her friends to splash over to Lapita, and the princess noticed the soft mounds of the child's wobbly breasts had grown, the nipples still pale. *My little friend will soon be thirteen, a young woman marked with monthly flow.*

A deep sadness overtook Lapita, and she leaned against a vesi tree shading the pool.

"Princess, are you ill?"

She folded Siga in her arms, the pure flesh against hers igniting a heat that burned through Lapita's being to consume her own childhood and memories of lost desire. "Be careful, manumanu vuka. Enjoy today, it is all we have."

Lapita assured her young helper that she would not need her until later in the day, and continued her walk to the headwaters of the stream to see who might be at the bathing pool for older women. In one corner among the rocks covered with bubbling water sat a thin marama Lapita had known as a youngster. Her skin was marked with ugly scars of the pox that suggested lonely days ahead. They talked about the past, the people who had died too early, the difficulty of adjusting to silence. At first the former playmate was hesitant to share with the princess, but Lapita's gentle questions opened a time of healing conversation.

When the woman left and Lapita was alone, she sat with her feet in the water and nurtured her own psyche, dreaming away the morning hours. She could not recall the last time she enjoyed the cool refreshing spring by herself, and she stayed longer than she intended. A break from Bahram's energy was welcome, but eventually she must focus on her responsibilities. She had planned to visit the fishing village, and if she didn't go now, it would be dark before she returned. Her legs seemed kaukaua but she needed to walk more often for longer stretches. She left the bathing pool and headed down the path. No young boys were watching from the trees.

CHAPTER SEVEN

1950: The Storyteller

I pause to consider the youngsters surrounding me, children who have already witnessed difficulties in their own lives. Tribal stories confirm that every generation has their struggles and the purpose of history is the recognition that together we can survive by learning from past mistakes. To do this, we must remember them. And draw our own strength and wisdom from the supernatural.

My duty is to retain and recite the story as told by the ancients, not my personal interpretation. I will be replaced one day by a younger storyteller, perhaps one who sits now before me. Only from a distance can a pattern be seen by weaving the past and future together.

Is it wise to tell the whole story? There are many disturbing truths but must they be shared? Will they understand? I know the traditional answer to these old questions, but some junctures carry more purpose than others. This is a difficult one: two babies, one frail and one bulu, a story common to every generation.

650 A.D.

Lapita

In the fishing village, Lapita and her helper cared for the woman whose labor pains were close together, her body wet with perspiration. Siga rinsed a sea sponge in a bowl of cool water with lavender and gently bathed Maca Matanitu, a recent widow. Lapita was worried because the baby seemed very small, but the labor pains had progressed for a long time as though this peipei was definitely intent on coming into this world soon. All Lapita could control was the sharing of her experience and encouragement for the mother.

Maca Matanitu moaned and drew up her knees. Lapita gave her an infusion of rosemary and patted the hand that clenched the covering of the pallet. In spite of the difficulty, the princess was content to be back in a role of helping her people.

"It won't be long now, Maca Matanitu," Lapita said. She hoped. Perhaps they would welcome a new warrior like his father who had died from the pox.

Through an opening in the back wall, she saw Bahram lurking in the forest and went out to him when he beckoned.

"You go," she said, brushing the humid air with the back of her hand. Through Abu, Lapita had learned many Arabic words but relied on gestures in case she misused them.

"You avoid me." He fingered the cowrie shell necklace around her neck.

She stiffened. He had touched without permission, without respect. Like he petted Dedan.

"Go away. You worry mother. She should be calm," Lapita hissed.

"Princess! Come now!" Siga's voice was frantic.

Lapita hurried into the new mother's vale. Siga held a bloody infant still connected to his unconscious nana. Siga's eyes were huge, and she trembled all over. The baby was silent. Lapita took over, instructing her helper to get more water. The tiny boy was too fragile for this world, and his spirit soon departed. For several days, Maca Matanitu herself hovered on the edge of life. The women of the village kept her company, and the warm breezes flowed continually and the ocean murmured.

Melane's baby came three weeks later. A healthy boy. His was a special position, the eldest son of the eldest son, the hope of ni mataka, tomorrow and beyond. The news was joyfully taken to the island of Beqa where aunts, uncles, and cousins also rejoiced, making plans to travel to Vahilele with their gifts for the ceremony set with the next full moon. Mother and newborn stayed inside away from neighbors until the Gathering of Family, when his name would be given to him by his oldest male relative, Melane's father, Chief of Beqa, who was also Lapita's Uncle Momo.

Lapita was grateful to Bahram for diligently caring for her, bringing her from a desire for death to a desire for life. She willingly learned his language, adding new Arab words to the vocabulary of the traders' vosa she had learned as a youngster. But there was more to learn than words. She and Bahram came from different cultures, and he continually questioned what Lapita thought was fact.

He had said, "I haven't seen Melane out with her baby. Is something wrong with him that they would hide him?"

"Melane and peipei stay in vale until sevusevu. That is our way."

"Why?"

"Peipei eldest son, prince."

"Will somebody try to kill him? They tried to kill you, the elder child of a king."

Annoyed, Lapita had shaken her head. It was very difficult to explain the importance of the eldest son to somebody who showed little interest in understanding. Her people treated Bahram with much respect as though he were superior, but when the bure they shared was dark except for a mound of embers, and Bahram sought pleasure from her body, she had her doubts that he was sent from the gods. She could not help but compare her late husband's gentle touch to the rough selfishness of the Persian. Her spirit rebelled at being treated with disrespect, though her intellect told her to be patient and endure the moment. When he slept, she crept away to the nurturing harmony of her yanuyanu beach where she collected her strength, her kaukaua.

She was confused by two conflicting role models. Her father, Tui Turukawa, had encouraged her to be hospitable to visitors. "Women are soft and offer comfort. Tagane are strong and provide safety." Lapita received contradictory advice from her mother, sister of a tribal chief, who taught her to use her mind to lead the people. "Women are wise and work toward unity."

Lapita's husband had been an interpreter of messages from the makawa assembly, and as Bete, he nurtured the spiritual gift he saw in Lapita. Remembering this encouragement, Lapita continually approached the sun god for direction every morning. Lapita knew she was not content to serve a new mate, but she didn't want to be rude to the man who had encouraged her back to good health. The royal princess wanted to chart a course for her island's future and blend the lessons of her elders with the new lessons of the current world.

One night when Lapita crawled to the vale entry, swallowing sobs of despair, an unexpected movement in the shadows startled her. "Shh." Her shoulder was pressed gently and a familiar hand stroked her hair. Lapita did not cry out because she knew the touch of her sister-in-law.

Melane pulled Lapita to her feet, and they tiptoed behind the huts like children escaping authority. The newborn suckled softly, secure in Melane's embrace.

"Why are you outside my bure?" Lapita whispered as she took small steps along the path toward the beach.

"The little one was restless, and I was walking him. I heard you cry out." Melane adjusted the baby and brushed her hand against Lapita's back in the dark. "You have rarawa, a deep sadness?"

"I do not complain."

They walked on the beach's pale nuku in silence before Melane took Lapita's hand. "It seems our tokatoka forgives you. The gods blessed you with a new mate, like a new beginning. He has a soft tongue and strong directions." Melane put her arm around Lapita's waist. "Dear sister, does he hurt you?"

"It is my soul that is bruised when I am set aside as a broken bilo."

"I see the pain in your eyes."

"It gets harder to repair the damage."

"You must not allow yourself to be a prisoner. Tavale will protect you. He knows you suffer."

"My father expected strength from royal blood." Lapita gulped back a sob.

"Your father would not allow you to be a prisoner. Your days of mourning are soon over, and you can return to the home of a Priestess."

"I am not a priestess, Melane. I am a humbled widow with no children."

"But our mataqali clan needs a new Bete."

A murmur from the sleeping baby caught the smiles of the two women. They looked down at the baby bundle so content in the love that surrounded him.

"Sleep marau, tiny prince." Lapita brushed his soft head with her kiss. Although her body ached and bled from Bahram's pleasure, she drew comfort from Melane, the strength of the past. And for the sake of this infant hope of the future, she would work to be kaukaua and whole. The waning crescent moon reminded Lapita of a larger dependable framework in which she had a place. Her kai respected the order of the universe, and she must search for her purpose. She breathed deeply, seeking peace for that day only.

The morning of the day chosen for the Gathering of Family was bright and beautiful, befitting the start of a new era for Vahilele. As the eldest relative on the island, Lapita was in charge of the ceremony. She was still frail but she would not ask help from Bahram to make preparations for the sevusevu to be held at Tavale's hut. She was happy about seeing her mother's clan, but she yearned for independence. Since she could not find her young servant, Lapita was concerned she herself would have to carry the large Tanoa bowl. Until today, she had avoided the pyramid vale, Bure Kalou, home of the priestly implements. Now it was time to return. *Where is that child?*

Lapita pulled back the sun-bleached masi cloth that someone had hung over the doorway of the hut she had shared with her husband. The new panel through which spirits entered replaced the white linen cloth that had been burned with the Bete. Tears filled Lapita's eyes as she entered, unbidden scenes of past days flitted across the memory of her nursing newborn, in the comfortable companionship of a wise husband. His duty was to love Vahilele, but in this vale, he loved his family best. With the flame she carried, she lit a candle to scatter the shadows. The smell of sickness and death was a hurtful memory, cleansed by the scent of sandalwood.

Lapita heard a footfall and briefly closed her eyes, controlling a rush of nausea. She could not endure Bahram's disrespectful presence on her threshold at this moment, but the peaceful silence that surrounded her was assurance that it was only her young helper who stood courteously behind her. Siga was the energy behind cleaning the Bure Kalou and keeping it prepared for Lapita's return, whenever the Princess was ready. The pots of herbs were in their places, the floor mats swept clean, the Tanoa ready for the preparation of Yaqona for the family.

"You did well, Siga. Vinaka." Lapita's voice was shaky. She did not turn around.

A moment later, the masi panel was pulled back and a shaft of sunlight spilled briefly onto the floor. Lapita was left alone with her memories and her tears.

CHAPTER EIGHT

Bahram

Bahram wished he had put on his sandals made from the soles of the captain's leather boots. He could not go barefoot like many of his mates who had adapted to the rough sand. Bahram's feet were still tender. He hurried to catch up to Lapita on the sandy path from Maca Matanitu's hut to the main village.

When they entered privacy under a cluster of palm trees, Lapita turned to him, eyes narrowed, and spat out in Arabic. "You do not go to the bure of Maca Matanitu. Women care for mothers and babies."

"You avoid me. Are you angry because I want to help? Have you forgotten I took care of you?" His voice rose. "Nobody else would feed you, and now I need permission to talk with you?" He tried to take the handle of the basket she held.

Lapita quickly transferred the basket to her other hand. "I take herbs to sick. You help men feed village." She set a fast pace, and he followed.

"I am not a farmer or a fisherman. I am a leader." Bahram took a deep breath. "I saw your family arrive from Beqa, and I would like to meet them. Abu told me about an important ceremony today to name Melane's baby. I think it is appropriate for me to escort you since we live together. Why didn't you tell me?"

"You are not *tokatoka*. You do not know our language."

"I will stay in the corner and be silent if you wish." He grabbed her elbow. "Lapita, I care for you. You are still fragile, and I am concerned."

"I have Siga." She pulled her arm away from him.

A woman's voice blared across the village common ground among the larger huts. "Lapita! Here we are! Lapita!"

She could not ignore the trumpet of her Nana Hewa, and Lapita turned to wave.

"They are here. We show *marau* before them." She smiled at her mother's brother and sister bearing down on her.

"They hold hands as though they are still children." Bahram was surprised that Uncle Momo was so large. His sister was delicate with darker skin and fuzzy hair like Melane.

"Elders need help to walk on bumpbump path."

When they came close, Lapita dipped her head and reached out for their embrace. "*Cola. Ni Bula.* We are honored that you come to Vahilele." She spoke in their own vosa. Bahram had to guess at the conversation. Her aunt folded Lapita in a cautious hug and then passed her fragile hand to Uncle Momo's large one.

He held her at arm's length with a thoughtful gaze. "*Sa Bula, manumanu vuka.*"

Lapita's obvious pleasure in his greeting rippled through her laugh, and she directed them along the shell path to a bure where they could rest until the ceremony started. Bahram could only speculate and assume he knew what was said. It was earlier reported to him that Tavale had spoken with them at the lagoon and was taking the cousins to their lodgings for the week. One of them brought a pair of boa constrictors as a gift for the new prince, and Tavale gave orders to ready the pit next to the Bure Kalou. First, the snakes were brought to Lapita, and Bahram saw that she was pleased. He didn't understand why.

Bahram nodded to Lapita's elderly relatives, and they extended their hands to him. "*Saka,*" they said, followed by other words he didn't recognize.

Lapita translated. "*Vinaka* for help to Vahilele. They invite you to baby *sevusevu.*" She gave him a wooden smile.

"Tell them I am delighted to accept." Bahram gave the visitors a courtly bow. "I will get ready."

"Wear *sulu* to *sevusevu*. Do not shame *tokatoka*," said Lapita. "Siga take to *vale.*"

"Will she bring me one of your husband's dresses?" He spoke in Arabic.

"Husband?" Lapita's brow wrinkled for a second, and then her eyes widened. "Bete."

He shrugged.

"No!" She turned and left him alone while she walked arm in arm with family on each side.

The neighbors of Na Koro gathered outside Tavale's large hut in anticipation of the announcement of the child's name after the sevusevu. Bahram noticed the five visiting teenagers flocked to islanders of their own age as did the two younger children. All of them wore elaborate necklaces of hibiscus and fern leaves. Lapita escorted her aunt and uncle to her brother's vale.

Uncle Momo entered first, and bowed to Tavale who stood near the doorway. Lapita and Bahram entered next. Tavale gestured for Bahram to remove his sandals. Everyone else was barefoot. Nana Hewa immediately made her way to the sleeping baby wrapped in brown masi cloth.

"*Totoka peipei,*" she said. Gently she rubbed the baby's arm with her index finger which she put to her lips, then to his tiny foot.

Uncle Momo approached his grandson and smiled his approval. "*Tik hai gone.*" He took his seat at the head of the rectangular pandanus mat in the honored position for the Yaqona ceremony. Behind him Siga and two youngsters were ready to mix and serve the kava.

Lapita explained to Bahram that Tavale's family was responsible for putting on the floor new mats that Nana

Hewa would take back to the island of Beqa. Tavale's family also provided the food for the festivities which included all of yanuyanu Vahilele.

"Are you feeding everyone?" asked Bahram.

"Neighbors now family," whispered Lapita. "Pox took *mataqali* Vahilele."

Each guest greeted the parents and admired their son. When everyone was seated Uncle Momo started the ceremony with uplifted arms. The sevusevu participants sat cross-legged with wrists on knees, palms up, and eyes closed. Except for Bahram. He didn't understand the chanting and responses from the audience but he assumed it was a universal religious invocation. Soon everyone quieted and whispered to each other. Then Nana Hewa and Uncle Momo started talking at the same time. Bahram turned to Lapita for an explanation.

"They talk names for baby," she said.

"Uncle Momo shakes his head whenever Nana Hewa makes a suggestion," he whispered back and noticed that Lapita almost smiled. Maybe she was no longer angry at him.

"*Peipei* can have many names. Nana Hewa offers '*Nanoa*,' of the past."

When Melane was asked, she suggested "*Veiwali*." Bahram looked at Lapita.

"Laughter. *Peipei* brings laughter to clan."

Bahram saw the tear in Lapita's eye, but he knew not to touch her. He had noticed that touching in public was close to forbidden except for the elderly. He understood the word "*tabu*."

Then Tavale was asked if he had a suggestion, and he said "Tui Turukawa."

Lapita leaned close to Bahram to tell him that had been their father's name.

Uncle Momo and Nana Hewa looked at each other and both shook their heads. Uncle Momo suggested another name "Tui Waitu."

Lapita whispered, "Grandfather's name honors sea."

Nana Hewa nodded and suggested "Tui Buka."

"Grandfather from Beqa island. *Buka,* fire."

After other suggestions and conversation, Uncle Momo clapped his hands.

"What happened?" asked Bahram.

"*Peipei* has name. Waitu Buka for grandfathers. It is proud name."

Bahram watched the baby's parents whose broad smiles lit up their corner of the hut.

"We call him Yaca," said Lapita with more tears. "Now, Yaqona, to mark this day."

In a large wooden bowl, Siga mixed with water the kava root she had chewed. A younger girl helped her strain it through a cloth into the Tanoa bowl. When it was ready, Siga dipped some into half a coconut shell and held it high to slowly pour it back into the serving bilo. Tavale was the taster who decided when it was of the correct strength. He immediately nodded at Siga and smiled. "*Wai donu.*" Lapita circled the Tanoa with her hands to bless its effect on this family, and nodded for Siga to pour the first cup which was given to Uncle Momo. Before this highest-ranked family member received the cup of Yaqona, he cupped his hands and made a popping sound three times. He took the bilo and drained it without hesitation. Lapita said "*Maca*" and the entire group clapped three times. One by one according to tribal rank, the cup was shared with the rest of the family. Seven adult cousins from Beqa followed Lapita's turn. When each one finished, they clapped their hands and repeated "*Maca*."

Bahram was the last one to be offered the bilo, and he glanced at Lapita who watched him without expression. He nodded at her, clapped his hands and proudly drank his portion. It tasted like Po-Li coffee. His tongue was numb.

CHAPTER NINE

Siga

Siga came out of Tavale's hut to pour the pottery wash water on the lavender plants as Lapita requested. In the distance she heard the blast of the Davui, the royal trumpet heralding the progress of the royal family who was showing the new prince his island. They would be surrounded by their guests and a growing crowd from the three Vahilele villages. Siga was surprised to see her grandfather. Matai Malolo rested in the shade of a vesi tree.

"Grandfather, do you wait for me?" Siga offered her hand to help him up. He seemed to have gained back the weight he had lost with the pox.

"Child, you have brought honor to our tokatoka today. An honor surrounded by a sadness because your nana and grandmother were not there."

"But they were, Grandfather. I heard their voices in the wind."

Matai Malolo smiled and patted her head. "It is good you listen to the words of Princess Lapita."

"She is wise." Siga hastened to add, "And you are, too. I'm happy you are proud, but I only did what she told me."

"You mixed the Yaqona that Prince Tavale accepted on the first try. A very difficult task! I told Nana Hewa, 'That's my granddaughter,' and she said you are an excellent helper. And pretty, too."

Siga thought her heart would burst. Princess Lapita had also told her she'd done well. And now praise from the head of her clan. This was a day to remember because of good things. She did not have many of those. She hadn't seen her father in a long time, and she worried.

"I will help you return the Tanoa to the Bure Kalou."

Siga's smile wavered. She didn't want to hurt him. "No, Grandfather. The Princess told me to do this myself. She said not to let anyone help me."

"Manumanu vuka, she did not want one of your young friends to carry it. I am on the council. I am trusted to drink the Yaqona. I can be trusted to carry the bowl. It is too heavy for you."

Siga looked up and down the sandy shell path shaded by palm trees and tipanie bushes with their fragrant velvet flowers. The Princess was nowhere around. She saw only a large brown lizard skittering across the shells. It was hard to say no to Grandfather who had taken care of her since her nana died. He'd cleansed her hut so she and her father could stay in the home her mother loved. He was the head of her tokatoka and a trusted leader of Na Koro. Siga felt the weight of her basket.

"I'd welcome your help. Vinaka."

Together they walked the path to the temple. Matai Malolo carried the large pedestal bowl used for the ritual sharing of kava, and Siga carried several smaller bowls. On each piece of pottery was the significant stamped pattern of her ancestors, curved facial features amid a variety of squares and rectangles. Grandfather walked slowly, and Siga matched her pace to his. Almond eyes on the Tanoa in Grandfather's arms stared at her. They were the eyes of the makawa judging her disobedience.

"Have I told you about your name, little one?"

Siga had heard the story many times, but she knew her grandfather enjoyed the sharing. "Tell me, Grandfather." She turned to look behind them. Nobody was there.

"A very long time ago, our family lived where the sun retires. Not me, you understand. My grandfather's grandfather told this story, and it has been repeated. Our people lived on an island where they built vales on long poles above the beach. Every vale had stairs like our Bure Kalou. Many of our kai died from the sickness that flying insects brought, but a black people living there were not affected by these bites. We respected the gods' gift to them, and our people moved to yanuyanu Viti Levu. My grandfather told me about his grandfather's place where the river met the sea, where he and his family farmed salt to trade. He described the way the sun kissed their vale every morning and so they named the river Sigatoka. It was very peaceful there, and they felt safe. Until a dark tribe came out of the mountains and attacked their settlement. Many of our people were killed. These tall men were fierce warriors with large clubs that they used to crack heads like coconuts. Our people moved again. This time to Vahilele, and here you were born, a marau child whose sunny smile kissed our vale every morning. Siga."

She nodded. "It must be very hard to load everything you own on to a canoe and move to a faraway place."

Grandfather usually said that Vahilele was theirs forever. He did not respond this time.

At the bottom of the stairs to the platform of the Bete hut, Matai Malolo paused, breathing heavily.

"Grandfather, I'll take these bowls up to the top and come back for the Tanoa."

"Do not treat me as though I am useless. The Tanoa is safe with me. I am not so old I cannot climb steps and hold a piece of pottery at the same time." His vosa was sharp.

Siga bit her lip to keep from saying it wasn't a piece of pottery, it was the sacred Tanoa, over which generations of royal children had been named. Her stomach churned, but she respected the decision of her elder. There were only six steps she told herself. She hurried ahead. Surely Grandfather knew he should not enter the Bure Kalou when the Princess was gone. *I will put down my basket and hurry back to carry the large bowl.*

It only took one misstep and a heartbeat to shatter history. Siga heard the crash and burst out of the hut through the white covering of the entry. She saw Grandfather on the ground holding only a fragment of the bowl. A larger potsherd lay at her feet. She knew she would be punished.

CHAPTER TEN

Lapita

While her family strolled the island, Lapita went over the details of the feast and entertainment to be held after the sun slid from a purple sky. She thought it strange her young helper was missing. Siga would have been much appreciated at the large banquet where extra hands and young legs were needed to assist their elders. The twelve-year-old could have been anywhere, probably with friends and basking in the praise of her Yaqona performance, but Lapita was disappointed that Siga did not attend.

Tribal songs and dancing continued into the night. Baby Yaca was passed from one adoring nana to another until he grew fretful. Melane nursed him and offered him to Nana Hewa who received him as though she had won a prize. The elderly woman rocked him to sleep, refusing to allow anyone else to hold him. Tavale and Melane moved from one conversation to another until Melane was exhausted and took the infant home. Lapita retired shortly afterwards. She ached from the many days of preparation for the festivities, and she had to get up early to oversee tomorrow's competition between islands. Rivalries were long established. Under Tavale's supervision, four canoes had been readied for the races in the lagoon. Elder Dau had overseen the preparation of the competitions of a distance spear throw and a shell toss.

The last time Lapita saw Bahram, he was chatting with Uncle Momo about outriggers and tapa cloth on Beqa. With Abu as interpreter, it didn't take Uncle Momo long to launch into past stories of brave young men riding the South Pacific waves. Lapita knew he could talk until dawn.

The Princess removed her feather headdress and brushed her glossy hip-length hair, but it was difficult to braid without help. She gave up and lay down on her pallet, the fresh banana leaves cool to her skin, a lavender fragrance helping her fall asleep quickly.

She slept soundly, but at daybreak, as novice Bete, she stood at water's edge with arms upraised. Lapita welcomed the sun god rising out of the sea to greet her, early morning rays filling her body with light, but she could not connect with the wisdom it carried. She had not disciplined herself to focus completely, and she could tell she was not alone. The distraction behind her destroyed the fragile thread, and she broke the whispered chanting of her soul. Lapita lowered her head, opened her eyes and turned around.

"I knew I would find you here." Nana Hewa's smile was bright in her thin face. She hobbled forward. "You have your Aunti's devotion."

"I seek her wisdom." Lapita took her elder's outstretched hand.

"In time, little manumanu vuka. Walk with me. Tell me of your new life, how you survived the breathtaking loss of your family, how you rebuilt your villages."

Together they strolled on pale nuku that slowly absorbed the heat of the sun's strength. Arms wrapped around each other's waist, one much taller than the other, they shared the soft blending of sun and sand. The closeness bound Lapita to the comfort of family, the forgotten peace of sharing joy and pain without guilt.

"What is there to say, Nana Hewa? My family is with the makawa, and one day I will be with them. Until then, I live like other women, trying to be useful to my kai.

Nana Hewa stopped and took her niece's hand in hers. "You are not like other women, Lapita. The royal blood of a lost tribe makes you and Tavale different. You must have more children."

"I will leave that to Melane. Her blood is mine, and I love her."

"No, her royal blood is from the ancient tribe of Chief Lutunasobasoba. Your mother knew this, and she would want me to speak for her. My sister felt honored to be chosen by the King but she was not chosen by love. It was her blood connection to the Sawau tribe, their spiritual history, that made her the ideal mate for your father."

"My father loved her, Nana Hewa."

Her aunt looked out to the gentle swells coming for miles to break on this reef, throwing spray high into the air, individual drops sparkling like jewels before falling to become one force. The power of the tide was invisible as it churned downward, and out again in constant motion.

"Your father was peaceable and resisted conflict. He loved everyone, manumanu vuka, and he learned to love your mother because it was best for his people. My sister could be stubborn when she felt the direction of the Phoenix." Nana Hewa smiled. "She fought for the good of Vahilele even when the kai did not understand."

"What do you mean? Everyone should seek a wise path to follow."

"Some people see what is best for themselves, but others who are more generous want to make these selfish ones happy, and they give up their own best interests. Their weakness is loving others more than themselves."

"I don't see that as a weakness."

"If your father had made the laws, he would have decreed that each person do whatever made them happy. But joy is not the same for all. What makes one person happy will irritate another." Nana Hewa smiled. "I think of Dedan. Not everyone loves your koli."

"I know. Some want to eat him!" Lapita laughed and put her arm around Nana Hewa.

"There must be laws to live with others. Your husband's wisdom came from the makawa, and it gave your father a lifeline to hold on to. Your husband, as Bete, championed a strong foundation for your tribe, the wisdom of our ancestors surrounded by a King's benevolence."

Nana Hewa stopped, pointing toward the great reef that protected the lagoon from the white swells beyond. Her finger was adorned with the royal cowrie shell ring of her Sawau tribe. "Like this island in the midst of the sea. We are all islands unless we reach out to each other and share our strengths. The ancient navigators learned this when they travelled from one island to another."

They stood together for a moment until Nana Hewa patted Lapita's arm. "Now that is enough talk from an old woman. I must rest. I trust you will find your way alone."

When Lapita finished her devotional, she walked along the shore to the fishing village to check on Maca Matanitu before the canoe races. On the way, she heard an urgent voice behind her.

"Princess, I need your help." She turned to see Elder Matai Malolo struggling in the sand, waving to catch her attention. The corpulent elder was out of breath. They squatted in silence until his breathing slowed.

Lapita took the time to summon her own energy as it had been a long time since anyone asked her help. She did not speak until he started the conversation. In the distance, she could see a crowd gathering while teams assembled for inter-island competition.

"May I speak?" He huffed his words, his face still red.

"Of course." She was curious at the new respect this elder showed toward her.

"My granddaughter did not come home last night."

"Do you know the reason?" Lapita waited patiently for the story.

"Yes, but I do not know where she might have gone. I fear she is hiding because the sacred Tanoa bowl was accidentally broken."

In spite of the warmth of the sun, a chill seeped into her bones. Lapita said, "A very long history of royalty was named over that bowl. She has reason to be ashamed of destroying the memories of the heart."

Matai Malolo paused. "She is just a child, Princess." He looked down at his hands. "One wrong step can bring so much heartache."

"Do you know where she hides?"

"I think she looks for her father. Lalai has not been home since his wife died. He goes from hut to vale from vale to bure, whoever will feed him. It is one thing to be lazy and refuse cakacaka, but if he hurts my granddaughter, I cannot be silent. I am the only justice for his child who has the generous heart of her mother."

"We all have rarawa, sad times. Like our people of all ages. I am marau she has you to help her out of the darkness."

Matai Malolo picked at a broken fingernail and did not speak again.

Lapita stood.

"I will ask in the fishing village if someone has seen her. She must face the consequences of her mistakes in order to grow kaukaua."

"Vinaka, Princess."

The first vale where the Princess stopped was empty, and she continued to the next one where a young girl Siga's age lived. Lapita recognized the girl who had helped with the Yaqona at the baby's sevusevu. She stood as Lapita approached.

"Cola, young one. Is your nana at home?"

"No, Princess, she is at the water." Her large brown eyes stared at Lapita's royal cowrie shell necklace and bracelet of shark teeth.

"Have you seen my helper Siga?"

"No, Princess."

"Did you see her last night?"

The child lowered her chin. "No, Princess." She fidgeted with her sulu.

Lapita paused. "Vinaka." As she moved down the path she heard the swish of sand as the youngster fled in the opposite direction.

In front of the next hut, three women sat together mashing dalo for their midday meal. They had not seen Siga. Lapita went deeper into the palm forest to Maca Matanitu's hut.

When she approached the vale, she heard voices. A man's low tones and a woman's higher pitched answer. Lapita did not want to interfere. From the path, she called out. "Ni Bula. Ni Bula. I come to talk with Lalai."

While she awaited an answer, she lifted her face into the refreshing breeze, closed her eyes, and opened her heart. Yes, she felt assured this was the vale where Siga's father hid. But the voices died down, and nobody came to the entry.

Disappointed, Lapita continued down the trail that would take her to the lagoon where several boulders formed a natural pool protected from the force of the ocean tides. Perched on the highest one was Siga. An occasional large swell rammed the base of the rock, sending a spray over the child who sat cross-legged, upturned palms on knees. Lapita smiled, recognizing Siga's imitation of her own meditation pose. Lapita moved to the edge of a smaller rock and stepped up to its center. "Siga. Cola."

Siga jerked her head toward Lapita and away again to stare at the ocean. Not fast enough that Lapita missed the red eyes. The tears that had been on Siga's face no doubt were lost in the ocean spray. Siga gripped her knees tightly, and a small shudder went through her shoulders and back.

Beyond the reef, a seabird flying low on graceful wings suddenly dipped and caught a small fish from the surface. Tradewinds blew Siga's black hair across her face. She raised her chin and snuffled. Lapita waited to speak. "It is another beautiful morning that Tiki brings us. Yes, little one?"

Siga nodded. "Princess?" With trembling lips, Siga looked at her mistress. "Vohosia, vohosia. Do not send me away."

Lapita stood quietly, feeling the warmth in her soul, searching for wise words to share with this little sister.

Her experience with raising children was not limited to her own infant because the kai children were always shared by the community. There was never a formula for handling unruly behavior, but there was a loving pattern in a culture generous with patience. Lapita put out her hand. A spirit of forgiveness washed over her, sorrow for the pain that Siga must feel. She had suffered enough.

"Come down, manumanu vuka. We have cakacaka."

"You still want me?" The confusion on the child's face was replaced by joy, and Siga clasped the elegant hand as she jumped off the rock. "What work is there?" Siga hurried along, wiping her eyes on the edge of her sulu.

"We must make a new Tanoa. I have a design I want to use to honor Yaca. A flame coming out of the ocean waves. Waitu Buka." Lapita walked ahead. "There is an abandoned vale up this hill that might make a good location for a work area."

In the north center of the island, they found the hut taken over by forest vegetation. Lapita determined the nearby slope would accommodate an earthen oven for drying the vessels as she remembered. She knelt to inspect the sand, to squeeze it in her palm.

"This is a good combination of clay and sand for making pottery, and our freshwater stream is close by."

Siga took it all in, looking far to the horizon just as her mistress did.

CHAPTER ELEVEN

Bahram

While Lapita's family from the island of Beqa visited, most of the Vahilele natives stayed up late with feasting and conversation Bahram did not understand. In the middle of the day, it seemed the entire island slept before the inevitable contests between islands. Because Bahram could not accustom himself to that schedule, he left Na Koro every morning to explore Vahilele.

Bahram walked into the clearing shared by four huts repaired by the sailors for themselves, a home away from home. They called it Nabataea Village, a temporary base until they were able to leave. Breaker and Ghazi sat cross-legged, bowls in hand. Bahram sat down next to them. "Beautiful place for dining, is it not?"

Nawfal leaned against the framework of his hut's doorway.

"I'm trying to teach this slow learner how to eat gruel," said Breaker. "Three fingers, mate. Watch me and learn." He easily scooped up some of the breadfruit paste and put it into his mouth.

"It tastes spoiled." Ghazi's hooded eyes wrinkled as he unhappily followed instructions.

"Don't insult our hosts, mate." Nawfal settled next to the others. "This dish is the difference between life and death when they have a bad crop year. They bury this breadfruit underground where it stays cool and ferments."

"I told you. It's spoiled." Ghazi pursed his lips.

"No, it's ripe." Nawfal laughed. "I've seen you eat worse. Remember Java octopus?"

"What about the betel nuts? Now that was a reaction to remember!" Breaker's laugh was contagious.

Ghazi shuddered. "You harbor memories to use against me. I have to find different mates."

"And I was going to ask you to be on my canoe race team."

The sailors burst into laughter. The memory of yesterday's embarrassment for the outsiders generated sustained hilarity. They had learned that a sailor on a merchant ship needs different skills to pilot a canoe loaded with coconuts.

Avoiding the first two days of festivities, Bahram took easy paths to the south end of the small island to visit the newly planted taro fields where the farmers had placed suckers in holes made with digging sticks. The crop had a good start that promised a profitable harvest in several months after the new year. He had hoped to clear more land to extend the fields for export crops, but nothing would be done while revelry distracted the natives. In spite of Bahram's instructions, the workers in the field village were not going to be pulling weeds this week. There was little to see, and he was only bringing aggravation upon himself.

Eventually Bahram looked for a new route, and his attention was captured by the high cliffs to the north. He determined this a worthy goal for the following day and thus set out early in the morning with Dedan. The first sandy path he followed through dense green jungle met up with another, and he had to make a decision on which of these forks to follow. His choice did not lead to the top of the cliffs, as he had thought, but meandered down to a rocky beach strewn with boulders. When he got hungry, he cut a papaya fruit from its slender stem and ate slices with his knife.

The sun was still low on the horizon on the other side of the island, its rays subdued by vegetation upon the headland above him. The shore line narrowed here on the western side, and Bahram turned south to stroll under huge vesi trees that towered over palms and flowering tipanie bushes. The path ended at a pile of rocks of different size and shape, and Bahram's spirit of exploration convinced him to clamber over them. He smiled to himself as he ventured along the fractured limestone. Here was a tale to share with Abu who had become lazier and no longer interested in the wilds of Vahilele. Bahram's turnshoes were hot and heavy, but he was glad he wore them. He needed solid footing.

The salt spray bouncing off the boulders refreshed him and brought up memories of balancing on moving decks, wind caught in sails, the camaraderie of shipmates shouting at each other as they put energy into controlling the forces of nature. Later he had seen how powerless men really are in the path of a fierce wind and rolling ocean. But he loved the challenge, and he had survived.

The mariner faced the sea, his back against the cliff face, the pounding surf at his feet. He contemplated the explanation of his survival. Was he in better physical shape than the sailor he had seen whisked from the deck like a water barrel broken loose from its moorings? He didn't think so. He touched the back of his head where a knot had reminded him for weeks that he had received help from Nawfal when a loose plank had briefly knocked all sense from him.

Bahram moved on, his mind engrossed in the moment that his *Nabataea* captain no longer had. A sliver of smooth rock was like a wedge cut into the cliff facing west, and he paused again. Above this ledge a lawedua left her nest in a crevice not yet touched by the rising sun, and he raised his eyes to watch her flight. There on the face of the white limestone streaked with dark gray he glimpsed reddish brown paintings. He climbed his way closer to see the petroglyphs where former residents had depicted the story of the island of Vahilele. He counted more than fifty scenes grouped in panels and hidden in part by vesi trees clutching the foreshore. One painting showed two birds, beak to beak. One was a canoe with two sails facing north, taking direction from a star sketched over its bow. Another was a whitetailed bird, no doubt a lawedua. One of the images showed a side view of a warrior with club in raised hand, one knee bent in dance, mouth open under a long narrow nose. Another was an aristocratic head crowned by a headdress of feathers, with large almond eyes that seemed to stare into his soul. He felt fear and chuckled at his imagination. That same image was on the pottery that Lapita used. One panel had many figures including small ones, probably children. Near two tiny hands overlapping was an odd painting of a bow and a three pronged arrow aimed at a large dark shape Bahram did not recognize.

The Persian had a flash of inspiration that he could add to this historical record. He belonged in this legend, remembered as one of the greatest, a warrior rising out of the sea foam, a god who rebuilt an entire tribe ravaged by disease. His spirit soared with the white bird as he contemplated his immortality.

The following week the visitors who had come for the naming of the new prince left Vahilele to its own sleepy routine. Bahram walked with Uncle Momo and Nana Hewa down to the lagoon. Their large raft with the comfortable structure in the center was ready for them. Blowing in the breeze was a tapa cloth hanging from the yard arm. The activities of the busy natives were watched by a visage on this flag, a stern face with slanted eyes and dark eyebrows blended together in the middle to make a low wedge for a nose. Bahram decided this must be the talked-about Tiki god whose small mouth was hidden within a dark beard, not typical for golden islanders who had little facial hair. He considered using a similar design for himself when he added his likeness to the cliff painting.

Bahram examined the royal raft with the natural interest of a mariner. It had nine logs lashed together and the front was pointed like a canoe. In the center was a deck of split bamboo covered with loose mats of bamboo reeds. One of the natives showed him that underneath the platform was storage space. The bow and stern had no deck and provided sturdier footing to the lookout up front and the helmsman who operated the steering oar in the back. Hollowed-out vesi logs on either side accommodated rowers when the raft was not under sail. He could see how the ocean waves drained out between the logs. Abu joined him to help with conversation, and Bahram found out that the masts were of tough mangrove wood. Cracks were sealed with breadfruit sap.

When Nana Hewa was ready to board, Tavale steadied the elderly woman as she waded into the shallow tide. She gave no notice to the edge of her beautiful sulu soaking up the seawater. One servant knelt so she could place a bare foot on his knee, and another rower at her side gave her his hand. Two strong men lifted her with ease to the platform. She waved at Lapita and disappeared into the covered shelter.

It took six natives to assist the girth of Uncle Momo, but they had the procedure down smoothly, without conversation. He took his place on the platform in front of Nana Hewa's hut, a water gourd secured with coconut fibre over his shoulder and across his chest. A small wooly-haired man in loincloth nimbly climbed aboard and positioned himself next to Momo. Abu told Bahram that this was the navigator.

The rowers took their places, and Tavale pushed them off with shouts of good wishes. Two canoes moved into the breach of the coral reef leading the raft with the royal family, followed by several outriggers laden with gifts.

Bahram watched them until they were specks on the open sea, his thoughts of sailing again to unknown places contrasting with building a life on land. *How can a new life compare with the satisfaction I had with the old?*

CHAPTER TWELVE

Lapita

Lapita sat cross-legged in front of the spirit fire on the floor in the vale she shared with Bahram. So much had changed. This had been her brother's hut, now it was hers. She had been married to the Bete, the High Priest, the most powerful man on the island. Now she lived with a mua, a foreign sailor. The world was upside down, as though the gods had shaken it, and she had fallen head over heels into a deep hole.

Nana Hewa's words bubbled up over and over. "You are special. You are like your Aunti, your father's sister. You can speak to the wind."

Lapita shook her head. No, she wanted to go with the wind, to travel the waves like Tavale did, free from bonds to a vanua. She wanted to see the faraway countries that exported exotic wares, like the silk cloth or the bronze figures she had seen on the occasional ship anchored off her reef. Long ago, a handsome Captain Safwan had captured her imagination and for years she kept dreams of him in her heart, bringing them out for solace when her father gave her in marriage to the Bete, a much older man. The High Priest was a serious tagane who spent hours in communication with the spirit world. Hours in silence, hours in reverie, hours on the beach with eyes looking out over the ocean whether it was smooth or rolling water. As a younger woman, she assumed this a common bond, hoping that he, too, wanted to travel. But the Bete wanted to travel further, back to the world of the island spirits, the makawa, the land of the dead who advised the land of the living.

Lapita wanted an exuberant life, and she showed this patient man how to appreciate her gifts of love. In giving of herself, she learned to love him. Now, she missed him so. His absence was a ragged hole that would never be filled again. *How can I live with this emptiness, without my soul's mate?*

Lapita laid another stick of nokonoko on the embers. The Bete used to sit like this for hours. Whatever did he see in the flame, what wisdom helped him to share wisdom with others. She missed his patience, his confidence. He had gentle strength, not the domineering strength that Bahram brandished.

She shook her head again to dismiss this foolishness. Comparison was fruitless and would leave her in despair. Though Lapita might like to have an infant to love, she could never replace the son she lost.

Nana Hewa said she spoke for her sister, Lapita's mother, when she told Lapita, "You are the last of a golden race. Protect the blood of your ancestors." Nana Hewa had been gracious to Bahram, but she seemed to be warning Lapita to mate with her own kind. Did she mean her brother? Some royals on other islands married family to protect the lineage. Melane's great-grandparents traced their family back to Chief Lutunasobasoba, but Melane also had blood from the original golden settlers. She was of respected royal lineage but not a pure Golden.

Lapita could not change her island unless she changed herself. She had to strengthen her spirit. The Bete's memory, his pattern of living, would make her whole. She wasn't sure how, all she could do was reach out as he had done, as Aunti had done.

As she concentrated on the flickering flame, her spirit stirred. Lapita knew she was on the right path but she didn't know where it was going. It was time to put into action her plan for Aunti's old vale.

Lapita looked through the village for Siga's grandfather. She found him in the meeting area sharing stories with his neighbors. She motioned him over to her and politely asked about his health and his brother's family. They walked together as she first put her new project into words.

"Elder Matai Malolo, there is a hut on the slope midway between Na Koro and the South Village. It has been empty for a long time."

"I know the one, Princess. Your father's sister lived there. She was an unusual marama."

Lapita smiled. "When I was Siga's age, I followed Aunti around the island and learned how different plants could heal or poison. She was very patient with me. Her presence brought harmony. In my dreams she sits behind a mist, like a white veil. I can see only her shape, but I can always smell the lavender she kept in pots outside the door. Sometimes she speaks to me. Last night she told me it is time to prepare her vale to make a new Tanoa."

Matai Malolo looked away.

"You will be in charge. Get several tagane to clear the forest around the front of the hut. I will need space for six pottery workers."

"Yes, Princess, we will have to replace the walls and roof."

"No walls, Matai Malolo. Repair the reeds and sennit that roll up for light and air."

"But Princess, the blinds won't be strong."

"Only if they are stolen." Lapita laughed.

"Nobody will steal from you."

"Then the vale will be strong enough without walls. I don't want to be closed in. I want to watch the sky."

Lapita visited the work area every day, making suggestions. She remembered how the vale used to look and decided to leave two walls to protect the essence of history under its roof. The tagane tried to please her. Bahram did not meddle or ask questions, and the couple saw less of each other during the day. Lapita grew stronger.

One day he finally said, "You are gone every day. Is somebody ill and requires your care?"

"We need a place to make pottery before we lose the skill."

"Excellent," said Bahram. "Make a lot of it, and I can sell it at the bazaar in Viti Levu."

Lapita stared at this man she could not understand. Her pottery was for the kai, the new design in honor of Yaca. There was no need to make more to get gold coins that could not be eaten.

When the last worker left, Lapita surveyed the finished shed. She had changed her mind again and put up one long northwest wall with two squares that could open with bark hinges for a cooling breeze. Coconut trees were cleared around the vale so falling fruit would not damage the pottery or the workers. The two tiny islands off the small end south of Vahilele were now visible, across from the field village, and the vast ocean was beyond that. She could hear its distant heartbeat.

Lapita sat on the pandanus mats that Siga brought. The vista of traveling clouds over distant fields soothed her spirit. She could almost hear the soft laughter of her aunt. This hut was where she first heard the stories of the ancient ones, and where she received forgiveness when she admitted she put a hole in Tavale's canoe. How could she hope to fill the gap between generations like Aunti did?

A movement down the slope caught her attention. She watched Matai Malolo approaching, and she blinked away her tears. Her Aunti said to build a new Tanoa, and she would.

"You asked to see me, Princess?" He wiped the sweat from his brow.

"Sit and rest, Elder." She waited until he sat cross-legged beside her.

"Do you remember when we sat here and listened to the stories of the ancient ones?"

"Many times we listened to the stories. I must admit I could not repeat them as you did. Even as a small child, you seemed to breathe them in."

"I was anxious to please." She paused. "You were in the older group that took over the care of our kai Vahilele." A smile played on her lips. "I remember your wedding, Matai Malolo."

"A very long time ago, Princess."

"Your wife was admired for her golden beauty, like a soft sunset, and you were like a strong golden sandalwood tree."

His eyes sparkled like the distant ripples of waves, but he was silent.

"And I remember her soft glow brightened with age. Her words were true and became a piercing sun ray to light our way. Pure as air and water."

"Always true. Vanua, forever. Always vanua."

"Do you not think all our memories are connected like holding hands from the present to the past and beyond?" She waited for him to nod in agreement. "It is shameful to break that trust. Do you agree?"

Again he nodded, color slowly moving up his neck to his face. "Forgive me, Princess. It was my carelessness that broke the Tanoa."

Lapita nodded. After a suitable pause, she said, "Bring to me the pieces of the broken Tanoa that are in the Bure Kalou. Siga is there now, waiting for you to help her. We will make new out of old."

Her commandment became the beginning of a legend.

CHAPTER THIRTEEN

1950: The Storyteller

"Within three months, the villagers' lives slowly mended, and 180 survivors were handling the duties of the thousand who had lived there before the pox. Bahram could see in the faces and conversations of the sailors that they were ready to move on. Their work here was done. After their large vessel failed to provide safety in a boiling sea, few were ready to ride in a canoe until they witnessed the prowess of the healed navigators and understood the stability of the outriggers. Only one sailor bravely caught a ride, without farewell, on the second trading canoe that took taro to the neighboring island of Viti Levu. The others waited for a ship that never came.

"In the following days, Bahram and his shipmates had many discussions about leaving Vahilele. William still was tied to his son's grave, two of the rowers were enjoying the respite from grueling labor, and Breaker and his mate could not be convinced to board a small craft when their much larger ship had been broken into pieces. Every sailor gave their expertise to the repair of the fleet of double-hulled canoes damaged by the cyclone, but they all agreed that a successful trip with a loaded outrigger was dependent upon the skill of several healthy paddlers. The wind and waves of the open sea were a fierce challenge. When they had signed on to the *Nabataea*, they expected to be gone for two years. What difference would a few more months make? Now they were resigned to adapt."

650 A.D.

Bahram

Bahram frequently walked with his dog as he reshaped his plan to stay on the island, a decision fragmented by his years at sea. He was hesitant to start a new venture because he was comfortable aboard a ship, but this last trip showed him the true risk. Perhaps he should quit before he was lost at sea.

"What do you think, boy? Should we stay here or find a way off this island?"

His family had been traders on land. Maybe that's where he belonged. With heartfelt apologies to Captain Koch, he considered a new life. Among the crew there was continual talk of leaving, and soon that talk would generate courage. Since he was their leader, Bahram felt obligated to help them make a wise decision. He also missed the comforts of a more civilized world although he could think of nothing he could not live without, except meat.

Bahram wandered into Nabataea Village and settled himself among the five sailors lounging in the clearing. At a break in their conversation, he addressed the group.

"I have considered our plight. I shall go to Viti Levu myself and see what there is to see. I'll put a notice at the harbor that you are all interested in jobs. Somebody might be looking for experienced sailors."

"Why don't we all go?" Nawfal seemed eager to leave.

"Where would ten sailors live if the harbor is closed, no jobs, no food? Maybe the pox is still rampant there."

"I talked to the navigators who carried our mate to Viti Levu," said Abu. "Their friends offered him room and board until he was hired on a ship. But I have to warn you, the Vahilele navigators don't like to spend more time there than is necessary. They say it stinks from all the foreigners living there."

The men expressed bawdy responses to that proclamation.

"I need to send a letter to the *Nabataea* sponsor and Captain Koch's family. And I have to send off the pouches with our mates' effects. Since we cannot all get into one outrigger, I suggest that you stay here, and I will report what I find." Bahram rubbed his talisman, the button he had taken from the captain's vest.

Nawfal nodded. "That sounds like a reasonable idea. I can wait. For now, we have only canoes for travel and the weather conditions have to be perfect. Tavale tells me the repairs on the other two outriggers damaged by the cyclone are almost complete."

"I'm still hoping a ship will anchor, and we can all leave," said Breaker, rubbing his arm that had healed but was still not at full strength to row.

"While I am in Viti Levu getting you a job?" Bahram laughed.

"Little possibility of that happening, since there is only one ship a year," said Abu. "This is too small an island for regular trade, and the natives export on their own. But that would be a story to remember: Bahram returns to the island as we head in the opposite direction."

The men laughed at the image. On foreign soil, their bonds had strengthened.

At the base of the limestone cliffs, Bahram found a narrow ledge where he could walk above the spray. The rumble of the powerful waves crashing so close to his feet echoed in his dreams even when he lay far from them at night. At the end of the ledge, Bahram climbed past heavy vines with purple trumpet-shaped flowers, up a steep trail to a chalky cliff above the cave nests of the goshawks. From there he could see to the horizon for miles across an ocean whose colors changed from cobalt to jade to an aquamarine hue closer to shore.

Reliving his survival of the storm blamed on the local gods' wrath, he was filled with his old country's Vohu Manah, an ambition of grandeur. His parents had taught him that everyone had a place to serve. *It was no accident that I met the explorer who brought me to Vahilele*, he reasoned. *Surely I was spared to use my mind to rescue these natives. This is my purpose. It is my destiny to accomplish great things. Good thoughts, good words, good deeds.* He smiled. "Like Caesar."

His reverie was interrupted when he saw far below him six outriggers speedily approaching the island. Twelve brown navigators propelled the canoes one at a time through the surf into the lagoon. Bahram's breath caught in his throat as his memory recalled his deep shame when he made an error in judgment as a sixteen-year-old lookout. He was on a Persian rampart, and he dismissed as harmless an old man at the gate with a donkey cart. Bahram's attention had been on the game of chance below him, played by his brother against the village champion. When he looked out again, he witnessed this traveler slash the throat of a sentry. A second man threw back the produce covering him and plunged his knife into the other guard. The two assassins opened the gate to hundreds of enemies who swarmed in to take control of the city. Bahram fled when his brother was killed. He would never again underestimate strangers.

With Dedan leading the way, Bahram hurried down the slope toward the closest group of men, his mind churning as fast as his steps. It had taken him a long time to forgive himself, through the kind counsel of Captain Koch, but he had never forgotten this mistake made years ago. He doubted the families of the dead would ever forgive. Surely, his father had not. Bahram's nerves were wound tightly. *I cannot change a past mistake, but I will not repeat it*. His sandals stumbled several times on the rocky trail. Branches on the shrubs scratched his face; his breath came in gasps. Halfway down the steep path his view of the lagoon was blotted out by tall trees, and he could only guess what the foreigners were doing. Maybe a stealthy attack was planned at the southern village where the natives had not yet repaired their canoes. Most of the men were in the fields, huts undefended. The foreigners could grab the women and leave before the men could save them. His imagination ran faster than his feet.

To calm his fear, he chanted. *Today is my moment of redemption. I will save many lives. Good deeds.* The first person he waved at was Nawfal who had quickened his pace when he spotted Bahram charging down the hill. Nawfal hurried to meet him.

"What's the trouble?"

"There are outriggers approaching fast from the east, through the coral reef." Bahram gestured to the western cliff above them. His chest heaved in pain, his words forced out. "I spotted them from the rampart."

"Calm yourself. This isn't Persia, and we are not being attacked."

Bahram shouted. "It is foolish to assume these strangers are harmless. It is better to be alert for signs of attack than be sorrowful for negligence."

Nawfal cocked an eyebrow. "Think, mate. If they know how to get through the barrier reef into the lagoon, maybe they've been here before. Maybe they are relatives. Or traders!"

"We don't know where they come from, or how many more might be on the way. Our people are still fragile and cannot defend themselves." Bahram put hands on hips, leaned slightly forward, and gulped deep breaths. "The navigators may be here to spy on us." Bahram huffed and sputtered as his heart rate slowed. "Even if they are not warriors, they might steal our ideas. When we're ready to trade our fabric and pottery in Viti Levu, there may not be a market. We must seize the advantage."

"That's insane. But what do you want me to do?" Nawfal stood motionless.

Bahram decided to show strength like Tavale had done. When Bahram and his shipmates washed ashore, they were intimidated by the forceful presence of the prince. "Get a few of our sailors to surround these strangers. Don't hurt them in front of the islanders, but take them into the forest and convince them to stay with us. We cannot let them leave."

"How will I convince them?" Nawfal asked. "I don't speak an island *vosa*."

"Use your imagination. And take Ghazi. Let him question them, and take prisoners if you have to. Quietly." Bahram watched his loyal warrior take off on the run. He felt his blood churn with power.

CHAPTER FOURTEEN

Lapita

As her health steadily improved, Lapita took charge over the women's work force. Instead of a low-fire burn of coconut shells under the earthenware covered with kindling, a kiln that could accommodate more pottery was built into the eastern side of the hill near the beach.

Under the thatched roof of the new pottery shed, three women browned the shells that would be crushed and mixed with the clay, chatting comfortably with each other about the difficulty in preparing new dishes for their men. Lapita rolled the clay into coils, and Siga stood at the Princess' shoulder. By continually asking questions, Siga demonstrated that she took seriously her responsibility to the future of the tribe.

"Are you ready for a different design today?" said Lapita. "We will start by piling one coil on top of the other as we always do, and work the clay for the correct height. This one will have a flat base because we want it to look like the kuro in the corner." She nodded to direct the girl's gaze to the storage container that had on both sides the traditional face design with almond eyes and long narrow nose. "While I do this, you can make smaller coils that I will paint," said Lapita.

"How will you do that?" asked her apprentice.

"With the same clay and saltwater Matai Malolo uses on the cliff drawings. I want to stamp tongues of buka on this one. And I will color them red." Lapita dipped her hands in muddy water to prepare her board.

Their labor was interrupted by the approach of Tavale who stood respectfully outside until he was recognized. The other women put down their work and left the shed, bowing slightly as they passed him.

"You may go with them, Siga. We will finish this later." Lapita smiled at Tavale, and motioned for him to enter the women's work area.

"It is too early for kakana, my brother, and I have no bananas to give you," teased Lapita. "Do you stroll the yanuyanu because of the nice breeze?"

"Wandering the paths of a village is not my favorite way to spend a morning," said Tavale. "I would rather be breaking waves in my canoe. Remember when we would crowd around the fire in the koro, and the old storyteller with the wrinkled face would tell us how our ancestors travelled the sea? As soon as I heard that, I knew that's what I wanted to do."

Lapita rubbed and pulled the coils until they were the shape she desired. Only when she put the new pot in the sun to dry and wiped the clay off her hands did he come to his reason for the visit. They went outside the shed for serious vosa. Lapita waited for her brother to share his thoughts.

"I sat with our elders. I told them it is time to speak out against the foreign ideas that are changing our heritage. I was born to take care of my people, and I am ready."

Lapita squatted in the sun with her back against a palm tree. Tavale sat cross-legged next to her. They rested in silence for awhile, choosing their words carefully.

"Elder Bati said it is too soon for the people to have a new chief." Tavale was motionless, gazing out to sea. "Our dalo field was flooded. We have had no more babies on this yanuyanu. There is talk that the gods show anger toward us."

Lapita used thoughtful words. "These problems followed the pox and the storm. Not a punishment of the gods. Our people took care of those who were sick and did not have time to tend the crops or the desire to make babies."

"I know and you know." Tavale sighed. "Bati is old and stubborn. And he still blames me that his son drowned while on my outrigger."

"A misadventure of young men, many years ago. Fueling anger clouds reason. What about the other two?"

"Matai Malolo and Dau always agree with Bati."

"The first fruits sevusevu will be soon. Even though the crop of yams is small, there are enough for us until the next harvest. That is a sign that the makawa is taking care of us."

Tavale nodded. "We still have breadfruit in the stone pits. Fishing is good. Our tribe has enough food for now."

"We will wait for our time. It will come, brother."

Tavale took a deep breath and released it. A small smile erased the hard frown that had accompanied their conversation. "Our trading outrigger is ready to make a long distance trip. I tested it myself." His eyes remained on the distant spot of blue glistening through the rustling fronds. "Melane has many scars but you and I have few. From the pox." He smiled. "I think she is beautiful. She is fearful I will want another queen. She said that in some tribes brother and sister marry. I told her not to worry."

Lapita nodded. "When our ancestors came to this island, there were no other people. For a long time, only our golden kai lived here." She glanced at her brother's noble profile. "Our mother's grandfather said that the Phoenix led us to this island."

"But that grandfather thought it wise to marry a darker skin race to protect us from those who wanted to make war with us."

Lapita smiled. "I think families have wars also. Only spirits connect through the makawa. Not blood."

"Blood is important, but he had only one child. If we are to add to the makawa we must continue to have children. I want Melane to be the mother of my peipei." Tavale nodded to affirm his decision. There was no question.

"You and I are different, but we are both connected to the wisdom of the makawa. It is a choice of the heart. You are your best on water, and I on land. I know when I know the right path. I can breathe it in. My soul is warm within me."

"Sister, that is your place. I look to the sky for a dependable guide to steer my canoe. Stars guide a navigator by night and the sun is my constant during the day." He sighed heavily. "Underwater is another world with its own laws. By Dakuwaqa."

Lapita reached out toward Tavale but did not touch him. Her hand lay between them on the sand. "Together, we will do what is right for our people."

He nodded.

CHAPTER FIFTEEN

Bahram

When Bahram announced taxes on dwellings would begin immediately, there was heated discussion. Every vale was affected, including those in Nabataea Village, where he asked the opinions of his friends, Abu and Nawfal.

Abu commented, "This is not one of your better ideas."

"You have big ideas but no experience to implement them," said Nawfal. "The islanders go along with you because they don't like conflict. However, the result will be that some natives will have to borrow money on their hut to pay the tax, forcing honorable sons and daughters to be slaves, forever working off their indebtedness. And those who don't want to pay will move into the forest and build a new hut."

"They cannot argue their lives were better before we came. Give me time. I am willing to make adjustments."

Nawfal was a peacekeeper. "I don't deny some of your ideas are good."

Bahram changed the subject. "How did your interview with the foreign navigators go?"

"Not well. They would not answer questions, and acted like we owed them respect. Like they were better than us. So I thought a couple lashes would show them who was in command."

"And?"

"Ghazi got carried away and beat a couple of them severely. He has a cruel streak."

"Did they die?"

"No, but the Samoans couldn't understand the questions. And we couldn't understand their answers, especially when they feared Ghazi." Nawfal shook his shaggy head.

"How did you know they were Samoans?"

"I could understand that much. And when I was last in Palembang, I spoke in Arabic with a Samoan who had tattoos like theirs."

"Where are the Samoans now?"

"I put them in an abandoned hut in the field village with a couple of our mates to watch them. We gave them food and water, and we allowed one of the islanders to treat their wounds."

"I hope the Vahileleans don't tell Lapita. I don't want the Samoans coddled. Make them work in the fields. Ghazi showed strength. He did the right thing. Now you show the Samoans they will not be harmed if they work hard. Gradually increase their food and their privileges. They will grow to love us." He grinned.

The two sailors who shared a hut with Nawfal came into the clearing. The man who had saved Breaker, after their shipwreck, continued to wear a head covering as he always had before his years of sailing.

Bahram asked, "Isn't that thing you wear on your head hot?"

"At times, but I'm from a desert trading family like Captain Koch," said the former deckhand, "and accustomed to wearing it. You never know when you'll need a length of cloth for an injury to yourself or your camel. In the meantime it keeps my brain cool."

"I haven't seen one camel on this island," said Abu.

"No camels on the *Nabataea* either, but that turban saved my life, it did," said Breaker.

"Towed that big old camel Breaker to shore!"

"That's the truth." Breaker was not laughing. "This guy with a cool brain will always be my best friend."

"Breaker and Turban. Sounds like a pair of camels," said Bahram, and everyone agreed.

CHAPTER SIXTEEN

Lapita

Each day Lapita walked on the beach, venturing further from the central village of Na Koro to build up her strength. One morning she heard pounding from the tapa shed as familiar to her as the pounding of the surf on shore. For generations, Vahilele women had impressed other islands with their masi cloth. At the recent family gathering, Lapita heard many compliments on the quality of the sulu she wore.

The Princess turned off the beach path to walk to an area protected by the forest where a long, low thatched roof sheltered three women pounding paper mulberry bark. A year ago, there were seven or eight working their craft together.

"Ni Bula." The work stopped, and an older woman stood and bowed. Lapita recognized the widow of a fisherman she treated for the pox. Although many women without husbands must be dependent upon others for food, it was good to see the maramas once again making cloth for themselves and trade.

"What pattern will you mark on this piece?" Lapita examined an unfinished strip pounded to make a soft cloth, and its owner stood at attention.

The young woman raised her head. "Princess, I like many suns coming up over the water."

Lapita nodded. "I think this will make a lovely sarong. For yourself?"

"My tagane will take it to Beqa to trade."

"It will be good to see the outriggers go out again."

Lapita smiled at another marama seated with her legs to the side. "Do you also have a plan for your work?"

"No, Princess." She awkwardly got to her feet.

Lapita saw that her knee was wrapped in leaves. "You are injured?"

"It is nothing. I have my walking stick to help me, and I go slowly."

Lapita asked questions about the injury before she reached for the herbal pouch at her waist. "Try a poultice with this papaya sap. I will come back in two days to see if it helps."

"Vinaka, Princess. You are as kind as your father. Vinaka."

"And for your words, vinaka. I leave you to your work."

As Lapita continued her trek to the field village, she thought about how her father had always spent the day interacting with the islanders so that he knew their problems and successes. She was pleased that his reign was remembered by some as justice tempered with respect for each individual. *I would like to be as compassionate.* She was also pleased that more of her tribe was showing her polite deference, but she wondered if it was because her father had been the king, or because now she was a favored servant close to the current leader.

Lapita continually shared with the islanders the foreign words she learned from the mariners and encouraged her tribe to grow in understanding of their new benefactors. She tried to teach Bahram the words of Vahilele. He resisted. She was more successful with Abu although she was uncomfortable under the scrutiny of his beady eyes.

When she got closer to the field village, she passed dalo fields and spotted several men who were not from Vahilele. In the bright sunlight, red welts on their arms and backs were obvious. This evidence of brutality infuriated Lapita.

She immediately turned around and went looking for Bahram.

When she located him at the fishing nets in the lagoon, Lapita confronted him. "Our neighbor bring harm to you?" She had no concern that others were close and listening.

"Neighbor?"

"Cakacaka. Dalo." She pointed to the south end of the island, having difficulty in putting her angry thoughts into words. She made no effort to make her vosa private. "Work in dalo field." She sputtered.

His friendly smile turned to a fierce frown. He stepped closer to tower over her.

"Lower your voice, woman. I made a fast decision to protect Vahilele. I know the constant rumors of tribal wars between islands."

Lapita's right hand swept her left side from shoulders to hips. "I know tatau of Samoan. No warrior. Sega. Sega." She shook her head. "Trade obsidian for masi cloth." She took deep breaths to calm herself.

"They also brought the smallpox that nearly wiped out your clan," Bahram retorted.

"Sega." Again she shook her head, struggling with new Arabic words. "Pox from Viti Levu. Chief burned trader canoe." She spit out the bitter truth. "Late."

He turned away, hands on hips. "You do not understand. Take care of women's work. I am in charge of the crops, and we need more men. We will feed the Samoans and choose women to bed them." Bahram looked back into her narrowed eyes. "Next year we will have many male babies for our tribe." He cocked an eyebrow as if to end the debate with an indisputable fact.

Lapita regarded the rugged countenance glowering down on her, the long black wavy hair held back with a strip of cloth, his mouth drawn into a childish pout behind his beard, his eyes black with anger at her insolence. He was no longer polite. He did not pretend to respect her. She would no longer pretend to be his servant. In her mind, she was released from traditional hospitality. She was confident her father would approve. In her heart she felt the peace of a wise decision.

"Sega. We let them go." She pointed to the east. "Far away, family waits."

"These Samoans have no worries because my men take care of them. They are happy here." He put his face down to hers and growled. "Marau."

"They were free. Now you choose for them. Why you say marau?"

"Because I tell them they are marau," He snorted.

Lapita shook her head. "They go home. No bokola." She moved past him to the corner of the beach where pox victims from the field village had been cremated. Tropical winds now blew nuku across the limestone rocks that covered the area. Her breathing slowed while she stood reverently, looking out to the sea, the breeze caressing her long hair and carrying her soft words into the future. Her conversation with Bahram was in the past.

She left him to his study of the fishing pools, or whatever activity he thought made him look important.

Since the traditional one hundred days of mourning her husband had passed, Lapita returned to her pyramid hut surrounded by dark green pepper shrubs, ti plants, and saga seed trees, fragrant with orange blossoms. She told Bahram, "I go home. No bokola." But he did not understand the word "prisoner."

The Persian stayed in his own bure.

CHAPTER SEVENTEEN

Bahram

Several days later, Bahram walked across a clearing surrounded by paper mulberry trees. He saw Lapita enter the noisy tapa cloth work area tucked among the palms. The rhythmic pounding ceased. A trill of feminine laughter was magically woven into the threads of the sunrays, and his heart filled with longing. His bure seemed empty without her, but he would never beg for affection from a woman.

Bahram entered the forest canopy and waited behind a sandalwood tree, the two-sided shed still in view. When Lapita came into the sunshine, he casually walked around the kettle of water boiling on the fire pit, as though to inspect the area. Lapita had to pass by him on her route toward the ocean sparkling through the palms. Her brown sarong with the patterns of a boa constrictor back was accented with a long strand of coral. She moved like a proud queen with shoulders back and head held high. Bahram pretended a chance encounter, but she merely nodded and moved on.

Madam Princess thinks she is too grand for me. Bahram feigned indifference. *If she no longer desires me, I will find another woman. Someone who appreciates bold leadership.* When he passed the area where women wove pandanus mats, he paused to watch the women pounding fiercely, sweat streaming down plump cheeks and mingling with long black hair secured by floral headbands. Strength and beauty all around him. *This is a paradise, and I belong here.* He nodded to the women. Some smiled as their hands kept a steady beat. He came to a sudden stop. In front of him was another large pot sitting over a fire, the only use of metal he had seen on the island.

"Where did you get this?"

A woman nodded. "Sa Bula." Her toothless smile suggested years her smooth skin denied, but not everyone could be a part of paradise magic.

"No, not bula!" Bahram spoke sharply.

The woman's smile faded. She shook her head and continued pounding.

Exasperated, Bahram found Abu and sent him back to the pandanus work area. "Find out where they got the iron kettles. There has to be a trading center near Vahilele."

"When are you going to learn how to communicate with these people?"

"Not my place. They need to learn my language. It is good enough for other countries."

Bahram's answer came back to him later that day when he found Abu lounging under a palm tree. Bahram sat down next to him, and Abu told him, "Viseisei. The iron pot came from Viseisei in Viti Levu."

"Then we need to see what kind of marketplace they have. At first opportunity, I shall venture to Viti Levu with the trader canoes."

"I'll be ready," said Abu.

"No, I'm going alone. You stay here and become my ears and eyes. Specifically, watch Tavale. I do not trust him."

"You're right. I have seen him in the midst of solemn natives, and the conversation stops when I stroll past, but I pick up many of their words. He tells them he is ready to be King," said Abu. "I have also heard that the elders have their doubts."

"We need to keep the pressure on the council so they don't make him king." Bahram broke off a blade of grass and chewed it reflectively. "He will lead them down the dusty ruts of the past."

Abu made a lizard run with a well-pitched pebble. "The island women complain about too much work because Melane stirs them up. Most of them are willing to make us happy as long as they think we like them."

"Let them complain," said Bahram. "They are like Dedan. They perform for a pat on the head and a few kind words."

"They don't realize they are now occupied. They think we were sent by the gods." Abu snickered.

"Maybe we were. We're smarter than them because we know how to trade goods for profit. Before we came, they had no thought of monetary value."

"Right. I can't see my former neighbors in Egypt taking shells for cloth that they spent hours to make." Abu yawned and settled back. "I have to admit the islanders have all they need for a comfortable life. There's something good to be said for an afternoon nap."

Bahram ignored him. "There has to be a profitable exchange. If Tavale becomes the law on this island, he will tear apart all that we have initiated. The stockpile of masi cloth will rot in place. The natives will go back to sleep."

"They just want to be happy." Abu pulled his hat down over his eyes.

"They are children who can't see beyond today. I try to explain but they don't understand. I will have to show them."

He was talking to himself. Abu was snoring. Annoyed, Bahram decided to walk down to the fields where Nawfal made progress in convincing the natives to weed the taro. He found his shipmate in conversation with two of the native workers. Bahram waited until the discussion ended with shared laughter, and Nawfal came over to him. "Cola, Saca."

"What does that mean?"

"Hello, good sir." Nawfal grinned. "I'm trading words with Lalai and his mate. I never was a fast learner."

"I don't have time." Bahram gestured toward the emerald fields. "Evidence of a good harvest?"

"If the beetles don't get it."

"See that they don't," said Bahram. "I am on my way to inspect the pottery shed. Want to accompany me?"

"I will walk as far as the turn off to the lagoon, because I want to inspect the new outrigger I've heard about."

"Good thought. We shall walk together. I am heading to Viti Levu soon. I hope to make a trade contact for the taro but that transaction will not be until harvest, and it will help to know what is available for immediate sale. Also I'll take a couple pots that Lapita made with a new design. Some shop owner might agree to sell them for a percentage of the sale price."

"You are quite the merchant. Talent I never suspected."

"This is a new venture, and I have a lot to learn. Captain Koch got me thinking about an alternative to taking the same routes everyone else does. And the Srivijaya regime is growing strong. I think they will be the new China."

Nawfal looked at his mate. "If you are correct, we have an opportunity to get wealthy."

"You always were the sharp one."

"Hah! I'm the last one to catch on to a new idea. I have to work harder."

Bahram chuckled. "While I'm gone, I want you to watch Tavale."

Nawfal hesitated. "Why? Is he still a problem? I thought Lapita moved out."

"She did. I asked her to leave. She was too depressing." Bahram shrugged. "And I need a younger woman."

"So you won't mind if I ask her to shake her grass skirt for me?" Nawfal grinned.

"Nawfal!" Bahram rolled his eyes. "I was saying I suspect that Tavale is not in favor of developing trade on his island, and I do not know if he has local support."

"I can understand that. The islanders have been living the same way for centuries."

They walked in silence for a moment, and Nawfal added, "Because we are friends, I will warn you that little Abu is interested in the girls."

"Good for him. Will you try to focus on what I am trying to tell you about trade in Viti Levu?"

"Of course, Saca."

Bahram pointed at a large outrigger with a shelter in the center. "There is the outrigger I will ride into the unknown. Does she look safe?" They walked over to the large canoe, only slightly smaller than the royal raft that Lapita's family had travelled on. Natives in loincloths repaired a hole in the roof with plaited banana leaves. Bahram made a show of inspecting the hollow log near him. "A paddler sits closer to the waves than a rower on a merchant ship."

"The crew has to be fit." Nawfal pointed to the rail. "Bahram, see these eight marks? There are eight matching marks on the other side. They pair to a single point on the stern."

"What are you talking about?"

"Tavale. He is a genius. He knows the constellations that I do like Orion and the Southern Cross, but he has different names for them and maybe a hundred more. With these canoe markings, he can get 32 bearings in two directions. He calls them star houses. He can find his way all over the ocean without charts."

"Captain Koch could do that, too."

"Right. Just thought I'd mention, Tavale is not only a chief's son. He's a smart one."

"That's why I tell you to keep an eye on him while I'm gone." Bahram walked up the beach a ways, turned around and came back to Nawfal. "And stay away from Lapita."

"Yes, Saca. I will, Saca. You better mention it to Abu, Saca."

Bahram walked the path to the pottery shed muttering about people who thought they were humorous but were actually annoying. His aggravation stirred up a jumble of unhappy thoughts. The one most often examined was his relationship with Lapita. After his exclusion from her bed, Bahram released the Samoans. To his confusion, she never acknowledged this generosity. Days passed and Lapita showed no gratitude. Well, he would not lower himself to be dependent upon the approval of a woman. He was thinking a break from Lapita would be good for both of them. Time to make a trip to the island of Viti Levu.

CHAPTER EIGHTEEN

Bahram

Three Vahilele outriggers sailed into Vuda harbor. Bahram refused the offers of his navigators who invited him to the huts where they were staying with friends. He would not be able to understand their conversation, and he would always suspect they were chattering about him. He slung his travel pack over one shoulder.

"I will see you back here in ten days," he told them in Arabic. He held up ten fingers for clarity. They nodded.

Bahram found a marketplace near the busy shipping area and talked to a merchant with a variety of merchandise for sale.

Unwrapping a bilo of Lapita's design, Bahram placed it in front of the older man. "You see the superior workmanship on this bowl?" he said in Arabic. "This is from Vahilele, and there is much more to sell."

The merchant's pointed hat had a brim that shaded any expression in his eyes. "We have pottery here from Sigatoka." He motioned to another table.

"That pottery has no flair. Ladies want decoration. Have you not noticed they like the excitement of something unusual?" Bahram raised an eyebrow and stepped closer.

The trader's mouth twitched, and Bahram knew he had him hooked. Before the Persian left, they had an agreement that the bilo would be displayed for several days. If it were sold before Bahram returned, they would discuss more inventory.

He got directions to Viseisei, a close village where he could get a bed and meals while he conducted trade business. He had to walk several miles, past many thatched huts that looked similar to those in Na Koro. When he arrived, he found bustling activity reminiscent of the civilization he had left in Sumatra. Among the men in traditional island dress, some wore exotic robes. Two women had their faces covered with veils while they strolled the dusty roads. Bahram saw black Melanesian merchants. He saw flat-faced workers with pointed straw head coverings and brown women in colorful silks, with jewels in their foreheads. The ancient town was beginning to represent a new age of travel to this part of the world. Soon it would be like Palembang.

Bahram met a pretty local girl whose brother gave him names of two ship captains, merchants who came yearly across the Coral Sea to Vuda Point harbor. Bahram confirmed his suspicion that most of the trade was done with other islands on smaller fishing boats or canoes.

Wandering around the village, Bahram passed a large hut with a steep thatched roof and sturdy walls of woven bamboo pounded flat. A black sentry squatted in front.

"Cola!"

"Bula."

"Do you speak Arabic?"

"I do."

"Who lives here?"

The oversized man plunged three fingers into a bowl of taro paste and made a messy show of licking each finger before replying. "Governor of Viseisei."

"Can I see him?"

"Gone to Vanuatu."

"For how long?"

Another long pause before he answered, "Not for me to know."

Bahram felt he was being dismissed. Maybe Abu was right, and he needed to improve his communication skills. "I want to discuss trade."

"He will return."

Through the open entry of the hut, Bahram saw an oriental carpet covering the dirt floor. The owner may not have possessions in abundance, but he had quality. Here lived a man with whom Bahram could communicate, a man who made the best out of his location. He glanced down at his own dirty turnshoes, felt the heaviness of saltwater in his clothing and whiffed the sweat of a long journey. In his past life, he would celebrate a port layover with a bath, a shave, a drink, and a woman. The idea had merit now.

"Would you direct me to a suitable traveler's resting place, kind sir? Saca?"

The guard's suggestion turned out to be excellent, and Bahram enjoyed the benefits of city life although many desperate souls were anxious to earn enough for their next meal. The first night, his landlord sent an attractive girl to his room, but she was too tender for his taste and never returned. Bahram was not concerned, as there would be many women available to him. His mission was scouting trade partners, not entertainment. By day he walked the streets, and at night he socialized in different gathering spots, conversing in a civilized manner with men of means and intelligence.

Bahram spent many hours at an establishment stocked with western merchandise. He talked with the proprietor in the universal Arabic language, and to two visitors in his homeland's tongue, Pahlavi. *Good words*. He penned a letter to the sponsor of the *Nabataea* telling him of their shipwreck a few months earlier, at the first of the year. He sent the pouches of his mates with the letter, although there was no certainty that the package would be delivered. His obligation as the leader of the remnant was fulfilled, but he held on to the Captain's pouch because he planned to personally deliver it. *Good thoughts. Good deeds.*

Bahram bought leather boots for himself, preferring their weight to going barefoot. Even the sandals fashioned by some of his shipmates didn't keep the sand and rocks from irritating his toes. With the local currency of golden cowrie shells, *bulikula*, according to a shop owner, Bahram also purchased a traditional tunic and breeches that a merchant would wear. He thought it would be wise to have an appearance distinct from the islanders, to be set apart.

In keeping with his promise to his mates back on Vahilele, Bahram talked with several mariners he met in Viseisei about his small band of experienced sailors who were interested in being hired on as crew, but he found no opportunities. He did not meet anyone who could arrange transportation for his mates back to Po-Li or even Bali, and heard of no vessel that made scheduled stops at Vahilele. This worked for Bahram since he could use his men to build his empire. His dream continued to evolve and expand.

On the last morning of his visit, he gave a Sassanian gold coin to the hot-blooded beauty who entertained him. She gave him deep scratches on his face to remind him of the power struggle that he won and would not soon forget. He also paid for his lodging and food with a Sassanian gold coin. The surprise on the proprietor's face made Bahram realize he could have made himself a target if he had flashed the large coins earlier in his stay. He cautioned himself not to arouse the greed of an uncultured people. He didn't want pirates to descend upon Vahilele. On his next visit he would pay for services with smaller copper coins or trade with taro or masi cloth, to avoid scrutiny.

Before he left Viseisei, Bahram visited his favorite store to say farewell and to make last minute tobacco purchases for his mates. He wanted to prove to them there was a place of trade on Viti Levu, and to strengthen their loyalty. Also to encourage their participation in the plan that was forming in his mind, thanks to a captain now buried in paradise.

At the docks in Vuda Point, Bahram visited the marketplace alive with merchants hawking a variety of wares and animals for sale to travelers. When he saw a litter of piglets, he was inspired to prove to Lapita that he was as concerned as she was about the future of Vahilele. Her tribe needed more sustenance, and he had heard that in the past, for special occasions, pig roasts were popular although now the island had none. He bought two pairs, and the seller put the pink, wriggling, squealing babies into a jute sack. Bahram moved more rapidly because he was now prepared to return as a hero bearing gifts. He secured his tobacco packet to pad a pearl-handled painted fan for Lapita. He imagined her regally fluttering it before her beautiful face like an Empress of New Guinea.

When Bahram arrived at the canoe, one outrigger was loaded and waiting. The islanders had bartered for cassava to replace the crop damaged by the storm.

"Other canoes go to Vahilele ahead of wind." The navigator studied Bahram's face. "*Tagane* concerned, *Saca*. Viseisei holds much danger."

Bahram held aloft his moving sack. "I purchased a litter of pigs. Next year, we will have more meat for everybody." Because of their immediate joyful chatter, Bahram thought the natives seemed cheered by his revelation. Their attention was now concentrated on going home.

Bahram stood with one hand holding on to the shelter roof for balance and watched Vuda Point recede into the past as they left the calm harbor. His other hand fingered the captain's button on the shirt he paid to have washed. His eyes watched the scenery and the mariners while his mind was working out his future. After his four months in beautiful Vahilele, he was not impressed with the many squalid areas of Viti Levu civilization, but the businesses in Viseisei gave him a model to restructure his island. His investigative trip was successful.

CHAPTER NINETEEN

Bahram

When they moved out to open sea heading southeast, the air was still and the sea as smooth as a piglet. The pandanus sails were not useful, but the men took turns paddling efficiently and in good spirits. Rangi, the navigator, was unusually quiet. Bahram felt the change in wind when it came. He was concerned and seated himself in the stern next to the navigator, who pointed at approaching brown clouds. Bahram kept his eyes on the sky that grew more clouded and darker. The wind picked up, and the sails were hoisted.

Within a short time, the winds were erratic and rain dappled the canoe. Bahram stayed with Rangi, a captain of sorts, and with memories of Captain Koch riding the *Nabataea* to the ocean floor.

"How far are we from Vahilele?" Bahram asked in Arabic.

"Midway now," Rangi answered, rocking back and forth, keen eyes searching the sky.

In the mounting storm, Bahram sought a place to use his experience. He joined the men who were lowering the sails. The discipline came back immediately, and Bahram pulled and strained with the others. It felt good to be useful.

The winds were fierce and the outrigger rode swells that towered over it. Bahram again seated himself cross-legged by the navigator who had not moved. The double-hulled canoe ascended wave after wave that crashed down upon it, tons of water escaping through the crevices between the logs, sometimes leaving a fish or two. Bahram had to admit that the small craft handled the rough sea with more grace than a large ship.

They found temporary safety in each trough between waves before they were lifted up by the next one, and the ride continued. The storm whipped the outrigger from all sides, but the men kept paddling. Bahram remembered the native word, *kaukaua*, and smiled. These islanders were made of strong marrow and didn't leave their posts. Unlike one or two of the sailors on the *Nabataea* who had sought shelter in the cargo hold until the command to abandon ship. Memories of that fatal day had etched an internal scar that he did not want to duplicate.

"The gods are still angry with Vahilele. We are going to die." The navigator's loud proclamation ignited fear in Bahram's pounding heart.

What had they done to anger omnipotent gods? These were gentle people. Why would they be punished? Yet this was the second time this year that the sea rose above his own head. He had to ask himself. *Is it me? Am I the target of an evil spirit*? He searched his brain for an answer, for a solution, for a meaning. He recalled conversations among travelers who had argued the theological difference between peaceful Hindus and Muslims. Bahram was raised a Zoroastrian and taught the world was a battleground among men under a supreme God in heaven. Who was right?

His mind flashed back into his childhood when his father had lengthy rules for each step and every thought. Bahram tried to remember what rule he may have broken recently. His mother continually cautioned him that evil challenges good. "Man chooses and God judges," she said. Was he going to die because of his choices? He chest hurt as his heart pounded fearfully. He did not steal his shipmates' money. He had only helped the islanders. *Good deeds*. What god would find fault with him? Suddenly he could imagine his father's displeasure and raging anger, "Animals are sacred, not to be slaughtered." He couldn't remember why. He couldn't recite the exact rule about eating pork and which god that would offend, but it seemed many religions addressed it, and men went to war over religion. With horror he recalled his last action on land. He bought pigs for food. *Is my choice a sacrilege?* He twisted and pulled at the captain's button on his shirt.

With mildewed memory, he considered the wisdom of his parents. He had gone contrary to them for years, and he suffered consequences. His life lacked stability. Maybe now he should make a choice they would approve. *I have nothing to lose in a new effort. All might be lost anyway.* Bahram got to his feet on the bucking platform and fumbled his way into the small shelter that protected the cargo. He balanced himself by grabbing a bamboo pole and ducked through the heavy skin over the entry. Under the thatched roof, all was in darkness but Bahram could hear the nervous grunts and squeals of the little piglets.

A scream from one of the natives outside terrified him. Echos of the foundering *Nabataea* exploded in his mind. *Hurry! We're going down.* He felt around at his feet to find the right sack; he identified it by the movement. With one tug and with no other thought, he backed out of the shelter into the pelting rain. Gripping each slippery pole and sennit cord that he could feel, he crawled to the side of the platform lashed to a log. *Hurry*! Two paddlers huddled there, riding out the storm. The waves were too fierce to battle. Clinging to a rope with one hand, Bahram raised up on one knee and pitched the sack of piglets into the boiling ocean.

That's all I can do, if indeed I am the reason for the storm. God save me! He crawled back to sit by Rangi who observed him without comment. Time lengthened in a deafening roar until suddenly Bahram saw a glimpse of a lightened sky and then calmer seas beyond. The men cheered and set their sails for Vahilele, with only one injury. To Bahram, the trip home seemed to have taken much longer than travelling the other way, almost a lifetime.

Bahram stepped off the canoe on to land, happy his return to Vahilele was not like his first arrival when he was washed ashore. He had worked alongside the islanders, and he had demonstrated his faith in the spiritual. He felt revived, confident in his leadership, worthy of a position of power.

And Lapita stood on shore waiting for his return.

CHAPTER TWENTY

Lapita

The first week Bahram was gone, Dedan ran wild, chasing giant megapode chickens or frightened children. Lapita stepped in to rescue her beloved yanuyanu from this curious black beast who now slept on her doorstep. Bahram had shown her that the only care Dedan needed was fresh water and cassava, but when a storm came up on the third night, she pitied him outside in the weather that had taken his mate. The koli was invited into her bure, and he made himself comfortable next to her pallet. As the days progressed, Lapita grew accustomed to his soulful eyes and talked to him when she had a decision to make.

"Did you know that Bahram released the Samoans?" Dedan's ears pricked up, and his head rolled from side to side as though he was doing his best to understand the conversation. Lapita had forgiven Bahram's capture of the navigators. His had not been the cruel hand that had marked their backs. She had asked her people, and they told her it was Ghazi who wielded the lash at Nawfal's order.

While Bahram was gone, Lapita concentrated on the affairs of her kai without concern that an outsider would challenge either her authority or her knowledge. She had her doubts that this man was truly a god's gift to Vahilele as some of her neighbors believed, but if he returned, she had to make peace with him. There would be two strong leaders pulling against each other. Tavale would be the chief to keep the old social laws, and Bahram would run the merchant trade. *Where do I fit in?* She longed for the day when a Bete made her path clear. Recently her husband's words would come to mind to guide her, and she sought his advice as she always had. She continually called out to him. *Where are you now? I need direction to be a uniter for the good of the kai.*

The sound of drums heralded the approach of the trading outriggers. Outside the Bure Kalou, a frenzy of excitement carried the villagers along the path to the lagoon. Safe passage home was always a worry for those who awaited their loved ones.

Dedan appeared at her side, and she spoke to him. "We are not going to run. We will check on Yaca first." The big brown eyes seemed to understand the significance of this duty, and he followed her steps to the large hut on the other side of the clearing.

Lapita paused respectfully outside her brother's vale. There were sounds of discord from within, but they were all produced by baby Yaca.

"Melane, cola." She called softly to the shadows inside, "dua, dua, dua," although Tavale probably left the hut at daybreak to check his nets. The night before, he had shared meal time with Lapita as well as his apprehension that the pressure of foreign ideas had confused their kai. Lapita knew her brother would be seeking his own spiritual strength from the gods of the wasa. He continually spent hours at the fishing village or along the rocky baravi on the western side of the yanuyanu. As soon as his canoe had been repaired from the cyclone's damage, the Prince of Vahilele rode the waves.

With Yaca cradled in the crook of her elbow, Melane swung aside the brown curtain over her doorway, and motioned for Lapita to enter. When Dedan tried to come in, Melane shouted in fear. "Sega!"

"He is only following me," said Lapita. "Let him smell the baby's toes, so he gets to know the new prince."

"He might eat him," said Melane.

Lapita laughed, a sound that had not come from her in a very long time. The cousins exchanged glances. The seed of healing was fragile but it had been planted.

"He may enter, if he is quiet," said Melane.

"He is a well-behaved tagane," said Lapita. "Except when he chases the chickens." She reached for her nephew who put out his arms toward her. "Do you want to walk with me to the lagoon? Our traders are home from the sea."

"Are you eager to see one of them?" Melane looked closely at Lapita's face, who was careful to keep her emotions to herself. "Tavale just left here. He came to tell me that only two outriggers are home. Bahram's canoe was late in leaving and got caught in a storm."

"I shall go down to the shore to greet those of my kai who have returned safely."

"And I must prepare food to take to the pavilion for the festivities tonight. You can play with this peipei later; he needs to rest now."

Pretending to herself that she also had tasks that needed attention, the princess returned to the Bure Kalou. Lapita worked the soil and tended her kava peppers and ginger bushes that always did well. Her little herbal garden had almost collapsed. All she had left was lemon grass, garlic, turmeric and cardamom. That was a start. She needed someone with a young back to assist her, but it would feel good to be planting her herbs again. Baby Yaca had restored her torn spirit. Inside the temple, she took inventory of the medicinal herbs on her shelves, cakacaka that she had put off for too long. Soon she had a list of what she needed from the next trip to Viti Levu.

Lapita nudged past her white masi doorway and stepped into the late afternoon heat. The storm clouds had passed in the distance, and she could hear the steady rhythm of the waves lapping on the crushed shell and white sand baravi, the heartbeat of the earth bringing comfort to her yanuyanu and her kai. The threat of the cyclone season had softened, the roofs were repaired and the household belongings dried. The effects of the smallpox epidemic were diminished, although the loss of life had left scars on lonely hearts.

Hundreds of friends and relatives were gone. Lapita closed her eyes and lifted her arms, breathing in the fragrance of her world, open to spiritual guidance. Wrapped in harmony and a healing peace, she chided herself that she enjoyed Bahram's absence. *I have been too harsh, and I should give him another chance.*

The repeat of pounding drums announced that Bahram's outrigger had been sighted. In thanksgiving, Lapita released the burden of concern she had lifted. She called to Dedan and joined the villagers headed along the path to the lagoon. Many of the crowd had been there when the first two canoes landed, and had patiently waited for the last one that now breached the reef easily and turned toward shore. The sail was rolled up and tied down. All was well.

Lapita strained to catch sight of Bahram. *Did he return? Or was he captivated by a woman in Viti Levu? Had he found passage home on a large Arab ship?* She patted the head and rubbed the ears of the hound seated next to her.

There he is!

Bahram stood next to Rangi, a good mentor, a solid mariner. Of course, Bahram would seek his companionship. Two paddlers knelt in carved-out logs on both sides of the craft, swiftly propelling the outrigger toward the waiting crowd.

Women and children anxious to see their menfolk entered the water, crying out a welcome home. Young boys swam out to the canoe to give them an escort to shore, no doubt dreaming of the day when they would be part of the journey to the unknown. Lapita remembered her own thoughts at that age.

She saw Bahram stand up and wave. At her. Without conscious direction her hand waved back, and her feet waded into the water. She felt drawn to the craft now getting larger as it came closer. She looked around. The entire crowd surged forward. The return of a trading canoe was another joyful sign of a new beginning.

The great outrigger hit the sand, and Bahram stepped off the edge into the water, making his way toward her. He looked different, his hair was shorter, beard trimmed. He looked strong, and he had eyes only for her. A long dead need in her stirred. Was he an answer to her prayer? Was he really the savior that her people believed? Or the threat Tavale worried about?

She couldn't think it out. Her mind was confused by the urging of her body. She would have to be very careful.

CHAPTER TWENTY ONE

Bahram

Bahram caught sight of Lapita on the beach with the rest of the tribe when the outrigger breached the reef and crossed their lagoon. Six young women swam out to welcome the men home.

Bahram's heart swelled with desire at the sight of Lapita's willowy figure knee deep in the surf, hand shading her eyes as they sought him. His Princess was the most beautiful woman he had ever seen, more so after his two week absence and near-death experience.

While other men unloaded the cargo, Bahram waded to Lapita's side, drawn by the intensity of her gaze. He stopped in front of her, heart beating faster.

"Good travel?" Her smile was as vivid as the setting sun.

They spoke in Arabic.

"A storm came up, and I feared I would never see you again." The words tumbled out.

"That would bring much sorrow." Lapita nodded.

"Yes?" He stepped closer. He longed to crush her smooth skin against his chest but he had observed that was not acceptable in public. If she were to be his queen, she deserved to be treated with respect.

"Lapita, I have acted badly. I hope you can forgive me."

She smiled slightly. "You release Samoans. Wise decisions bring good will."

Dedan's sharp bark on shore drew his attention, and he coaxed the dog to meet him halfway in the water before Dedan whirled and galloped down the sand and back again, barking excitedly.

"Was he much trouble?" Bahram squatted to jostle the dog in friendly battle.

"We are friends. At day he kept to my side, and at night he slept at my feet."

"He is a fortunate dog." Bahram rose to stand over Lapita again, closer this time, and she had to look up into his face. He heard the intake of her breath, saw a vein in her neck pulsing.

"You come to Bure Kalou? We share *yaqona*. You tell stories," she said.

Together they started the path toward the village. Bahram's skin tingled.

Lapita motioned to Siga who hovered near. "Prepare yaqona for Saca."

Siga chattered excitedly, and Bahram didn't understand a word.

Lapita's gaze over his shoulder showed alarm and made Bahram turn. Natives at the outrigger were removing a man and carrying him to shore on a litter. She turned back to Siga with an abrupt question.

With eyes lowered, Siga talked in island *vosa*.

Abu came up from the other side, eyes widening when he looked at Bahram's face. "You must have had quite a ride."

"A storm came up."

"I heard. The pretty little girl is telling Your Highness that her uncle's foot was crushed between two logs on the outrigger. It sounds like he's in great pain." Abu snickered and lowered his voice. "But I was referring to the scratches on your face."

Bahram ignored Abu's comment and told him briefly about his new business contacts while he waited for Lapita to finish her conversation. "The trip to Viti Levu was a success.

I figured out how we can make a fortune. Now I have to convince the elders."

Lapita gave a sharp command to Siga who took off running toward the village.

"Uncle broke leg." Lapita said to Bahram and walked quickly away, looking grim.

Bahram was speechless. What had just happened to cool his warm welcome?

"Do you think she understood what I said?" Bahram asked Abu.

"She understands more Arabic than she speaks, and I think she is concerned about Siga's uncle and wonders why you are not. You could benefit by learning more island language, *vosa*."

Dedan ran after Lapita until Bahram called him back. The dog hesitated. He watched his new mistress follow the cluster of men carrying the injured man, and then he returned to Bahram, back to his master's heel. Bahram took him on a long walk as a reward for his loyalty.

CHAPTER TWENTY TWO

Siga

"Princess?"

Silence. Siga fidgeted behind Lapita's back. She didn't know how to interrupt with her important message. She paused, moving her weight from one foot to another. In frustration she blurted out. "Grandfather sent me to remind you about the council meeting."

Lapita made no comment or movement for a long while. Siga stared at the horizon like Lapita did. The waves beyond the reef rippled and sparkled in the sun. *Just like every day.* Eventually Lapita lowered her arms and turned to Siga. *She looks happy.*

"Princess, what do you see when you look across the water?"

Lapita chuckled. "Very good, manumanu vuka. You are opening your mind to ask questions. Wisdom does not depend on any one opinion." Lapita turned away.

"Princess, you do not answer."

"Walk with me and I shall consider a response." While the rising sun kissed the horizon and crept along the ocean to touch white sand, they strolled past the canoe building area and past the fishing village tucked into the jungle of palm trees. The north end of the lagoon narrowed as the barrier reef crowded a shore assaulted by the open sea pounding the huge rocks that kept the waves in their channel.

Lapita paused to look out over the breakers. "This is the same water we saw earlier. It looks different. So fierce."

"Yes, Princess, we are closer to the coral reef here."

"Ahh, and what does that mean?"

"I don't know."

"I will wait for your answer." Lapita smiled.

Soon the white beach was only a narrow path amid huge boulders with dark gray streaks. Siga followed close to her mistress walking tall and strong ahead, her skirt flapping in the breeze. Siga was not allowed to come this way on her own but she was not afraid. On one side was the comforting presence of vesi trees whose roots demanded a tight hold upon scarce soil. On the other side of the narrow path was a steep drop to boulders pounded by the surf. One careless step or a sudden forceful wave taking a bite of the island ledge could be perilous. Siga stayed close to the cliff side of the path.

Lapita stopped and pointed out across the sea. "Viti Levu is across this water. Although it cannot be seen, we know it is there.

Siga flung her long hair out of her face with the force of the sea breeze and made herself look out, not down. A red footed bird with long black neck and back and white chest plunged into the waves and then rose again with a fish in his mouth.

"Often I have wanted to cross the watery divide by myself, to have the courage to set forth in an outrigger. But my arms are not strong, and I would need a man's assistance," said Lapita.

"Tavale has strong muscles."

"Yes, he does."

"And he is brave. Does he fish close to the shore?"

"No. The waves here are too much for even Tavale. He takes his canoe further out, where the bale of sea turtles swim." Lapita took a deep breath. "This way." She weaved her way among a grove of trees that hugged the cleft of the rock. "Look up, Siga. What do you see?"

"Paintings, Princess. Nana brought me here once to show me that history was written on our cliffs. She said this is a very special place for our golden race."

"Your nana was wise. She gave you a key, little one. These paintings were made by more than one golden who could see the importance of a foundation. It is good to travel and see new things, but if you know not where you started, how can you find your way home?"

"What do you mean?"

"A good question, Siga. And I am sure you will have a good answer when you think about it." She pointed at figures that had one knee bent and arms raised. "See the dancing men?"

"Are they warriors?"

"You have a keen eye. Yes, this one holds a war club."

"Who do they fight?"

"Another good question. The paintings have no answers. They portray the legendary lives our ancestors had on this island. Not much different from ours."

"Grandfather says we live in peace," said Siga.

"I would say we do not use war clubs."

Siga also tucked away that comment to think about later, and maybe ask for Grandfather's help. "What does this man have on his head?"

"That is a crown of feathers," said Lapita.

"You have a smaller one like that."

"Yes. It belonged to the Bete of many generations back, and it tells of the judgment of the Phoenix. It is not worn often."

Siga's finger stretched toward a dark form drawn on the cliff. "Dakuwaqa."

"Yes, always there is Dakuwaqa."

On the way back around the northern point of the island, they passed a grotto at the mouth of the stream that surged from the highland through limestone caves, finding its home within the ocean. A teenage couple sat close together in the sun, their feet in water that had been cooled inside the earth.

"Princess, my friend Dede Nikua said that the king was buried in that cave. Is she right?"

"There are many caves in there, and some of them connect with the pools of the red prawns."

"We didn't walk that far."

"We will do that another day. Above the cliff paintings is a cave where the kings and queens of Vahilele were laid to rest. The Kalou-Vu ni yalo."

"How do you get there?"

Lapita gazed at her steadily. "One day I will show you. You must not go there alone."

Siga's heart fluttered. She knew that would be a special day. *I can't wait to tell Dede Nikua!*

CHAPTER TWENTY THREE

Bahram

Days before the first fruits ceremony, Bahram met with the three elders who had experience in uniting the 180 natives on Vahilele. Each elder represented a village, a small group of huts in different areas. Bati was from Na Koro, the central village, Matai Malolo from the north and Dau from the south. Bahram had asked Lapita to include all the native leaders in this discussion. He even asked her help with the language barrier, and bribed her with the painted fan. But she was not here for his first council meeting.

"Where is Tavale?" he asked the elders, shrugging with palms spread upwards. Two of them shook their heads, and one pointed toward the beach. Bahram settled cross-legged facing them and motioned Nawfal and Abu to sit down behind him on each side.

"Bad start," murmured Abu to Nawfal. "This will be a short conversation."

Bahram silenced him with a glare. To the men seated in a line across from him, he said in Arabic, "How are you?" He flicked the sand off his new trousers.

"*Ni Bula*," whispered Abu.

"Yes. *Bula*," Bahram inclined his head, without lowering his eyes, and the elders murmured. He pointed to himself. "Bahram." And then gestured palm up towards the hunchbacked man in the center. "I remember your name is Bati, but I do not know the others."

Elder Bati waved a hand toward his right. "Elder Matai Malolo." And to his left. "Elder Dau." Each one nodded.

Bahram repeated the names as they were told and added, "*Bula*." He pointed at his mates who made their own introductions.

"We are friends," Bahram said, bowing with palms together. He relied on Arabic words and spoke slowly. "We talk about the future of Vahilele." He remembered Lapita's word. "*Ni mataka* Vahilele."

Elder Bati answered, "Vahilele *marau*."

Bahram had heard *marau* but could not remember its meaning, so he pressed on.

"Work. What work do you do? How you feed your people?"

Abu leaned toward him to give him the island *vosa*. "*Cakacaka*," he whispered.

"Vahilele *cakacaka*?" said Bahram.

"*Cakacaka* all day." The corpulent Matai Malolo used a cane to draw in the sand.

To his relief, Bahram understood the sketches depicting the island life of canoes, fish, taro and celebration. "Old way of life. You fence shallows and spear small fish." Bahram gestured with his hands and pointed at the drawings for reference. "Why not take canoes into sea and catch big fish? Vahilele *tagane* make fine canoes and nets," he said. "Very good."

"Very good canoe," said Dau. He sat twisted like a snake charmer Bahram once saw in Palembang, with his feet placed on the opposite thighs, soles facing upward.

"Everyone *cakacaka*," Bahram said. "Big world wants Vahilele *cakacaka*." He hoped his expansive arm gesture would get his words across.

The elders talked among themselves. When they gave Bahram their attention again, he picked up Lapita's sarong of brown *masi* cloth with black designs of four intersecting tracks containing circles.

"This would please the *marama* in Sumatra. Or India. Or

China." Bahram saw the confusion on their faces and interpreted that they were unfamiliar with these countries. "We start with Viti Levu." He smiled. They smiled and nodded. Then he held up an earthenware bowl with a Lapita design with almond shaped eyes stamped upon it. "Very good *bilo*," he said. "Viti Levu need." He smiled, and they smiled. And nodded. "I go Viti Levu. I see Viti Levu *bilo*." He shook his head. "Not good like Vahilele. I see *masi* cloth." He shook his head. "Not good like Vahilele." Their faces frowned but Bahram didn't know if it was because they didn't understand him or didn't agree. Frustrated at the difficulty of communication, angry at Lapita, his emotion boiled up. Bahram rolled to his knees in front of the startled natives and erased the sand drawings with a swipe of his hand.

"Lapita should be here," he muttered. Then he took a deep breath, settled cross-legged, flashed a fake smile and tried again. *How do I get this across to simple peasants?* He wiped sweat from his brow.

Then he took a knife from its sheath on his waist, and the elders sat in cautious courtesy to watch him sketch in the sand his vision of prosperity for their island. Bahram used sign language to strengthen his words. "Little *marama*, clean *vale,* clean *bure*. Big *marama* make *masi* cloth, make *bilo*. Old *marama* cook *kakana*." As he spoke, he drew columns of stick figures to represent workers under rough symbols of huts, dresses, pots and bananas. "*Marama cakacaka* for Vahilele. You men, *tagane*, take *bilo* and *masi* to Viti Levu bazaar." He held up the pottery and sarong. "Trade at bazaar." Bahram pointed to the symbols drawn in the sand. "*Tagane cakacaka* for Vahilele. Take canoe and nets to marketplace in Viti Levu."

"I trade *dalo*," said Elder Dau, with wrinkled brow. "No *bilo*. No *masi*."

"Now we trade together. All share *kakana*. All share *cakacaka*. All share profit." He placed a gold coin on the sand and drew lines connecting it to the stick figures. "Vahilele make good *cakacaka* for Viti Levu bazaar."

Then he drew six large faces, three on the natives' side of their circle, and three on his side. Bahram pointed to each man and then a correlating face drawn in the sand. "You three watch. Council." He pointed to his eyes. "We three watch. Council." He pointed to his eyes and shook his head. "Council no *cakacaka*." Pausing to see their response, he saw a small smile play on Matai Malolo's round face.

They all nodded. Did they understand?

To set them apart, Bahram presented each of the three natives a Sassanian gold coin on a sennit cord, like his own. Nawfal and Abu also were given coins to hang around their necks and were appointed to this new council of six watchmen. The three elders suddenly wore big smiles.

As they examined the coins with the image of a fire altar guarded by two figures on one side and a man wearing a crown on the other, Bahram said, "Need honest *tagane* to watch people *cakacaka*." He tapped his eyes and ears because he had not learned the word for spy and did not know how to communicate his thoughts. At the corner of a hut squatted a younger man Bahram had seen frequently loitering near the elders or walking with Matai Malolo along the path to the fishing village. Bahram pointed at him.

"You. What is your name?" he shouted.

The startled man looked at Bahram and then at the elders.

"Lalai," said Matai Malolo. "*Tokatoka*." He pointed to himself. One of his family.

"Excellent," said Bahram. "We have an overseer."

CHAPTER TWENTY FOUR

Siga

Siga could hardly wait to show her friend Dede Nikua the pocket doll Nawfal had made. Her bare feet lightly skipped along the path to the swimming hole where young girls gathered in the late afternoon. It was Siga's favorite part of the day. Her chores for the Princess were done until mealtime, and she was care free.

It was an exciting time to live in Vahilele. Everything was different from the year before because so many had perished with the pox. Children her age were assigned duties that in the past belonged to young adults. Now that there were only six her age in Na Koro, they depended upon each other, closer than they might have been before the tragedy. Twenty-four young girls from all three villages had more responsibility, and Siga passed on to them Lapita's stories of resilience and courage, a history of the tribe adjusting to previous hard times. Only at gatherings of the entire island were more than ten girls at this creek together. The last time was the day when baby Yaca got his name. Siga looked forward to the First Fruits Ceremony when she would again see friends, girls who were too old to play with toddlers, but not yet ready for marriage. An awkward, in-between age.

Before she even reached the rock pool surrounded by lush vegetation, Siga felt the change in temperature. The shade of the forest canopy preserved the coolness of the spring tumbling over rocks on a higher ledge to fall sharply into a hollow it had gradually carved into the coral limestone. She removed the new sulu her Princess had helped her make, placed the folded cloth on a dry rock, and stepped off the bank into the little stream of freshwater. Siga loved this hideaway and its exclusive freedom. Here secrets could be shared among girls only. They were a sisterhood that would remain a secure foundation in the tribe as they grew older together.

Her bare skin tingled from wafting cool air as she splashed upstream to the pool underneath a waterfall. Between her budding breasts, Siga's shell necklace swished back and forth. It was a recent birthday gift from Lapita, and Siga treasured the trust and love it signified.

She seated herself directly under the cascading water needles that prickled her head and shoulders, alone for now but expecting Dede Nikua shortly. Siga soaked up the musical sound of the falling water curtain that guarded the youngsters' secrets from those at the shallow baby pool down the hill where mothers watched infants and toddlers. Young married women bathed even further downstream or swam in the lagoon with the boys and were not interested in juveniles. Except to tease them.

When Siga was pounded limp by the waterfall, she stood and moved away from the cascade, where she settled down again with her head on a rock, arms floating lazily in a purling eddy. She was in a dreamy state when she thought of a game she could play, hiding the doll to make Dede Nikua search for it. She giggled and opened her eyes. As she excitedly scrambled to her feet, she saw a man squatted on the other side of the pool. His unexpected presence took her breath away. Siga recognized Abu, Bahram's friend who often joined a group of young people to teach them Arabic, especially when all the villages gathered. Siga had seen him walk by this pool several days ago when she played with her friends, but he had not stopped.

Today he watched her, and she didn't like it. She lowered herself in the water. It seemed strange that he was silent, but maybe he spoke and she didn't hear him because of the noise from the waterfall.

"Cola, Saca," she called out.

"Cola. Siga. I hope I did not disturb your bath. I thought you might be asleep." Abu rose and crossed the stream, moving slowly in sandals slipping on slick rocks, his agate eyes on Siga, his mouth turned up at the corners. "I was here yesterday but didn't see you. It must be difficult to work long hours with no time to play with your friends." He perched on a rock above her. A gold coin hung around his neck like the one her grandfather now wore. It signified importance. "You look so relaxed."

Siga scooted closer to within an arm's length so she could hear him over the falling water. Abu watched her every move.

"Your necklace is lovely." He reached out to gather it in his fingers. "Did you make it yourself?"

"The Princess made it for me. Golden cowrie shells are for royalty because they are..." She didn't know the Arabic word for valuable or scarce. Besides, he made her nervous because his knuckles rubbed against her chest. She experienced an uneasy fear and wanted to pull away. *What did he do?* He didn't hurt her, but he was breathing funny. She was suddenly afraid. The lonely pool was now too dark and too empty.

"Siga! I'm coming!" A familiar voice came from the forest, and Siga heard the pounding of feet on the path. Dede Nikua!

"My friend is here." She looked directly into black eyes that had no depth.

"Well then, I must be going," said Abu. "It was so nice to see you. If you have any questions about your Arabic, come to see me. You are one of my brightest students." Abu stood and nodded.

How foolish I am. Abu means no harm. Siga also rose to her feet and splashed out of the pool. "Dede Nikua. I brought you a doll. You liked mine so Nawfal made one for you." She took the wooden toy from the pouch she had placed with her clothing.

Her friend squealed. "I love her. Our dolls can talk together like we do."

Dede Nikua removed her sulu, and placed it next to Siga's.

An older girl came up to the stream that murmured over rocks on its way to the lagoon. "What's he doing here?" She paused to stare past Siga who turned in time to see Abu slide into the forest.

"I think he's lost," said Dede.

The pool was once more a place of laughter.

CHAPTER TWENTY FIVE

1950: The Storyteller

I interrupt my tale about Lapita, Bahram, and Siga because some of the children are having a hard time sitting still. One little girl buckled and unbuckled her red shoes, over and over, and then pulled the ribbon out of her hair and wound it around her legs. It is time to get them involved. I remind my audience that centuries ago our ancestors celebrated First Fruits as we still do today. "You know this is a ceremony to honor the gods for our harvest, but who can tell me how to get all the people together at one time without a telephone?" As expected, the answer is shouted out. "*Davui! Davui!*"

I choose one child, a polite well-mannered listener, and I tell him, "Since you have been especially attentive, you may have the special privilege to blow the tribal *Davui*. Blow as hard as you can so they can hear it for miles." I hand him a large conch shell trumpet. "This was a signal to get together in Na Koro, the central village, but the kai in the other two villages had to hear it, too. Blow as hard as you can."

When this child manages one significant sound, I encourage the other children to applaud the feat which is very difficult for young lips. We cheer, "Well done!" Some of us jump around.

"You will all get a chance to blow the *Davui*. Later. Now back to our story." While I wait for their excitement to calm, under the twinkling stars, I add kindling to the Spirit Fire. It must never go out again.

FIRST FRUITS CEREMONY
650 A.D.

Lapita

When they heard the Davui at the sun's highest point, the natives proceeded from their villages bearing yams in baskets, making their way up the hill to pass in front of the burial ground. Around the cemetery were huge slabs of rock carved with detailed human figures with uplifted arms and faces. Lapita watched from her position near the empty graves of her cremated husband and son marked by remnants of masi cloth. Her parents should have been buried in the ancestral cliff tomb for kings and queens, but only a marker lay there also. Because of the pox, there were many empty graves. Although she was saddened by the loss of her family, strong warmth wrapped Lapita in the approval of those who had traveled on. Last year at this time, there had been so much joy. One day all traces of her own life would be gone to dust, and this night would be the new past.

Lapita was flanked by Tavale on one side and Melane on the other with Yaca cradled in the folds of her garment. Lapita admired the kaukaua faces of the islanders who waved palm branches and sang makawa songs as they paraded in front of the sacred enclosure and past the royals. Many older friends of their parents bowed to Tavale and Lapita and wished them well, promising they would beseech the gods for wisdom and protection of the royal leaders. They graciously received the words of support.

One by one each family brought forth an offering to thank the gods for watching over their yanuyanu. They wound past the cemetery, laying the long, orange uvi they carried in a pile next to the natural rock platform for the speakers. Elder Matai Malolo directed the pacement of the growing mound of yams offered in humble gratitude to the gods. Elder Dau instructed the large assembly to move downhill so they could hear the speakers standing at the top. The women responsible for spreading out the feast for the islanders after the speeches were encouraged to stay near the path. These maramas would need an early start on the crowd to get everything ready to serve two hundred.

At the end of the procession, Elder Bati walked with head bowed forward under his humped back, one hand gripping his walking stick. He wore the traditional necklace made from parts of the banana tree, as did Matai Malolo and Dau. They also wore their coin necklaces. Bati, as leader of the council, stepped up to the flat rock outcropping where he could see over the heads of the crowd. Tavale and Lapita made their way to be near him, ready for their turn to address the islanders. Tavale wore the family Tabua, a whale's tooth hanging from a braided coconut fiber over a brown masi sheath formally draped over his shoulder. Lapita's sarong displayed a new design created for this event. She had accented her customary brown and black stripes with touches of damudamu, like flames of a buka. She and her brother stood in regal serenity.

Lapita noticed Bahram elbow his way to the front, followed by Nawfal and Abu close behind. The Persian wore his coin necklace with merchant attire, standing tall and solemn. Other sailors took places in the back of the congregation.

Elder Bati held up a hand until all the people were quiet. "People of Vahilele. Villages from the lagoon, the fields, and here in Na Koro, the oldest settlement. From all yanuyanu homes, together we offer a portion of our harvest to the royal family. It is only a small sample of the blessings we have received from the merciful bounty of our gods. We are deserving of their judgment, and we are grateful for what we have.

"Together we endured a tremendous loss of numbers. Together we mourn our diminished families, especially the young ones who departed so soon, but we did not allow weakness to defeat us. Perhaps the gods are pleased at this. We opened our hearts and homes to foreigners who endured the loss of their friends and have difficulty travelling back to their countries. Perhaps this also pleased the gods who have now blessed us with a new heir to the throne."

Tavale held baby Yaca aloft, over his head. The crowd rejoiced and called his name. When Yaca's head wobbled with a big smile, there were cheers and encouragement to have many more babies. Melane laughed and shook her head. Tavale nodded and the crowd cheered. Lapita tried not to think about her own barren future and applauded with the others.

Bati mentioned happier events from the past year, and the mood of the crowd remained cheerful. When he finished his oration, he stepped off the rock, placed his hands on the pile of yams, and bowed his head.

The next to speak was Tavale who also touched the offering of uvi before ascending the speaker's platform. "People of Vahilele, friends and council members," Tavale's vosa was soft with inexperience but gradually picked up volume. "You bring honor to our ancestors. Because of these gifts, our vanua will prosper. The last season of pain and suffering is past. This is a new beginning. Tavale cannot accept gifts in the name of Degei because the council waits for wisdom. I am not yet your king." He glanced at Elder Bati who stood near him. "But I will accept the offering as a Vahilele son whose blood came from an original golden tribe." He lifted an uvi above his head. "Those who protect this yanuyanu from harm bring me whispers in the cagi. They tell me you have done well, my kai. You will be rewarded. When our sun rises in the morning, everyone come to the field village to share our Vahilele harvest."

The crowd raised their hands, breaking into noisy appreciation. "Dua, dua, dua." As they chanted the traditional respect to leaders, Tavale raised his own hand in salute and relinquished the platform to his sister. Lapita took his hand to step higher on the rocks to address the crowd.

The tribe's enthusiasm brought a warm smile to her face, and she waved to the people as they cheered. It had been a long time since their last festive celebration. "Oi...Dua!" When the noise died down, she spoke from her heart.

"Beautiful people of the yanuyanu Vahilele. My home forever." Tears welled up as she looked out on the smiles of hope and love focused her way. "The family of the Turaga ni vanua wishes to offer our gratitude for standing kaukaua with us in this time of recovery."

Applause and shouts of "Bete" covered the hillside.

"You are always in our hearts. We ask the makawa's gods for happiness and prosperity for Vahilele." There were loud cheers of "Phoenix Vanua."

"The beautiful women of Vahilele prepared a feast for all. Come now to the center of Na Koro, the heart of our island. Let us celebrate all that unites us. Vanua forever."

In the emotional wave of applause that erupted, Lapita turned to take Tavale's hand to step off the rock and noticed Bahram trying to get her attention over the heads of the tight congregation in front of the platform. Lapita thought he looked ready to speak when introduced.

His Arabic words were drowned out by native noise. "Lapita, wait...I want to say a few words!"

Lapita pretended she didn't see him and bent her head to speak to Tavale and Melane while they blocked the entry to the rock platform. Just by standing still and ignoring Bahram, they diffused his attempted takeover of the ceremony. As the crowd broke apart, the royal trio hurried to maneuver into their customary positions at the head of the procession.

"We act like children," Lapita whispered to her brother. But the camaraderie they shared was more satisfying to them than having one of Bahram's shiny coins.

The royal family led the tribe down the path without pretention, single file at narrow steep spots expanding to allow chattering groups where the path widened.

"You spoke well. You have a gift for touching the hearts of our people." Melane whispered to Lapita.

"I can only share what I know and stand true to the lessons I learned as a child. I was fortunate to have wise teachers." She playfully tapped Yaca's nose. He gave her a tiny smile and tried to suck on her finger.

When the young prince fretted in Melane's arms, she shifted him to face over her shoulder. At the sight of the women coming down the hill behind them, the four-month-old was distracted, especially when they waved and laughed at his laugh. He kicked his legs and windmilled his arms in the air hitting his mother's head.

"Tavale," Melane called out. "Carry your son."

Tavale stopped to seize the infant and hold him high. Yaca gurgled and made swimming motions in the air, to the merriment of the islanders who missed all the children taken by the pox. Each one born now was treasured.

The descent down the hill was more festive than the procession past the burial ground before the speeches. As they walked, Melane hung back to chat with other maramas, allowing Lapita a few moments alone with Tavale.

"I hope you have many more peipeis," Lapita said to her brother. "Yaca makes you smile. You are too serious for such a young tagane."

"A chief has to be serious. I am charged with the care of many," said Tavale.

They walked in silence, Lapita wondering if Tavale knew that Bahram planned to be the island's leader. Surely the elders had told her brother about the council meeting. How could she approach Tavale about a decision handled by the men in the tribe? *How can I be a bond between two leaders? Only as Bete would I be allowed to voice an opinion.*

"I was thinking about our childish behavior that prevented Bahram from speaking. Father would not have approved, and our grandfather Ratu was gracious and noble."

"Mother would have laughed, and she was wise," said Tavale, and the siblings smiled as they recalled the joy their parents shared. "And your husband would have told you the First Fruits Ceremony is not for foreigners."

"Tavale, not long ago you thought these foreigners were very generous to our kai. I will try to be more gracious." She spoke with determination although doubts clouded her soul. Even as Bete, she would not be able to persuade either Bahram or Tavale to change.

"It is wise to be gracious but you cannot praise Bahram more than he praises himself."

Lapita smiled and nodded in agreement.

"You forget the lesson you taught me, sister."

"Which one?" she teased.

"When a canoe has a hole in the bottom, it fills up with water. The hole has to be plugged so it can ride the waves again."

The two golden royals burst into laughter, a delightful beginning to a celebration of life.

For two hours the megapode chickens, fish, cassava, dalo, and yams wrapped in banana leaves had been lying on hot stones in deep pits covered with leaves and coconut stalks. The procession came into the pavilion area of the main village, and the women hurried to lay out on long planks the many kakana bowls filled with all that the yanuyanu provided. As the sun set, the contented people of Vahilele embraced renewal.

CHAPTER TWENTY SIX

Bahram

Bahram helped himself to the smorgasbord laid out before him, his anger at Lapita and Tavale slowly receding as the sun slipped over the horizon. He rationalized that the natives would not have understood him anyway. *Why make a speech?*

A lovely young woman came over to him with a big smile above her bare breasts. Her hips gyrated beneath a grass skirt, and he did not need a translator. When he grasped the hand she held out to him, she led him to the light of the fire where natives danced away the night. For awhile, he enjoyed keeping time to the rhythm, stomping his feet and wiggling his shoulders and hips, encouraged by those around him. When he saw Breaker and Turban clapping and heard the obscenities they were shouting, he decided he looked foolish. He left the festivities, alone, since Dedan stayed near Yaca who dropped most of his food on the ground.

As he walked, Bahram recalled the dark days before celebration. Because his arm was broken, Breaker would have been lost at sea when the *Nabataea* went down except Turban hauled him to shore. Breaker was forever that man's devoted servant. There was a lesson of dependence there. Bahram considered the man whose ankle was broken in several places on the recent trip to Viti Levu. Siga's uncle. It was doubtful he would ever paddle again, and he would be bitter and depressed. Bahram thought about gaining his loyalty.

He wandered over to the cluster of huts used by the sailors. Bahram found Nawfal lying in a net fastened on both ends to the poles holding up the roof.

"Is this your bed?"

"More comfortable than lying on stone." Nawfal rolled out and gestured toward two wooden benches against the wall. "Have you come to dance?"

Bahram gave a short bark of laughter, in spite of himself. "I guess my reputation precedes me. That was not my finest moment. I looked like a clumsy simpleton."

"Because you were being lighthearted? There's nothing shameful about carefree enjoyment that harms no one else and balances sadness and hard work." Nawfal offered him a cloudy concoction one of the comrades had made with the spirits salvaged from the *Nabataea*, and they settled outside in the cool of the night. Other sailors joined them, and they shared stories of home and families, waiting or not. Bahram shared his plan for the island's future amidst the distant jungle background of beating drums.

"I have been to Viti Levu, and I've seen the trade coming in from Srivajaya, New Guinea, Sumatra. When I compared the quality of our pottery with others displayed at the bazaar, there was no doubt ours was superior. I can say the same for the masi cloth. Also, I think we can increase our production of outriggers for commercial trade. In fact, our little island has an abundance of desirable resources. Look at the sandalwood and vesi trees. Those alone are worth exportation."

"The natives don't want to work all day, Bahram," said Nawfal. "Maybe you want them to have more sophisticated lives, but they are happy with what they have." He broke a branch from an ironwood tree, got a small knife, and sat down to whittle.

"Most of them have not been off this island, and they don't know what they are missing. When I showed Lapita the Chinese fan I bought her, she couldn't keep her hands off it.

She expressed admiration of the colors and the design, probably never saw one before."

"Did you ask her?" William was direct, in his Nordic manner.

"He doesn't know the words yet," said Nawfal.

Ghazi laughed in spite of Bahram's scowl.

"What do you think about staying here and making an effort to build the economy of Vahilele?" Bahram was ready for business, but he needed a team. This was as good as any. "The natives don't understand commerce so they need administrative help."

One sailor nodded. The others were silent.

Bahram said, "I left word in Viti Levu that we have sailors looking for work, so it is possible you can leave at some time in the future."

"We know that. Didn't you notice that another mate has gone?"

Bahram's eyes widened. "When?"

"Shortly after you came back. For a jug of honey from the storeroom, he bribed a native to get passage off the island. We don't know what became of him."

"I guess Abu did mention it, but I was obsessed with planning a new island. I hope the rest of you stay because I'll need your help. Each of you outworks any native, and they need your leadership. And you are not going to work for free. There will be enough profit to pay you handsome wages."

"How handsome?" asked William.

"I don't know exact numbers. The details will have to be filled in as we progress." Bahram gave them the bare bones of his idea. "There is no doubt that the natives have the skills and patience for making outstanding outriggers and cloth. Our job is to increase their productivity and export the products on a larger scale. I will be a broker for them to improve the quality of their lives."

While the men talked among themselves, Bahram asked Nawfal, "What are you whittling? It has a face."

"Just a pocket doll. I gave one to Siga and Dede. Now another friend wants one. Very simple, no arms or legs, more like a totem to hold in your hand. And I'm not making them to sell."

"I wouldn't ask you to because there is no market." Bahram winked at the *Nabataea* rower, a man too big to dance.

"Good. I hope they are appreciated only on this island as my gifts to the Vahilele natives," said Nawfal.

"No need to get prickly." Bahram chortled. "One moment. You said natives. Have you given these to the boys, too?"

"Yes. The boys use them for good luck charms. With the girls, no doubt."

"I need one next time I get on a canoe."

"Get in line. I'm working as fast as I can, and there are hundreds in front of you."

The listening sailors hooted in their beards at that remark. Bahram left them in good humor to talk about what he proposed. When he got back to his vale, he considered his hard sleeping bench that leaves did not soften.

Maybe tomorrow I will sleep in a net.

CHAPTER TWENTY SEVEN

Bahram

The next morning, when Bahram and Dedan left Na Koro, Abu passed them, going the other way.

"Where are you headed now?" Abu asked.

"To inspect the crew building canoes."

"The natives will not work until after they collect their share of the harvest. Tonight will be another celebration. I'm going home to bed so I will be rested. I'll see you later."

Bahram shook his head and continued. The decadent manner of island living was affecting his comrades. He strolled past a small fire where a woman stirred the mangrove roots to make masi cloth dye. She used the iron pot Rangi brought her on the last Viti Levu trip. Her harelip was a jarring blemish in his perfect world, and he wondered if she had children. He gave her a nod and continued on the trail that took him through tall cane grass to the shore on the northern edge of the island.

One of his shipmates approached through a grove of pandanus trees whose webbed roots tangled above the ground, twisted together like the past and future of Vahilele. Ghazi gripped a necessary tool of his trade in one hand, a stone adze used to hollow out a canoe or cut firewood.

"I want to talk with you." Ghazi's voice was sharp. The former blacksmith was a stocky man whose chest and back were forested with black curly hair. "Tavale does not cooperate. He disrupted our work, encouraging the men to go to the field village to get their share of yams. They are still gone. Abu thinks they will celebrate again tonight."

"Abu is sleeping off the palm wine from last night's "fruitless" ceremony" and, like them, ready to drink again tonight," Bahram mocked. Requesting help from an invisible spirit made little sense to him when the success of the yam harvest was the result of his good management of the field hands. When he became the King, the Kisra of Vahilele, he would eliminate this archaic ritual. "I think it is a useless event that should be cancelled."

"That might improve production from some, but Tavale is a troublesome vassal who doesn't recognize his place." The blacksmith tightly gripped the adze's wooden handle to slash at the grass next to his feet. "He will not follow instructions." The sharp stone responded. Whack. A small tree was cut in two.

"Convince him there's a price for disobedience."

"He frightens the others with tales of a shark, and they don't listen to me." Whack.

"I'll talk to him. When the others pause for their midday meal, send Tavale to me."

"If I see him."

Bahram took a long walk to consider this insubordination and how to handle it. He could not afford a mutiny, but he must be firm. At water's edge, he advanced past towering vesi trees and slogged through sand and over rocks to take another look at the petroglyphs. The Persian mariner stayed there a long while, examining the rock art and contemplating a spot for a figurative addition. He would sketch his own design and appoint a team of artisans to start working on it. A new project to keep his tribe busy would be prudent.

Last night's heathen babble alerted him to the incipient stirrings of discontent. Bahram no longer knelt in homage to Mazda, but he would not allow superstitious nonsense to be the religion of his kingdom. New ideas might arise from conflict, but it was best that these natives know he had ultimate control. He aspired to be a benevolent commander, but he would dispense rapid justice to those who sought to diminish his authority. Including Tavale who kept him from speaking at the dedication of the yams.

CHAPTER TWENTY EIGHT

Lapita

Returning from her daily devotion on the beach, Lapita greeted one of the workers from the pottery hut. "Bula."

The woman approached with lowered gaze, taking careful steps along the path. She glanced up with a brief smile. "Bula, Princess." She carried wai in earthenware jars suspended on rope from each end of a bamboo pole balanced over one shoulder.

"I heard laughter in the forest and thought of our children. How quickly my mind recalled a time before our great sadness. It is still like a bad dream to me." Lapita inclined her head to acknowledge that she knew that this nana, too, had lost her son. "For all of us."

The villager nodded her head. She pointed into the palm forest. "Muas chase chickens."

"Like children," said Lapita. "They do not know control."

"They celebrate when the black koli kills a megapode chicken."

Lapita hesitated, taking in the marama's words, realizing it had been a long time since one of the large red-headed birds strolled across the Na Koro common ground. They were unable to fly and at the mercy of carnivores. The woman walked on, and Lapita continued down the path. She didn't know what to say about Dedan. She was fond of him.

And how could she demand that the sailors leave these flightless birds alone when the natives themselves would eat them on special occasions.

Her inner spirit was anxious. This was something Bahram would have to address, and she would have to use the right vosa to get his attention away from gathering wealth. She sought Melane's wise support. As she approached the hut of her brother's family, she heard the little one whimpering.

"Melane. It is Lapita. Do you rest?"

"Come in, Lapita."

She slid the brown fabric back and entered. The bamboo side facing the forest was rolled up to encourage the passage of cool air. Those travelling along the path could not see the linterior.

"I teach Yaca that tavioka is tasty." Melane put a tiny bit of pudding on his lips, and he spit it back at her. "He does not agree."

Lapita laughed. She reached out to pet the chubby leg that kicked his nana. "You are like your cousin." Her words caught in her throat recalling her own child was now a whisper in the wind.

"Lapita?" Melane reached out to caress a graceful golden shoulder destined to carry the future of her tribe in spite of the burden of internal scars.

"It is true." Lapita put on a marau face and worked through the despair that had threatened to repossess her. "He would eat only small grains of dalo at this age." She smiled at her gentle sister-in-law. "I am not sad. I remain kaukaua. I will show Yaca how my boy liked tavioka."

"Can you watch him while I get prawns for dinner?"

"Of course. We will do well together."

She was so entranced by the peipei, Lapita forgot she had come to Melane's hut for advice.

CHAPTER TWENTY NINE

Bahram

Bahram roamed the island to encourage his tribe to work faster after their days of indulgence. From the tapa shed came the sound of robust women pounding the bark, its inner layer having been soaked and scraped with shells. He stopped to observe the pieces being overlapped and beaten at the joints. At the other end of the shed, the dry cloth was decorated with a pattern of canoes, or turtles, or flowers to become masi cloth used for trade.

He was pleased with the progress here, but then he walked to the eastern side of Vahilele. At the lagoon, he viewed with contempt the customary fences that trapped fish for spearing at low tide. He had continually told the fishermen how they could catch more fish using nets. His advice was ignored, but he decided he would have to reform this tradition at another time. *I cannot change everything at once*. At the moment, he had a more important project to develop. He would have to find the words to spark Lapita's imagination so that she could envision Vahilele's possibilities and share his dreams. As Bahram made his way along the sea trail with Dedan, he rehearsed a proposal of marriage to the princess.

Bahram thought Lapita did not understand her role in his future. *She is governed by memories of ritual and tradition. If only she could see that my reforms would greatly improve the daily lives of the natives.*

He was so engrossed in his internal dialogue that Melane's sudden appearance coming out from behind the tangled vines at the bottom of the cliff startled him. And her. She carried a large basket of red prawns.

"Melane, do you have a secret place to harvest your dinner?" He smiled.

"Red prawns. *Uradamudamu*. Tavale." She kept her scarred face bowed in his presence. "And Lapita. *Kalou-Vu ni yalo*."

Bahram would not ask what she had said. "I approve the good care of your family. Move along." He stood in the shadows while Melane hurried up the path, casting furtive looks over her shoulder. When she was out of sight, he followed Dedan behind the vines into a mangrove forest where ocean tides met the freshwater within the island. He saw the hiding place where the heron laid her eggs. Here intricate caves among the roots and rocks protected shallow pools that the wind and sea could not destroy. And below the clear water were hundreds of red prawns, a delicacy Bahram had heard sailors describe. He emitted a long low whistle into the dank cavern illuminated by light shafts eroded through the limestone cliff. "This is incredible! I thought it was merely a legend," he whispered.

Bahram walked back to Na Koro, absorbed in a strategy for a new commercial venture. The first to get his bowl filled by the busy women who had prepared yams for the workers, he carried his meal to his hut and sat outside cross-legged to watch his people mingle and relax in the common area. He told himself he learned more from watching than through conversation. *Observation is a wise advisor, and here comes trouble.* He studied the approach of a proud man, loin cloth revealing sinewy leg muscles. Tavale had recovered his good health and now looked menacing in his determined gait. Against his golden arm the jagged scar showed vividly. His countenance showed neither fear nor friendship.

Bahram deliberately remained seated and did not speak. When he felt as though he had established dominance over the moment, he motioned to his left.

"Sit with me, and we shall talk."

Tavale squatted with his back to the vale, balanced easily on bare feet. He waited.

"I understand that you once explored different islands. Did you learn Arabic?" Bahram looked at Tavale while he spoke, but the native prince did not give any sign he understood the question.

"Are you happy here? Marau?" Bahram patted the ground.

"Home."

"Yes, but do you like your home?" Bahram thumped a fist over his heart in an effort to communicate.

Tavale nodded. He swept his hand around the clearing where islanders ate and chatted. Then he pointed at Bahram and crossed his wrists over his chest. "Na Koro, friends."

"Yes, friends. We saved you. Without us, you would be gone." Bahram gestured over his head, assuming the tribe's belief in an afterlife.

Tavale did not respond. He watched the common area activity before he spoke with deliberation, "Tavale, *Ratu*. Lapita, *Adi*. Melane, *Adi*." He smoothed the brown linen sash tucked into his waistband and paused.

This man is dimwitted. "I don't understand. I know the chief was your father." Bahram spoke slowly. "I thought Lapita was your sister and married to the High Priest. Is Melane your sister too? You are married to your sister, or is she your cousin?"

"Yaca, *Tui*."

"Your son. Tui?"

Tavale moved his hand motioning waves and pointed northeast. "Beqa."

"Lapita told me your mother came as a bride from the island of Beqa."

"Sawau."

"I thought it was Beqa." Bahram shook his head and snorted. "Your family history is not important." The tone of his voice was harsh. "Truthfully, you are not important. You had nothing but misery when I arrived. I showed you how to enhance the fortunes of your people. They could be wealthy if they turned loose from your moldy ideas from the past." He pointed at himself. "You work for me now. You should be thankful to me, not to invisible gods."

They sat in silence until Tavale rose in one motion and moved away, head held high, thick black hair like Lapita's controlled with a slim coconut fiber coronet.

"Go to work, you ignorant peasant," Bahram shouted at the retreating back. "I'll talk to your sister or cousin, whoever she is, about this shark nonsense." He muttered to himself as Tavale's long strides took him swiftly along the path into the surrounding forest. "She has the intelligence to show homage to her master." He quieted when he saw that some of the natives looked toward him and talked among themselves. He silently twisted the captain's button.

For a long time, Bahram sat in the narrow shade of his hut sipping the yaqona he had hoarded from the previous night's ceremony. The kava beverage prepared from pepper shrub roots was intended only for the elite because it had a mellowing effect on the average islander. As the sun rose higher, he resumed his inspection tour and walked south to the taro fields. He had heard that Abu took the place of a group leader, a *Nabataea* sailor who said it was too difficult to make the natives work. Bahram wanted to support Abu's decision to take a man's job instead of giving language lessons all day.

The midday break was over, but one worker still lay under a palm tree at the edge of a clearing. From a distance Bahram saw that Abu stood over him and kicked his leg.

"Get up, you lazy cur," Abu shouted. As Bahram came up behind the two men, the native roused himself to roll over. "Lalai, you are worthless." Abu kicked him again.

Lalai stood. He frowned at this little man who wore the golden coin of dominance. He rubbed his stomach and uttered a complaint.

"You are not the one doing the labor. We made you the *boso*. Get over there and tell your friends to cut down those trees. We need a larger field." As Abu gestured with hand in the air, he noticed Bahram watching them. He slapped Lalai's golden face with the back of his hand. "Get to work."

Abu turned towards Bahram, shaking his head. "The natives are slower than usual today."

"The next time there's a ceremony, we will plan for a day off."

"They celebrate everything." Abu grimaced and wiped the sweat from his forehead.

"They need direction like children," said Bahram. Together they watched Lalai talk to his crew.

"Why do we have a council meeting tonight?" asked Abu.

"Exports are doing better, but we are still a small operation dependent upon canoes. The elders can tell us the contacts we need to make in Viti Levu and other islands to attract a company with a large trading vessel. Then we could multiply our profit."

"Can't argue with that. What would we use for incentive?"

"A festive celebration with good food and beautiful women." Bahram grinned. "And there's a small amount of gold left from the shipwreck." *Thanks to the good captain.*

"Is that the gold you promised me and Nawfal if we stayed here?"

"Don't worry. There's enough left to divide. Have you collected everyone's property tax?"

"Most of it. Tavale is difficult. If we force him to pay, then they all will."

"Take his hut and give it to Matai Malolo. That will get the attention of these natives." Bahram looked directly at Abu. "If that doesn't work, Nawfal can pay him a visit."

Abu shrugged.

Bahram completed his rounds and returned to Na Koro. Lapita was outside her hut, talking with a thin wooly-headed man who dissolved into the forest when the Persian approached. Lapita's brow was furrowed.

"I will rest while you prepare my dinner." Bahram slowed his steps to admire his favorite scenery although his view had been limited since she moved out of his hut.

"You push my people hard. They have *rarawa*." Her words were short and crisp, but she was learning his language. And he had heard *rarawa* enough to know it meant sadness.

"They will change their minds when we are the wealthiest island in Srivijaya." He inhaled the seductive fragrance of the tipanie garland she wore. "One day ships will be lined up to enter our lagoon."

She shook her head. "That is not what we want."

"You have no imagination." He reached for her hand, but she put it behind her back.

"You do not understand because you do not listen." Lapita stood tall, and a scowl gave her a fierce look. "Tavale talked with you. Tavale is royalty, and he merits honor. He is one with the sea. Sharks protect our reef, and he respects them. Tavale's son will one day be our chief. Our story will be carried into *ni mataka,* tomorrow and beyond."

"Yes, we talked. We sat down together, as friends, and he agreed that I know what is best for the good of all," Bahram lied.

Lapita shook her head again and looked past him. She sighed deeply, ignoring his ardent gaze. Then she drew her fingertips across her cheekbones. "Waves pound in my ears. Fire grows inside and my eyes burn." Lapita tucked her chin. "Siga prepares dinner for you."

"Of course, my dear. You had too much sun today." He snatched her hand and smiled triumphantly. "Stay where it is cool, and I will return to soothe your pain." He kissed her fingertips and rubbed his full dark beard with her knuckles. The musical notes of her speech had stirred a desire to hold her closely, as he had before she moved back to her temple. "The council meeting will not take long."

Lapita withdrew her hand from its prison, and brushed back her curtain to enter the Bure Kalou. Bahram watched her retreat. Once she had been a hostess grateful to Bahram, but now her intense headaches had become a barrier between them. These episodes were more frequent, and lately she avoided his company, isolated in her hut, like a brooding tigress. Bahram resented the rejection. He often felt her stealing his thoughts when he should be concentrating on policy decisions for the island. His focus was compromised by uncontrolled memories of the touch of her fingers, the comfort of her generous breasts.

Fire grows for certain, woman.

CHAPTER THIRTY

Lapita

The next morning Lapita poured her bath wai into a basin that Siga had placed on a stand in her bure. The stream that ran under the yanuyanu had never run dry. It was a blessing they depended upon, a sign of favor from the gods.

Outside, Bahram's call to Dedan as they left Na Koro for their daily inspection tour reminded her that Melane had met Bahram on the path to the cliffs outside the mangrove forest. Melane was sure he went behind the vines that protected the pool of the red prawns, after she was out of his sight. This was a problem more serious than Dedan chasing chickens.

In the past Lapita would have discussed a wise solution with the elders, but it was obvious that they regarded Bahram as a temporary chief and would allow him special consideration. She could involve Tavale but her brother tightened his lips and stalked the other way whenever she mentioned Bahram's name. The day before had been filled with tension. Several men had walked home rather than complete their cakacaka for someone who shouted in a vosa they did not understand. But that was on the baravi of the lagoon, and Tavale would have to handle it as the boso of canoe builders.

Lapita reasoned. *I was schooled in tribal history not canoes.*

As a youngster Lapita had listened to the talk around her grandfather's Yaqona circle of counselors. All her life she had heard tales of different lands, and she had met people of different religions. Grandfather Tui Waitu had treated them all with respect. He had taught her there was a natural rule of behavior shared by all people, no matter their origin. The differences in people were demonstrated by their choices.

Lapita decided her place was to confront Bahram and tell him the legend of the red prawns and endure his usual scorn for their traditions. *I will give Bahram a choice.*

Late in the day, Lapita saw him at the tapa shed watching the women work. She invited him to her vale where she offered him yaqona without the ceremony. They sat outside the circle of stones enclosing the live embers. Siga stood in the shadows.

"Were decisions made at the council meeting last night?"

"We discussed the good news of babies and their care. One in Na Koro and two more in the fishing village. Since women are needed to prepare food for the men who work, the care of children must be shared by the community," reported Bahram. "Maca Matanitu has not recovered from the death of her infant months ago so the council excused her from heavy work. She was assigned the duty of watching the youngest children in the afternoon while their mothers work shifts to prepare dinner for our tribe. Two hundred and growing."

"She cannot care for many at one time. Her legs are weak."

"We will see. If you want a voice at the council, you should attend."

"A woman's voice is not welcome," insisted Lapita.

"You are as wise as any of your elders."

Lapita considered this flattery, not praise. "It takes little wisdom to see that Dedan is killing more chickens than he can eat."

"I will tie him up."

"He will not like that."

"I shall not give him a choice."

"Your sailors encourage him to chase the chickens."

Bahram smiled. "I cannot tie them up."

"Should I bring this to the council, or will you?"

"I will have a discussion with the sailors and Dedan about chickens. This is why you wanted me to come to your vale?"

"No. Soon we will have a planting ceremony and celebrate the special blessings here. Then we ask for a successful crop of prawns. There will be a meke dance about an important tradition to Vahilele, the legend of the prawns. They are protected by the Phoenix."

Bahram did not mention to her that he already knew about these prawns. Instead he asked, "What Phoenix? The mythical firebird that rises from the ashes?" He snorted.

"The spirit that Degei sends to watch over the people of Vahilele."

Bahram sipped his drink in silence.

Lapita also was silent. Important words required thought.

"Are you angry at me for trading megapode eggs?"

"I speak about prawns. Not eggs," she said.

"Are you certain?"

Lapita motioned for Siga to leave. The white veil fluttered and brief sunlight accompanied the girl's departure.

Lapita had not intended to address this rumor now, but here was a choice. "Tell me the reason you traded eggs for Tongan war clubs."

"Because I admire them, and we don't have weapons to defend the island." He shook his head. "A woman does not understand."

"I understand they have spikes to break men's heads. Again I ask. Why did you trade eggs for war clubs?"

"If we have their clubs, the Tongans shall not be using them on us."

"The Tongan traders said they wanted an outrigger."

"Why can they not build their own?"

Bahram's expression mocked her, and she grew impatient with him. "They do not have vesi trees on their island. There is much you do not understand about our kai."

"I think they heard we were vulnerable and planned an attack. They are a war-like tribe."

"You said that about the Samoans. Not everybody is looking to fight."

"You are naïve, my dear. I lost my home and family to invaders. The rest of the world is continually at war."

"For what reason?"

"Life is better for the strong because they make laws that the weak have to follow."

Lapita stared into the spirit fire. "I can see we need to defend ourselves."

Bahram took Lapita's hand, and she pulled it away. "Do not worry, my love. I would not hurt you nor my people of Vahilele. I am here to help you." He smiled as he stood. "You will see."

CHAPTER THIRTY ONE

1950: The Storyteller

Adults straggle in behind the children to hear the familiar story. The little girl with red shoes is curled up on the ground, asleep.

I tell my growing audience, "The rhythm of Na Koro lives changed, but the faster pace always played out against a natural backdrop of brilliant green and gold amid the warm comfort of whispering breezes.

"The salvaged portion of the *Nabataea* cargo included luxury barrels of dates, leather and copper. With worldly experience, the newcomers transformed the lifestyle of an ancient people who had never desired more than basic sustenance, peace, love and joy. Beware temptation, my children."

650 A.D.

Bahram

On his next trip to Vuda Point, Bahram took Abu and a second outrigger.

"Why do we take two canoes, Saca?" asked Vunde Moto, the navigator in charge.

Bahram clapped him on the shoulder. "I will make large purchases to bring back to Vahilele."

Vunde Moto looked confused.

"Abu, tell him."

"Do you want me to tell him what you are buying?"

"Tell him we are trading copper for a cauldron."

Abu launched into an island vosa that cleared the navigator's furrowed brow and had him nodding.

When they reached Vuda Point, Bahram gave the crew five days to trade taro like they had always done. Two of the natives transported a barrel filled with Lapita's pottery to the merchant that Bahram met on his first visit.

"Do you have a place for more Vahilele pottery? The best in these islands, I assure you."

"Ah, yes. The man who bought the last piece asked if there would be more available. I told him to come back next time his ship harbored at Vuda Point."

"There is plenty more. My man Abu will take care of delivery and inventory."

Introductions were made, and Bahram travelled to Viseisei.

The native sentry he had seen before was again stationed in front of the governor's house.

"Good day to you. Thank you for the excellent advice on accommodations you gave me last time I was here." Bahram spoke in Arabic. "I am back to confer with the Governor on a business opportunity. Is he available today?"

This time, Bahram got to walk on the oriental carpet he had only glimpsed before. As expected, the governor was open to discussion about projects that would initiate more commerce for the area. Their conversation gave Bahram new ideas, but his initial purpose impressed the governor and heightened an alliance.

"Have you ever grown rice?" The well-fed man preened his mustache.

"At this stage it is an experiment. I oversee the taro farming on my island, but I see a future in rice production. We have experienced a labor shortage, and I will need skilled workers."

"I heard about your tragedy. We, too, were hit hard by the pox. The locals are especially vulnerable to disease brought from other countries. It will take years to recoup our losses, and I plan to bring in new workers." The governor sat on a tapestry upholstered chair whose high back and arms were ornately carved.

"I am an investor, Saca. I create jobs for those who have special skills. For example, I have a pottery factory in Vahilele and also a shipyard for construction of double-hulled canoes, the best on local water."

"Possibly we could work out an agreement. We have an advantage with the accessibility of our harbor which I understand you lack."

"I hope to take advantage of your expertise in these matters. If the price is right, of course."

The governor brushed crumbs from his silk sleeve. "I understand we are speaking about the necessity for farm labor."

"You are correct."

"My price is standard for this commodity. I have an established Bali contact for experienced field labor. However, at this time, I suffer a shortage. Perhaps I could release four of my own workers to get your venture started. They are all healthy Bali men well experienced in the planting and harvesting of a rice crop."

"You are a prudent man. I will take your advice and go slowly. Certainly there is no guarantee of success, but that is an elusive goal for gentlemen of vision like ourselves." His thoughts were less generous. *I could probably do this without your archaic assistance.*

The rest of the afternoon was spent in touring the governor's holdings, examining his records on rainfall and crop production, and enjoying the generous hospitality afforded a man of means, a new perspective for Bahram.

The next day four male workers were selected to make a move to Vahilele. The governor made it clear to them they were being ordered to leave. They were confused and asked questions that were never answered. By the time Bahram escorted them to the harbor at the end of the week, they were openly rebellious. Bahram sought help from Abu, his language expert.

"Abu, take control of my new friends here. I cannot understand what they are saying. Explain to them where they are going and that they will not be hurt. If things work out, their families will come to join them. If not, they will be returned here."

Abu pieced together words of unknown origin, and Bahram could tell the effect on the Balinese men. They quieted and even smiled. He told Abu to tell them they would make real money, not shells. They were soon willing to leave Vuda Point.

The Vahilele crew solemnly made room for them.

The day after Bahram returned to Vahilele from his second trip to Viti Levu, he awoke rested and motivated to work. He left his hut to walk the path to the lagoon. Dedan galloped toward him from the direction of Melane's vale.

"So that's where you sleep when I'm not around. I thought you stayed with Lapita." He leaned down to rub the silky black ears. "You're with me today."

It felt good to be back on his island. He waved to several women congregating at the pavilion to make the tribe's midday meal. The air was soft, stirred by an ocean breeze that was fresh, without the spicy odor of Viseisei. He approached the thatched roof of the area where the mats were made from leaves of a saltwater marsh plant, boiled and pounded with a heavy stick. He could hear the team of women already at work. When the pulp had dried in the sun, it was rolled into bundles and cut into strips to be woven and decorated with tiny shells around the edges. The rhythmic beats of the wood stirred in his mind a birth ceremony of the night before. He had not stayed long. This morning the breeze and sunlight cleansed the atmosphere of the ominous current Bahram had felt when the dancers, shiny with coconut oil, lunged with their decorated spears to the beat of the bamboo sticks on hollow logs.

He stopped to gesture at the new kettle delivered that morning. The women were still filling it with water, but the fire underneath was burning. "You like?" He said to a woman close by, and she nodded, never missing a beat with her stick. Bahram envisioned their handling larger orders for outrigger sails. He would begin negotiation on that contract after he set up the construction of the new pond they would need for the rice farm. So much to do, but this ex-sailor enjoyed every minute. He thought his father would be surprised at his success as a merchant, maybe even pleased.

Bahram entered the forest travelling downhill, his heavy soles crunching sand on the path. Several yards in front of him, Lapita glided, as graceful as the palms she passed. Her swaying hips drew his attention. Bound in tight fabric they moved seductively back and forth, and he averted his glance lest he be tempted. She had been polite last night, but he would not act as though he needed her attention. He had a satisfactory diversion in Viseisei.

At the water's edge, Lapita stooped to speak to Melane, washing baby Yaca.

Abruptly it occurred to him that there was a natural succession of leaders. After Tavale, this child would be next in line to be chief, followed by any brothers that would be born, and then Tavale's grandsons.

From the shadows, Bahram observed the women's heads close together over the gurgling child splashing in the pool of seawater his mother had trapped in the sand.

Bahram mused. *An attractive tableau for the petroglyphs, if it were Lapita and me and our son.*

He kept on walking to the canoe building area, where he talked with Nawfal who used an adze to hollow out a log for a new canoe.

"How is Tavale doing?"

"He is very happy. He takes great pride in building canoes." Nawfal did not look up from his task.

"But did he pay his taxes?"

"Not yet, but he will. I told him there would be a severe penalty if he did not. I was clear and forceful." Nawfal stood and looked down at his shorter friend. "But I was respectful. He is the leader of the tribe. Soon to be chief."

"Right."

Bahram continued along the shore for a mile and then picked up the track that coursed the perimeter of his kingdom, shaped like a footprint in the Pacific. He never yearned for the noisy dust of his own country; he was willing to remain in Vahilele forever. Nor was there a comparison between clear aquamarine water and the crowded filth of his recent home in Sumatra. Some of his shipmates had given up families when they sailed, but he himself only relinquished a life of hardship. He fled the abuse of men who enslaved others to make money. Captain Koch provided an opportunity. *Now I will make the rules.*

CHAPTER THIRTY TWO

Lapita

Lapita ventured down to the common area where workers laid out food for the midday meal. Already diners waited with mother-of-pearl shell scoops or bilos, while they shared memories and debated current events with each other. They carried their own gourds with water. Some stood as she passed, while others inclined their heads and lowered their eyes. She greeted all with a smile and a nod.

As she approached a cluster of men lounging among the palms near the dining area, she heard snippets of conversation.

"Our kakana is slow today. Marama must have slept too long."

"I'm not in a hurry. My boss is always saying no cakacaka no kakana." The speaker was behind a tree but Lapita heard his comment. "That works two ways. No kakana, no cakacaka."

"No worries," said another. "Cakacaka is forever."

Another one in the group had his back to Lapita, and she clearly heard his complaint. "That is the worry. There is too much cakacaka. My aches grow pains." Several swallowed their laughter at him as she walked past.

Lapita nodded to them and entered the covered shelter where a throng of women prepared the meal of fish kokoda.

Before her presence was known, conversation among them was loud and unhappy.

"How can one tagane command thirty?"

"Why do thirty Vahilele men obey? And allow one tagane to shame our Royal Prince?"

"A foreign mua." Someone spat. "And now we have four Balinese workers! And we have to feed them while my grandmother starves."

The vosa stilled as Lapita came into sight.

"Sa Bula, Princess," an elderly woman said. The gaps in her teeth did not slow her smile.

"Ni Bula," Lapita responded. "I am looking for an extra candle. Is there one here?"

One islander found a candle for her. Three others found large bowls of heart-shaped taro leaves, rourou, to silently rush outside to serve the waiting crowd.

As Lapita left the common area, almost in front of Bahram's hut, she heard a voice behind her.

"Princess, may I see you?"

She turned to wait for the approach of a canoe worker who still had an abundance of sand on his arms and legs. "Sa Bula. How can I help you?"

The islander held up his arm to show Lapita a large discolored swelling above his wrist. "Do you have something to cleanse this bite? I disturbed a sea krait hiding in the shallows, and he attacked me. Tavale said you had a magic potion to take so I can go back to work after kakana."

Lapita heard Bahram's voice thunder behind her. "That is a serious injury. Surely you don't expect the princess to have a solution to every problem. She is not a sorceress as her brother suggests," Bahram snapped.

Lapita ignored him. "Nevertheless, I have a poultice that has worked on bites before. And ginger to cleanse your system. You are fortunate the little snake did not get you between the fingers. They carry a powerful poison but their mouths are too small to do much harm to a tagane arm."

"It still hurts."

Her tinkling laughter joined the music of the birds. "You must be brave." She led him back to the Bure Kalou.

Bahram walked between the princess and the native wearing the loincloth.

Later that afternoon a shower interrupted the first wedding preparation of the year, a celebration for the entire yanuyanu because it had been such a long time since the last one. Melane darted from her vale to Lapita's, carrying Yaca on her back.

"Why are you out in the rain? Peipei is soaked." Lapita rescued the little one from his sack and nuzzled his fat neck. Yaca chortled and flapped his arms.

"He will dry. I will call it his bath. I finished my chores early and picked up Yaca from Maca Matanitu. But Tavale is at the baravi. And I need help with Yaca so I can prepare myself for the wedding. If there is going to be one."

"What do you know that I do not?"

"The bride complained about the size of her salusalu necklace and threatened to run away, so her mother told her to sweep the floor and put down clean mats for the guests. Now they scream at each other."

Lapita laughed and tickled Yaca. He giggled with her. "I also need assistance. Siga is ill."

"What troubles her?"

"She could not settle her breakfast."

"Ohhh, sega. She is very young, and she has no special tagane. Who could it be?"

"Do not vosa about what you do not know, Melane." Lapita said sternly. "It could be something she ate. Not the seed of a peipei."

Melane nodded. "You are wise as a substitute mother. Siga thinks only of your comfort, and she spends little time with any cauravou who plays such games, although I have seen a special smile for Rangi's son." Melane laughed at Lapita's frown.

"I carried to her a potion to make her better. Now she is at the lagoon bathing Dedan. He rolled in chicken droppings." Lapita put the baby on the floor and gave him a rattle of snake vertebrae to shake. "After you dress my hair, I will rock Yaca to sleep while you get ready."

"That's what sisters are for. Substitute servants." Melane's grin revealed her tease.

Lapita sat cross-legged next to Yaca and captured his attention with her shark tooth bracelet.

"I would like to have straight hair with gentle waves like yours, not this tangled mess." Melane pulled at her own curls.

"Tavale loves you the way you are. Even your flat nose. He told me."

Melane jerked her sister-in-law's hair, and Lapita fell over laughing. Yaca squealed with delight.

Bahram

When he returned to Na Koro from his daily inspections, Bahram paused to give homage to the colors of the setting sun, more glorious in the steamy aftermath of the recent shower. He removed his crusted sandals outside the Bure Kalou. The operatic carol from a swallow perched on the roof made him smile. Today he would impress Lapita with his inspiration to market the masawe that grew wild on grassy slopes.

From within the Bure Kalou, Melane's agitated voice attracted his attention and he paused outside the doorway. Bahram hesitated to interrupt the women's privacy, but he did not hesitate to listen. He moved the white curtain a tiny bit so he could peer inside, as he struggled to understand the conversation.

"I am a stranger to Yaca." Melane fretted as she coiled Lapita's shiny hair for the wedding festivities. "He sees Maca Matanitu more than me. I must carry jugs of *wai* in the morning and then prepare meals for the men. I work hard for this new commune. I refuse to call it our tribe because there is no good will."

"It is good that you are *kaukaua*. Our council leaders say to help each other," insisted Lapita.

"And not our *tokatoka*? Families need each other. Maca Matanitu cannot love my son like I do," Melane grumbled. "He is pale and sickly because he stays inside all day."

"Maca Matanitu sits to rest her legs. She is weak."

"Too weak to care for babies. Children quickly move toward danger. When our grandfather was Ratu, he understood these things."

"Grandfather Tui Waitu had the *mana* of the gods but he is gone. Now Bahram takes his place."

"The gods do not give him power," protested Melane.

"He has the experience of other countries."

"Is that why he brought in foreign workers? You forget. Our old way was better," Melane scolded. "The council is slow to make decisions, and slow to change. Tavale must be our *turaga*. He has the blood of a chief."

"Give Bahram time. Vahilele had many problems when he came. I pray for wisdom."

"Why does the Persian listen to the words of Lalai who sleeps all day and spies on neighbors? My husband left his nets to harvest *dalo* as he has always done. Bahram heard lies, and Tavale was punished when his nets were empty."

"How was he punished?"

"We did not get our share of *dalo,* and his nets were given to others. Now he works at the canoe yard." Melane sighed. "Your brother does not complain because he is *marau* when he builds canoes. He loves the ocean."

"What can we do?" Lapita asked softly.

"The gods will raise up a wise *turaga*. And your body gets *kaukaua*. *Nui taka* grows, our hope for a wise Bete." Melane secured the royal cowrie jewelry upon her sister-in-law and fondly squeezed her arm. "Now it is my turn to dress. Do not forget to take the sandalwood dust for the bride's hair."

"Yes, Queen Melane."

Although Bahram didn't understand everything he overheard, he caught enough to change his mind about talking with Lapita. He understood rumbles of discontent, and he wanted to reflect upon them.

Nui taka? Queen Melane?

CHAPTER THIRTY THREE

Bahram

Bare feet pounding down the path outside his bure awoke Bahram at daybreak.

"Get up!" Abu shouted as he burst his way inside the vale. "Get dressed! Hurry!"

"Quit shouting! When I am King, I will make you a general with your own army, and you can shout at them," Bahram joked as he staggered to his feet. He heard more noise outside. "What is going on?"

"Tavale's body washed up on the rocks below the cliffs." The whites of Abu's eyes glistened in their dark sockets.

As Bahram pulled the fabric of the entry aside to look out, Abu continued. "Nawfal said his arms were cleaved from his sides."

Bahram grimaced. Men and women hurried through the common area between huts, heads down, voices urgently speaking to one another. "What do my people say?"

"They think their legendary shark god punished Tavale because he did not pour a kava tribute into the sea before he took his canoe out last night."

"Let them believe that. He had teeth marks from his last shark encounter." Bahram decided this solemn occasion required native dress. He took care to wind a tapa sheath around his waist and over his shoulder. Since the religion of his childhood revered humility, he may adapt to the practice of removing his new sandals to enter a hut, but he would not secure his sulu at his waist. In his eyes, that showed a pagan lack of modesty. Also, he felt vulnerable when the old scar on his back was exposed.

"Now they want another ceremony." Abu wrung his hands.

"Of course. It will calm them." Bahram headed down to the shore. "Have you seen Dedan?"

"No. Why are you so calm? The Prince is dead."

"And this is regrettable, Abu, but I cannot change it. I must respond to reality. I shall never be a prince, but I can be a good leader who moves his people forward."

They crossed the village green to approach the path to the ocean. Two women holding the hands of children mumbled a greeting and hurried around them.

"Where is Lapita?"

"She is down at the lagoon with the others," reported Abu. "No one is working."

Bahram followed Abu past the quiet huts. When they left behind the palm trees framing the beach, Bahram joined a subdued throng. He looked to the litter where Tavale lay, covered with masi cloth, his blood drained into the ocean he had loved. Abu groaned and turned back toward the village.

Bahram politely made his way through the crowd, patting shoulders, murmuring soft, soulful greetings. He approached Melane, whose tears pooled in the scars on her cheeks. She stood to the side, flanked by women of the clan. Everyone's gaze was directed toward the lagoon. When the Persian came toward her, she turned from her support group, spitting angry words in his direction. Without waiting for a reply to an epithet he did not comprehend, Melane turned toward the village, baby on her hip and head held high, taking the path to the comfort of her home, away from the disturbing sight of her dead husband. She was surrounded by a retinue of helpful neighbors.

Curious as to what held everyone's attention, Bahram broke free from the crush of the crowd. He saw Lapita was ankle deep in gentle waves. A shark fin was moving through the breach in the coral barrier.

Siga

The sound of running feet and suppressed cries also woke Siga.

"Grandfather, wake up. Our neighbors rush toward the beach."

"I hear no alarm from the *Davui*." Matai Malolo rolled over and lay on his back, delaying the struggle to stand up.

Siga went to the entryway. Two women trotted past, holding hands, one leading the other whose tears seemed to blind her. "Marama, what is the news?"

"Our Prince is dead. They say it was Dakuwaqa!"

The shock punched Siga like a blow to her chest. She drew a painful breath. "Grandfather! Prince Tavale is dead." What happened? "I have to find the Princess, but I cannot take anything to her but the Truth." She left while Grandfather dressed. As fast as she could, she ran toward the beach with the other villagers. *What happened?*

Already on the shore, the Princess stood straight and proud, eyes glistening with unshed tears. "Siga, get the yaqona. Quickly."

Back Siga ran, up the path, past her hut, not daring to slow to tell Grandfather. She was entrusted with a mission. Anxiety sped her up the stone steps into the Bure Kalou. Only a small amount of yaqona was left from the day before. *Is this enough? Should I make more? I don't know if she means to share with the elders. Perhaps for Tavale. What shall I do? I am too young for this decision.* She poured the yaqona into a jug with a spout while she thought. "No! I will follow instructions. If this is not enough she will tell me. The Princess said to run fast. I will fly like a manumanu vuka." And Siga picked up the jug, covered the small opening with her hand, and ran as fast as she could, the precious elixir sloshing inside.

Now there was a crowd, and Siga could not see over them. *Where is the Princess?* She circled a cluster of islanders, passed a mother whose children clutched her sulu and whimpered. Sega skirted two men grumbling in hushed angry vosa.

When she was closer to the shore, Siga saw Lapita in the water, golden arms raised. A great dark fin neared the breakers. Inside the lagoon. Lapita stepped further into the water, calling out. "Dakuwaqa, have mercy!" The fin glided toward her. A shout of alarm came from the mesmerized crowd.

As noiselessly as she could and as quickly as she dared, Siga carried the jug to the side of her mistress. "Princess, I have the yaqona, but it isn't much."

Without comment, Lapita took the jug. She advanced into deeper water, the bottom edge of her sulu first dampened and then weighted by the waves that swirled around her legs. Siga followed to hear any other instructions. The shadow of the underwater monster came closer. Siga trembled for her mistress. And for herself. She retreated. *Princess, forgive my fear*.

Lapita raised her voice. "Dakuwaqa! Have mercy!"

A murmur from the crowd echoed, "Dakuwaqa! Have mercy!"

The fin came closer as Lapita earnestly chanted. "*Dakuwaqa, Dakuwaqa.*" Her slender fingers lifted the yaqona high, waving it towards the azure sky. "*Dakuwaqa, Dakuwaqa.*" The people wailed, picking up the chant, "*Dakuwaqa, Dakuwaqa.*" Bodies swayed in tempo.

Siga whimpered and looked around for somebody strong to help her mistress. She was the closest, but she was not brave. Matai Malolo was bending over the body of the Prince. He was too slow. Bahram moved toward the shore quickly, followed by Elder Dau. Siga saw that they also hesitated at the edge of the water. Lapita's shout caught Siga's attention again. It was a vosa that Siga did not know. She was entranced by the fin that now circled the golden beauty who slowly poured yaqona into the sacrificial water. The fin disappeared for a hushed moment and then reappeared moving majestically out of the lagoon into the deep.

Bahram waded into the water to support the Princess who wavered on her feet and looked as though she would sink to the bottom. An excited babble broke out among the crowd. Elder Dau came to help. And then Elder Bati and Grandfather. Siga didn't know what to do. She didn't know the herbs that would help Princess Lapita. She waited.

Next to her, somebody said, "Siga, come quickly." A touch on her elbow turned her face to face with Savu Vatu. "Hurry. Dedan is dying."

Lapita

Lapita was weak. She had reached deep down into her soul to meet this shark god, and it seemed her spirit had soared up and out of her. Now her body was drained of emotion. Bahram's hand kept her steady, kept her from falling, helped her to sit in the white sand. She felt him wipe the sweat from her brow and heard him murmuring how everything was going to be all right, as he had months ago when her body raged with fever. This time, there was no pain, only an empty place where her spirit and body had separated and now strained to reunite. She closed her eyes and lay her head on the sand to end the whirling. She lost consciousness. When Lapita jolted awake with a sudden awareness of duty, Bahram was still at her side, holding her hand. Her first thought was for Tavale. Her brother was dead, and her duty was to prepare his body for burial. She attempted to rise.

"Lie still. You have had a shock."

"I must be strong for Melane. Help me to stand." As Bahram gently pushed her back down, she asked, "Where is Siga?"

"I don't know. I am here, and I will help you."

Lapita continued to struggle, so he stood, and she pulled herself up by his hands, hesitantly, to make sure her shaky legs would hold her upright.

Elder Bati hovered, approaching Lapita when she looked his way.

"Princess, we mourn the loss of our beloved Prince Tavale. With your permission, our maramas will prepare him to ascend to the makawa."

"Vinaka, Elder. Take the Prince to the Bure Kalou.

Bati gave immediate instructions to the islander standing nearby, and he trotted off with his message.

Bahram helped Lapita move along. Bati depended upon the help of his cane to slog through the sand on her other side. The hushed crowd parted as they made their way.

"Where is Melane?" Lapita asked.

"She took the young one to her vale. She is not alone."

"See that somebody stays with her."

"Yes, Princess." Elder Bati passed this word to another messenger who hurried to do his part.

Words of condolence surrounded her, and she drew strength from the presence of her tribe. "Is Elder Dau preparing the headland for a ceremony at the royal cave tonight?"

The moment of silence told her the conflict that she feared. "Prince Tavale was royalty. He was our Chief even though he had not yet been formally recognized."

"But there was no ceremony." Edler Bati spoke gently. "And therefore, he will not be buried in the cave. The law is clear. He will be buried near the graves of your husband and son. And my wife. Elder Dau is in charge of the details."

Lapita was silent, trying to convince herself these men were wise but she had serious doubts. By the time she reached her Bure Kalou and readied the room for the bier, purpose had swept the shadows from her mind. She knew her way forward, and Savu Vatu's grandmother brought comforting experience and utensils to help.

Dede Nikua appeared with the Prince's sarong he had worn at the First Fruits Ceremony. "Princess, Melane said she will be here soon."

"Vinaka." Lapita looked at her brother's mutilated body. Her stomach churned. She was overcome by thoughts of his last moments of terror. She trembled. "Tell Melane that I will send for her when we are ready. Then bring us more water."

The Princess assembled the containers necessary for preparing the body to join the makawa. She noted two jars were missing from the neatly organized row, and she thought again about her helper. *Where is Siga?*

When the women had done their best and wrapped the Prince in a ceremonial shroud for royalty, Lapita sent for Melane. Their broken hearts mourned his loss in private, before the men came to bear his body to the cemetery where his litter was placed on an elevated bier.

Melane prepared to return to her vale. "Princess, you must take care of yourself. Where is Siga? Your hair is still wet, and your skin is cold. If you need healing, what would we do?"

Before Lapita could answer, she heard the scrambling of bare feet at the entry. Siga cautiously pulled back the curtain and stood there, shaking.

"Where have you been?" shouted Melane. "You are close to worthless!"

Siga burst into tears.

"I will handle this, Melane." Lapita handed the widow a packet of herbs. "Go rest and hug little Yaca. I will come to get you, and we will share tonight's vigil as sisters." She hugged her brother's widow with compassion, trying to give what little strength she had left. As difficult as this was for Lapita, she knew from experience it was a world-altering event for Melane. A widow's grief had many aspects and a potent finality.

Siga looked down, still snuffling when Melane whisked past her. "Take care of your mistress."

"I will. I regret my absence."

A brief glance at her helper annoyed Lapita who saw scratched legs and dried blood splotches, evidence that Siga had been playing around in the underbrush. "Either you are with me or not. If you are not, I must find somebody else. I must have a helper who is dependable."

Siga fell to her knees and bowed her forehead to the floor in front of Lapita. "Have mercy, mistress. Have mercy. Please do not send me away. While you were weakened by the shark god, I tried to give aid to a friend who would otherwise be overlooked."

Lapita was so weary. She prepared a restorative of honey and ginger for herself. "Go out and gather more nokonoko for the spirit fire." When Siga left, Lapita took Melane's advice to wash and change clothes but she would not lie down. *If I sleep, I will never awake. I must prepare myself for the evening ahead.*

Lapita settled in front of the embers. *My brother is gone amid a struggle so terrible I must not imagine it. I cannot help him. I must clear my mind.* She struggled to put her questions to the side for now, but it was close to impossible. Nor could she forget her harsh judgment that so distressed a goodhearted child. *Spirit, help me.*

When Siga returned with a basket of ironwood, she prepared a meal for her mistress and yaqona to take the chill from her bones. "May I dress your hair, Princess?"

"Vinaka."

Siga got a comb from Lapita's sleeping area and returned to slowly and carefully attend to her grieving mistress.

This would be a very long night but the ancient ceremony itself would bring comfort. Lapita would wear a heavy royal headdress and watch the dances of different tokatokas expressing their sorrow. Tomorrow, family from other islands would arrive and the burden of feeding everyone would fall upon her. There would be a four-day ceremony, and the Tabua would be presented to her, the last of the golden royalty until Yaca was of age. But for now, fingers stroking her hair were calming, and while Siga wove a rope of fragrant herbs into her braid, Lapita rested, eyes closed. It was just the two of them in a quiet vale.

Abruptly Lapita spoke. "Tell me your story."

Siga

When the command came, Siga was ready. "While Saca was with you on the shore, a friend told me that Dedan was hurt. Princess, I should have stayed with you and not run away. I thought I could help Dedan quickly." She swiped away hot tears that splashed down her cheeks, and took a deep breath. Seated in front of her, Lapita was silent.

Siga got her voice under control and continued. "I followed Savu Vatu to the shelter of boulders on the beach. Another boy had used his own sulu to warm Dedan, but the dog lay there with his eyes shut, barely breathing. He had a deep cut on his shoulder. He was weak, and his life force bled out to the ground. We feared he would die." Siga paused to take a deep breath.

"Princess, I remembered how you helped my uncle, and I hurried back here to get the same herbs to help Dedan. I didn't know if they would work on a koli, but I had to try. I told the boys to keep him warm and dry.

"Please forgive me, Princess. I was not with you when you needed me. I was a stupid child. I am ashamed." Again she swiped at her tears that would not stop flowing.

Lapita was silent, sitting straight while Siga continued to work the herbal rope into her braid. Siga could not see Lapita's face but when her shoulders shook, Siga knew her mistress was also crying. *It must be horrible to administer to your brother's savaged body.*

Siga finished her task and backed away, thinking about the honor that was hers to touch the head of royalty. Now she had ruined her position of trust on this day of great sorrow. Why did she make such foolish decisions? *The Princess forgave me once when I did not follow instructions. How could I leave her to take care of a koli that some people like my father would eat? I am worthless, like Melane said.*

Siga was filled with tremendous sadness at this realization. She loved Dedan, but she loved her Princess more. Now Lapita would know how stupid she was and find a new servant.

"I will go now." Siga managed to choke out the words into the already heavy air. She waited to be dismissed. Lapita rose and turned.

She's going to strike me, and I deserve it.

Siga shook with deep sobs and covered her face in shame.

The Princess embraced her. "Little sister, you have deep feelings for every creature. That is a gift to be treasured, as it will light your way. Do not apologize for your spirit. Be true to it."

Together they wept for the painful loss of a kingly man.

CHAPTER THIRTY FOUR

1950: The Storyteller

Throughout the subsequent four days, the people of Vahilele held a celebration of life, a reguregu for Prince Tavale. Uncle Momo and Nana Hewa journeyed from Beqa to Vahilele with crowds of people. Royalty from Samoa and Viti Levu came to pay their respects. The lagoon was littered with boats and canoes of all shapes and sizes. The men of the fishing village worked many hours to catch the number of ika necessary to feed a large gathering. Many of the visitors brought gifts of food to share, and each local marama cooked for days. Several megapodes were roasted, and royalty dined on boa constrictors. Siga took the remnants of the snakes and carefully dried out the vertebrae for later use.

650 A.D.

Siga

While her mistress sat with the members of the council during the reguregu, Siga saw Rangi's son motioning to her from the shadows, but she looked away. She had to choose who she served first even though she wanted to help Dedan. When she thought she could slip away without reprimand, she joined him and spoke in a low vosa, "I can't do anything more."

"But Dedan is hot and weak." Fourteen-year-old Savu Vatu looked fearful of the responsibility he carried. "Why can you not come and look at him to make sure I am caring for him properly?"

"I cannot leave the Princess. With all the visitors on the island, there are many duties, and I must be here." Siga put her head closer to him and whispered forcefully. "She said either I am with her or not. I have to show her I am dependable."

"But you are the healer, not me! Dedan will die!"

"Change the poultice often and keep the wound clean. Make certain he has fresh water to drink. That is all I know, all that I can do." She looked over her shoulder. Nobody on the council looked for her. They were still seated around the fire, silently sharing a spirit pipe. "Vinaka. Dedan will live because of you."

"I can't do this," he hissed.

Savu Vatu's fear breeched Siga's gentle heart. She must be strong for him.

"You have to. You're the only one with the time. Dede Nikua and I have to serve the elders."

"I don't know why I bother. It's just a koli."

"That is true. And you are just a boy looking for a way out. Run and play if you want."

He shifted uneasily on his feet. "Give me the herbs. I will try."

"I cannot get them now. Later tonight the elders will meet at the Bure Kalou, and I will send the herbs with Dede Nikua after she settles Elder Bati for the evening. Then we take turns sleeping. I will try to check on Dedan before morning."

Savu Vatu shrugged. "My father is one of the night guard for Prince Tavale's bier. I will stay with Dedan." He watched his bare toes make tunnels in the sand.

She reached out to touch his shoulder. "Because of you, he will live."

He looked up at her and shrugged again.

"I have to get back to the Princess," she said. When he eased among the shadows of the forest, Siga took a deep breath and returned to stand behind Lapita who knelt in front of the ceremonial spirit fire.

Siga watched the flame dance in the night breeze. The elders were quiet with their thoughts. *What do they see when they stare into the flame?* She knew Lapita would speak to the Phoenix spirit if she were alone. The Princess exercised her faith, not her power. Siga had heard her say many times, *Hear me, Spirit. I am unworthy of your attention. You know all I need. You know where I walk before I step. Guide me so I do not fail.*

Siga recited this in her heart until she felt calm. Her experience with her uncle's crushed foot came to mind. He was better and now able to help Bahram with shipping masi cloth. *I used the same herbs so maybe Dedan will get better.* She sat down to rest her legs. It would be a long night.

Then she thought of Maca Matanitu's baby the Princess tried to help. And it was not to be. *I have so much to learn.* She recited the words again. *Hear me, Spirit...*

Lapita

On the last evening, Siga was excused to retire after the dancing. Lapita expected to be up all night with the elders surrounding the fire, the buka.

The Princess accepted the clay pipe from Matai Malolo. She traced her finger over the ancient dentate pattern on its stem. Almond eyes and a long nose on the bowl looked out at the three council members, one across the fire, and two on either side. If Tavale were alive, he would be seated here. But then the balance of earth's circle would be interrupted. North, south, west and the stem to the east. Four directions of the wind, four people at the buka. Perhaps it was the will of the gods to have only four. She shook her head. Those thoughts were not worthy of a granddaughter of Ratu, whose

Yaqona circle included many. Her father also had sought wisdom from every corner. She inhaled.

Not knowing the precise moment of moce, farewell, when the body separated from the soul, Lapita kept a prayer in her heart. In her spirit, Lapita apologized to Tavale for a woman's voice that was not respected enough to have him buried in the royal ganilau, a cave on the cliff.

They said you were not yet a king. We are all lesser for that in my humble mind. You had the heart of a warrior and would have been a strong leader. Have you found our father yet? He will welcome you, and I will let you go. She had no more tears to shed.

A bitter smoke rolled over her tongue, through her cheeks up her nostrils and lifted like a mist into her brain. She exhaled the smoke and wished she could so easily rid herself of a tangle of thoughts. There were so many, in such disorder. Many choices like trails leading away from the center of the earth. Nana Hewa had added to her burden when she had cornered her and whispered, "Lapita, take special care of Siga. A betrayal was prophesized by our Bete at Bequa." Now Lapita wondered if Bahram was right about the Tongans waging war. Worry would not help. She would wrap a candle with an herbal wreath to protect Siga from unknown danger.

Lapita advised herself. *Sit here until there is only one thought left. The kaukaua one.*

She passed the clay pipe to Elder Dau on her left. And dwelt upon sorrow, rarawa.

CHAPTER THIRTY FIVE

1950: The Storyteller

It is important to remember every word in The Story that describes the sadness of that time. I tell the children, "The tribal flame was carried by torch to light the ceremonial fire in the late afternoon. At dusk, the Davui sounded and a crowd surrounded the bier. The islanders wore leaf bracelets around their ankles and wrists. A meke group swayed to the chants, dancing individually in a loose circle. The men carried long spears and wore skirts created from the bark of the vau tree, and each woman wore her best sulu. Everyone had small circles drawn on both cheeks made by a black paste of charcoal and coconut oil. Around Lapita's neck resided the ancient Tabua, formerly worn by Prince Tavale. In this way, the natives released a young chief's soul to its guardian spirit, and buried his body on Vahilele.

"Bahram thought this elaborate service appropriately marked an end of the opposition to his leadership and the tribe would see the wisdom of the new plan for their lives.

"After a respectful time of four days, the council adjourned. Within the week, visitors left the island.

Remembering Nana Hewa's warning, Lapita gave the candle she made to Siga."

650 A.D.

Lapita

When a daily routine was back to Vahilele slow normal, Lapita visited the canoe yard.

Men straggled to their work stations, but when they saw the Princess move among them, conversations ceased. In the rustle of the tropical breeze, only the sound of adze on log could be heard. Lapita touched each canoe in progress and offered a brief prayer for the protection of its navigators. She was pleased that Vahilele men worked on each island canoe. Unlike the new rice pond that was being built by foreigners.

You must have loved it here, brother. The beginning of so many adventures. Why have I come? What hope does a woman have to understand this place of exacting measurements?

Lapita sensed a presence near her and turned. Rangi's hooded eyes looked out to sea, his long hair tamed with a masi headband.

"Rangi, may we vosa?"

He nodded and walked away from the industry that resumed amid whispers and the sound of rock on wood. Lapita joined him at a respectful distance when he stopped, facing the ocean. *Always looking to the sea, just like Tavale. She felt a great loneliness. Tavale will never stand next to me again.*

Lapita chose her words carefully. "Rangi, I understand you found my brother. Vinaka." Her words were a formal acknowledgment that Rangi acted with compassion. Her father taught her that people ought not be taken for granted. He had said that small acts accumulate to bind men together, and every man appreciates a nod of recognition.

"Did you see anyone else that morning?" Lapita asked the question that burned her soul.

"Only Nawfal," he said.

"The mua? Isn't it unusual for him to be on the beach so early in the morning?"

"No, Princess. Every morning he came early to talk with Prince Tavale."

"What did they have to talk about?" Lapita glanced at Rangi.

"The stars." A shadow of a smile touched the navigator's weathered face, like a secret to be kept. But he answered, "Nawfal was eager to learn. Sometimes they would be out here late at night." He shrugged. "Sometimes I am restless and walk along the baravi at the lagoon."

Lapita considered his words. Tavale always laughed at her inability to see a difference in the position of stars. "It is wise to be more attracted to nature's power than to man's."

As Lapita walked the path back to the Bure Kalou, she thought of her helper's constant devotion to her in the past few days. And again she thought of her father's words. *Small acts bind us together.* Lapita cut through the forest, making her way to the children's hideout where Dedan lay recovering. Siga, Savu, and Dede were all there keeping him company. Lapita settled herself among them.

Her words were shared with children.

Her thoughts reached out to the makawa for guidance.

CHAPTER THIRTY SIX

1950: The Storyteller

"Prepare to dance the legend of the prawns, young princes and princesses." They busy themselves donning sulus and hibiscus and shell necklaces to participate in the drama of the uradamudamu, the children's favorite part of oral history. While the designated drummer boys give me background rhythm, and the dancers come forward on cue, I continue The Story. My fingers tap my ankle to the beat of the drums, but I remain seated. My role is telling the story. Their role is learning the history to repeat to children in the next generation.

650 A.D.

Bahram

Shadows slipped around the corners of the huts in Na Koro, and a southeast wind still had a delicate bite to it. It was the time of year for the people of Vahilele to plant their crops, starting with a ceremonial fire on the white sand beach before sunset. When drumbeats signaled the beginning of the festivities, Bahram was prepared to leave his vale. He wore a brown sash to differentiate his island sulu from Elder Bati's dress, and he wore his sandals.

Islanders from all three villages gathered in response to the call of the trumpet, the *Davui*. One by one, they tossed a seed or a root on the fire and mumbled with head bowed or cried out with arms upheld. Then each moved on to find a place to sit. There was no talking until the entire assembly was settled. Bahram made his way to the front row near the council members, but chose a place between two attractive teenage girls who exchanged surprised wide-eyed glances. He patted the ground in front of him, and Dedan lay down, ears perked, eyes on the musicians and their sticks. While the crowd settled, Bahram showed the youngsters how Dedan appreciated their gentle strokes. An ugly wound on the dog's shoulder was healing.

Lapita was the last one to make her offering to a goddess of fertility. She threw two hands full of seeds into the fire and pronounced "*Mana* Vahilele." As she turned and walked toward Bahram, her eyes locked on his. At her gesture, the two girls stood and disappeared into the shadows. Lapita seated herself gracefully and placed wrists on knees, palms turned up, back queenly straight. No conversation. Dedan thumped his tail in welcome.

At last, my future queen takes her rightful place beside me. This is how it should be. With pride, Bahram scanned the sea of brown faces around him, some with eyes closed in reverence. He imagined stolen glances at him and his slender princess.

Having spent the afternoon going over financial numbers with Abu, Bahram was tired but excited about the profitable commerce opening up in Viti Levu trade. *In less than a year, my fortune has changed. Once I had only a future randomly tossed my way, and now I could rule this island and marry into royalty.*

Bahram watched Melane in the front row on the other side of the audience. She and her neighbors giggled at baby

Yaca who stood shakily with her support, clapping until he collapsed into her lap. Over and over again.

Soon the drums changed tempo, and several young women, wearing grass skirts and salusalu garlands, danced their way forward one at a time. Behind their right ears, each wore a single hibiscus bloom. The crowd sang, as bare heels alternately lifted and pressed the sand. Hips rotated continuously. The beautiful performers moved independently of one another, hands gesturing and bodies swaying until the beat of the drums changed again. Then they moved in unison. Bahram did not understand the song that accompanied the dance.

Lapita whispered, "They dance the legend of the red prawns."

Bahram felt a tingle of apprehension. *Does this involve me?* He tried to understand the movements. Open palms circling their own smiling faces would indicate beauty. The grinding hips seemed expressions of wanton prowess that elicited encouragement from the male spectators. And laughter from the women.

"There once was a Vahilele Chief with a beautiful daughter who attracted marriage proposals from all surrounding islands," interpreted Lapita for Bahram.

Several men played the part of these eager suitors by jumping in front of the dancers, wriggling their shoulders and gyrating their hips. The female dancers, each playing the same role of the princess, shook their heads and pushed their palms outward, and the rebuffed suitor exaggerated a fall to the ground and rolled to the side. The crowd responded with amusing suggestions and ridicule.

Lapita had to raise her voice to be heard over the merriment of the natives. "One day a young chief from Viti Levu came with many gifts in his canoe."

A painted-face warrior wearing Trochus shell arm rings danced his way forward accompanied by rhythmic clapping from the tribe. He pretended to give each dancing girl a gift, as though he were offering different gifts to the same princess, but each gift was refused with a shake of the dancer's head and a flip of a wrist. Undaunted, he went to the next one and tried again. Each time he met rejection, the girl turned her back and danced with prissy steps in a circle away from him.

"Nothing is good enough for this princess." Lapita's laugh tinkled like chimes, a rare sound lately.

Bahram looked at her lovely eyes glowing in the firelight, her lips parted, ready to smile. Even if this was a foolish ceremony, he was glad she was enjoying the performance. Next to him.

In front of the last dancer, the young suitor pivoted several times with his hands behind his back. When he stopped, the crowd grew silent. With great flourish, he elevated his hands, palms up as though he held a treasure, toward the lovely lady who kept the beat of the drums with her hips and stutter steps. As one, the crowd shouted denial. "*Sega!*"

"He offers giant red prawns cooked in coconut milk. They are found in fresh *wai* and are very special on the islands," said Lapita near Bahram's ear.

"Yes, you told me." He breathed in her scent and leaned his shoulder into hers.

The young women danced their way into a line and ceased movement. They crossed their arms over their breasts and shook their heads. The drumbeats softened.

"*Sega, sega, sega, sega.*" chanted the crowd as one.

"The princess says 'No!' and refuses all gifts," explained Lapita.

In unison, the dancing girls struck the air with both palms outward to their left and circled around the suitor to the right. The drummers hit their logs harder and faster.

"To the cliff," shouted the excited assembly. "To the cliff."

Bahram put his lips close to Lapita's ear, "Is she tired of his arrogance or insulted by an offer of food cooked by another woman?" He laughed at his own wit.

"No matter." Lapita had to shout to be heard. "He and his prawns will be thrown off the rampart."

"Ahhh," said Bahram.

Two warriors danced their way into the circle and escorted the unhappy male dancer out of the firelight. His scream was heard and imitated by the people who were now on their feet, chanting and laughing. The dancers pretended to swim and the crowd mimicked them.

"The prawns fell into a pool at the base of the cliff and came to life," said Lapita. "Forever ours on Vahilele." She got to her feet with the rest of the crowd, straightening the hibiscus lei around her neck. Bahram took her elbow to help her up but she stood gracefully without him, clapping and chanting with the audience.

Bahram did not want to squander this moment. "What happened to the man?"

"He lived to tell the people of Viti Levu that he was attacked by a Phoenix that protected the Princess of Vahilele." Her bright eyes pierced his. "It is true that anyone who tries to steal these prawns will sink into the ocean."

Not when I am King. He broke eye contact reluctantly. Her gaze was too intense for her childish words. Charming superstitions were unworthy of discussion, but he would pretend respect for tonight.

The dancers were joined by everyone, stomping and moving in time to the drums. The laughter and gaiety of the evening was in sharp contrast to previous somber ceremonies, and the celebration was destined to continue long into the night.

1950: The Storyteller

I drink my yaqona while the children calm themselves and settle around the fire. The youngest boy has to be tackled by his brother before he quits his enthusiastic leaping and stomping. "I am Savu," he explains to giggling girls. "And I am happy I saved Dedan."

"You are lialia," snaps this brother. "Stupid like your sister."

"Am not." Little brother pouts.

When all are quiet, I continue.

650 A.D.

Bahram

Without further comment to Bahram, Lapita glided over to Melane's side and gathered her nephew into an embrace. She put herself into a family group that did not include him, and Bahram felt forsaken, surrounded by natives losing themselves in emotion.

They are a weak people, given to drama. It will be a challenge to rescue them from their bleak future.

In dismay, he watched Ghazi join the twitching, swaying crowd. He emulated the hunched over stomp of a warrior, shaking his fist as he made circles around the fire with the other men. The drum beats got faster and the men straightened up with twisted movements, arms raised, shouting as women came forward to dance among them. Siga's uncle, the outrigger paddler with the injured foot, stood to the side, eyes closed, unable to dance but still participating with ecstasy etched on his face, arms raised, head shaking.

Bahram considered a permanent life in this setting. If he were to have children with Lapita, they must be taught self control. In cool disdain, Bahram left the scene with a trembling Dedan who did not seem to like the noise either.

Passing Abu as he strolled home, Bahram grumbled, "Expect tomorrow to be another day of low production."

"Stay in bed." Abu shrugged and kept walking toward the noisy festivities on the beach. He was late for the event, as usual, and already fortified with strong drink.

CHAPTER THIRTY SEVEN

Lapita

The morning after the planting ceremony, few of the men reported to work. Siga was faithful to her mistress and came early to prepare her bath and breakfast. When Princess Lapita was dressed, she gave Siga permission to visit her tokatoka. Before the servant left, there were visitors at the door. Siga stepped outside the white curtain, and Lapita heard her ask the men their business at the Bure Kalou.

When her servant reentered the vale, the Princess was told that outside there were three men from the field village who had a dispute to settle.

"The tagane should go to the elders of the council," said Lapita. "They sit every day at the same spot to pass judgment on island concerns."

"These men are from our mataqali, and they would like your opinion as part of the extended family. It is a father and his two sons."

Lapita suspected their identity and agreed to see them. She seated herself by the live embers and added kindling, preparing her mind to concentrate on prudence and justice. Siga showed the men to their places and receded to the background.

"Bula," said Lapita. "You may be seated."

"Bula, Princess," they said in unison. The tagane sat,

waiting for her permission to speak.

She watched each one as they settled.

Lapita studied the fire that drew to the smoke hole in the pyramid roof. When she was ready, she said to them, "We will pick apart the knot that has tangled your family and thereby your neighbors' families. The younger son shall speak first."

This cauravou had rough hands and a chunk of ear missing near a long scar down his cheek. He addressed her with shaky vosa. "Vinaka, Princess. I am a low tagane. I seek your wisdom for my life."

"How so?"

"I was foolish. I went to Palembang because I heard it was a place of adventure. I left my Vahilele home before the pox infected our people."

Silence soaked up his confession.

"Princess, I was in error. I looked for a life of pleasure and little effort. I traded all that I had here for choices that brought me unhappiness."

Lapita waited patiently.

"But I dreamed of my home in Vahilele where I always had kakana and a bure. I made better choices here because my father guided me. By myself, I had nothing."

He bowed his head as Lapita considered his words. She nodded at the father.

"All this is true, Princess," he said. "This one was always trouble and taking what did not belong to him, disrespectful to me and his nana. One day he stole our canoe, and we did not see him for a long time. His mother died of the pox, but she was weak from a broken heart. And then his sister died also."

A lament of deep grief escaped the lips of the younger son. "You always allowed me to borrow your canoe. I did not steal from you." His shoulders shook and tears rolled down his cheeks. "How was I to know about the pox?" He wallowed in grief for his lost family, for his lost years.

Lapita waited quietly, studying the smoke plume, back straight, searching for wise yalo words to share.

The elder son interrupted without permission.

"Princess, do not be swayed by tears and false mourning." His father turned to him and shook his head, but the son's words came tumbling out. "I stayed with my father and did not take anything for my own gain."

Lapita closed her eyes.

"I accepted what was given, and I accepted more than my share of fieldwork and my place at the nets. Until the new laws demanded equal distribution." He paused for her comment, but there was silence. "I swallowed my grief when I lost my mother and my sister. Still this brother did not return." Fresh outrage at this neglect sharpened his vosa. "And now my father has many years, and I must care for him. But I do not ask for special consideration. I know my duty."

She opened her eyes to regard this haughty young man whose attitude blazed and whose vosa quivered in anger.

"My brother returned on the day of the planting ceremony. And he was welcomed with great honor. I sacrificed every pleasure to stay with my father, but I was never honored. I did not marry. I have no children. My question to him and to you great Princess, where is my reward for my faithfulness? Where is my justice?" He glared at his brother.

Without thought, the younger man turned to snarl. "You have no idea what I endured to return to Vahilele. You sulked away to complain to all who would listen. Of course, our father is happy to see me whole and back at home."

"Where is the canoe that you 'borrowed'?"

"You give no thought to the dangers I faced in foreign ports." His hand went to his damaged ear. "You are selfish."

"Me? I never took anything that did not belong to me."

"You think everything belongs to you."

Their father spoke out. "Princess, forgive me for disturbing you. These angry words have no place in your presence."

Lapita signaled her servant to prepare the tea made from orange tree leaves and sweetened with boiled masawe. And then she spoke sharply.

"Elder son, did your father ask you not to marry?"

"No, Princess."

"Did your father beg you to work for him?"

"No, Princess."

"Why did you stay and forsake a life with a family of your own? Was it because you loved your comfort? Were you too timid?"

"I loved my father."

"Do you not love your father now?"

"I love my father now. I have no regrets at staying."

"Therefore, rejoice with him that he has two sons who will care for him. A burden will be shared. You did well to stay. Vahilele men help their tokatoka, but why did you not find a wife to give your father a grandson? Was it easier to stay at home and lay claim to your father's vale, his canoe, his nets, his name? Everything your father owned was yours, and you did not want to give a portion to anyone else?"

The young man dropped his chin. "I am ashamed that I was selfish, Princess."

"And you, the father. Why did you allow your sons to put themselves first? Children are greedy by nature. Parents must train them to give. Pride has diluted the harmony of your home."

All three men hung their heads because of her harsh words. Lapita gave them time to think about their situation. She concluded with a softer tone.

"I cannot answer these questions for you. I cannot see into your hearts, but you know the right choices. Elder son, I expect you to honor your father and love your brother. You will be one of the leaders of our kai one day. Younger son-- you who spit on the gifts of your father and the sacrifice made by your brother who stayed behind when he too could have deserted his yanuyanu--I expect you to honor your brother and take care of your father as he ages."

Then she clapped her hands, and Siga served them. Lapita's first judgment was agreed upon by the acceptance of refreshment at the Bure Kalou.

CHAPTER THIRTY EIGHT

Bahram

The day after the planting ceremony, an early inspection of the commercial areas confirmed Bahram's expectations that few reported for work. At Nabataea Village, most of the sailors slept late, and Bahram returned to his vale and sat in the shade to watch his people and make new plans. Even Dedan deserted him, disappearing on his mysterious rounds to visit favorite places. He noticed three natives go to Lapita's doorway, and he was concerned for her safety. He approached the Bure Kalou, but Siga would not admit him.

"The Princess has guests, Saca."

Bahram sat outside on the steps until the visitors left at midday, but Lapita did not venture out.

The commune women in charge of meals at the pavilion gathered to prepare the afternoon dinner since everyone still expected to eat. For most of the island, it was a lazy day, and many congregated in the central village to trade stories until they were served. Bahram walked down to the shore.

At the lagoon, Bahram saw Maca Matanitu staggering along the trail from the lagoon to her hut in the fishing village. In one arm an infant was slipping from her grip. He ran to her assistance.

"Please help me, *mua*," she wheezed. "I could not pick up Yaca and this one together. I was afraid to lay baby Moto helpless on the shore. But I am weak. I had to leave Yaca in a pool by the boulders." She gestured behind her. "He does not walk, but he loves the *wai* and will sit and play by himself. Will you bring him to me?" Her eyes were recessed and surrounded by dark bruises.

Bahram picked out familiar words, Arab mixed with Vahilele language. He understood she needed help and she was worried about Yaca. "I will take you home, *marama*." Bahram cautiously took the infant from the babysitter's arms and carried him up the path while Maca Matanitu plodded behind. Bahram looked for other people to take over for him so he could return for Yaca, but there was not a soul in sight. When they got to her hut, Bahram secured little Moto in a basket and helped Maca Matanitu lie on her pallet. He wiped his hands on his tunic. "I will be back. Rest."

Bahram hurried back to the beach. Still he could see nobody else. Maca Matanitu lived alone in the first vale on the path to the shore. He would have to venture further into the forest to find the next hut and maybe someone to care for her. But how would he ask for help? It was easier to handle the task himself, and he could use the story to brag to Lapita and Melane how he saved Yaca, the Prince of Vahilele.

When he grows up, he will make the decisions and lead the council and be indebted to me. But...will Yaca listen to revolutionary ideas? Or will he be thick-headed like his father?

Bahram's thoughts churned.

When he got to a ring of three boulders, where the seawater formed a shallow pool, he found Yaca slapping the water and happily squealing at the splash he made. Bahram heard Dedan yip near by. He had wondered where the dog had run off to this time. When Dedan yipped again, Bahram peered around a rock and saw him prancing in the tide as a branch swirled in the foam. Dedan thrust his head down and flipped the branch to the sand. It was a sea krait.

"Leave it alone, stupid dog," he shouted. "That snake is venomous." Bahram halted in his tracks, and the black mist that had clouded his mind for weeks suddenly took shape.

"Bring it to me, Dedan. Baby Yaca wants to play, too. Good dog."

The devil himself made Bahram's feet fly to the hut. He did not remember the walk, but there he was. And he knew what he had to do.

"*Marama*, are you ready to die?" He whispered.

"The *makawa* comes soon," Maca Matanitu said and closed her eyes. "I hear the *cagi* blowing."

When Bahram's hand closed over her mouth and nose, her eyes opened in surprise, but she was feeble and not able to struggle for long. He arranged her gaunt body to look as though she were sleeping, like Moto, too small to be a witness. Maca Matanitu was the only one to connect him with Yaca's unfortunate accident.

Bahram quietly eased to the threshold and peered outside. He didn't see anyone. Hastily he circled the hut, and plunged into heavily wooded terrain, putting as much distance between him and his deeds as he could. As quickly as possible. The heat of the moment passed. The fervor of danger drained and left him cold. He was terrified by what he had done. He was not a violent man; it was an impulsive choice. *Surely I was controlled by an outside force.* Bahram walked slowly and considered the consequences. *As sick as she was, she was useless to the tribe, almost dead anyway. Mine was an act of mercy.* He vomited into the dense scrub until his dry heaves exhausted him.

And then there was Yaca. *What will I say to Lapita?* He reached for the captain's button on his shirt. It was gone.

CHAPTER THIRTY NINE

Lapita

Lapita put aside the necklace she had worked on all afternoon. The ritual dinner she had served to their family had produced many gata vertebrae from a snake offering, and the princess worked on a gift for Melane. She measured the length by trying it on, and was pleased at the result. Her sister-in-law needed special care right now.

The day was pleasantly warm, but hot humid weather was on its way. It had been seven moons since the outbreak of the pox. Last spring, she had lived with her husband and her young son. They had hoped for more children, but it was not the will of the gods. She learned to be at peace with her life. *Nature moves forward, and so must I.* Her glance was drawn to a basalt mortar and pestle, a treasured gift from a former suitor she had not forgotten. Perhaps over the years, he had forgotten her.

"Look forward," Tui Turukawa, her father, had advised her when she was younger. "Like the hawk sees into the distance." Her thoughts moved to a cousin's wedding scheduled in Beqa after the cyclone season, and Lapita would prepare to celebrate with the mataqali, relations from all the islands. She had to carry gifts to everyone.

Before dinner, she had time to walk to the inlet to inspect the new outrigger about which the men bragged. She needed to support their efforts in spite of the continual complaints about the sailors. Now that Tavale was gone, she must show even more strength. *Change brings new problems, old temptations.* Preceding generations of her family had laid foundations of a life pattern that had served them well. Built on dedication to tokatoka and respect for each other. *I am not alone.*

Lapita ceased her reverie.

Along the trail, she saw Siga walking with her young friend Dede and two mua who tracked them closely. One made a comment that caused an outbreak of giggles.

Lapita called the servant to her side.

"I forgot my golden cowrie necklace. Kerekere, can your fast legs help me?" As Siga hurried to do as her mistress asked, the sailors disappeared. "I heard your father call you," said Lapita to the other youngster. She scampered home.

When Siga returned, she glanced around for her companions but made no comment. She carefully slipped the shells over Lapita's lowered head.

"Vinaka. Did you see my present for Melane? I will pick a special time to give it to her."

"She will be surprised, Princess." Siga smiled. "She will cry."

Lapita looked into her servant's lovely chestnut-brown eyes, "Be careful, yalewa, my gentle young lady. The foreigners use totoka vosa, sounding very sweet, but they will steal your heart and leave you empty."

Siga slightly nodded. A red flush crept up her cheeks.

Lapita shifted to resume her walk. "I am going to the lagoon and then to see Yaca."

Siga said in a soft voice. "Princess. Vahilele tagane also know those touching games."

Lapita stood still, eyebrows raised.

Under her gaze, Siga dropped her chin. "My friend told me," the girl whispered.

A scream hastened Lapita's footsteps to the area where the fishermen lived. Her heart pounded. It was an unbearable replay of the morning when Tavale was found.

Which of her kai had to deal with heartache now? In the distance, she saw Melane seated near a circle of rocks, scarred legs bent in the nuku, wild with grief, clutching a child to her scarred heart. Lapita ran faster. A woman rocking them both gave way to the Princess who kneeled to embrace her family. Yaca's head lolled backward on Melane's elbow, eyes glazed, little lip black and swollen. Lapita gasped. *The mark of a poisonous gata.*

"A sea krait bit my baby." Melane threw back her head and wailed. "Ahhhhh, help us, Degei. Why, Degei? Why Yaca?"

"Who was responsible for watching him? How could this happen?" Lapita shouted at the gathering crowd. Someone pointed at Dedan lying at the tidal pool, head on paws, whimpering. Lapita moved closer to the dog, wondering how he was involved. Near him was a silvery blue snake with tiger stripes, bitten in half, its head crushed. She kicked its body with the side of her bare foot. "Where is Maca Matanitu?"

"The koli must have frightened the gata," said someone in the crowd.

"That koli chases anything that moves," was another comment.

"It's time to kill him," grumbled somebody else.

Lapita looked around for the caregiver. In the distance, she glimpsed Bahram advancing from the dense scrub brush where there was no path. Melane's rising lament turned Lapita's attention back to her sister-in-law. The tribe was once again moving together to share Melane's grief. The princess picked up a wooden doll from the sand. *Nawfal's work?*

Elder Dau came to Lapita's side and repeated her question. "How could this happen?"

As two women helped Melane stand, cradling her silent baby, Lapita spied a paw print near the little eddy where Yaca had played. Lapita's glance moved from the paw print along the wet sand exposed by retreating water. A depression in the packed sand slowly drained, and she could see the shape of a large sandal. Gentle waves softened a footprint too large for Melane. Or Maca Matanitu.

"Elder Dau, what does this mean?"

He crouched next to her and touched the print. "We do not know how long it has been here."

As Lapita watched, the tide erased it, and all doubt drained from her spirit. Her heart ached.

"Elder Dau, go quickly to Maca Matanita's vale. I must see to my tokatoka."

She knew that she knew: evil lived on Vahilele, and she could no longer ignore it.

CHAPTER FORTY

Bahram

From the cane grass, Bahram was close enough to hear Melane's cry. He had seen Elder Dau and a few canoe builders pitch their work to the side and respond to her alarm coming from the shelter of the rocks. When he saw Lapita rushing to help, he came forward acting as surprised and as concerned as the others.

He circled around to come out on the beach near the main trail as Lapita embraced her weeping cousin. It was too late to save Yaca. Bahram hoped his presence would convey condolences he would not have to put into words which might betray himself. He looked to the cloudless sky for distraction. The sun was making its way to meet the sea. His newly planted yam crop needed rain, and there was none in sight. *There is no reason to feel guilty about Yaca. I made a business decision like any other and seized an opportunity.* Abu would understand, but it was best not to give even a friend information that could be used against him. It was done.

A crowd gathered, and Lapita turned over the care of mother and child to others and strode to Bahram's side. "The *peipei* was alone in the *wasa*. We must ask questions. The snake is deadly but it has a small mouth and only bites in defense." Lapita looked over Bahram's shoulder at a roof peaking through a break in the foliage. "Where is Maca Matanitu?" Her almond eyes flashed in a tear-stained face. "Yaca was the great grandson of Ratu, a tribal chief. Why was he alone?"

"Have you not heard that Maca Matanitu is dead? It is good she is no longer in pain." Bahram put his arm around her. His flesh tingled. "Compose yourself. You are too important to create chaos with criticism."

"The *marama* was too sickly to care for babies any longer, but your council refused to make changes." Lapita studied Bahram's countenance, and then glanced back to her cousin who was being assisted by their clan. "If Maca Matanitu decided to bring the boys outside, she should have stayed with them. And where is the baby, lailai Moto?"

"It was an accident. We all watched her grow steadily weaker. Maybe she felt sick and lay down." Bahram gently pressed Lapita's shoulder to guide her towards the path, and they walked together toward the central area of Na Koro. "Maybe she fell."

"Why do you look for an excuse?"

"How can you be so cruel? She and her husband had the pox. He died. You know how difficult it is to lose a husband and child. You almost died." He paused and softened his voice. "Since she lost her infant son, she couldn't overcome the despair." He hesitated again. "Perhaps she forgot he was outside." He lightly touched her elbow as they trudged side by side.

"A *peipei* is dead." Lapita's words quivered. "Yaca." She leaned into him, and he struggled not to put his arm around her. He knew tabu.

Quietly he said, "If she was outside with two babies, perhaps she could only carry one child back to the hut before she collapsed. She had to choose."

"Why do you say that?" Lapita demanded. She stopped to stare at him.

"Would you be happier if someone else's child died?" Bahram kept moving, his emotions of fear and lust scrambling his thoughts.

"No. I want to understand how a child was bitten by a snake. Melane was right. Maca Matanitu was too sick to work." She was now behind him and could not see the inner turmoil revealed on his face.

"Your cousin requested that her child be outside. An accident occurred." Bahram took a deep breath. He was the superior here, and he would make decisions for those who depended upon his leadership. He turned to wait for her. "And now we will make certain that this does not happen again. Melane shall watch the babies." He noticed tiny beads of perspiration on Lapita's lip and imagined the taste of salt.

"You are too late with ideas. That is not wisdom." Lapita's eyes blazed darkly.

"Complaints are not ideas. What is your wisdom?"

"This commune idea does not work because of selfish desires." She mixed her native *vosa* with Arabic.

He controlled a flare of anger, lips pinched. He could hear Lapita breathing heavily. They tramped through the common area. Dedan drooped between them.

"We need competent labor. We need honest workers. We need intelligent people." Bahram composed himself. "We shall console the islanders and go forward in harmony."

"Your council said that when Tavale died. But questions need answers. Why was my brother, a Vahilele Prince, in the *wasa* at night?"

"You must have compassion, dear Lapita."

"We must have justice! Dear Bahram!"

Bahram's head snapped back. "On this island, there is justice. We are equal. We share the work and the results. Your island was nothing when I came. Now it thrives." His tone grew louder. He grabbed her arm. "Every Vahilele man now has the coins of the seventh century civilized world." He snorted. "But there are many who do not know what to do with them."

She jerked away, her eyes narrowed. "Some tagane are lazy. They rely on the hard work of others. They cannot be changed, and their sloth is resented by those who work hard. This is a truth. Men are not alike." Now she spoke only in Arabic. "Vahilele used to be an island of free men. That is the way we are the same. You made us all slaves because we were weak in mind and body. All men have the same choices, but we choose differently because we are created differently. We must be free to choose. A man forced to share is never free."

"Peaceful men are proud of this island."

"Pride can destroy!" shouted Lapita.

"Shaking spears and beating drums stir up angry emotions of a warrior people. There is your destruction!"

"This warrior people was promised equal shares. Not larger ones for deceitful men like Lalai. Or for his wife's father, Matai Malolo, because he sits on your council." She stomped toward her hut. "Greed births your ideas, Bahram, not the future of Vahilele. Is that how kings rule? The strong on top are most important?"

Her vibrant beauty tempered his anger. Bahram wished to pacify her. He followed closely. He didn't know whether to smother the sparks between them or fan them to ignite passion.

"*Vosa* with you will not prepare me for my nephew's *reguregu*. I must seek harmony with the spirits. *Moce!*"

Bahram stared at the fluttering curtain where she entered the Bure Kalou. He smiled. She was a spirited match for him, but she would bend. She was worthy to follow at his heel, a crown on her beautiful long black hair. He imagined his portrait, and a family painting on the rock with the others.

CHAPTER FORTY ONE

Lapita

At the sacred enclosure, where Yaca's body was buried, covered with masi cloth weighted down with golden cowrie shell fringe, Lapita sat with the elders. Melane stayed for three nights before Siga took her home and put her to bed, understandably devastated by the harsh loss of her husband and then her son.

Lapita served Yaqona to the elders as they comforted one another, facing the bleak prospect of the end of an era, with no royal blood to continue the lineage on this yanuyanu.

"We have mataqali on the island of Beqa. There will always be family there," reasoned Elder Bati, hunched over the pipe he packed with tapaka.

"It is too early to require anything of Melane, but we can ask questions about a suitable mate." Lapita stared at the buka in the center of their circle, and muttered, "If the council feels it can ask questions in this matter." She knew they spoke of her but she would not be used by these men.

The elders were quiet.

"Do you mock the council?" asked Elder Bati.

"I ask only for Truth. In all things," said Lapita.

"Will you know it when you find it?" said Elder Dau. "Can you accept truth?" He lowered his eyes because he had talked out of order. He was the youngest of the elders, and the thinnest, all knees and elbows. There was a long stretch without words.

"Trouble comes to everyone," said Elder Bati, stroking his chin. "If you ask too many questions there might be more trouble. Tavale always looked for a spirit of ca in a new plan. He did not look for the good." He passed the pipe to Elder Matai Malolo on his left.

"Is that why he is dead, Elder Bati? Because he questioned the wisdom of replacing old customs with a new way of life?" Lapita glared at him, and he frowned.

"Demanding that a kai follow you, because of your position by birth, is living by the sword. Tavale required action that our tribe did not support. We are a peaceful people. We believe in harmony. We do not fight each other." Elder Bati stretched at the waist. Dede Nikua draped a tapestry over his humped back.

"I do not want to fight. I want Truth. Someone may have seen Tavale go into the wasa. Someone may have seen Yaca play with the gata. I found a wooden doll. I saw Dedan's paw prints near the hole where Yaca played. And I saw a man's sandal print. Maybe someone saw the koli with the snake. It will help to talk with each other without trying to persuade minds," said Lapita.

"What difference does it make at this point to understand these things? Do we not notice when the herons leave the yanuyanu before a brutal storm? What can we do about it? Nothing. We see many signs we do not understand," said Elder Dau.

Lapita adjusted her position and settled. "We keep faith in the signs of harmony from a source more powerful than man," she murmured.

Elder Matai Malolo waited for a pause in the discourse before he offered his opinion. "We are only tagane. We are weak and make mistakes."

"You are a watchman," Lapita snapped. "You are entrusted with the care of our yanuyanu."

Matai Malolo leaned toward her. "I do not say that you did wrong, Princess. Perhaps someone in your tokatoka ignored a sign given by the gods. Perhaps someone in your family was proud and did not accept a new leader. The Prince suffered for his lack of faith because he lived in the past where only some benefit. That is what I think."

"And do you think this new way of life is ordered by the gods? Which god would kill our chief and his son?"

"Tavale's death was an accident!" Elder Matai Malolo fingered his gold coin.

"Was it?"

"Our new leader is wise. He knows what is best for the mataqali. All work, all share. All are the same. It is the new way," said Elder Matai Malolo. "Many places have these laws."

"How do you know this? Because Bahram spoke it?" Lapita scoffed. "At the request of this foreign tagane, you have made many laws that must not be questioned. How have you saved the arm that lacks strength? The new way of life makes no exception for sickness on our yanuyanu. No cakacaka, no kakana. No respect for the elderly. Except you three with gold around your necks." Lapita impatiently shook her head.

Elder Dau responded. "Look to yourself. Do you ask questions to find truth or to pretend you are our leader?"

"Why do you change our vosa?" Lapita now spoke softly. "Two deaths need to be investigated." She grew quiet, very quiet, looking inward. She was weary of conflict.

"Did you not hear the navigator Rangi tell how Bahram threw piglets into the sea as sacrifice to gods? The storm ceased. That was significant," said Elder Dau.

"I heard the story. Perhaps the storm had already passed over," said Lapita. "Bahram has faith in nothing but himself. He warrants my compassion because he is confused, but one act of faith does not make a religion, nor does one act of desperation indicate one. What god did he call upon? In whose name did he act? I have questions before I believe."

"Of course you do. You want to make Bahram appear small so you look big in comparison."

Elder Bati cast his gaze upon Elder Dau and frowned.

Lapita responded with bitterness because Dau's face was like stone, his eyes dull. "You will never see Truth if you refuse to look for it. Finding fault with me makes you feel better but does not move you down a path of discovery. You are blindly tearing down the bushes along the path. This does not make you look important. It is a useless activity that does not advance your journey."

"I do not pretend I am on a journey."

"I see that. You forever move in circles with no purpose."

"Should you not be rebuked for mocking the council?" Elder Dau fumed. "Why should your empty talk make elders hold their peace?"

Lapita sighed loudly. "Old men are not always wise men. Kalou-vu gives understanding." She closed her eyes and turned up her palms.

The elders remained quiet while Rangi's son, a cauravou charged with serving them, put another branch on the buka. It took a few minutes for the embers to blaze. Lapita sat motionless, inhaling deeply.

Elder Matai Malolo said, "Do you think a mua is responsible for Tavale's death?"

"I think the gods are not happy. All I know is that we brought in foreign workers and soon my brother was dead and today my nephew. That is the Truth."

"You could have a bright future if you were not blinded by the past. Many on our yanuyanu think you are afraid to change, and you do not consider the rest of our mataqali." Elder Dau pointed a thin finger at Lapita. "You want control."

Elder Bati glared at him. "Enough."

"Have you given good advice to help my kai?" Lapita's voice was slower. "What kalou vosa shares with you the wisdom of gods?"

"Be grateful. Our leader favors you above all other women," said Dau. "You must see your gift of a new life."

"You want a priestess who humbles herself to a man with no power over the cagi or the buka? Bahram is weak because he loves himself first. He has power over you because you permit it." She began to close her ears to the council.

"If you were worthy of secrets, you would hear from the Phoenix," spat out Dau.

Lapita experienced a warmth growing within her. "Ahhh. Now you speak Truth."

CHAPTER FORTY TWO

1950: The Storyteller

"In Nabataea Village, the sailors stayed out of the way. They sliced breadfruit and fried it in coconut oil as they had seen the natives do. They roasted chestnuts. They ate pineapple and papaya and bananas, played knucklebones and slept long hours. Although the tribe had always been friendly to them, they were well aware that the mood could change quickly. A chief was dead and now his son. Hundreds of visitors from other islands had come to mourn. The sailors were uncomfortably in the minority."

650 A.D.

Bahram

"What about the Balinese men you brought in?" Nawfal asked of Bahram.
"They are in the taro village."
"Locked up?"
"No. There's no place for them to run, " said Bahram.

"I meant for their protection since they are outsiders, too. Is there any place for them to get food?"

"That is Dau's problem. He is in charge of them." Bahram leaned back against a palm.

Turban helped himself to pandanus kernels and passed the coconut shell bowl to Breaker next to him, two sides of a coin.

"How is the rice pond coming along?" asked the cook, a timid man who rarely spoke.

"We need more workers to build a sea wall," said Bahram.

"The taro field workers are idle right now. We can use them," suggested William who had recovered his strong constitution.

"They are lazy. Malayasian workers move fast," said Bahram. "It was a good idea to bring in the Balinese. It made the Vahilele men jealous."

"I don't see signs that they are concerned," said Breaker. "You treat Dedan better than the Balinese."

"The Viti Levu natives understand that every tribe has a lower class that is bred to be servants. They know their place."

"I heard there are tribes in the hills that use live servants to fill the holes made for the foundation corner posts of the temple. The blood of sacrifice." Ghazi snickered.

"The blood of religion," said Nawfal, casting his eyes down at the vesi bird he carved.

"Blood is a necessity of life, a trade for duty, a trade for consequences, and the purpose of a bloodline. Like Lapita." Bahram looked at Nawfal without smiling. "Or Melane."

"Vahilele natives do not require blood letting." Nawfal stood.

Bahram said, "What does that…"

Nawfal said, "They want to live in peace. They welcomed outsiders like us, and look at what they got. Disease and turmoil. I don't think much of this commune empire. It is weak compared to their heritage."

"You are wrong. In a commune you share all the work, but you share all the profit, too."

"Really? How much is my share?" Turban's eyes widened.

Ghazi and Breaker laughed.

"There is no way to make everyone equal," said Nawfal. "Vahileleans do not believe that. They pretend to please you because if you aren't happy, they all suffer. Keep Saca happy. Marau, for your language lesson." He got to his feet and stalked off to be the cook's teammate against Breaker and Turban in a game of shell toss behind their hut.

Abu and Bahram sat without speaking for awhile.

"He is a problem," said Bahram.

"Do you want me to solve the problem?" asked Ghazi.

"He sees things differently because he was in love with Tavale," sniped Abu. "Give him some time. Meanwhile, what about getting more workers from the Sigatoka salt mines?"

CHAPTER FORTY THREE

Lapita

Lapita awakened to a stillness which told her that Siga was late and her breakfast of pineapple and banana was not prepared. The Bete would have admonished Lapita. *The Tiki does not wait for fruit. Why should you?* She understood but it was early, and she was drained of energy and purpose. Nevertheless, she was on the beach with arms uplifted as the sun rose to kiss the yanuyanu shore with life-giving warmth. The Bete-in-training absorbed the promise of faithfulness to all living things and expressed gratitude for another day.

On her way back to the Bure Kalou, Lapita visited Melane's hut. She heard a rustling within and assumed that Siga had come to help Melane first. From outside the brown curtain, she softly called, "Siga, are you there?"

Melane herself came to the entry. "She is not here this morning, but I could not sleep. Come in for tea."

"I thought Siga was more dependable, but she proved me wrong."

"Do not be angry with her. She has been here every morning since my son's reguregu, and there are days when I would not have gotten off my pallet without her encouragement."

"I am happy to hear that. But a few days of dedication does not excuse a day of abandonment."

"I told her not to come, Lapita. I need to move forward."

Lapita reached out to stroke Melane's shoulder. "I know it's hard. I had both you and Tavale at my side to get me through my rarawa." She seated herself next to her sister-in-law to share what solace she could muster.

An hour later, Lapita left Melane's vale without mentioning to her the footprint that the tide dissolved. An accident was hard enough. Murder was unthinkable. The loss was forever, no matter the reason. Other questions must be asked, and she decided to go to Bati's vale. If he were seated outside, she would be able to talk with him. By this time of day, Dede Nikua would have him up and dressed.

Indeed, Elder Bati was soaking up the morning sun but it was Siga attending to him. Lapita approached and nodded her respect for the elder's position.

"Bula." Bati was the first to offer greetings. "Do you look for your young helper? She has done well and may go with you." He looked clean, his frizzy hair groomed to support a top knot.

"I did not know she was here."

"She took the place of Dede Nikua who is not feeling well, I am told. Be seated then, and she can serve us both at the same time. This new generation likes efficiency."

Lapita seated herself and hid her aggravation at Siga's taking care of everyone but royalty. *How quickly I have become dependent upon a younger sister.*

"We have spent many days together lately. I am surprised to see you seek my company so soon." The hunchback gave her an amused smile.

"I have a small problem to bring to your attention," said Lapita.

"Ahhh. Is this a new one? Already you have more decisions to put before the elders? Is this again about the sailors eating chicken, or have you found somebody else who saw a disappearing footprint? That was an especially entertaining story."

"I suppose it is bula for someone of your age to find humor in unusual places."

Bati stiffened, and his smile disappeared.

Lapita continued. "My purpose this morning is to ask if you have seen the Tanoa?"

After a long pause, Bati said. "I have not seen the Tanoa since little Yaca's reguregu. Have you lost it?"

"No. I remember yaqona was prepared in it the last ceremonial night at the Bure Kalou, but it is not in its place on my shelf."

Siga came out of the vale with two bilos. She presented one to Lapita first, and Elder Bati snorted. "Little girl, I will be glad when my helper feels better. Will she return tomorrow?"

Siga stood before them with head bowed, hands clutching the sides of her snugly wrapped skirt. "I do not know. But if she cannot walk, I will be here."

Lapita was alarmed. "Did she hurt her leg?"

A red flush crept up Siga's face. "No, Princess," she whispered.

Silence.

"Well then...what happened?"

"A man forced himself upon her at the pool."

"Where she was no doubt prancing around without a sulu. This was to be expected." Elder Bati shook his head as though disappointed in his helper.

"Was it one of our kai?" Lapita stood up.

"A mua."

Bati commented immediately. "He would not understand our language. Probably thought she was agreeable to his proposition." He shrugged. "She does look older than she is."

"I will go to see her. Her mother is dead, and her father is the navigator on Bahram's trip to Sigatoka. She has to care for her little brother." Lapita used the restraint practiced for years in a tribe where men are dominant. "Come with me, Siga. Elder Bati has released you."

Lapita and Siga walked first to the Bure Kalou to get the herb basket to deliver compassion to the confused child abruptly exposed to the cruelty of man. They found Dede Nikua sitting silently, holding a sleeping Moto whose natural selfish expectations had been met by his sister in spite of her own bruised psyche.

Lapita's heart went out to her. *My father was right. Women move instinctively to comfort. Is this my role?* "Come back to the Bure Kalou, Dede. You and Moto can stay with me until your father returns."

Before Dede could respond to Lapita's invitation, an elderly neighbor stopped in with food and clean wrappings for Moto. Her sulu was worn but clean, and she wore a small tipanie bloom in her hair. She greeted Lapita with a smile.

"Princess, it is good that you visit the sick and the injured, but our yanuyanu changes with new rules, and I do not know our people because there is too much rarawa, and too much fighting, but can you help us?"

"Nana, I will ask questions to see what I can do. What do you suggest?"

"I am a plain marama, but I can see that some people work hard and some people do nothing, but when the sun goes down, they have the same food and pay the same taxes." She rambled on. "My son no longer tries to fish, and he and his friends see that life can be short, so why not enjoy it, even when neighbors argue over who should be most important, but if Prince Tavale were King, he would be the most important because he had wisdom."

"You are right, nana. We must take care of our neighbors like you do for Dede and Moto. Everyone has a place in our mataqali, but it isn't the same place. We are all important in different ways."

"Prince Tavale was a quiet man, and I knew him as a brave boy with an active curiosity, but he was respectful of our gods, and I will say what is on my mind because I cannot believe he was a victim of Dakuwaqa. Now I will be quiet." The elderly woman bowed her head and backed away. "I regret any disrespect I have shown you."

"Do not apologize for speaking your heart. You are also brave, and I am pleased you spoke out. Too many whisper behind curtains and run from conflict. Dede Nikua will do well in your care. Vinaka."

CHAPTER FORTY FOUR

1950: The Storyteller

"Lapita was concerned about the dissatisfaction growing within her tribe, but she did not know how she could change things. As a woman, she lacked the strength and the voice to intervene in the council. As a royal seeking to take the place of a Bete who could direct her people with wisdom, she lacked experience. Every morning she sought the will of Tiki. Every day, she sought supernatural direction for her spirit. She did not know if she would recognize an answer if it was provided. But she kept asking and stayed open to a response."

650 A.D.

Lapita

Under Lapita's creative supervision, a new pottery design with a pattern of feathers replaced the familiar dentate motifs. The firing in the new kiln took longer, but the sea salt in the driftwood fire glazed the feathers to shine like flames, which Lapita preferred for the Tanoa.

"Siga, did you hear me request more water?"

"Of course, Princess. Forgive me." She bowed quickly and scampered off with a water jug to do her mistress's bidding.

"What is capturing your thoughts, child, to make today's lesson so difficult?" Lapita murmured to herself. She looked around. Only two islanders had come to work today, and they were unusually quiet. *I don't know why I cannot concentrate. I cannot blame chatter.*

The old Tanoa had not been recovered, but the new Tanoa sat before her, a symbol of the future generations of leadership. This one was on a pedestal rising gracefully from a central foundation to spread upward and out, like the sides of the lagoon. It would shelter the yaqona to be shared with the decision makers before the spirit fire. The bowl had been fired over a low heat, and the flame design, pressed on the outside with a stamp, was ready to paint with liquid red clay. She envisioned a sun glowing from the interior of the bowl, spreading from the bottom up the sides. Lapita prepared a special yellow dye from boiled turmeric roots. Surely the wisdom of Tiki would enhance the yaqona. The god's visage on the flag of Uncle Momo's canoe could be added.

I must consider this with care.

In the preceding days, Lapita had practiced on three smaller bilos while waiting for the new Tanoa to dry. Bahram would probably want to sell them, but he might honor her decision to use the extra pottery in the Yaqona ceremony. She was unsure what to do about the traditional almond shaped eyes.

Why am I unable to go forward? It is a small decision.

Lapita studied the design variations in her trial pottery, and finally selected one to use on the larger bowl. She decided to make the eyes rounder to suggest a decision made with all the facts. When Siga returned, Lapita told her, "We will use the dye from mangrove roots, but I want to put more thought into this important design. I cannot work while this heaviness surrounds me. Let us rest awhile. Do you want to practice your Arabic words until midday break?"

"Yes, Princess." Siga somberly followed her outside to sit in their meditation spot. The view was a peaceful lagoon and two coral islands off the small rounded end of Vahilele's heel. Together they sat motionless until the worker maramas took their leave.

"What troubles you, manumanu vuka?"

"You tell me we are a people who love peace and harmony."

"Yes, that is true."

"Grandfather tells me we moved to Vahilele because the hill people of Viti Levu wanted to hurt our kai."

"That was a long time ago. Does that sadden you?"

"Why do we act like hill people if we don't want to live with them?"

"How do we act like hill people?"

"Our people buried a worker at the foundation corner of the rice pavilion. My friend's father says it is the old way because the spirit of the worker strengthens the new building. He said sometimes four are buried, one at each corner."

Lapita shifted, her thoughts tumbling, a feeling of great disturbance like the water of the sea receding quickly and then rushing the island with one overwhelming assault. She closed her eyes until the image was replaced by silky smooth water. "Yes, that was the old way of the hill people. They had workers born for that purpose. You were told that our kai did that?"

Siga's words came fast, unburdening herself to somebody who cared, who could right the wrong. Her tears came faster. "Yesterday. My friend heard screaming. The worker was alive but everybody stood and watched the dirt cover his mouth and eyes. Nobody helped him. "

Lapita struggled with the tightening of her chest. "Your news troubles me greatly, Siga. I must ask Elder Dau what goes on in his field village." She reached out to caress the back of a child who carried a heavy burden.

"These strangers must be fearful of us," said the child.

Lapita studied the hopeful young face next to her. "I am very pleased that you know this is an unacceptable sacrifice. Before I respond, questions must be asked."

"But Princess, will our men answer?" Her whisper was as soft as air.

"My little one, you get wiser every day. I will do my best to seek the Truth in their hearts."

"Princess, can you make them stop the hurt?" Tears coursed down her innocent cheeks.

"I am neither a king nor queen to suggest the wisdom of a law to the elders." Lapita put her arm around her charge. "A Bete keeps the peace with laws and can instruct elders, but I have not proven myself worthy of that position. I seek mana, a touch from the Phoenix. Until then, I am only a princess who loves her people."

When Lapita could breathe without anger, she told Siga. "I need to consider my words before I question Elder Dau, and I will consult the spirit fire. We both must take time to calm our minds. You are not able to learn with these thoughts swirling in your head."

Lapita watched Siga leave the pottery shed, dragging her feet, head down. *This thoughtful child will grow through the trials of time to be a wise leader. She takes others' pain upon herself, but she offers more than just comfort. She will be like obsidian to Vahilile.* Lapita wondered at the source of this clear insight.

Lapita seated herself again before her new design. She took a cloth to dip in the red dye of flames that would surround the outside of the Tanoa bowl, the wisdom of the tribe purified by fire. Anger welled up within her and exploded. The flames looked like feathers.

"Brengsek!"

With one swipe of her arm, Lapita swept the bowl off the table. Without a backward glance at the shattered pottery, she headed to the field village for a discussion with Elder Dau.

CHAPTER FORTY FIVE

Lapita

On the windward side of the island, the rice pavilion under construction sat on the edge of the forest cut back to allow cultivated fields.

Lapita walked past it quickly and up toward the hole where men labored in the midday sun. Elder Dau walked down the slope to greet her. "You are indeed returned to good health, Princess, to accomplish a long walk from Na Koro."

"I have been spending most of my days at the pottery shed, Elder Dau, half way between here and the Bure Kahlou."

"I heard you have had much success in trading your pottery. We are all doing our part to move Vahilele into a new world." As he stepped closer, the gold coin around his neck glinted in the sun's rays.

Three Balinese workers scrabbled around the hole they dug, filling containers with sandy soil, hoisting them to others who passed them on to the next in a line all the way to the lagoon.

"Why is this soil needed on the shore?" Lapita shaded her eyes to observe the organized effort.

"We are building a sea wall so our crops are not flooded easily. All the big cities have them, according to the mua.

This pond will catch extra freshwater to use in our planting season for rice."

"I didn't know there was such a plan."

"At the council meetings we talk about the future of Vahilele. Saca Bahram has revealed to us how the rest of the world lives, and encourages us to imitate the success of other cultures."

The pretentious words contrasted with the horror that had hastened her steps to investigate Siga's report. *The worker was alive but everybody stood and watched the dirt cover his head. Nobody helped him.* Lapita lashed out. "It must have been an unpleasant shock to Saca when your men reverted to an ancient custom of the hill people. Or did he approve it? After all, they live in the rest of the world."

"If a problem was not discussed, perhaps it does not exist. Let us retreat to the cool of my vale, Princess. I would be a poor host if I did not offer you refreshment."

Lapita kept her lips pressed tightly to keep ill-tempered words under control. This man she had known forever had worked hard to oversee an excellent quality of dalo cultivation. The emerald fields could be seen in the distance, waving their way up the slope, more than enough for the tribe and for trading after the harvest. But lately he was an arrogant tagane proudly in charge of Bahram's new rice crop. Nobody mentioned it would require more effort than dalo and much more water.

When they were seated in the cool shade in one of the largest vales on the island, Dau's wife provided a hot tea of fresh lemon leaves along with grated cassava sweetened with masawe. "Our grandson no longer has headaches." She bowed to Lapita. "Vinaka, Princess." When Dau frowned at her, she left them alone.

"You have come a long way, and I will hear what you have to say." Elder Dau's respectful welcome gave her own critical words a dark contrast. His words made her appear to be a troublemaker, inciting unrest where there was calm agreement among men. She knew his goal was to control their conversation and make his point of view more attractive even if it meant lying.

Perhaps he misrepresented reality this way unconsciously, but Lapita wondered what Dau gained by ignoring the unhappiness of his tribe. Her gaze focused on the intricately carved wooden tray that sat between them. "This is beautiful wood, Elder Dau. What is it?"

"Teakwood from Java. A present for my wife who abides my frequent absence from the vale."

As her eyes grew accustomed to the dim interior, Lapita saw beautiful cloth covering the walls, some pieces whispering around separate areas as large as her bure. This silk was first quality, not water-stained from the *Nabataea* cargo.

Dau studied her as she looked around the vale. "Princess Lapita? Is there a purpose for your visit?"

Her gaze traveled back to Dau's lean face, a man of industry and integrity, long honored to represent this village at the council. "Elder Dau, I wish to understand the sacrifice of a foreign worker in building the rice pavilion."

"How did you hear the business of our village?"

"That is not of importance. It is Truth that holds my attention. A visitor to our island died."

"You would wish an islander take his place?"

"Your place on the council has given you much experience at twisting words to avoid honest discussion. I will not play those games." Lapita lowered her eyes and tried again. "I respectfully ask you, Elder Dau, how do you explain this sacrifice by a peaceful tribe? She raised her eyes and waited for his response.

Elder Dau examined the bilo in his hands. "Not all of our people are connected to the Golden tribe like you are, Princess. I myself have the wooly hair of the Lutunasobasoba people, and I am proud to have their blood." He paused. Lapita waited. "Some of our kai Vahilele had grandparents who were hill people with servants whose blood was used for sacrifice. These clan members thought it a good idea to show which part of the tribe owns this island after the loss of Prince Tavale. They do not want foreigners to become part of our mataqali. They want them separate. And if they are marked for sacrifice only, they are separate. There is no question. The Balinese are not part of Vahilele, nor will they ever be."

"Kai Vahilele is not hill people in customs or thoughts. We teach our children to respect the land and all living things. Why would we confuse them by murdering those who have ideas, dreams, and emotions like our own?"

"Everyone has a purpose, Princess."

"And what is yours, Elder Dau?"

His eyes snapped. "I do not have time for your cutting words."

She rose before he could. "I hope you recognize Truth before it destroys your lovely family." She shook the dust from her sandals before she put them on at the door. She could not leave as quickly as her head commanded.

Lapita's walk back to the pottery shed became a march to the drumbeat of her heart. She looked forward to calming herself by creating something of beauty. Siga had already returned and put the shed back in order. Lapita started over to craft a new Tanoa.

Later that afternoon, Bahram entered the pottery shed empty-handed. "My dear Lapita, I have a surprise for you." Lapita expected his return from Sigatoka and looked forward to whatever trinket he would bring her, but she saw nothing in his hands.

"I see you are back safely. Is everyone else walking?" Lapita murmured in island vosa. Although she still held a grievance toward him for not tending to Siga's uncle on the last trip, she was annoyed at herself for speaking childishly. Her late husband had always focused on one task to the exclusion of everything else, but he never excluded the welfare of those around him. *Did he? I must be careful. It was so long ago that my memory is making him perfect.*

Bahram's forehead furrowed, as though he was puzzled at the words but he was distracted by the islander behind him, carrying a container he handed to Bahram.

Bahram busied himself in connecting pieces of wood, and she watched with curiosity.

"I have looked forward to showing this to you, Lapita. I hoped to have it put together before you saw it. I found a woman in Viseisei spinning her potter's wheel and thought of you. She said it came from Palembang. She had clay up to her elbows and sang as she worked. Not as beautifully as you, my dear.

"It will take time to learn to use it but it seems so much faster." Bahram stepped back. "Try it out." He took the soft bowl she was working on and slapped it on the new board. It tilted.

Lapita cried out. "Ahhhh! I spent much time shaping that bilo. Brengsek!"

His look of disappointment shamed her. Until his dark eyes lost their sparkle, and his fists clenched. It was good that he walked away.

CHAPTER FORTY SIX

Bahram

Angered at Lapita's ungrateful response to his gift, Bahram stomped the path to the southern part of the island, past the uvi field, to the isolated Nabataea Village. He looked forward to chatter with his shipmates, people he understood. He had been so busy he had not been here since the reguregu for Yaca. The reminder of his evil deed filled his mind with black thoughts. He saw a collection of huts in disarray and needing repair. In areas of tall grass, two huts had large holes in their cane walls. *Fighting among sailors*?

Nawfal shaved out a short vesi log with his knife, while Ghazi and Abu watched. William and Breaker stretched out in the sand, eating the meal that had been handed out at the pavilion. Bahram was hailed with weak greetings.

"Good day to you, Saca," said William. ""Welcome to our neighborhood. Cola!"

"We are very fortunate," Breaker spoke up. "The big man comes to visit."

"Nabataea Village looks like the slums of Viseisei," said Bahram.

Nawfal looked up from his carving. "Home away from home. Make yourself comfortable."

"This place is a pig sty. Why would I want to come here? At least the natives are neat."

"Thanks to Melane." Nawfal smiled. "I've heard her reproach her neighbor for apathetic hutkeeping."

"Well, I understand that you spend too much time in Melane's company," said Bahram. "That is a lost effort. She is a hard, bitter woman."

"Melane is very strong. *Kaukau* for your information. How many could lose a husband and a son and still keep a religion?"

"Are you helping her to keep going, mate?" Bahram sneered.

Nawfal put his bowl down and slowly got to his feet, towering above Bahram. "Saca, you are getting into dangerous territory. I shall warn you to back away."

Bahram studied his friend and snorted. "Forget it, Nawfal. I'm aggravated because my own men do not honor a commitment to support a project we talked about. I understood that everybody was behind a plan to make extra coins since we had to sit around here anyway. But you've grown lazy like the natives. Now, it's difficult to get cooperation to do the minimum that you did without comment two months ago. Like that unsightly pile of coconut shells."

"Those are for starting fires at night, but you work us such long hours, nobody wants to sit around and talk. We eat our dinner and collapse. We work harder than the natives. Why do you want to constantly complain? Last time it was about lady visitors, the only entertainment we have if we run out of palm wine and betel nuts."

William and Breaker left the area with their shell plates, headed to the lagoon, and away from altercation.

Bahram backed up and squatted. He shook his head. "It is an old coxswain habit. I have better things to do now, but I want to share my vision with all you mates who came here with me. I want to see you succeed. Since I travel so much, I depend on you to manage our business here on the island. I can't do it all."

"We have to wait for the rainy season to fill up the new pond for irrigation of the rice field," said Ghazi.

Bahram nodded and took a deep breath. As Nawfal gathered up his tools and partly hewn vesi log, Bahram asked him, "What are you making?"

"Tanoa bowl."

"Why?"

"Because the old one is missing. In a few days Lapita will need one for a meeting with the elders, not enough time to make another one of pottery."

"Some brengsek thief probably stole it," said Ghazi, his mouth twitching at one corner.

"Probably." Nawfal scowled at him.

"With no thought to others."

"Business is business." Bahram winked at Ghazi.

"Pride makes greed," commented Nawfal before he went into his hut.

Bahram regarded Ghazi lounging in front of the small fire that took the chill from the night air. The big man shrugged. Bahram glanced at the hut, back at Ghazi, at the forest, and finally said, "Nawfal is not the friend he once was. He forgets his allies because his heart is controlled by island voodoo. Have you noticed?" He walked around the fire to sit next to Ghazi. "There are too many religions to keep up with, and they are all superstitious nonsense. Nothing but meke believe. I am glad you are not corrupted by ceremonial doctrine."

"I don't know what that is. I have to see to believe."

"Exactly! That is why we get along. And why I will tell only you about my new venture." He revealed the hiding place of the large red prawns and explained how rare and how valuable they would be in foreign ports. "I will be going back to Viti Levu soon. After the next council meeting." Bahram regarded the hooded eyes and full bearded cheeks of his henchman. "I think it's time for you to be in management and wear a Sassanian gold coin."

CHAPTER FORTY SEVEN

Lapita

Footfalls hesitated outside the pottery shed where Lapita bent over her work. She used paint made with charred coconut husk and banana sap to repeat the same design she had stamped on a water jug. She decided to make the flames twice the size on this new Tanoa. Stronger power was necessary to rid Vahilele of the evil that had escalated.

"Princess, there is somebody here to see you." Siga waited for direction.

"Vinaka. I cannot stop what I do. Ask them to enter."

Soon a man stood next to her. Lapita's eyes travelled from the deep brown eyes of Dede Nikua's father to the old Tanoa bowl he held in front of him. *Here is a story.*

Lapita put down her tools, and wiped her hands. She stood, and the rustling around her told her that the other women in the shed were leaving silently. Siga stood at attention in the corner awaiting her mistress's request.

"Sa Bula, my old friend."

"Sa Bula, Princess."

She reached out to take the Tanoa, examined it, and identified the irregularity where she had patched it. Carefully she placed the bowl in Siga's hands. "Take this to the Bure Kalou where it belongs." Motioning to her guest, she led the way outside where the ocean could be seen stretching to forever. "This is my fount of inspiration, Vunde Moto." She seated herself cross-legged, back straight, hands on knees covered by the grass skirt she wore when painting. Her visitor followed and seated himself next to her at a respectful distance when she gestured permission. "Tell me your story."

"I am a navigator, Princess, and make many trips to other islands."

She nodded. This man had been Tavale's playmate. She had grown up in their shadows, but always on the outside of their exuberant games, never allowed to compete after she was ten. She once beat them in a foot race, and her father punished them all. "A princess does not behave like a tagane," he had said. But she was secretly included in the telling of their tales when the adults were distracted by their own conversations.

"In past days, I journeyed to Sigatoka, Princess. I was instructed to wait near the harbor for our trading delegation's return. My duty was to safeguard the outrigger but I was not alone, and we took turns."

This was a storyteller, and Lapita settled in for a lengthy account of his trip to Sigatoka. As she gazed at the changing blue expanse highlighted by shimmering gold from the rays of an afternoon sun, Lapita felt the tug of the past, an unbroken cord that anchored her to childhood days when memories were woven with innocence and adventure. Her brother was near. As he should be. She nodded again. Lapita already knew the ending. The Tanoa was now returned to her possession. As it should be.

"In my wanderings through the stalls of the marketplace, I came upon a beautiful bowl with flames of passion. I thought of you, Princess."

A long silence. Lapita did not move. She patiently awaited his purpose.

"I heard of your kindness to my daughter while I was gone." He paused again. "When my Dede Nikua was abused, I feared she would never recover. Little Siga was a true friend. Like we used to be to each other. Your brother and you and me. We shared our questions of an adult world, our experiences of triumph and sadness. We were close. Prince

Tavale's death grieves my soul." He took a deep breath. Lapita waited. "We each had a path to follow and our lives separated long ago. I thought we had grown apart."

A catch in his voice reverberated in Lapita's innermost depths, a pull on that tie they had created as youngsters.

"As always, you recognize what is true. You gave good counsel to Tavale when we were younger." She smiled. "He had only one scar." They chuckled together, the tension released from weighty words.

"After Dakuwaqa bit him, I told Tavale he was spit out because the shark didn't like the way he tasted," said the navigator. He sniffed loudly.

"I remember. You said he would always be safe because Dakuwaqa didn't like breadfruit."

Neither one laughed. Lapita's heart hurt with the memory.

"When I saw that Tanoa, I recognized something precious, something never spoken. The bonds that held our generation together are weakening. Our respect for each other is overshadowed by selfishness."

After a long pause, Vunde Moto continued his tale.

There is no hurry for important thoughts and words. Lapita felt the stirrings of Truth in her soul.

"My Dede Nikua is broken. She will forever have a scar inside that no man can erase. She will survive. But she has lost something of value, the trust in a world of love and order that the three of us had.

"Dede Nikua told me about the broken Tanoa and how you made a new one with flames, but I heard that it disappeared. And then a merchant in Sigatoka tried to sell me a bowl that looked like our Tanoa. He called it 'a Samoan creation,' but my heart said it belonged in Vahilele. I hope, Princess, I did not make trouble for you."

She did not comment because she was in awe how this miracle had unfolded.

"Princess, I saw those flames. I don't know why you chose them, but they are right for this time. I have known you a lifetime, and a bright light has always been a part of your soul. This is your time. You are on the right path, and I will follow wherever you lead. And there are others who feel the same. We depend on your wisdom."

Tears streamed unchecked down Lapita's cheeks. *I don't want this lonesome path. I want to be a friend, not a princess. This path ends in heartache.*

Her heart told her differently. This was her journey.

"You have a way with words, old friend."

"They burdened me until I shared them, Princess. Now I am empty, and I can sleep."

She turned to his strong features, the dark eyes under curly black eyebrows. His mouth turned up slightly, reminding Lapita of the young boy who once chased her with rocks and then with flowers.

"I miss the old times. My world cracked when Tavale was killed," he said.

There was a pause. Lapita took a cautious breath. "How do you think he died?" She whispered.

His eyes moistened. "At man's hand, Princess. And we cannot set evil aside."

Abruptly he stood and left.

The sounds inside the shed told her that Siga had returned and was cleaning up, attending to her mistress's abandoned project again. While the air cooled and the sun dropped below the high cliffs behind her, putting the eastward sloping island in shade, Lapita remained immersed in thought. Golden rays still kissed the water farther out, deep blue to the beyond.

CHAPTER FORTY EIGHT

Lapita

Days unfolded as Lapita experimented with new designs and shapes, an outward expression of her inner conflict. Although she was often unaware of those around her, Siga was ever at her side.

One afternoon, Lapita felt the need to connect with her people. She was weary of seeking answers to fading questions. She said to her young helper, "I hear that you gave Dede Nikua a candle with an herbal wreath. The one I gave you?"

Siga lowered her gaze. "Yes, Princess. I didn't need to be healed but she did."

"You are very thoughtful, manumanu vuka, but those herbs were for protection, not healing. We will have to make her another."

"Yes, but I am not in harm's way so I do not need a protection candle."

"We all need protection from the unknown." Lapita straightened, pushing away from her tangle of thoughts that brought more questions. She sighed and looked around at the women who surrounded her, a growing number required by the higher volume of pottery sales they had made on the last order. They were each focused on the task before them, working together although different in age and experience.

One of the women had a new infant being cared for by her lame grandmother who could do no other work. Another marama left her small children with her husband who had been crippled in an accident logging huge vesi trees. Bahram's new venture had frightened some islanders who refused to do it, and who, therefore, were refused food by the community council.

"Do you not have to go home to prepare your grandfather's dinner?"

"Not yet, Princess. He will be late because of the council meeting this afternoon," said Siga.

"Yes, the council meets to make rules to tell the rest of us how to live."

Lapita rinsed her hands in the reddish water by her pottery board. As she picked up a cloth to dry them, she said, "I am going to a meeting. Carry on." Eight pairs of eyes looked at her and comments were whispered among the women. There was an air of excitement, a few smiles. Lapita knew that she knew: this was the right path. Her heart swelled.

"Princess, I will help you get ready," said Siga.

"I am going as I am, wearing a common grass skirt and a dirty face. They cannot ignore a golden heart."

The women laughed. One clapped her hands with delight.

Lapita walked back to the Na Koro village center where the meetings were always held out in the open but opinions never sought from those without a gold coin necklace, the badge for inclusion.

Elder Dau's quick eyes were the first to see her striding off the path toward their huddle. He looked startled and glanced away when she stared back at him. Elder Matai Malolo turned to greet her over his shoulder.

Bahram was speaking and suddenly broke off, "What catches your attention...ahhh, my lovely Princess joins us. The day I have been awaiting." As he bowed in her direction, his necklace of snake vertebrae caught her eye, and she wondered where he found it.

She ignored his friendly welcome and Abu's surly

comment, "What are you doing here?"

Lapita glanced at Elder Bati, who looked amused. She nodded at Matai Malolo and Nawfal and seated herself in the space next to Lalai who fidgeted with his hair and clothing. She was thankful that today he did not smell sour.

"We are discussing new possibilities for farming, my dear," said Bahram. "Elder Dau reported that the rice fields are prepared but we cannot plant until next year when we are sure to have enough water in the pond. I have suggested we plant kava in the meantime but there is no agreement among us."

Lapita looked at each of her kai, deliberately excluding the sailors from her response. "Kava can be very potent when used for healing and prophecy. Yaqona is offered to our tribe for ceremonial occasions, but our forefathers did not think it wise to make a powerful drink available to everyone all of the time. It is possible that some might drink too much. This is part of our heritage." She spoke her opinion in island vosa and then again in Arabic. Elder Bati and Elder Matai Malolo nodded. Everyone looked at Elder Dau who hesitated before he nodded in agreement and untangled his legs as though preparing to flee.

"Well, it looks as though the lady influences this discussion." Bahram chuckled. "Tell me Princess Lapita. Do you have a better suggestion for a crop?"

"I have not put much thought into changing what we have. I see you have brought in foreign workers, and I've seen that they are well fed. However, that does not erase their fear that they will be sacrificed like their friend."

"That was an unfortunate incident now in the past. I brought in only four Balinese workers because we needed their experience. I soon will travel back to Viti Levu to secure the help of more Malaysian workers because our kai is very busy and cannot handle the farming of crops and logging the forest. But that was the business at the last meeting. We have moved on to a different agenda. You do not want to farm kava. What do you suggest?"

Lapita gave a cautious response. "Ginger shrubs grow well with little oversight. There must be a market similar to the other spices exported from China, but I wouldn't know about that."

The men were silent. Elder Bati nodded agreement.

Elder Matai Malolo said, "The Bure Kalou is surrounded by medicinal plants and the Princess would know about the importance of ginger root." He nodded his agreement. "I suggest that I accompany you on your next trip to Viti Levu, Saca. I could make inquiries among my friends there as to the success of production on other islands."

"I will consider that suggestion," said Bahram. "Thank you, Princess Lapita. Before we decide what to plant, we must make a decision on how we will pay for the new workers. I think it is fair that each native tagane is taxed for his plot of land where his vale sits. I do not want to add an unfair tax on our maramas because they rely heavily on the strength of taganes. Therefore, let us make the tax only on taganes. Do we agree?" He spoke in Arabic and kept nodding and smiling while he talked.

Lapita said, "There is already a tax on each vale."

"Of course, but this would be a one-time additional tax like the Romans and Muslims and Greeks put on their people when they need to make improvements where all people share in the result. All countries do this."

The three elders nodded in agreement.

"Then we are all agreed."

Lapita shook her head. "There are some who are not able to pay more."

"We will work with them so they pay their share only a small amount at a time. I am willing to make adjustments. You have seen that more people benefit by living in a community than under the old way of individual choice."

"I have seen that you create conflict and call it progress. My kai goes along with your ideas because they don't like conflict."

"Consider your cousin Melane, who has no tagane to provide food for her, but because of our community rules, she always gets a share," said Bahram.

"Melane takes care of small children as the council requested when Maca Matanitu died. But she gets her share of food because our tribe has a traditional commitment to care for widows and children even if they do not work," said Lapita.

"Some of the council's new laws are good," said Nawfal in Arabic and nodded at Bahram. "We discuss the import of more field labor because there is a slowdown in production." He added in island vosa. "Princess Lapita is a wise leader. She knows Vahilele tagane realize the hard workers get the same reward as the lazy ones. Therefore, they ask themselves: why work hard? That is a separate problem."

Lapita interrupted. "Nawfal, I strive to be a spiritual leader. That is my place, a mediator between our mataqali clan and our gods. I do not wish to be part of this council that seeks control of its brothers. There is a plan of division between the workers and the few at the top who do no work but still get a large part of whatever is shared. I speak plainly. Theirs is the portion used for bribes. For controlling those who get less."

Lapita paused to weigh her words. She thought of Tavale. "Equality among us is not a virtue because we are not a flock of clucking megapodes. We are a kai with hearts and souls." Lapita noticed Elder Dau and Elder Bati exchange glances. "There will be no harmony until we value the unique contribution each person makes." She stood gracefully, nodded respectfully, and went back to the Bure Kalou.

"The lady speaks her mind," said Nawfal. "Tagane perspective does not own wisdom."

CHAPTER FORTY NINE

Siga

The coming of age was upon Siga, and she went to her vale to look for cloths to staunch the flow but they had all been used during her mother's sickness. Her grandfather was gone to Viti Levu and Siga left by herself. *I am thirteen, old enough to handle problems. A woman. What shall I do?*

Months ago when she helped her mistress deliver Maca Matanitu's baby, Siga had seen many cloths at the vale.

They were still there when she helped prepare the sitter for burial. Her need increased, and Siga hurried to that hut, but it was not vacant as she expected. Her father was there, sleeping and snoring loudly. She tried not to disturb Lalai but he awoke, angry at the intrusion even though she explained her reason.

"I look for marama cloths. I need them today. Now."

"Why did you not go to your royal highness who pretends to know everything?" He raised himself on his elbows and squinted at her. His words were slurred. "She says she is a healer. She killed Matanitu with her stupidity."

"Father, do not speak about the Princess with scorn. Our future depends upon her."

"No, we have real leaders now. Royalty is shallow, worthless." He lay down again. "My blood runs more Golden than hers," he muttered. He turned over and closed his eyes. "Get what you want and leave. Don't bother me."

Siga took the basket of cloths back to her vale. When she emptied the basket to neatly fold the cloths, she found an odd bone, what the foreigners would call a button. She could not understand its presence in Maca Matanitu's vale, but she had other things to think about.

Why does he hate me? Siga was besieged by memories of her father's old refrain, "You're just like your mother." When she was a child, she took that as a compliment until she noticed that Lalai continually treated her mother with contempt. *He is my parent, but I am alone.*

Siga's stomach hurt, and now her heart ached as she walked to the children's boulders. Depressed and low in spirit, she climbed over the outlying rocks to the high one in the center where she could absorb the sun and dream of what lie beyond the horizon. *Not even Savu or Dedan care about me.*

"Siga. Cola." It was Abu, standing in the nuku. She waved, anticipating that he would move on. But he stepped up to the rock below hers, sandals slipping. "I'm glad I found you. I have a question about island words." He spoke in Arabic.

"Which island words?" She answered in Arabic.

"What?" He cupped his hand behind his ear. "Please come down so I can hear you. The pounding waves are too loud to shout back and forth."

There was nothing to do but scramble off the rocks. He was older, and his words were important. She liked him less every time she saw him, especially after he hurt her friend Dede. But that was not for her to mention.

"I cannot remember the word for sand," he said.

She knew that wasn't true. Unless he suddenly had a lapse in memory, which sometimes happened to her with Arabic words. It didn't matter. He was a man, he was a friend to the island leader, and she was nothing. She was like the worker born to be buried alive to capture his spirit. At that thought, she trembled. Could she be tricked into being a sacrifice? Would she be able to get away? Was that how her life would end?

I am only thirteen.

She scrambled down. "Nuku."

"Nuku. Of course, I knew that, but I couldn't remember. Does that ever happen to you?"

"Yes, Saca."

"Really? And you are so smart." Abu showed his teeth in a slit across his face.

It was not a friendly smile, and she felt uneasy. She stood across from the break in the reef where canoes entered the lagoon. The pottery shed was hidden in the jungle up the path behind them, and the fishing village was out of view around a bend in the shoreline. Not another person could be seen. She was afraid of this skinny little man with matted hair and smelly tunic, but she would not make him angry.

Abu is the man who hurt Dede Nikua, and the council did nothing.

"This is a wonderful day to be alive," Abu said, wading into the waves that lapped the nuku. "The breeze is cooler here than in Nabataea Village."

"Your sulu is very high on your chest." Siga's face grew warm. She may have offended the mua with her careless comment.

Abu laughed. "That is why I wear nothing underneath, just like the Greeks." He flashed the garment up and down and laughed. "Do you know anything about the Byzantine Empire, little girl?"

"No, Saka." Siga decided she didn't want to know anything about Greeks if they did not wear breechcloths. *Perhaps I should go to the pottery shed now.* She looked that way again.

"I will give you a history lesson."

"History?"

Was this the language lesson he wanted to ask. Maybe he would talk about the makawa. She was curious, and she didn't want to anger him.

"Yes, I come from the Kingdom of Aksum far away, across three seas."

"Three? I thought there was only one."

"Oh yes, there is the Indian Ocean, and then there are the Red Sea, and the Mediterranean Sea, and the Arabian Sea and the China Sea and many more."

Siga was astounded. She forgot her discomfort in being with this strange man who really did have interesting stories to tell.

"In Aksum, we had different traditions than you have in Vahilele. This garment is called a lungi."

"I do not know Aksum. Is it a yanuyanu, an island?" The world was so much bigger than she had imagined. *This is what Princess Lapita talked about. Traveling to other places.*

"No, no." He laughed again and sat down on the crushed shells and coral sand, the tide creeping in to cover his legs and rushing out again. "Sit with me, and I will tell you all about my home."

"Vanua." She smiled.

"Yes, my homeland."

Siga settled herself near him to better hear his stories. Nobody was around, but what harm could there be? Soon the water gently lifted her sulu and his skirt, swished out, and came back again to cover their legs, and still Abu kept on describing ships with dragon heads and the sight of shore property with acres of grapes. A wave came in that knocked them backward, and Abu hooted loudly. Siga giggled, and turned loose of her father's criticism that had soured her attitude. Abu was fun, and she was glad she was brave enough to try something new.

"I left Aksum at an early age. There was a warrior people who invaded and they took me, at age fifteen, away from my *vanua*." He smiled and nodded at her. "They taught me much about sailing and trading merchandise along the Red Sea, but I was lonely. I didn't have the friends you have."

She felt a spasm of pity for this man she had described as ugly. She could feel his pain.

"Your princess reminds me of Empress Fausta. I saw her once in Constantinople. From a distance. She wore a diadem of gold, studded with emeralds and ropes of pearls hung from it."

"What is a diadem?"

"A crown, or headdress like Princess Lapita wears."

"I know pearls. Perhaps I could make a rope of pearls for the Princess." The possibility excited her, and she listened with great attention to this new teacher.

"The Empress was the only one in the kingdom who was allowed to wear a great purple cape. She was the most beautiful woman I ever saw. Except for your princess, of course." Abu winked at Siga.

"What is purple?"

"A color as bold as the red feathers in Lapita's headdress, but mixed with the blue of the sky. The color of royalty."

"My Princess should have that cape."

Abu laughed. "It would be too warm for Vahilele. But it was beautifully embroidered in gold thread with the figures of the Magi."

"What are the Magi?"

"So many questions! They were wise men from the Parthian Empire who were interested in a Jewish baby they thought might be a monarch one day. They put great faith in dreams."

"As does my Princess!" *These other worlds are not so different.*

Abu smiled and looked out across the lagoon, and the breakers, into faraway lands. Siga sensed his despair even before he spoke.

"As a youth, I was passed from one ship captain to another, usually as a prize for a game of chance. It was in this way I met Captain Koch who treated me well and taught me to read and cipher. He was a great man. But too late to save me," he whispered.

Siga was sorrowful that his abusive past had crippled him. Her spirit was burdened for him. *If he finds happiness in Vahilele, his soul could heal. But I will not tell Dede that I am his friend.*

Abu abandoned his story. Siga examined his profile, the small eyes and hooked nose. His mouth turned down now and his shoulders hunched over.

His sadness surrounds him like a dark cloud of tears.

A wave swept over them at that moment, and he took a deep breath.

Abruptly he stood and held out his hand to Siga. "Let me show you a game we played in Egypt. He pulled her into the lagoon until they were standing knee deep in the surf.

"Do you believe in fate, Siga?"

"I don't know what it is."

"No, of course, not. I get my religions confused. You believe in the Tiki god? The mana of the Phoenix?"

"Yes. But Degei knows all."

"Really. Does he see all?"

Siga was now chest deep in the water and stumbled.

"Don't fall." Abu hooked Siga closer to him with one hand and stroked her neck, down to her breast, with the other. "You are also a beautiful woman. Has anyone told you that, little Siga? You can help me escape my prison of memories."

She felt a tight grip that wriggling would not release.

Abu sniggered and pulled her closer. "Will you do that for me?"

She felt a heavy shadow move from him to smother her. He was not a friend, and she was afraid.

Lapita

Lapita had been listening for the arrival of her helper and not concentrating wholly on her new bowl. Since the deaths of Tavale and Yaca, she often had dark thoughts. *When was my peaceful island overcome by evil?*

As though she had been expecting it, a sharp scream punctured the quiet morning.

"Continue your work, maramas. You do well without me." Her words were to the ladies who worked with her on the large order of pottery they hastened to fill. "I must go where I am most needed."

The Princess started down the path, her steps faster and faster, fearful of the unknown and mindful of the last time a scream made her run. Another piercing wail of fear penetrated the hazy thoughts that she tried to clarify with her prayers.

From the edge of the forest, Lapita saw Abu in the lagoon, gripping Siga's arm and pulling her farther out. The girl shook her head and struggled to break free, but Abu laughed. When he forced her into deeper water, she struck at him and screamed again. He secured both her hands and squealed in laughter.

Lapita tried to hurry her footsteps through the soft sand.

When Siga lost her footing, waves up to her chin, Abu put his hand behind her head and shoved her under, drawing her towards himself. He hollered out, laughing insanely as she struggled up, gasping for air.

Two of the island boys ran down the beach and waded forcefully through the waves toward them.

Lapita stopped at water's edge.

They will rescue her. I must ask for the help of the Phoenix for them. She elevated her arms, searching for a spirit connection.

Before she felt control over this evil, she heard one of the boys shout, "Dakuwaqa." Fear opened her eyes. One boy pulled his friend to a halt by pointing toward the reef.

A dark fin passed the opening of the coral barrier straight ahead. Abu appeared unaware of the ominous presence of the huge tiger shark. Lapita stepped into waves lapping on the pristine sand as though nothing unnatural was happening, as though the gods turned their heads and ignored the cries of anguish.

"You boys get out of the water," she told them while she took long, strong steps in a steady course toward Siga. She continually chanted, "Dakuwaqa, Dakuwaqa. Protect the Golden child."

Abu pushed Siga's head under the water again and whooped when she came up gasping. She no longer cried out, she only had time to catch her breath before he plunged her head under again. Lapita held her own breath.

He pulled Siga up, leered at her. "Don't know that game? It's all right. I know another one," and he clutched Siga in front of himself and carried her deeper.

"Abu, let her go! She is a child." Lapita tried to keep fear from her voice.

He turned toward her. "The great Princess is here to watch. And she can't do anything to stop this game. Maybe she wants to join us. Come on out, Princess. I'll trade the child for you."

"Abu! Let her go!"

But he didn't respond. His eyes were closed, and he smiled as Siga struggled against him. He didn't see the new blood of a virgin in the water. He didn't see the dark gray fin slowly breech the lagoon passage.

Suddenly, Melane swished past Lapita, arms pumping, sulu pulled up, knees high above the water, and then she swam toward Siga as efficiently as any fish in the sea.

Lapita stood in place, arms raised. "Dakuwaqa, Dakuwaqa, have mercy, we honor you." She could not close her eyes. She quit breathing when the sailor and his victim disappeared underwater and a red streak grew wider and brighter, but she continued her prayers.

Siga came to the surface, eyes enlarged and blood streaming from the top of her head. She flailed toward Melane.

"Slowly, slowly. Do not kick," shouted Melane, straining to reach the child's outstretched hand.

Lapita saw another fin coming through the passage. "Dakuwaqa, Dakuwaqa, we mean no harm to you." Her attention was mesmerized by the swirling water where Abu's arm appeared and then snatched from below. Her chest ached, and she felt dizzy. "Spirit of the Phoenix, watch over this child of the blood." There was no need to shout. Her heart communicated with the spirits of the sea.

Disoriented now, she waded out toward the churning red water. *What is my purpose? Dakuwaqa, did you come for me? I do not think you took my brother, but must you take me with you, O Great Dakawaqua?"* More fins closed in on the reef.

Siga floated toward Melane who stretched out to grab her hand and slowly pull her away from the bloody froth in the water now attended by two sharks.

Retreating to shore past Lapita, Melane held Siga out of the water, one hand under her knees and one supporting her trembling back, Siga's forehead tucked into Melane's neck, mouth crumpled with sobs and coughs.

The Princess did not follow them. Shouts from Melane and Siga fell on Lapita's deaf ears. She was transfixed now, and she spoke aloud. "Are you my jailor, Dakuwaqa? Or do you want me to follow you?"

The water was colder now, up to her waist, and the great fin approached her.

"Have you come for me? I am ready to go."

Siga's wail pierced Lapita's core. "Princess! Princess! Come back!"

A tug on the back of her sulu held her captive. It was followed by gentle, low words in her ear. "Sister, I hold you fast. Come back. We need you."

Lapita was pulled slowly backward, step by step, and the great fin turned to greet the others coming through the reef. The lagoon foamed, and quieted when the sharks left.

"Lapita, it will not help Vahilele to kill yourself." Melane released her and they walked to shore hand in hand. "You must think of others."

"I am weary of thinking of others."

"Come. We will talk."

"I am so tired of being kaukaua, Melane. It's time for me to go to the makawa."

"Sega! It is time for you to fulfill your destiny as our spiritual leader. We need a Bete!"

Lapita sank to the beach where Siga shivered, and held the child tightly to her breast. "You are favored, little one. Dakuwaqa found another sacrifice for his displeasure." The assembled crowd watched the horror slowly disappear into quiet seas and soft breezes. Some were crying, some stood in stony silence.

The sailors talked among themselves, soon retreating to Nabataea Village.

In dry clothing before the comfort of a Spirit Fire, Melane and Lapita silently sipped yaqona. Siga was wrapped warmly and slept on Lapita's own bed. An herbal infusion would keep her quiet for awhile.

"Melane, you were very brave. You will make a good leader."

Melane sniffed. "Very brave or very stupid."

"Sometimes, it's the same thing." Lapita's mouth curled slightly, and she nodded. "You were brave when you put Siga's safety ahead of your own."

"Any mother would do the same. It's natural."

"Did you notice that I did not? Nana Hewa told me I am different. She was right."

"Lapita, you were offering yourself as a sacrifice. That is very brave."

"Is it? I think it takes fear to be brave. I was never afraid for myself." A trace of smoke ascended like a kalou seeking release. "I am afraid for Siga's future."

Melane crawled over to sit close to Lapita and warm her icy shell. "My sister, you are more distant now. You stand for long heartbeats on the shore, looking out to sea. What do you think about?"

Lapita looked to Melane's love shining out from large dark eyes. She deserved the truth. "I think about escape, looking for my husband, for my mother, for my father, for my peipei. They are not buried in earthly graves."

"They are right here," Melane whispered. "Stay with us, sister. Help us. We need you."

That afternoon, Lapita went to the graves searching for wisdom and direction that she did not find. Now she started the uphill climb that started benignly like other paths leading from Na Koro. Soon it became rocky and treacherous.

"Brother, do you wait for me? You again are free. You always go first, always go farther. Again I am left behind to wonder where you are while I am trapped in this beautiful cage. But there is nobody to stop me now, nobody to pull me back and tell me my destiny is for the people." Lapita stood on the judgment rock. Below, the surf smashed into the base of the cliff. "There is nothing to keep me from spreading my wings. I long to fly out over the crystal water below, away from this island of deceit and conflict to follow the sun that Tiki pulls across the sky. Tomorrow he will bring it up again but I won't be here to see it. I will finally catch up with you on your travels." She smiled sadly at her foolishness and finished her climb to the rampart of Vahilile.

Princess Lapita watched the setting sun, rays of light that slowly lost its hold on land and slid over the horizon followed by its own radiance. At the edge of the highest peak, she raised her arms and cried out, "Spirit of the Phoenix, what is my purpose?"

Over the pulsating roar of sea and wind, she could hear her husband's voice. "You must stay. It is your destiny to lead our people." He spoke to her heart, and she understood.

CHAPTER FIFTY

Bahram

It was late afternoon when Bahram directed two islanders to put his new possession in front of his vale and gave each of them a copper coin for their service. The burden was not extremely heavy, but he wanted to train them to be dependent upon him for rewards. He removed the wrapping that had protected the upholstery from seawater on their outrigger journey back to Vahilele. Seated on his new high-backed chair, he congratulated himself for having the wits to include this symbol of power in his negotiation with the Viseisei governor. The carved armrests were comfortable, exactly what he needed to spend hours in intellectual pursuit. Like Caesar.

Bahram moved his throne so he could see the steps going to the door of the Bure Kalou to his left, the best scenery in the village, and he imagined his princess descending the steps to walk seductively toward him. To his right he could see part of the common area around the kitchen pavilion where the three elders still sat among a small group of men. It was too early for the usual crowd. Melane's hut was partially visible down another path. As he rested from his voyage, he saw Elder Dau stand and come toward him, probably with a report of his taro field production that he continually boasted about. Bahram waited for his approach, like a king waiting for a steward.

Elder Dau nodded to him. His eyes took in the chair but he made no comment. He squatted without asking the permission Bahram had observed in similar situations. *Dau looks unhappy. Maybe the old man is ill.* They sat in silence until Bahram decided it was his place to start the conversation.

"Cola, Elder Dau."

"Sa Bula."

"I trust our dalo crop is doing well. Are the water trenches finished?"

"Yes, Saca."

"Good. Good." Bahram was glad it was Dau who came to him because he knew Arabic better than the others. "We will have plenty of water next season for a rice crop."

"Yes, Saca."

There seemed to be a restrained effort from the elder to communicate, a hesitation in his voice. *My imagination most likely.* "What about the sea wall?"

"No, Saca, it is not done."

"Well, no worries. I have contracted for more workers who will be brought in soon. The project will proceed faster."

"Vahilele men are fearful that Dakuwaqa does not want a wall. He swims the shore with his children."

Bahram paused. Perhaps he misunderstood what the native said, but here was a progressive islander who had backed all commercial decisions wholeheartedly in council meetings. "Elder Dau, I have had a long journey. I must need rest because I thought you said something about a shark."

"Yes, Saca. Dakuwaqa came to our lagoon and took your friend Abu. He is no more."

Bahram felt dizzy. He turned to the elder as the shocking news roared through his head into his body. "What happened?" But he was on his feet rushing to Nabataea Village to get a trustworthy account. Plunging through the forest the path was too long, the birds too shrill, the breeze too sticky, the fragrance of tipanie too cloying. Nothing was right. A dependable friend was gone.

Ghazi reclined against a log clutching a wooden bowl of dried pandanus kernels and a bilo of spirits, judging from his lethargic appearance.

Bahram bellowed as he entered the clearing in the middle of the four huts. "What happened?"

William and Turban appeared at the sound of his voice and stood without speaking as Ghazi waved his hand and stuttered. "You return! And I assume you are asking about the fate of our shipmate, little Abu. Poor devil." He took a sip from his bilo. He shook his head. "He was splashing around with a young girl and 'poof' he was gone." Ghazi's glazed eyes attempted to stay focused on Bahram for a moment before he looked away.

"Where's Nawfal?" Bahram glanced at the hut Nawfal shared with Breaker and Turban.

"With Melane, where else?" William muttered, swirling the contents of his bilo.

Turban shrugged his shoulders.

The *Nabataea* cook came to the entry of his hut, wooden bowl under one arm while he stirred with the other. Bahram asked him if he had seen what had happened to Abu, but he shook his head.

Bahram sat down heavily and watched slack-jawed as William started a small fire, the everyday routine that made Abu's absence seem an outrageous possibility. Indeed, Bahram almost expected the jokester to come wandering up with a humorous comment about one of the natives. "Of all of us, he was the one who was most comfortable in this new world. I can't believe he's gone," he said, voice breaking.

"No way to recover from a shark bite on the neck." Ghazi slurred his words. "At least he was dead before the feeding frenzy."

"Disgusting." Bahram felt nauseous and had to leave. He headed down the path to his own hut and encountered Nawfal who showed a strained countenance. Both men slowed and came to a halt.

"I can see by your face you have heard about Abu," said Nawfal.

"I can't even imagine how terrified he was."

"I don't think he saw the shark. He was preoccupied with scaring the hell out of Siga. Abu didn't suffer long. Probably didn't know what happened."

"And Siga?"

"She was unharmed because of Melane's quick action to rescue her."

Bahram snorted. "I'm not surprised you would make Melane the heroine of the day. I understand you spend a lot of time with her when I'm gone."

"She thinks her husband was killed by a shark. Perhaps now you understand how hard it is to push aside dark thoughts when imagination unexpectedly brings horror to mind."

Bahram had nothing to say. He shoved Nawfal out of the way in his effort to escape the feeling of helplessness and despair. Avoiding the village, he walked from one end of the island to the other along the lagoon, not returning to his hut until he was so tired he dropped asleep. No dreams.

CHAPTER FIFTY ONE

Bahram

The following week, the natives abandoned their work to assemble on the sand and watch a merchant ship navigate the barrier reef. Lapita and Bahram stood together at the edge of the crowd who welcomed these dark foreigners landing small boats on shore.

""The gods provide a calm sea for our visitors." Lapita wore a formal masi sarong embellished by the red flames of her new pottery design. It covered one shoulder, a good background for the Tabua around her neck.

Bahram's sharp eyes watched the captain of the ship headed their way. The community separated to let him pass, and the Princess moved toward him, her elegant hands outstretched, a welcome lululu for the rugged man who moved with the easy gait of a prowling lion.

"S*a Bula.*" Lapita spread her arms gracefully to include the island. "*Vanua tu*, Captain Owen Safwan."

"*Vinaka*, my beautiful Vahilele Princess." The tall mariner bowed and presented her with a gift of kava, never taking his eyes from her face. It was as though the two of them were aware only of each other. "I am honored that you recognized me and remembered my name."

Bahram pushed forward through the throng to shake the Moor's hand, irritated that he himself was not given an introduction. To the the seaman's credit, it seemed he had taken care to wash before greeting the princess, but that made Bahram more suspicious.

"*Vale. Yaqona.*" Lapita led a procession to her home. Melane walked beside her, Dedan trotting behind.

"Native traditions, you know. It won't take long," Bahram commented to the captain. "We'll talk later about news from civilized ports."

"I admire these island people. They know how to enjoy a simple life." Safwan gave him a cursory glance. "And they honor their visitors."

"They do not miss what they do not know. I am in charge now." He fingered a necklace of sperm whale teeth, graduated in size. It had been removed from one of the smallpox victims near the snake pit, and the Persian wore it on special occasions, along with his gold coin that he never took off for fear of someone stealing it.

"Are you? We can talk after we have a grog with the lady." Safwan's gaze brushed over the new tunic and trousers Bahram was wearing, but he never looked him in the eye.

Annoyed by the newcomer's dismissive tone, Bahram dropped behind the captain and trailed with the two elders, Bati and Dau. "Did you complete the inventory of the shipment going to Beqa?" he asked Dau in a loud voice.

"Yes, we are ready," said the elder who assisted Bati along the rocky path.

After a period of silence, Bahram surged ahead of these slow walkers to get a seat close to Lapita. He understood the importance of ceremony to his people, and he would allow their tedious rituals if they did not interfere with his plan to increase commercial trade for Vahilele.

When Bahram entered the Bure Kalou, Safwan was chatting with Melane at one end of the semi circle of woven mats whose decorated shell fringes faced Lapita in the center. Bahram sat on the other end. The sevusevu began when the elders took their places in between the foreigners.

After the ritual drink in a common bilo, they each clapped their cupped hands and responded, "*Maca.*" Lapita waited for her last guest to finish his *Yaqona,* downed all in one swallow.

"You are thirsty, my friend," she said to Safwan.

"It has been a long time at sea without refreshments this pleasurable."

He returned the ceremonial bowl to Siga who then served individual bowls to Lapita first, Melane and guests. No one spoke as a bowl of taro paste was passed among those relaxing in the temple. Elder Dau dipped his fingers in it immediately as though he were famished.

Lapita kept her eyes lowered, watching the embers that Siga stirred in the center of their circle.

Bahram started a conversation in Arabic. "Stranger, please enlighten us about the ports you have visited."

"We anchored at Vuda Point in Viti Levu before coming here. The harbor was crowded with canoes carrying island produce." Safwan smiled at the princess. "None to compare with that from Vahilele."

Bahram sat up straighter. "We work hard to present our best wares at their bazaar."

The captain didn't look toward him, nor did Lapita. They gazed at each other.

"Why did you come here? Do you know Vahilele?" asked Bahram, fidgeting with the mat shells.

Melane remained mute, eyes closed, palms on her ankles crossed in front of her.

"I heard stories of your hardship, that smallpox left only a remnant of your tribe." Safwan glanced at Bahram, then back to Lapita. "I heard that your honorable father and husband are now gone." He spoke to her in island voice, and Bahram had to guess at his meaning.

Lapita's mouth turned up slightly. "No dear friend, they live on. As does my son. Whenever we remember them."

The captain nodded. "I also heard about Prince Tavale. I was touched by your loss."

Bahram watched Lapita carefully for clues to her relationship with this worldly stranger. She bowed her head slightly, eyes narrowing, reflecting the red of the flames. The wrists on her knees quivered, and he noticed her palms moved upward to a meditative position. *Back to her old religion.*

"My people are all dead now. But they will long be remembered. It is time for new blood."

Bahram saw her make a tiny motion with her head toward Melane who sat motionless. *Was this a reference to Queen Melane? Nui taka?*

"You are an excellent queen." The captain nodded again.

"No, a queen directs her people," Lapita murmured to the firelight.

"What then?" The captain gently asked.

Bahram sighed.

"I am a spiritual guide, my friend. *Kaukaua yalo.* Soon I will be of the wind. I must be cautious and listen to the *cagi.*"

Bahram snorted.

Safwan cocked his head at Bahram, but watched Lapita. "This gentleman is uncomfortable with talk of the spirits."

"Those who hold fast to earth cannot see beyond," remarked Elder Bati in Arabic, breaking from his solemn reverie. He sat with eyes locked on the tiny breath of fire before him.

Captain Safwan paused, but the elder did not expand this unexpected pronouncement.

As hostess, the princess asked questions of the visitor about his travels, and he entertained them, in native language, with engaging stories of faraway lands. During one of them, Melane silently left the hut with a polite bow toward all.

Bahram interrupted in Arabic. "Tell me about Srivijaya, mate."

"The empire is growing. The capital on Sumatra is full of people, mostly warriors. It appears the king is planning expansion. But there are *vales* like this one where a man can get refreshment and peace."

"And other entertainment?"

Safwan laughed. "Yes. Right you are. Coxswain, it seems you are very interested in worldly places. What binds you to this secluded island?"

"I would not be a gentleman if I left two widows in distress, now would I?"

Captain Safwan cast him a sidelong glance, took a deep breath and rolled his shoulders. "Lovely Princess, with your permission, I would like to rest now. May we continue our fellowship at another time?"

"Our guest is weary," she announced in Vahilele *vosa*. "Siga, accompany him to his *bure*." In Arabic, Lapita said, "She will escort you." At her words, Siga came out of the shadows. Safwan inclined his head, stood, bowed again and backed to the doorway.

Elder Dau assisted Elder Bati to his feet.

Bahram waited until they shuffled out before he spoke. "I suspect you know the Captain well," Bahram commented as he reached forward to help Lapita stand. "Is that true?"

Lapita shook her head and stared into the dying coals. Melane returned and sat next to her cousin, and Bahram asked no other questions. He left the Bure Kalou to instruct William to make the captain comfortable in a guest hut and to keep an eye on him, and then returned to the Bure Kalou to linger outside Lapita's doorway, waiting for Melane to leave. Bahram wanted to warn Lapita that a man without roots might try to take advantage of her, but as a neighbor and gentleman, he would protect her with his life. He easily heard the intense conversation between cousins inside the hut, and most of it he could understand.

"The Persian is angry you shared *Yaqona* with the Moor." Melane spoke sharply. "He wants to control you."

"He does not have that power. Only spirits have control over me now, and I must listen for their direction. The wise Phoenix lived within grandfather Ratu. He did not rule his people with laws but gave them freedom and choices because we each have different skills. He gave them an example. Not for his gain, but because he loved them."

"Your headaches announce the arrival of the same *kalou* in you, dear Princess," insisted Melane.

"I must be careful because there are those who would rule over our yanuyanu with force. Tavale defended our heritage. Now he is gone."

"You are wise. And *kaukaua*. It is the golden blood that binds you to your *kai*. You will be Priestess, and one day, my *peipei* will be *turaga*."

Bahram walked in without warning. The two women stood near the shelves of herbal jars, startled to see him. Melane's hand was on her slightly swollen abdomen.

"What conspiracy is this?"

"What do you see?" Lapita stroked the smooth shell at her throat, her *bulikula*.

"I see you and Melane whispering in your hut," said Bahram.

"Women whisper. Wise words are not loud words."

"And I see the way people pass you now, with eyes down, heads bowed. What does that mean?"

"Do you not think I deserve respect?" Her eyebrows elevated.

"Lapita. If I didn't respect you, I would force you into my bed." He cupped the back of her neck and pulled her close. She stiffened and did not lower her challenging stare.

"You have changed in the last few months," he said. "These headaches you're having must be a sign of something wrong. Perhaps the pox is returning."

"Perhaps," said Lapita, still rigid.

Melane stepped forward clutching a cane stick at her side. Bahram relinquished his hold and backed away.

"Why do you no longer drink coconut milk? It helped you get stronger."

Dark eyes scrutinized his face. "I need a different strength to prepare for my destiny."

"What is your meaning?"

"You shall see." She swept back the cloth door and left her hut. Melane followed with an angry motion at him with her switch.

Bahram considered Lapita's words. Perhaps she drew away from him because she thought he was weak. The death of her brother may have confused her. And there was no doubt in his mind that the arrival of the Arab ship disrupted the orderly system of the island. Any of these reasons was a possible explanation for her strange behavior.

If this will be my kingdom, I must take charge. It is time to show power. Anger bubbled to the surface. His chest hurt, and he took quick short breaths. A glance around the room found an earthenware bowl with the new flame pattern Lapita designed. Bahram snatched it up and smashed it to the ground. "I shall take control of this island, now and forever!"

CHAPTER FIFTY TWO

Lapita

Lapita did not sleep well that night. It was as though her memories took on human shapes and swirled in conflict around her vale. She surrendered to exhaustion shortly before dawn. When Siga entered the next morning, the Princess was still in bed.

"Are you ill, Adi?" Siga called out.

Behind the veil that shielded her pallet from the public room, Lapita awoke. "Enter, Siga. I will rise soon."

"I will put your wai here and go now to the fishing village. I heard there was a big walu catch in the outer reef nets." Siga spoke in the measured tones she had been using since terrorized in the lagoon, as though she tried to subdue her memories by controlling her outward manner. Lapita had seen her spend more time in meditation, often accompanying the princess to the beach on the mornings Siga had no pressing duties. She stayed a respectful distance behind her mistress. It was both poignant and frightening to have somebody mimic all that you did.

"Yes, go. I will be fine." Lapita slowly sat up, her eyes heavy, her long braid undone around her shoulders. *What are my choices? Where is my path?*

By midmorning Lapita was prepared to walk her yanuyanu. When Captain Safwan called politely from the base of her stone steps, she pulled the white mazi cloth back and left the Bure Kalou to greet him. He had rinsed the sea from his hair and wore clothes that did not smell of six months of travel. Sandals replaced heavy boots. With heart pounding, she stared at the handsome visitor.

He broke the bond of their gaze first, with a low chuckle. "You have not changed, Lapita, except to grow more beautiful."

She tossed her dark mane into the wind, glancing at the vales circled around the Na Koro common area. Nobody was outside. "I was a young yalewa when you first came. You make pretty words, Captain Owen Safwan, but you do not know my yalo of this day." She moved towards him. "Walk with me," she said, and he backed up to let her descend to the level of the path where he stood. This experienced gentleman held out his hand to assist a lady, but she did not reach for his touch.

"I know you are now a marama with a past," he teased.

"My past makes me wiser. And you Captain?" She smiled without looking at him.

"My past makes me more careful. I keep on the move so it won't catch up."

She laughed with him as they walked the path upward to the cliffs.

"If I had stayed longer, those many years ago, I would not have those regrets."

"We live our choices," she said.

"You were wise to stay in Vahilele. I have never seen a more breathtaking landscape."

"I agree. I have seen Viti Levu, and Beqa, and other close islands. I choose to remain on this yanuyanu."

His eyebrows elevated. "I thought Degei ruled your world. Does he not choose for you?"

"Yes, when I ask," she said.

They walked slowly, gaining elevation to where the trail turned sharply to traverse the hill, from which point they could see over the tops of trees to the Arab ship anchored outside the barrier reef.

He reminded her of a conversation long ago. "You told me Bete was chosen for you."

Her shapely lips parted. Eyes sparkled. "He was. And so were you. It was a test of wisdom."

It was Safwan's time to smile. "Ahhh. I didn't have a chance." He laughed loudly then.

His nearness made her uncomfortable, and she came to the odd truth that she was vulnerable. It would be best to stay closer to her clan. "Let us walk back to Na Koro," she said. "I will show you new choices." The currents of his dark eyes were deep enough to swim. And drown.

"I shall go anywhere with you," he murmured. "Lead on."

When Lapita showed him the pottery shed at the outer edge of Na Koro, she picked up a kuro and explained how this flame motif was popular with customers in Beqa.

"I never thought of you as a merchant," he said. "Do you stand behind the tables covered with masi cloth and sing out 'Get your pottery here. Come to my table, young man, don't you want to take a kuro home to your nana'?"

Lapita's mellifluous response carried through the shed and into beyond. She had forgotten how easy it was to spend an afternoon with this charming mariner. "I do not leave the yanuyanu for the marketplace. We have traders for that."

"I, also, would keep you hidden away," he whispered.

She glanced at him, seeking a deeper meaning for his words. Captain Safwan's large stature made her feel unusually delicate. His hand brushed hers as he took the kuro to glance at it. But his gaze brushed her face, her neck, her breasts. Lapita could not deny the swirling current that stirred her loins. He moved closer. Slowly. Heat from his body enveloped her in a spicy aphrodisiac.

A cold nose on her ankle startled her.

"Dedan. What are you doing here?" She stepped back.

Bahram dipped under the low edge of the roof shed. "Good morning, my dear. Captain, do you wish to buy our pottery? We have the best in Srivijaya," he proclaimed. Today he wore the island attire of sarong and sandals, with a brown sash tied at his waist.

"Not today, sir. This lovely lady is showing me the island sights," said Safwan.

"It has changed, I am sure. When were you last here?"

"Many years, perhaps five or six?" For confirmation, he looked toward Lapita who rearranged pots and bowls on a shelf. She was mute, struggling to recover her emotional control.

"We are greatly improved, sir. I have brought Vahilele into the seventh century," said Bahram.

"Then I am not certain I will admire it as much as on my last visit," said the captain.

Bahram hesitated. "What are you saying?"

"The charm of Vahilele was its determination to avoid the sins of those around her. She kept her people isolated and held them fast with the attributes of truth and love for one another."

Lapita turned to regard Safwan's face, the familiar scar that hinted of battles won. He was speaking in Arabic, and she caught most of the words. She was flattered that this foreigner was ably defending her way of life.

Bahram crossed his arms over his chest. "You talk strangely for a merchant for whom commerce is a necessity. Do you not trade your best product for the highest price that is offered? Securing that high price takes effort. Concluding the trade takes skill."

"Yes, everyone benefits." Safwan pointed at Bahram's chest. "Especially the person in the middle who has no investment."

Bahram stiffened his spine, threw back his shoulders, and clenched his fists. "My service is necessary to arrange the trade, whether it is for spices from India, Oriental silk, copper from Pashtun tribes, or Egyptian gold."

Lapita intervened. "Gentlemen, you have common ground. Sharp voices are not needed."

CHAPTER FIFTY THREE

Bahram

Bahram stomped along the path, headed to the high point where he could breathe deeply and calm himself. He had seen the fire in the Moor's eyes and did not fault him. The same fire was surely in his own eyes when he looked at that infernal woman. She forced his mind from control. Especially when she laughed. Her pleasure pealed like perfect chimes, and he never tired of the melody.

As he passed the Bure Kalou, he heard a rustling noise inside. *An intruder*? He stepped up the stones and threw back the curtain. Siga was at an elevated rock grinding roots with a pestle in a shallow mortar.

"You make kakana for your mistress?"

"I crush ti leaves. Saka."

As he closed in, she trembled, arms at her side and head bowed. He reached out to touch the blossom behind her ear.

"You're a pretty little thing. I bet you're not as cold as your mistress, eh?" He rubbed her chin with his thumb, drawing it up so he could see her golden brown face. He stepped closer and her fragrance reminded him of Lapita. He stroked her cheek. His breath caught, and he tangled his thick fingers in her dark tresses to pull her forward and cover her tiny red mouth with his rough beard. His other hand briefly caressed her small breast then hastily moved behind to her backside, pushing Siga into his taut body, fully alert now. Siga struggled, the movement increasing the Persian's desire. He squeezed her against a post thrusting his tongue inside her virgin mouth, his hips trapping hers like a tiny bird. She was stilled.

He eased away, breathing heavily, and looked at her bruised lips, the tears blurring her eyes and spilling down her soft cheeks. Bahram snorted. "One day, little girl, when you're older. I'll teach you how to serve a man."

Siga turned to flee. She tripped on a garden basket and the palm of his hand slammed into the post in front of her, delaying her flight. "Don't worry, it will come easy to a girl like you." He patted her small buttocks.

She ducked under his arm. Her feet carried her swiftly across the room and out the white panel, her whimper drowned out by the Persian's coarse laughter.

Bahram stepped over the basket and scattered yams, walked past the white curtain and paused to watch her flee through the forest. He took a deep breath. The sight of the garden surrounding the Bure Kalou caught his attention. He recognized the kava pepper shrubs which were most plentiful. He looked for the ginger Lapita had mentioned at the council meeting.

"Are you a farmer now? Or a healer looking for herbs?" Nawfal's voice turned him around. His shipmate came down the path with a large net in his arms.

"I am inspecting the ginger plants."

"What is your conclusion?" Nawfal waited for Bahram to descend the steps.

"They must be planted on a slope for better drainage. Elder Matai Malolo talked to a farmer near Viseisei who has a profitable concern with little labor. Perfect for slow-moving natives."

Nawfal scowled. "You still don't give their culture any credit for the traditions that have worked for them in past generations."

"Who are you to pretend such moral superiority over me? I wager that net is going to Melane's hut."

"I am a friend making hut improvements as Tavale would have done. Sometimes I take firewood. Sometimes I repair the roof. What happened to your mantra, good thoughts, good words, good deeds? Don't you recognize compassion?"

"Did that compassion make her with child?"

The shocked expression on Nawfal's face told Bahram that his old friend did not know what he himself overheard Melane tell Lapita. Bahram's shame was brief.

Well, he deserves a shock, the self-righteous turncoat.

CHAPTER FIFTY FOUR

Lapita

Two days later, the captain called again for Lapita. She went outside carrying her sandals and a basket woven of dried coconut leaves.

"I have searched the island for you, lovely lady."

"I have many people to care for, and my helper did not come yesterday."

"May we see more of your island today, another beautiful day in paradise?"

"I carry herbs to a marama on the southern end of the yanuyanu. You may walk with me."

Together they crossed the village center and caught the path that took them to the beach. Laughing and teasing each other, they shared the wonder of the perfect sky and warm breezes. The hot nuku burned her feet as Lapita walked the eastern baravi, and she stopped to put on her sandals, leaning into Captain Safwan's support. When she heard his deep breathing, she suddenly feared he would inhale her if she allowed it. She could release herself to become part of this handsome man's life, part of the air he breathed, and he would take care of her. He would protect her. Burdens would be lighter because there would be two to carry them. She had once known a union where two parts became one, like lock and key. *My husband is gone, and I am alone now.*

Lapita's long legs took strides matched easily by her companion. They skirted the fields showing the new growth of the season. Islanders pulling grass from between dalo plants shaded their eyes to look toward the handsome couple, then dipped back down to their chores, making low comments to one another. Lapita barely noticed their presence. The totoka ship captain at her side absorbed her attention. And he watched her with open adoration. She felt young again and desirable.

"Captain Safwan, do you see that we have planted more dalo than before?"

"I confess I have eyes only for you, my Princess." The captain grinned, but dutifully examined the expanse of cultivated fields, dotted with workers. "And your yam crop?"

"We have more than we need," said Lapita. "Still our people work long hours. Bahram explained that we share cakacaka, and then we share the profit from selling the uvi."

"And who determines this share, and this profit?"

Lapita looked up at him, brow furrowed. "Bahram."

"And you trust him?"

"The council does." Lapita hesitated. "And they make Vahilele laws."

"These are the men who wear the coins around their necks?"

"Yes." Lapita turned off the beach path to enter the edge of the village.

"That should tell you something. My dear." Safwan mocked the phrase Bahram had used.

She glanced at him and kept walking. "Do other countries have laws like these?"

"Do not strive to be like other countries. Their leaders come and go because men are cursed with a passion for power. To possess it, they would dance with the devil."

"And you, Captain. Are you cursed?"

"Right now, that seems to be true. I am cursed with a passion that is ignored." He touched her arm and stopped in the cool shade behind a screen of tipanie shrubs. She slowed her steps and looked up into his tender gaze.

The sharp squawk of a lawedua overhead reminded Lapita that she was not an ordinary yanuyanu marama who could play in the sun and lust in the dark. She was the last royal of a great people. The end of their story rested upon her choices. With a long sigh, she broke away from his silent entreaty.

When they reached the hut where her patient waited for her, Lapita went in alone. A short time later, she rejoined the captain. "We must start back. Siga watches for me." Her admirer reached out to move the flower nestled over her right ear, but Lapita turned from him, walking steadily toward the worn inland path. He followed.

Inside her head a drama played out. *Why must I be different from other women? Why can't I live a life of love and simple pleasures? I have had more than my share of rarawa, too much sorrow. I deserve marau, some happiness in my future.*

In her soul, the question was already answered. *Not, why was I chosen to sacrifice my heart? Instead, why was I honored to serve so many? And I am not alone. I have the collective wisdom of the makawa with me. Always.* Her spirit warmed with the Truth of her thoughts. The white bird took flight from her perch in a chestnut tree, leading their way back.

When Safwan escorted Lapita into the pottery hut, the workers nodded and returned to their assignments. In their silent presence, Lapita felt her face flush, grow hot with madua, as though she had a shame to hide. She had teetered on a precipice but she had not fallen. *Not one can fault me for what they cannot know.*

Captain Safwan left immediately. "I will leave you to your work, Princess. May you all have a pleasant afternoon." He smiled at the ladies working in the shed.

With dignity, Lapita replied, "And you as well, Captain." After he left, she seated herself with a kuro bearing the new flame design. Avoiding the curious glances of the other women, Lapita immersed her hand in a bowl of red wai to dampen her pottery board. There was no evidence of wrong doing, but she had been tempted by desire. Now she did feel young. And foolish.

Bahram came stomping up to the shed. "Where have you been all morning?" he growled at her. "We have orders to fill. Your absence has caused us delay." He loomed over Lapita's table, hands on hips.

The Princess did not raise her head. She focused on arranging the clay coils Siga brought to her.

"No. Don't do that now. Paint the design." Bahram's words bit into the salty air.

"I thought this was women's work. Am I in charge here, or are you?" Lapita stood balavu, as tall as he.

"You work for me. I supervise all projects." He stepped closer.

"You are the expert?" she said in Arabic. "You paint the design." Lapita turned away and left him standing there, ignoring his command.

"Lapita! Come back here!"

Siga ran out the other side of the shed to trail behind her mistress, a smile playing on her lips.

CHAPTER FIFTY FIVE

Bahram

The following day, Bahram went to Lapita's doorway and called to her. He trusted that time softened a woman's mood. He would be patient. Siga stood on the other side of the white panel and whispered a response, "My mistress rests."

He repeated the overture later with the same result.

The next time, he took a yellow clay jar with turquoise glaze that he bought in Viseisei for Lapita. "This is for you, Siga." She took the gift and closed the curtain.

Bahram shrugged. He studied the situation and came to the inevitable conclusion this was unacceptable behavior. Lapita must understand that she was not as strong or as competent as a male leader. He had given her ample time to heal. Perhaps he had treated her too softly, and she misunderstood kindness to be weakness. But Lapita was like no other woman he had met, and she stayed in her bure for two days speaking only to her servant.

When Bahram came through the center of Na Koro on the next morning, he saw Captain Safwan standing at Lapita's steps. As Bahram watched, Safwan backed down to the rock path. It was apparent that he, too, had been rebuffed. *Maybe he and I do have common ground.*

At the midday meal, Captain Safwan told Bahram that his ship would be sailing north on the following week. Bahram was ready with a reply.

"I have a business opportunity to discuss with you," Bahram said. He made certain there were no ears to hear his proposal. "If you are open to pursuing a profitable venture, meet me at sunset on the boulders at the northwest shore."

The captain nodded.

Later that evening, Bahram secretly showed Captain Safwan the island's treasure of red prawns, and a trade was arranged.

A lululu between worldly gentlemen.

CHAPTER FIFTY SIX

Lapita

As Lapita approached Melane's vale, Dedan ran out, followed by Nawfal who smiled and waved to her. His hair was shorter than she remembered, as was his black beard.

"Sa Bula, Princess."

"Sa Bula." Lapita nodded, but she was concerned. What business did this mua have in her brother's hut? Nawfal walked across the common area toward the path that would take him to the lagoon. Lapita stopped at the brown tapa entrance to the vale. "Melane? Cola?"

"Enter, Lapita."

By the doorway rested a carved war club, the length of Lapita's arm. Fine narrow bands of braided sennit were evenly spaced on one end. On top a round knob graduated into two spikes along one side, created to do serious damage. "What is this?"

"Nawfal gave it to me after Tavale died because he thinks I need to protect myself. He put it by my pallet, but I move it where I want, out of the way."

"Where did he get the club?"

"It is one of the war clubs Bahram got by trading megapode eggs with the Tongans."

Lapita could see the glow in Melane's face, and she worried. If her baby was Nawfal's, what consequences would besiege the royal family? "I can see that Nawfal cares for you. You may have to use the club on his head."

"Did you not recently tell me, 'Do not vosa about what you do not know'?" Melane said sternly.

"He is the only man who comes to your vale, isn't he?"

"Lapita!" Melane scowled at her. "He brought to me hermit crabs that he and Savu gathered this morning." She walked behind her privacy curtain and returned carrying a carved doll. "I found this on Tavale's grave. Nawfal did not put it there to get favor from me."

Lapita took the effigy that showed almond eyes and a sharp nose, a slender headband over long hair. On its chest was carved a five point star on the left side of the totem. "A fitting tribute to my brother. He would be pleased that Nawfal knew his heart."

"Nawfal loved Tavale," Melane's voice wavered. "But I couldn't leave an idol there and offend a spirit."

A great sadness curled around Lapita. She remembered the wooden doll in the sand. "Nawfal will be cast aside."

Melane stared at her. "How do you know this?"

"I listen to whispers in the wind. And I had a dream where Aunti warned me about a betrayal, like Nana Hewa did."

"A kaukaumata? A Bete omen?"

Ignoring her cousin's question, Lapita asked, "Do you and Nawfal plan to leave our island?"

"That is hurtful, Lapita. I am carrying Tavale's child, and I will never put the peipei at risk. He is the future of the royal Goldens. You misunderstand your wandering soul."

"Nana Hewa told me to take care of Siga, and I did not. She was marked for attack by Abu, and I failed to protect her. If not for your courage, she might be lost forever because of my disobedience. I have to ask questions, even if they are hurtful."

"I understand you did not correctly interpret an important omen, but you should know I could never betray Kai Vahilele."

"I am learning to be a Bete. I have to find my way. I cannot be close to anyone."

"If Aunti warned of betrayal, perhaps Bahram or your Captain Safwan have a plot against us."

"I know they do, but this omen was something new, an unexpected evil."

Lapita turned to leave. Melane held her arm and said, "You must take the tribe in hand before it is too late."

"There are still many who distrust me," said Lapita.

"You have to do something!" Melane took a deep breath and lowered her voice. "I am not wise like you, sister, but I can see the mana of the Phoenix growing in you. We will recover our culture. Once again Kai Vahilele will be kaukaua."

"I do not have mana."

"Find it! Take it! Put it on! I do not care how you do it." Melane waved her arms wildly and paced the floor. "All that interests you is the dead past. You close your mind to the change on this island. Your people need you! Your living people will be sacrificed because you do nothing. But, if they see the power of your mana, they will follow your lead."

Lapita considered this strange outburst from a usually calm marama. "I do not know that I am ready."

Melane shook her head. "What do you fear more than the loss of our heritage?"

Lapita saw desperation in her cousin's eyes. "What brings you despair today?"

"There is talk that when Safwan leaves here, he will return with workers who will take over the masi trade and the building of our outriggers."

"Where did you hear that?"

"From Nawfal."

"He is Bahram's friend. Why would he tell you that?"

"He loved Tavale, and he loves me."

"He may have killed my brother."

"Do you not think it was Dakuwaqa?"

"No, Melane." The pain in Lapita's heart brought to her the shadowed glimpse of Tavale that she had tried to bury with him. The image would not leave her, and she spoke out in frustration. "His arms were cut off straight. He could not save himself but Dakuwaqa did not harm him. He drowned because he could not swim."

Melane's face contorted in horror, and Lapita embraced her. "Vohosia, forgive me. I regret speaking out. I meant to carry this burden myself and never tell of it."

Melane's tears streamed from closed eyes as she pushed away. "You have carried it long enough. I would have heard the story somewhere, sometime, and I need to know the truth to handle it in my own way, in my own time." Melane retreated to a corner where she squatted, fingering her bone bracelet from her Beqa homeland. "Do not punish yourself for me. It was my news to hear, and it was better I heard it from tokatoka, my close family. I have no more tears left."

Lapita squatted close to her. "We survived disease to rebuild our culture. I thought that lesson difficult, but it is worse to be attacked by men who share our home and our food."

"I knew the sailors were guilty, but I didn't know how. I could not go close enough to see my husband's body."

"I am glad that memory cannot fix itself in your dreams to keep you awake. It forever comes to my mind unexpectedly."

"I was holding Yaca, and concerned about his memories. I didn't know my baby's short future." Melane wiped her face.

"Remember how much Tavale loved you. That memory is your keepsake."

"He loved you, too."

Lapita nodded. "Our connection was blood and bone. When they killed Tavale, they killed a part of me. I will not rest until I avenge his death."

"Your father would tell you to forget what is past."

"It is not in the past, Melane. Tavale's death is now. It is the beginning of evil growing on this island. I can feel it like a darkness sliding over us. We will all drown."

"Cease this vosa, this language of tragedy," Melane snapped. "You must prove to the tribe you are worthy of their trust."

"You don't trust me, how can they?"

Melane stood. "If I didn't trust you, why do I beg you to be the High Priestess?"

"You doubt my timing." Lapita prepared to leave. "I will not make a move until I know I should. You are not in charge. Nor am I. I take direction from the Phoenix. His time, not ours." She nodded and left for home.

CHAPTER FIFTY SEVEN

Lapita

In the glow of the setting sun, Siga blended with mortar and pestle herbs that were spread on a mat stamped with a turtle image. Lapita sat inside at the Spirit Fire, searching for wisdom. She heard murmuring outside, Siga's polite refusal to allow entrance. The princess had confidence in Siga's efforts to filter nonsense from her attention; they were both learning new patterns to their relationship.

Like her husband, Lapita habitually turned her back to the doorway to eliminate distractions from outside. He had told her it helped to focus on a central thought as Bete and also to build up awareness of the unseen. She smiled whenever she remembered how annoying it was to be shut out by a focus on the invisible. Now she was guilty of the same offense.

Siga stood beside her, waiting for recognition in the pale firelight. Without lifting her eyes, Lapita shifted. "Yes?"

"A mua wishes to speak to you."

"Bring him here."

Siga escorted Nawfal to the opposite side of the flame but did not suggest that he be seated. The sailor stood patiently. It was a test of Nawfal's intention that he respected silence and time. He was thoughtful, as she would expect of any of Tavale's friends. Lapita motioned permission for him to sit down. Siga took her place in the shadows, waiting for a command.

"Sa Bula." Lapita spoke first.

Nawfal responded with an incline of his head. He sat cross-legged, settling the anxiety that brought him to the Bure Kalou.

"You are far from home, mua. Why do you seek me?"

"I owe a debt to your brother, Princess." He paused, seeming to struggle with words to use, combining Arabic with island vosa. Lapita waited. "Prince Tavale taught me much in a short time. Not only about canoes. Not only about the natural order of sun and stars and sea. But also about people. He lived with honor."

Lapita waited, wanting to hear what this sailor knew about Tavale's death. She knew Tavale's life. She shared it. But she didn't share his association with foreigners. And she was certain the clue to his death lay somewhere she could not go.

"I suspect that one of my own shipmates killed your brother because of Tavale's closeness with you. I assume you share that suspicion." Nawfal fidgeted with the shells on the fringe of the mats, clicking them together. "It is possible that others will blame me."

Lapita waited until he quieted his fingers and put his big hands together, resting his elbows on his knees. "Why would you be suspected of this crime?"

"My concern for Melane's safety," he responded. "At first I wanted to show her that I shared her grief as though Tavale was my brother. His loss diminished us all. And to think that his life was taken brutally and selfishly...I have no words." He choked and sputtered.

Lapita raised her eyes to Nawfal's face. The tears on his cheeks said more than words in any language. She signaled for Siga to leave them alone. "You do not believe Dakuwaqa took his life?"

"I never did, even after Abu was killed. I am ashamed to think it was one of my people. But it was not me. It is important to me that you know. It was not me."

"Why is that important?"

"I leave tomorrow. I care too much for Melane to make her part of an intrigue whispered about over cups of yaqona and palm wine."

"Does she know your plans?"

"No. I could not trust myself to carry out a wise decision. If I saw her one more time, my defense would weaken, and I would open my heart to her. I worry that her life is in danger. It seems a killer wants to eliminate the royal family. She would be next."

"I am confused. If you think your friend's life is in danger, would you not stay to protect her?"

"I think my presence makes it easier to kill her because then I can be blamed, like I am for Yaca's death. I've heard the rumors. If I am not in Vahilele, the task is harder." He paused. "I am here tonight to request that she be invited to move in with you. The more people around her, the safer she will be. And Dedan will come, too."

"You plan to vanish? What proof of your innocence does that provide?"

"Yes, I will vanish, but two mates will come with me to Viti Levu. And your Ranji can spread the word." Nawfal removed his gold coin necklace and gave to to Lapita. "This is for Melane. For her baby."

How does he know about a baby?

Lapita considered the unexpected plan. She was relieved Nawfal was leaving the island. His growing relationship with Melane was part of the chatter at the midday meal.

But she is not the royal power. I am. Would that matter to an outsider? Am I the next victim?

CHAPTER FIFTY EIGHT

Siga

Siga listened to the sound of Grandfather's relaxed breathing, a deep inhale and exhale, a rhythmic cadence that brought comfort. There were so many nights not very long ago when a pause in her mother's erratic breathing alarmed Siga, and she lay awake to count the beats, listening to its fluttering, wondering how long the diseased heart would pump. Every fluctuation was a cause for worry.

Now all was well. Siga reflected on her own adult body so she wouldn't think about grandfather. She had passed into womanhood like others before her. She had gained a new wisdom of the frailty of man, fighting among themselves for stronger position even though that position was temporary. Princess Lapita told her it was futile to argue with peers while an enemy outside gathered forces, and it was time for action. Siga didn't know what that meant. She turned the idea over in her mind.

Many times Siga watched the Princess focus her eyes and ears to the invisible, but she did not understand what Lapita was seeking, or why she spent hours searching, staring into the fire, or at the horizon before sunrise, waiting for light of a new day. Was Lapita worried the sun god would forget to ride across the sky or change his course? His dependability was a solace just like grandfather's regular breathing.

But rest was elusive for herself. She was no longer sleepy, although she had no immediate concerns, no fears about displeasing the Princess as she had the season before when she had experienced Lapita's forgiveness. She knew the Princess loved her, as did Melane. Siga had lost her own nana but had gained two strong sisters to care for her. She learned from them that there was no greater love than sacrifice and forgiveness.

Siga felt the need to rise, perhaps to walk and get tired again so she could sleep. Dawn was a long way off. She didn't want to spend the night with her spinning thoughts.

Grandfather's steady breathing brought to mind the rhythm of the waves on the shore. *Maybe a walk would bring harmony to body and spirit and allow me to rest.* She eased off her pallet, crossed the room and through the doorway. The sweet fragrance of the soft South Pacific night under a nearing-full moon brought a thankful response for her beautiful island home. How fortunate her tribe was that all they had to do was accept the gift and care for the yanuyanu. She had heard Nawfal call their way of life angelic leisure. She did not know these words, and she asked for his explanation. His words were true.

From the black forest, Siga saw a tall shadow detach itself from the trees and head toward the Bure Kalou. Her pulse quickened. Who would walk through the underbrush, where poisonous centipedes lived, when they could stay on the path, assured of good footing? Someone who wanted to hide. Siga considered returning to the safety of her hut. She chastened herself. *I am thirteen. I know the secrets of womanhood and how a man seeks company in the dark. That is all this is, a sailor looking for comfort from a marama's soft embrace.*

Siga made light of her childish fears and an urge to run and hide. *You are grown now. You must be strong like the Princess.*

At the thought of Lapita, Siga's fear flashed bright. The shadow had angled through the sandalwood grove in the direction of the Bure Kalou. Thoughts of Tavale and Yaca spread alarm directly to her feet to move faster, to break into a run.

Siga kept to the path until the last turn. Anxiety nudged her to take a shortcut. Siga ran the last few steps through underbrush, unconcerned about the snake pit nearby. She came out behind the silent Bure Kalou and listened intently. There was no sound of disturbance. "Princess Lapita?" she called out. "Are you all right?"

She padded outside to the front of the temple, quietly so as not to awaken the Princess, if her fears proved foolish. Through the white spirit curtain rushed a bony native who didn't see her. He ran hard into her, surprising them both. With a sharp intake of breath, his hands braced Siga from falling. The man turned and ran.

Tears pooled to blind her. Not because her twisted ankle hurt but because she recognized her father. His presence here in the dark did not bode well for anyone, particularly Lapita. Siga shut her eyes and made herself a grownup promise. *If he has hurt my Princess, I myself will kill him.*

She listened for sounds of distress, but did not hear anything. She could not leave until she saw that Lapita was not harmed. She wiped her eyes. She crept into the temple, picked up a piece of kindling that lay in the pile she made earlier in the day convenient to the Spirit Fire. She touched it to the embers until she had a tiny torch to carry behind the sleeping curtain where Lapita lay, and she listened. Lapita's breathing paused as she turned over in her sleep. Deep breaths resumed.

Siga held her light aloft to assure herself that the Princess was alive and well before she backed carefully out of the room. She left the temple but sat outside on the rock steps and waited for dawn.

A gentle shake of her shoulders chased the dark shadows from her dreams, and Siga awoke.

"Manumanu vuka," said the Princess. "What are you doing here?"

Siga sat up instantly alert, although her body felt the soreness from a hard bed. Lapita crouched next to her.

"Princess, I could not sleep, and I came early. But I did not want to disturb you before daybreak."

Siga felt the intensity of Lapita's gaze.

"Siga, you were protecting me, weren't you? Did you see who dropped this?" She held up a war club as long as her arm, the handle carved with turtles.

Siga had seen it in Melane's hut. Fear closed her throat. All she could do was shake her head. She could not look into Lapita's eyes. She could not tell tales on Lalai, her own father.

"It is time to ask questions." Lapita showed her the wooden doll. "I found this in the sand by baby Yaca. Do you know who made it?"

"Yes, Nawfal made it for me, but I gave it to Yaca. He liked to chew on it."

Lapita took a deep breath and nodded.

CHAPTER FIFTY NINE

Lapita

Dedan came running across the clearing to lick Siga's face.

"Where were you last night, Dedan?" Lapita leaned over to fondle his smooth long ears.

Nearby, Bahram appeared at the entry of his hut, eyes squinting, rubbing his face. He ambled up the path. "Good morning, lovely ladies. I see my best friend has already greeted you. He's faster." Bahram's eyes focused on the war club. "What is that?"

"You know what it is."

"Yes, it's used to split the heads of enemies. Why is it in your hand?"

"I tripped over it when I got off my pallet."

"That is not humorous."

"I do not laugh."

"May I look in the temple?"

There was a long pause. Lapita was finally getting a serious response to her request for an investigation. How could she refuse?

"Yes. Enter."

Bahram's inspection did not turn up new clues to explain the presence of a war club, but Lapita didn't expect any. She waited for him to leave so she could confront the owner of the club. Melane.

"If you lived with me, you would be safe." Bahram grabbed her shoulders.

Lapita stiffened.

"When the council asks me to be the king, I will accept. I want you to be my queen. You will have everything you desire." He gently moved the strand of hair that blew across her aquiline nose.

"What do you mean?" She was rigid in his disrespectful grasp.

"What is it you do not understand?" asked Bahram. He released her and raked his fingers through his own disobedient hair. "I want you to be my Queen. Most of the women on this island would line up for the chance."

"You are offering me a duty that I already have because of my bloodline!" Lapita snorted. "You are right. I do not understand."

"You want to be a Priestess. A Bete. You can do that by yourself. You need me to make you a Queen."

"No Bahram. You are confused. I am the first born of a king. I can be a Queen without your permission if that is what I want. A queen distributes food and enforces rules pronounced by the gods through the Bete. You try to make yourself valuable by giving me what I already have. I seek the power of the Phoenix to be the Bete, power that exceeds your imagination. It is you who does not understand."

Bahram shook his head and looked away.

Lapita did not tell him she had seen the club in Melane's vale. She first wanted to talk with her cousin without Bahram listening to their conversation.

"At least keep Dedan with you at night," Bahram grumbled. When he concluded the mystery would not soon be solved, he went back to his hut.

Lapita went to see Melane.

"This is yours." She held up the war club.

"You know it is. Where did you find it?"

"Close to my head."

Melane stared. "No. That couldn't be. Although I have never heard you utter one untruth."

The shock on Melane's face convinced Lapita that her cousin was blameless. In spite of their bitter exchange of words the night before, Lapita did not really suspect her, but an investigation required orderly thoroughness.

That afternoon, Captain Safwan stopped at the Bure Kalou to check on Lapita. "I heard chatter about a war club in the temple. Were you injured?"

"No, the hand of Degei disarmed my attacker while I slept." Lapita motioned across the Spirit Fire. "Sit and talk with me."

The captain seated himself. "I have not had opportunity to tell you we will weigh anchor in two days."

Lapita nodded. "May you have safe passage." She paused. "You are always welcome in Vahilele."

"Princess, I have been to many remarkable places and have often imagined how much my visit would be enhanced with you at my side."

The world is so far away from my island.

The flame held Lapita's eyes. "I dream about busy cities. Bahram told me about the bright colors in Viseisei and how the village grows and changes to handle visitors from other countries. It must be exciting to be in their midst." She smiled weakly. "He described the different ways of the people, all jostling to communicate without being overtaken by the strong or the cruel."

"Bahram's words are light and fleeting. I will show you wisdom and beauty you can hold in your hands." Captain Safwan opened the pouch at his waist and removed a small bundle of yellow silk. "Artwork from an exotic civilization."

Lapita restrained herself from touching the shimmering fabric before it was presented. The color was extraordinary, but forgotten when she saw the article it protected. "What is this animal like a koli with tall legs? If this is an idol, I will not touch it."

Safwan laughed and placed the figurine in her hands. "This is a horse. It is five times the size of a dog like Dedan.

The Tang Empire in China has lost their senses over horses. They bring in hundreds at a time. That is the talk I hear, and this vosa gives the artist ideas for new wares to sell at bazaars."

Lapita turned over and over the smooth statuette in her hands. It was the red glaze that captivated her attention. How did the Chinese bring such a shiny color to the earthenware?

"Why do they need so many horses? Do men eat such magnificent creatures?"

"War, gentle love. Of course, you do not hear of such things. These animals are loyal and brave, charging swiftly wherever they are commanded by the men on their backs. Sometimes a thousand together."

Lapita stared into the fire while caressing the tiny horse. "It seems nothing could slow such an army." She shivered, imagining the thundering hooves of a powerful herd, the cries of the common people trampled in their path.

"In that part of the world, the horse is a symbol of power and virtue because they do not question their destiny. They are trained to obey."

"My father told stories of faraway countries where people of long ago fought to control land they did not need. Our people made strong canoes to find a new place to live in peace. My grandfather remembered coming to Vahilele, and his stories came with him. I did not know of what he spoke." Her brow wrinkled as she watched the flame. "I remember his lesson." She could hear the lament of the ancient ones. She breathed deeply.

"An army on horseback is a fearful image," said Captain Safwan. He took the hand holding the figure. Her other hand was turned upward on her knee. "You are trembling. What do you see?"

She did not immediately answer him, but he waited.

"You said power. And virtue?" Her voice was strained.

"It seems virtue is a reason to use power in civilized countries. The meaning changes with the speaker."

She closed her eyes. "Where is wisdom applied, my friend?"

"Nowhere at times." Safwan chuckled and released her hand. "Men debate wisdom. The stronger decide."

Lapita shook her head. "The gods decide."

"Do not be worried over matters that are far away. You are safe here."

"The strong decide here also. There is no safety from man."

"You would always be safe with me, beautiful Princess. I shall be proud to show you new countries, and if we suspect danger, we will sail away."

"That is a pretty dream, Owen Safwan," she said. She turned from the fire to the smoldering heat in his eyes. *I am so weary of conflict.*

He put out his hand, and she took it. Until Melane glided into the room and sat down next to him, scowling fiercely.

CHAPTER SIXTY

Siga

"Grandfather, I need council."

"Come, child. It will be sweet to talk with you," said Matai Malolo. I have missed our chats. It is not so long ago that you crawled onto my lap, and we watched the stars line up."

"You taught me much, Grandfather."

He smiled at her, and they walked in the shadows to the beach that picked up the heavenly lights shining on the magic carpet before them. "We will sit together and tell stories. I always have much to say to you."

He held her hand as they settled themselves on the nuku still warm from the heat of the day. Siga nestled close to him. As her mother had taught her, she breathed deeply to calm her mind before opening her mouth. And she waited for her elder to speak first.

"You grow more beautiful, manumanu vuka. Like your dear nana."

"Vinaka. I miss her." Siga's fingers massaged the pox scars on her forearm.

"As do I. She did not have a choice as to how long she would stay in this world. She is with Grandmother now." Matai Malolo sighed. "You are of the age when you need her help to make decisions." He turned to her. "Would you listen better, dear child, if she were here talking instead of your old grandfather?"

Silence. Siga felt his warm smile touch a corner of her heart.

"Our people have always kept to themselves. I hear rumors of war in the deserts. And even closer is a king who wants to have power over more islands than he already rules. I am marau to live here in Vahilele, a yanuyanu of peace."

"Grandfather, what is war?"

"A good question, peipei. I have never seen one, but I would say it is when one kai uses weapons to try to control another kai. They cannot change others with vosa so they steal and kill. Our ancestors have moved many times. We do not want to live where we could be diminished."

"Which do we fear most? Steal or kill?"

"Another good question."

"My Princess teaches me many things, Grandfather."

"Ahh." He waited awhile to speak again. "I have a question for you, Siga. I walked near the Bure Kalou, and I saw you run from it. Your hand covered your mouth as though to swallow your cries. You ran to the forest, not to your father. I saw our master come out, and he seemed amused."

Silence.

Then he spoke again, "Sometimes old eyes do not see clearly."

Silence.

"You saw clearly," she whispered. She pinched her scar.

Matai Malolo drew a deep breath and fingered the gold coin that hung from the fiber around his neck. "I went to the bure and looked for the Princess, but she was not there."

Silence.

"You were alone with the Persian?"

A small voice peeped. "Yes."

"Did he hurt you?"

The silence spoke clearly.

"Did you go to your father?"

"No, Grandfather."

"He should be told."

Silence.

"I will go with you, lailai manumanu vuka."

"He does not care."

"You are his daughter."

"My father lay with my friend. She is ten. He would not find fault with a powerful man."

Siga heard Grandfather's sharp intake of breath. And felt his arm around her shoulders pulling her against his stout chest, but she was not afraid.

"I put the uvi that were strewn on the mat back into the overturned basket. But I did not come after you and ask questions, Granddaughter. For that I have levu madua, a great shame. You were right to come to me," he said.

Siga thought of Dede Nikua weighted by a great shroud of sadness. Her friend no longer went to the virgin pool, and she rarely smiled. Her words were soft and halting.

Where is the harmony sought by the Princess?

Matai Malolo kissed her forehead and sang the makawa song of the stars as he gently rocked her until she slept.

Bahram

When Bahram returned from a meeting with Lalai, he sat awhile on his throne outside his hut in the dark, Dedan beside him. When two of Bahram's former shipmates came by and asked to speak to him, the dog growled. Bahram silenced him with a cuff to the head and invited the sailors into his hut. Dedan left.

"We've been talking." Their eyes shifted everywhere but on Bahram's direct gaze. They glanced at each other and the dirt beneath their feet. The heavier one spoke first. "What's going on is..."

He was interrupted by the shorter of the two. "Look, we don't like the way the islanders are treated by some people."

"I have heard nothing." Bahram shrugged. "Who do you accuse?"

"We don't know who is guilty, or of what," quickly said the ship's cook. "But the natives used to trust us, and now they're afraid."

"I will have Nawfal investigate," said Bahram.

"Nawfal disappeared today, and we don't know what happened to him." The large sailor shifted from one foot to the other.

"Nawfal? Did he take inventory of the cargo going to Viti Levu this morning?"

"Yes." An awkward silence followed until it was broken by a confession. "Sir, the main thing is ...we are going back to Po-Li with Captain Safwan. William, too."

"Not because of any trouble here, you understand." The cook shrugged. "We miss our families."

"Is that all right with you?" The rower's huge hand tapped on the *bure* framework.

"Of course," said Bahram. He stood with hands on hips. "You are not slaves."

"No, of course not." The man looked down on him. There was nothing left to say.

The visitors left and Bahram returned to his throne where he collected his thoughts. When he saw Safwan leave the Bure Kalou, he followed. In the shadows of the forest, they made their plans.

CHAPTER SIXTY ONE

1950: The Storyteller

I place another branch in the flames ringed by stones, not for warmth on this tropical island, but to unite the Spirit Fire with The Story. "The past stretched generations before the years when Lapita first heard the stories. Our ancestors brought this flame from Viti Levu where it had been carried from islands in the northwest. From Vahilele it was carried to the east and beyond by a nomadic seafaring people centuries old. Along with the flame, secrets of healing were meticulously passed by every Bete to the spiritually gifted of the next generation. As a spiritual leader, Lapita's privileged priority kept a flame alive in her vale, a tradition preserved by generations. It was not a matter of warmth in a tropical setting. It was the tie to the past and to the future.

"Listen carefully now my children. Listen with your hearts."

The children draw closer and settle in for the end of the tale that never fails to enchant them. Darkness surrounds us.

650 A.D.
Lapita

When Captain Safwan left the two cousins at the Bure Kalou, previously unspoken thoughts became intense conversation, flames became a fire.

"Was it Bahram who brought you the news of Yaca's death?" Lapita asked one of the questions she had fearfully kept to herself.

"No, it was Lalai." Melane glanced at her. "Do you still care for Bahram?"

Lapita was startled by the question. "What? I never did. I felt obligated. Do you forget my crawling out of his bure? You were there."

"Do you fear him?"

Silence.

"Lapita. Answer me."

"I am surrounded by the makawa. Their strength is in my bones and in my mind." Lapita took a deep breath and considered the dark face that Tavale had loved over all others, a scarred face that had thinned and hardened under stress. Lapita had seen the pain in Melane's eyes when they had argued before. Now there was a softness, a shine to her skin, a subtle change seen on several maramas recently. "Melane, my fear is not for myself. I fear for your baby." Lapita did not tell her she suspected the father of the baby was Nawfal.

Melane's mouth turned up slightly. "Yes, the unborn royal. Nawfal told me before he left that Bahram will stop at nothing to take over Vahilele. That is why other sailors left. They have seen our people mistreated. We are captives on our own yanuyanu. Nawfal warned there is violence ahead."

"Melane, let us take this problem to the Phoenix. We need wisdom. I am not ready for war, but I know Bahram and Safwan will destroy our culture, one family at a time. It is time to confront them."

Lapita signaled to her helper. "Prepare yaqona, Siga."

The two cousins sat before the Spirit Fire and waited. Lapita occasionally added a twig. Melane squirmed.

"You talk too much." Lapita smiled. "How can I think with all your chatter?" She heard Melane snort, and she looked up.

"You act like a chief." Melane's eyes glittered in the firelight.

Lapita gestured for silence and returned her gaze to the fire before them. When Siga presented their bilos, Lapita said. "Sit outside to prevent intrusions. Vinaka."

Lapita blew on the surface of the kava and studied the pattern made by the bubbles. "Ahhhh. This is Tavale's baby." She closed her eyes, and a tear escaped. "He will be strong. Thanks be to Degei." She reached for Melane's hand, and in silence they drank their yaqona. Dedan whined from the shadows.

Before Melane left the temple, she told Lapita. "Nawfal asked me to go with him, but I refused. He did not want to be part of what is happening because it will cause great pain. Lapita, if you do not obey Bahram, there will be bloodshed. Your blood will spill first."

"But this is not about me."

"Yes it is," said Melane. "You are the last of the Goldens."

"No, I am not. I am the last of the royal family. You know my mother was Sawau."

"The Sawau tribe shares the heritage back to the first Golden on Viti Levu. So your mother, my aunt, was also a Golden. There are none without the blood of the Melanesian somewhere," said Melane.

"Yes, there is one. I am the last of the royal Lutunasobasoba Goldens. But Siga is the only one with a pure bloodline." Lapita motioned for Melane to wait while she went behind her privacy curtain. When Lapita returned, she handed Melane the gold coin necklace. "Nawfal wanted you to have this."

"It brings heartache. Nawfal loved Tavale. And he loves me, but I could not love him. He reminds me of the change that is taking over our island, the loss of our heritage."

"He meant this as a gift. Keep it to remember this time of conflict. And love."

"Gold brought evil to Vahilele."

"No. Men did." Lapita sighed deeply. "Nana Hewa said to secure Siga's future. For that I am ready. True faith requires obedience."

"But who should we obey?"

"We obey the Phoenix."

Melane retired to her hut. Lapita sat before the Spirit Fire until it was time for her to tend the fire at the new kiln built into a hillside so that the earth could provide insulation.

The kuro assortment was clustered on flat stones in the center, and grass and twigs piled on top, similar to the old pit kiln. A log fire around the lovo burned hot, and it was the duty of the craftswoman watching it to keep it fed. Lapita had arranged shifts for the pottery craftsman so there would be someone there all night and the next day to tend the blaze until the pottery cured. She put herself in the long five-hour period that preceded dawn.

Bahram

When Bahram returned to his hut after his meeting with Captain Safwan, Ghazi intercepted him. "One of our outriggers is missing. I think the Tongans stole it when they left this morning."

"If you remember, weeks ago I prophesied war with them."

"There is more bad news. Nawfal is missing. Along with Breaker and Turban and a large portion of our money. The natives aren't talking now, but I'll find out what happened."

"Brengsek! There are only two of us. Keep asking questions." Bahram searched the shadows around them. Ears seemed to be turned against them. "Ghazi, do not hurt anyone. This recent contract for more men was fortunate. But until they get here, we cannot hold back a mutiny."

Alone in his bure, Bahram fretted over his choices until the early morning hours when he finalized his plan. The islanders' main problem was lack of direction. The council had lost their enthusiasm for new ideas, and without guidance, the natives milled around like sheep without a shepherd.

It was time to assert new authority. He decided his course, and his first step would be a meeting with the elders to award them shares in the development of a red prawn industry. In exchange they would support Bahram's suggestion that he shoulder all responsibility for the future of Vahilele, protecting the elders from any criticism from their neighbors. Bahram would take the title of King before they understood the extent of his domination.

I must keep Lapita and her questions away from council meetings.

He awoke refreshed, confident in the future. His future. It was a busy morning. In exchange for a jeweled bracelet, Bahram presented a cargo to Captain Safwan for transport to Srivijaya. Lalai had been bribed with gold to package the prawns in earthenware shipping containers with a flame trademark, proof of the significance of the new King of Vahilele. Bahram would be that King soon after the Moors sailed.

CHAPTER SIXTY TWO

Lapita

Lapita's vigil of the flame came easily because she practiced it daily. In the darkest morning hours, Lapita heard the heavy tread of Matai Malolo approaching the kiln.

"May I speak, Princess?" He whispered.

"You are up early, Elder."

He came into the firelight. "I do not sleep well." Matai Malolo folded his hands and bowed his head, but not before Lapita saw the tears in his eyes.

"Are you in pain? I have herbs that can help. Is it your back, Matai Malolo?"

"No, Princess. Pain in my body I can endure. It is my lost soul that cries out."

"Sit by the flame, my friend."

Matai Malolo awkwardly settled his bulk on the nuku. "I have a knot that I fear I must cut away."

"Talk with me first. We will try to untangle this knot. Together."

"I made a promise to my daughter when she lay dying. I told her I would care for Siga. I have failed."

"I listen."

"Princess, I come to you to beg your forgiveness. I have been blind to an evil that crept upon our beaches and into our huts. This ca came so slowly. And it came with gifts." He removed his Sassanian coin and slung it into the fire. They watched the fiber cord burn. The image wearing the crown was distorted before embers hid the gold from view. He spoke again. "I am to blame. I encouraged the union between my daughter and Lalai because he was a Golden, as she was. My decision was based on the purity of the blood, not the best life for my daughter. Lalai made ca choices. I will not be part of this new freedom that tears down trust in our tokatoka."

"What do you wish to do, Elder?"

"I ask your permission to restore the cliff paintings. The past life of our tribe is drawn there and should not be lost."

"That is difficult work for a man of your age."

"I shall do it with pleasure. We must never again forget nanoa, our past."

"Is that the end of it, Elder Matai Malolo? Is that all you want?"

"Justice," he murmured.

"Elder. Do you have the courage to shed blood?"

There was a long silence. And he spoke the words louder. "I want justice."

Lapita regarded the indulged flesh of this man she had known forever. She had doubts of his commitment. Until he raised his tormented eyes to look into hers. And her kalou rejoiced at his intense conviction. Nui taka.

Before dawn, Lapita made her way to the lagoon. As she marched along she concentrated on the familiar, the feel of the cloth skirt that pulled against her knees and rubbed against her hips, her feet steady and sure along the path. The rhythm of her breath, the touch of a palm branch on her arm. Her thoughts tumbled like the waves that drew her closer. She sought guidance from the cagi. She prayed to touch the invisible current that held the wisdom of the Spirit.

Her choice was not one to be made as the daughter of a chief but as a spiritual leader, who felt the weight of ni mataka upon her shoulders. She was not distracted by the possible consequences of a poor decision she might make. She closed her eyes in complete surrender to the moment. To the confirmation of her path. Her heart sparked and the warmth spread into her shoulders and down her arms as she lifted them. She knew what she had to do. For her people.

Lapita stood on the baravi, greeting the morning sun with golden arms upraised. She did not hear Safwan approach. No, she felt his presence. After completing her prayer, she turned.

The captain stood at a respectful distance. "My lovely princess greets a lovely morning. This is a sight to remember."

"Some days the sky is so clear I imagine I see the land where the breezes begin."

"Maybe one day I will take you there."

"Vahilele is my place in The Story. Melane and her baby will travel far." She knew when she spoke, this would not be true. Each day, she became more intuitive, more receptive to unseen Truth.

"You are alone now." Safwan moved closer. He took her hand. "My lovely princess. Come with me." His tone was urgent. His eyes burned black. She felt nothing and looked out to sea again.

"My yalo tells me that you search for meaning. Do you look in a good place?"

"Your spirit? Sweet lady. Those are the words your late husband used. You know that I am a simple man with simple desires. I do not search for meaning in what I cannot see."

Lapita raised her eyes to examine his face. "That is sad. Do you fear that faith will take control of your simple life?"

Captain Safwan chuckled, looking away from Lapita, smoothing his beard.

Lapita decided to give him an opportunity to make a choice. "Before you leave, I will share a Vahilele legend." She removed her hand from his.

"Of course." His eyebrows elevated.

"Walk me home." She would honor their long friendship.

When they were seated and Siga served both a bilo of yaqona, Lapita began her tale about a Vahilele princess who refused the gift of a young royal from another island. Along with a proposal of marriage, he presented her with cooked red prawns, na ura. She was not impressed. She ordered him and his giant prawns tossed off the cliffs. The suitor survived to testify that the prawns came back to life when they fell into the pool at the base of the cliffs.

Lapita ended her story. "Forever after, the prawns are cultivated for the enjoyment of the Vahilele royal family and are protected by the Phoenix."

"Oh, yes, the firebird that rises from the ashes. An amusing ancient legend. The Egyptians, the Hindus, and the Arabs have variations of the same theme. I am glad to learn that the bird roosts in Vahilele."

"I did not expect your ridicule." She studied him closely. New furrows marked his handsome forehead, and puffy skin surrounded dark eyes that continually shifted their attention from one spot to another.

"Forgive me. I have much on my mind. Did you know that I will have extra passengers on board?" The captain stared into the dying embers.

Lapita silently studied the hot stones in front of her.

"Three of Bahram's sailors asked for portage to Po-Li," said Safwan. He looked around the vale.

Still no response.

"I am honored that you have the mortar and pestle I brought you years ago. Although it was nothing exotic like red prawns."

"It was a thoughtful gift, and I use it often."

"Do you think of me then, when you are grinding bananas, or whatever you do with it?"

She looked up at him. She no longer shared in his amusement with life. "Yes, sometimes I do."

"I suppose you told your husband it came from me."

"It was only one moment out of my youth. It had little significance. He had the rest of my life." Lapita paused. *He only had the rest of his short life, and he lived each moment with care.*

Safwan withdrew from under his collar a coconut fiber necklace with a single golden cowrie shell. "I still have your gift to me. I thought it significant."

Lapita considered her childish desire to please. She had grown in wisdom. She felt no need to respond.

Captain Safwan soon rose and bowed out of their strained conversation.

"I leave now," he said into the stony silence. "We will be loaded by nightfall and sail with the tide in the morning."

The differences in their spirit paths were clear, and Lapita felt a lighter burden when he left the Bure Kalou.

CHAPTER SIXTY THREE

Bahram

The soft morning breeze accompanied Bahram as he strutted past the enlarged fire pit, now about twelve feet in diameter and three feet deep. Heavy stones had been recently collected and piled on top of cold ashes. Two men squatted in the dirt, no doubt telling worn-out stories. He spoke to these islanders who rose when he approached. *Good. I am still revered by some.* They moved between him and the raised pit.

"A wedding tonight?" He twisted his hips, but the men did not respond. Bahram was undeterred. "Foreigners leave. I shall gather all Vahilele." He spread his arms and waved them back together into a circle. "Gather." He pointed in the direction of the sea, and used his hand to imitate the motion of waves. "Ship sails. We start over." He touched his own headband and sash. "All drink *yaqona*."

"Ah, *Yaqona*." The older man smiled and nodded.

"Two days." Bahram smiled.

"*Tu*." The younger man wiped his brow, calling attention to his scar and missing ear.

"Tell others," said Bahram, gesturing as though he were casting seeds. He strolled along, pleased with his communication success.

Coming toward him from the north were several natives, each carrying a large limestone rock, white streaked with dark gray.

"*Cola*. Where are you going?" Bahram asked.

"*Cola*." They smiled and nodded, standing to the side to let him pass. They did not release their burdens, nor did they answer him. He did not notice. He was headed to his favorite rampart.

From a twist in the path, Bahram could see the harbor, where the last of the cargo was being stowed upon board. In short sleeve tunics and narrow trousers tucked into heavy boots, Safwan's Moors struggled with barrels packed with red prawns. Their strenuous labor looked jerky in contrast to the fluid movements of Bahram's bare-chested island people who moved easily in patterned tapa cloth secured around the waist, bronzed muscles rippling in the sun.

Natives in loincloths waded through the surf with yams and bananas they offered to sailors. Young men with coconut fiber armbands observed the scene from double-hulled canoes, now a trademark of Vahilele. Around them were spectators making a holiday of this unusual event. There were few children old enough to splash without supervision in the baby blue water. Bahram recalled the lost generation especially vulnerable to the disease that surged through the island at the beginning of the year. *I shall build a new generation, starting with a son of my own.* His heart swelled with pride.

The confident future Kisra continued across the island through the breadfruit trees and palms to the western beach where a heron fished in the shallows. Its mate called out from above. Before Bahram continued up the trail, he slipped behind the vines where the prawns had been harvested from the pool. Lalai left a few to spawn a new crop. His plan was in motion.

Earlier in the year, the Persian thought his shipwreck on a barrier reef was a tragedy. Now, he recalled how his family in Merv perpetually prepared for another season or another war, and his young ideas and talents had been rejected. His new people of Vahilele gave him the recognition he deserved.

Here, Bahram was a magistrate in peace and soon to be a king honored almost as a god. His success would be legendary. He reasoned the loss of life had been minimal. From today's vantage point, it was obvious that his arrival on the island was fortuitous.

When the last of my comrades leave tomorrow, the tribe will believe that evil is gone and rely more heavily upon me. Out of chaos comes change. A mission I am eager to embrace.

His former mates were ready to make the journey north, but a life of grandeur appealed to Bahram. He would wear the mantle of a benevolent leader. *The Kisra of Vahilele.* He stood taller with good thoughts.

CHAPTER SIXTY FOUR

Lapita

On the way to the lagoon, Lapita stopped by the fire pit, the center of surging activity, and instructed that masawe roots be buried within the fire. She continued on for her afternoon walk on the shore between villages. Instinctively, she sought the coolness of the waves lapping her feet as a contrast to keep in mind later as her feet burned.

Captain Safwan intercepted her before she got to the fishing village. "We leave at sunrise." He wiped away beads of sweat with his forearm.

Lapita was engulfed by a sadness she could not alter. "You have had a difficult day?"

"Swabbing the decks, filling water jugs, the usual preparations for a sea voyage. The men are rested and ready to return home. We will take three of Bahram's men back with us."

"You told me." *Here stands a stranger, once an admired suitor before our paths separated.*

"Lapita, be wary of the Persian. He has plans for this island that will not prosper you. Your family's peaceable legacy is in jeopardy."

"Captain Owen Safwan, would you be in alliance with those plans?" Her heart ached.

"I would never hurt you. I am a merchant. I do not aspire to be a king of anything. Except my own bure." He stepped into her space, seawater washing over his boots, so close there was only a sliver of light between them. "Come with me. Be my love."

"I choose to stay," said Lapita with chin up, looking squarely into agate eyes. "I am married to my kai. Vahilele trusted wicked men from other places who trade their lives for wealth. We learned from our mistakes, and Degei will give us favor again. Through the Phoenix who roosts, as you say, on this yanuyanu."

She saw his face flush and his jaw move as though he would say something else but he nodded curtly and backed away. "Maybe next time," he said.

Before she returned to the Bure Kalou to prepare for her crucial spiritual passage, Lapita watched the sunset settle on a lagoon as smooth as satin. She prayed that knowledge give birth to wisdom, and she waited for a second confirmation of her difficult decision.

A hesitant shuffle caught her attention. She did not turn her head to recognize another's presence. She summoned her protective spirit and waited.

"Speak," she said.

"Bula, Princess."

"Bula."

"May I address you?" The hesitant vosa came from a man who stayed behind her.

"Yes."

"Trouble comes to Vahilele."

She remained silent, prepared to obey an omniscient presence.

He continued, "Our treasure of red prawns was stolen."

Lapita did not move. She moaned.

"Loaded on the Arab ship today," he said.

"You saw this yourself?" she asked.

"It was told to me."

"It is good you share this knowledge, but the tagane who witnessed this betrayal must come to me himself."

There was a brief pause before his revelation. "He stole them."

"Why?"

"For gold."

"And who is he?"

"Lalai. From the tokatoka of Elder Matai Malolo. He said he followed our master's orders."

"Bahram? The Persian?"

"Yes, Princess."

Several deep breaths calmed her soul. "You serve your yanuyanu well. Vinaka."

Footfalls receded. The last vestige of cloistered forgiveness seeped from her heart. Lalai. The ultimate betrayal by a parent. *Nana Hewa's prophecy is confirmed.*

Lapita looked to the baravi where she had just said her last goodbye to Safwan. The evidence of their footprints was already slipping away. Tears of disappointment prickled her eyelids, but she would not allow them to fall.

She stood kaukaua, arms stretched toward the heavens, and spoke into the wind. "Loose the power of the enemy's influence, great Degei. Bind this kai to Truth and to the purpose of our vanua's heartbeat."

CHAPTER SIXTY FIVE

1950: The Storyteller

As storyteller, I am the voice of Bahram, Lapita, Melane, Siga and the elders, but the children now prepare to act the parts of the villagers at the end of The Story. Dramatizing the ceremonies helps them to remember. This is a vital portion of tribal history, dependent upon them to pass down to the next generation so that their descendants preserve the heritage of our beautiful Vahilele.

The most able child blows the trumpet shell, an assignment of honor, as I open the scene. The crowd around our fire is large now, and very serious. Little Miss Red Shoes is awake and holding the hand of her friend, and our youngest boy is somber. He has not made a peep since the mention of Yaca's snake bite.

The grand finale begins.

650 A.D.

Bahram

The seafarers were aboard their ship, resting for an early departure the next day. The *Davui* called the villagers at dusk to gather near the firepit. Several musicians seated themselves together with their instruments of hardwood gongs and bamboo cane tubes. Bahram crossed the clearing and mingled with those in the back of the assembly responding to the beat of sticks on logs. Singing started spontaneously. The fire burned brightly before the crowd, highlighting the sweet smelling coconut oil worn by the meke dancers and others.

Bahram was drawn by earnest smiles into the beauty of movement. The graceful island women wore headpieces of white hibiscus for their meke and wove a charming tale with hands and arms, bare feet prancing in small steps, hips swaying under grass skirts. Each wore a salusalu, a single white shell peeping from the garlands of flowers that draped over bare breasts. Even though Bahram was still angry at Lapita's rejection, his body ached for her soft pleasure. She would be a fine queen for a new monarch.

The men wore bark skirts and leaf bracelets, and they performed an aggressive dance with spears, obsidian points decorated with blood-red flowers. One of them was Vunde Moto. The crowd chanted and cheered when spears were replaced with torches. Bahram could not understand a word of it, only the fervor. He looked around for the couple to be married.

Many of the village people sat to the side, but some stood to participate. Bahram did not see Lapita or Melane. As the crescendo built, four men with long poles approached the stone platform where the blaze had sizzled into embers. Leaves and vines were fastened to the tips of these poles, and the men used them to sweep the stones, clearing away burning sticks. The villagers gathered around those tending the fire. An enthusiastic chant turned to "O-vulo-vulo." A thick vine was dragged across the stones knocking a loose one to the side. "O-vulo-vulo." Deeper voices took on urgency. As it fell, sparks flew, but there were no flames. "O-vulo-vulo." Only the heat. Bahram took a position at the edge where the base of a tree fern lay across the pit. "O-vulo-vulo."

Over the heads of the shorter natives, he saw a gap opened by the community on the other side of the pit, making an aisle for a man trotting across the dark clearing, ushered by Melane. In the flickering torch light, Bahram was stunned when he saw Melane stop before the platform over the fire and offer a hand to Lapita. At the signal "Vuto-o," the tree fern was quickly removed, and Lapita stepped onto the hot rocks and circled around the edge of the pit. Her breasts were held flat with tight fabric, and her bald head glowed in the heat. The Persian was horrified.

"Stop! No, No!" He reached for her, but he was restrained by those close to him. "No!" He screamed. "Cease and desist! No!"

The costumed tribe loudly chanted over him. "O-vulo-vulo. O-vulo-vulo." Hands were elevated with voices. "O-vulo-vulo." One woman dropped to the sand, her fall softened by friendly support. She lay there twitching and ignored. The chant escalated with the rapid rhythm of sticks on logs. A young man with half an ear and a long scar on his face spun into frenzied dancing emboldened by shouts and moans. Lapita held arms upwards and cried out. *"Mana."* Frequent shrieks from the restless group alarmed Bahram.

"This is sorcery!" Bahram's shout was overwhelmed by the hysteria of the natives. "This is the sin of the archaic magi." He pushed his way to the boundary of the pit. Every arm Bahram touched, he shook with a direct order. "I command you! Abandon this evil from an ancient Druj."

Melane stood at the edge where she last held Lapita's hand. Next to her, Dedan paced, releasing an occasional howl. Eyes closed, Melane did not acknowledge Bahram's presence. The black circles of soot on her cheeks shone with tears. One hand cradled her womb and the other rose to beseech a dark heaven. She cried out, *"Mana.* Vahilele. *Mana."* The dog silently pressed close to her side. The hair on the back of his neck stood straight up.

Bahram resisted the urge to shake her. His eyes were on the fire pit.

Bundles of wet grass and leaves were thrown into the center of the stones where Lapita nobly paused within clouds of steam. The delirious mass chanted "*Bete. Bete. Bete. Bete.*" Until she descended from the hot platform. A village of helping hands steadied her. Elder Bati removed the band of dry fern leaves from around her ankle and buried it deeply in the coals with four clusters of roots. A necklace of snake vertebrae was lowered over her head. Siga hovered near her mistress, bearing a coconut cup. Melane supported Lapita whose body trembled, her eyes opaque, her jaw slack.

Bahram reached out, whimpering, "Oh, no. My lovely queen." Tears washed his cheeks. He gently brushed the stubble above the narrow coronet. A low growl came from the dog.

The natives close to them fell silent. Bahram felt an ominous warning he did not understand.

Melane shoved his arm away from Lapita who leaned heavily upon her. "Do not touch *Bete*." In the hush, Melane's words rang out. "Vahilele welcomes the Spirit of Degei." The crowd cheered.

Bahram ignored the glare of hatred directed toward him. This was his island. He raised his voice to be heard by his people. "I shall not allow this pagan worship." He turned to the tribe. "Go home, all of you. Go. My queen is injured." Flapping his hands, he succeeded in making some of the people move back. But they stared at him. "Go. The spectacle is over." The smiles disappeared in the sparse light of the torches. "There will be no more ceremonies. Never again."

Into the silence of the black shadows came a husky imitation of Lapita's voice. "*Mana.*" She clutched at her heart. "*Mana.*"

And a shout went up. "*Mana.*" Elder Dau screeched and tore his clothing. He snatched his Sassanian coin from his neck and pitched it into the fire. He pranced and chanted with the others. "*Mana. Mana.*"

Lapita called out clearly in deep tones. "*Mana*. Vahilele!"

And the people answered her, "*Mana*. Vahilele."

"*Vanua.*" She called out.

"*Vanua.*" They responded, over and over. "*Vanua. Vanua.*"

Siga lifted *Yaqona* to Lapita's parched lips, and she drank, her eyelids fluttering. Bahram hunched away, past the revelers who threw offerings of kava, coconut, dalo and wreaths of flowers into the coals. "*Mana. Vahilele. Vanua. Vahilele.*" The blaze grew higher.

Bahram ripped aside the masi cloth over his doorway and felt his way to his bed. He kicked off his sandals, slinging them into a dark corner. The pagan thumping from the Na Koro clearing accompanied the throb of firelight squeezing through his bamboo blinds and into his head. He closed the shutters to block out the light that reminded him of the earlier scene, his queen's beauty desecrated by foolish allegiance to voodoo nonsense. Eyes narrowed, lips tight, drawing deep breaths through flared nostrils, the Persian flung himself into his sleeping net and crossed his arms tightly over his chest.

"That brengsek woman!"

"I should leave." *Go to the lagoon and create a commotion until someone comes from the ship.* He paused to consider a retreat. *Probably the sailors wouldn't hear me. The ship is too far away, and the waves and wind would suffocate my shouts.*

The crew had gone back and forth to the shore on small boats, not risking damage from the interior reef. Those boats were now stowed on ship. Bahram reviewed his options.

I could steal a canoe.

No. He couldn't leave now. Not while his dreams of masterdom were still possible. He understood why the natives would cling to their past. It had taken him a long time to cast off his own history. He struggled to reach for a new beginning while holding on to the familiar. Until he turned loose of one of them, he was suspended between.

Besides, I shall not quit in shame again.

CHAPTER SIXTY SIX

Lapita

As the natives retired the firelight for the light of a full moon, Lapita motioned Siga to carry a torch from the sevusevu for their walk to her vale. Siga silently lit the path for her mistress and awaited instructions.

Lapita pulled aside the white panel. "Put flame to these embers. I will listen for those who come."

Siga obeyed quickly, then shrank into a dark corner. Lapita sat with palms resting on her knees. She knew her empathetic cupbearer trembled with a vision of conflict. She could not yet help her.

Soon afterwards, the three elders stood outside and requested entrance. At Lapita's direction, Siga opened the white veil over the doorway and escorted them to the circle of bright Light. She waited outside for new instructions.

Bati, Matai Malolo, and Dau seated themselves across from Lapita, and the four of them sat in silence for a long time before the new Bete opened the discussion.

"You may share your thoughts," said Lapita.

"Bete, we await your wise instruction." Bati spoke for all.

"I will make an offering to purify our vanua, our sacred land," she said.

"Yes, Bete," said the elders in unison.

"You will take part. It is time to put flesh to our vows. Matai Malolo, bring Lalai to the headland at the highest rise of the moon."

"And if he will not come?"

"This is also your trial. You must bring him before you can be forgiven your failure as a watchman. I will not close my eyes as you have done to the treason against Vahilele. There is only one consequence for this treachery. The laws are clear." The Bete's eyes held his, until Matai Malolo solemnly nodded. "You may go now."

While Matai Malolo left the hut, Bati and Dau sat motionless, eyes riveted on the flames in front of them, bodies shiny with perspiration.

Finally Lapita addressed them. "There is no redemption for those who glorify their own lives at the expense of others. They worship themselves although none of them has ever made a dalo seed or a banana tree. None of them has brought the rain or sun upon command. I have sorrow for their choices. But they are freely made."

She paused to allow them time to speak. They had no words to offer a High Priestess.

"Dau, get three kaukaua Vahilele warriors from your farming village to bring Ghazi to the headland. Do not involve the foreign workers."

"You can depend on me." Dau promised.

"Bati, the judgment must be carried out by all. We will need a supply of firewood on the cliff. See that three stakes are set deeply into the ground. It is time to gather the makawa."

Bati gave Dau a sidelong glance. "Three?"

"Yes, we must be prepared for judgment after questions and testimonies."

"Understood." Bati removed his coin necklace and tossed it into the fire as though it were already hot to the touch.

The Bete acknowledged his commitment. "It is time."

The men left to accomplish their assignments, and Lapita continued to sit, whispering to the flame. *Phoenix Spirit, make my thoughts pure, my words true, and my deeds wise. Fill this servant with your power over evil.*

Immersed in ritual, she did not hear when Melane's slender frame eased beside her. Together they prepared themselves for the difficult task of leadership, intoning an ancient prayer. "Spririt of Phoenix, speak to me. Live in my heart and give me strength to obey." Melane repeated the words but her eyes were on Lapita.

Dedan kept guard with Siga as the hours passed and the moon rose.

"I know the toll the firewalking ceremony placed on you." Melane spoke quietly, as a sister. "I held your quivering body and worried about each breath you took before your eyes found my face. Lapita, perhaps we need to wait until tomorrow. It will not be wise to fail."

The Bete straightened up and sighed.

"The moon is high. It is time."

Moving up the path to the headland, fueled by determination, confident this was necessary, Lapita set her feet on the path, and they performed with muscle memory, her way lit by the torch that Siga carried. Her head and heart communed with the supernatural. *Hear me, Spirit. I am unworthy of your attention. You know all I need. You know where I walk before I step. Guide me so I do not fall.*

The elders were ahead of them, the tribe behind. Few words were spoken. All knew the somber consequences of this mission. All knew their responsibilities on Vahilele's highest rock, not used for a judgment in decades. It was time. What was the charge? Who was guilty? The clearing at the top of the cliff was trampled down, barren, like the souls sacrificed here.

Her father had never convened a trial. If he had inherited the hot-steel backbone of her grandfather, he would not have hesitated. A judgment would have been quicker, a tokatoka saved from extinction. Gone was the chance to save a remnant of the Golden race, but their culture could be preserved if action was swift now. The makawa whispered in her heart. *The power of mana is only as strong as your belief in it. Stand kaukaua.*

CHAPTER SIXTY SEVEN

Lapita

Elder Bati's shout commanded attention. "Truth gives us Faith! Faith gives us power! Let the power of the Phoenix move among us!"

The natives hushed each other and gathered closer when their royal leader softly sought spiritual guidance. She set the tone for a righteous trial. "Spirit, give us wisdom."

Surrounded by her restless tribe on Vahilele's bald rocky pinnacle, Lapita confronted their prisoners, one in island sulu and one in trousers. Princess Lapita motioned to the sailor secured by burly warriors. "Let this man step forward and speak for himself. Everyone else be silent." The islanders stilled. "Ghazi, sailor from the *Nabataea*, what can you tell us about the death of Prince Tavale?"

Defiantly Ghazi regarded those who surrounded him. He tried to shake off their grip but they stood firm until Princess Lapita nodded. When released, he rolled his thick shoulders and his coin necklace glimmered in the torch light. He took a step toward the front of the crowd. Tagane stepped with him on both sides. Ghazi pleaded with open palms. "It was an accident, and I knew that nobody would understand."

Princess Lapita questioned him. "How could an accident cause a man to lose both arms?"

"Tavale was showing my friend how to navigate by the stars, and a shark unsettled the canoe. Nawfal told me that Tavale fell into the lagoon and cried out for help. Nawfal swung his adze at the shark. When Tavale went under, Nawfal knew nothing could be done in the dark. He saw only a great fin moving away. My mate was so troubled, I knew he told the truth."

Princess Lapita asked, "Why is this the first time I hear this story?"

"Nawfal knew you would not believe him. He swore me to secrecy, and I agreed that it was better to keep silent. I was afraid for my mate. This trial proves the need for that concern." Ghazi glared at the men around him. "Nawfal felt guilty, but it was an accident."

"Nawfal is not here. Who can speak for him?" Lapita turned to the faces of the crowd softly lit by moonlight and torches.

Silence. A few looked at their neighbors. Who would stand up for a mua?

Princess Lapita ascended the natural rock risers to look out over her kai. Elder Dau accompanied her with a torch. Melane and Siga remained at the edge of the gathering, flanked by Elder Matai Malolo and Elder Bati.

The Princess turned to this congregation of witnesses and jury. "Did anyone here ever see Nawfal use an adze?"

There were murmurs of disbelief. Nawfal was a woodworker. One of the canoe makers testified that Nawfal was proficient with an axe. Someone else shouted out that Nawfal carried only a small knife.

When Lapita pointed at Lalai, Vunde Moto shone a torch light on his face. Lalai stiffened between the two islanders who held tightly to his arms, and his eyes blinked rapidly until he looked downward.

"Lalai, look at me."

He obeyed. Princess Lapita could see his mouth quivering, his chest heaving. She regretted that his daughter had to witness such weakness.

"Lalai. What do you know about Prince Tavale's death?"

"Nothing, Princess. I was nowhere around."

"That is not true." A deep strong voice came from the crowd. Rangi stepped forward. "It is time to recognize lies. Too long we have politely turned our heads." He addressed the crowd. "It is time to confront the evil among us before we are a part of it."

There were a few who voiced support in the dark, and Rangi continued. "I found Prince Tavale on the shore, washed up on the beach like a dead fish, not the brilliant man that he was, not the fearless leader who loved this island and our people. We should all be ashamed we ignored the manner of his passing and did not ask questions. Only Princess Lapita showed bravery. We men were weak and stood by. We didn't want to cause trouble. How did our silence keep us from trouble? I do not know who killed our Prince, but I want to find out. I want justice." He turned to Lapita amid murmurs of assent from those around him.

"Princess, I left Prince Tavale's body for my son to guard while I went for help. Lalai was nearby, but I didn't think to ask him the reason. I told him to go after somebody with a litter and bring help back to the beach. I didn't tell him who was hurt. I couldn't bring myself to say, 'The Prince is dead.'" A sob escaped from the innermost part of his soul. He quit speaking.

Lapita could hear other wails and cries of "Ratu Tavale." It was like reliving her brother's funeral. The wound had not healed. Grief had not been forgotten. His people lifted up his memory. Lapita's eyes burned and her throat closed. She struggled to maintain control. She concentrated on the power of the Phoenix. She could not do this alone.

A voice from the crowd questioned loudly. "Lalai came to my hut for the litter and told me it was for Prince Tavale. How did he know that?"

Siga

Siga knew then what she had tried to push from her mind the night outside the Bure Kalou. Her father had come to kill the Princess but changed his mind. *Why? Where does evil begin and where does it end?* At that moment Lalai's eyes found hers. He looked totally beaten, filled with shame, devoid of hope. He hung his head, and her heart broke for him. There were not enough tears to make up for what he had done and the punishment he would have to bear.

Lalai cried out. "I didn't hurt Prince Tavale. I swear it! I didn't hurt anybody."

From the darkness, somebody shouted, "You showed the mua the sacred prawns."

Somebody else voiced the accusation. "You're a thief!"

"I showed Captain Safwan. I didn't steal them."

Another voice shouted. "You helped them load the ship." The crowd pressed together, closer to the accused, anger sparking action.

Princess Lapita commanded, "Enough!" She stood with staff raised until the tribe calmed. "The investigation before the tribe is the death of Prince Tavale." The elders nodded. "Lalai. How did you know Tavale's body was on the beach?"

Lalai's chest quaked, and he made high-pitched whining noises, rocking from one foot to the other. "Ghazi told me he wanted to talk to Tavale. I knew that anybody that talked to Ghazi got hurt, but I couldn't refuse or he would hurt me."

"Are you telling us that Ghazi told you to bring Prince Tavale to the beach?"

Siga held her breath.

Lalai nodded.

"Speak up!" The Bete's voice dominated the hush like a thunderclap.

"Yes, he made me deliver a message to the Prince."

"What did you tell him?"

"I told Tavale that Rangi's son and his friend damaged a canoe they had stolen."

"And then what happened?"

"When we got to the beach, Ghazi was crouched down by a canoe. Tavale didn't know who it was. When Tavale got close, Ghazi jumped up and hit him with his adze. They fought, but Tavale was not armed. When Tavale lay still, Ghazi put his body in the canoe and launched it into the lagoon. I was hiding in a grove of mangrove trees and saw Ghazi return by himself."

Lapita interrupted. "Did you do nothing to protect your Prince?"

Lalai hung his head. "I saw what Ghazi did to that dog when he tried to protect Tavale. I didn't want to be slashed. I waited, thinking I might see the Prince swimming ashore. But I didn't. I waited and waited. Until the tide brought in his body, and when I saw him, I was afraid. I didn't know what to do. You have to believe me, Princess. I never would have hurt him." He glanced at his daughter.

A thought moved Siga's lips without sound. *That's a lie. You would have killed Princess Lapita if you had not heard me call her name.* Lalai took a heavy breath and watched Siga. Her eyes held his. She straightened her shoulders and moved purposefully to the front of the crowd. She must show herself loyal to the Princess. To the Truth.

Suddenly Lalai shook off the lax grip of his captors, and ran towards the cliff where rocks met sky. With one screech, he snatched destiny into his own hands, but he leaped into a dark sky that refused to hold him.

A collective gasp ran through the crowd. Those closest to Siga reached out to stop her run toward the cliff. At the edge, Rangi firmly grasped her arm. "It's for the best, little one. He knew what his portion of justice would be." He gently turned her away, into the arms of Matai Malolo.

Her grandfather said, "For the first time in Lalai's life he acted honorably, and he will carry that one moment into the beyond. Let us go home, manumanu vuka."

"No, Grandfather. It is not finished."

More torches were lit, and the cliff was bright.

Princess Lapita stood kaukaua.

"I have one more mystery to be solved, Ghazi. Who killed our Yaca, Prince Waitu Buka? Who killed Maca Matanitu? Their deaths must be investigated."

The tribe stirred with the question. "Yaca was killed?" A woman wailed and the crowd pressed closer to the three empty stakes, only one accused.

"I don't know," said Ghazi. He snorted. "I understood it was an accident. It wasn't me. A child killer is a monster."

"I agree, and I intend to administer justice." The Princess struck the ground with her staff. "Why should we believe you? We just heard you deny that you killed Prince Tavale. But witnesses cast doubt on your testimony. Why should we believe you are innocent of another killing? Perhaps two more."

Vunde Moto stepped forward. "I heard Ghazi talking to Abu. He said that a woman as sick as Maca Matanitu didn't deserve to live and eat the food of workers. He said, 'That's the way of nature'." Murmurs arose in several areas. The people pressed forward, sticks in hand.

"Silence!" Lapita motioned to the agitated crowd and everyone halted. "Ghazi. Is that true? Did you say that?"

Ghazi's shaky voice sought to deflect blame. It was obvious he would lie to protect himself.

"That isn't what I meant. I said it was merciful that she died. I didn't know somebody killed her. Maybe it was Abu. He was sick in the head."

Princess Lapita's expression hardened, and she thrust the point of her staff in his direction. His guards tied Ghazi's hands and feet to a stake. The mua gasped when the first islander threw a piece of kindling at his feet. His heavy eyelids widened with terror when a second man stepped forward and put a stick on top of the other. Ghazi's mouth trembled, and he shouted, "I didn't kill a baby."

"Why did you kill Prince Tavale?" Lapita's measured tones escalated.

"I hated him," Ghazi's voice broke. He paused and got control of himself. Staring at the crowd, he bellowed. "He acted like he was better than me, but he was just another savage. Like the rest of you! Look at yourselves! Barbarians!"

A nearly silent void held only the whisper of a slight breeze rustling the dry bushes that struggled to live on barren soil. Ghazi pleaded. "Don't you see? Tavale was a stumbling block. If it weren't for Bahram's ideas and the hard work that us sailors did, you would still be burning corpses and repairing huts." He whimpered. "I beg you for mercy. This is inhuman."

Siga hung her head. She could not look at the accused, but her Princess spoke forcefully into the shadows. "Ghazi, intruder from faraway lands, if you are guilty of this treachery against our royal Prince, on the island that gave you refuge, you are not worthy to be buried among us. Your spirit must wander until you find another home."

Ghazi's tears flowed freely. "Bahram is going to be the King of Vahilele, and new workers will eat your food and take your women. You will be treated like the lazy animals you are." He shouted as loud as he could, "He will be here soon and punish you all! You deserve hell on earth!"

His voice rose into a scream that ascended to the heavens. Siga looked up. Above them the stars remained in position, the full moon shone steadily, unchanged.

The royal leader lifted her staff and declared. "The just shall live by faith. The just are obedient. Peace comes from a clear conscience as the Phoenix spirit moves among us." Her words struck a deafening silence. Her staff struck the rampart where she stood.

The crowd moved as one, multiple brown and black and golden hands, throwing firewood at Ghazi's feet until the pile reached his knees. Siga felt the emotional significance of the moment, as though the entire kai hovered at the edge of an abyss awaiting to hear a final judgment. She could barely breathe.

Ghazi squirmed and cried out, "Where's Nawfal? Ask him who killed Yaca. Ask him whose baby Melane now carries."

Princess Lapita did not acknowledge the prisoner's accusation. She chose to proceed with law and order. "Kai Vahilele, those who are certain of this man's guilt, show your decision with a stone."

Whack.

Ghazi shrieked when the first rock hit, and the blood trickled down his cheek. Then a second, and a third. Shouts from an angry crowd overwhelmed his cries of pain and fear.

Whack. Whack.

All he could do was scream, as one rock after another pelted him, the fury of the crowd releasing judgment. Siga watched her people demanding revenge for their Prince. At the edge of the gathering, Melane held tightly to Dedan who howled his own outrage. As a united kai, they found Ghazi guilty of murder, and their laws justified punishing his violence with a retribution he did not survive.

Then came a fearful calm. Lapita took the torch closest to her and held it high, illuminating the upturned faces around her. "Man's judgment is finished here. Return to your huts and never mention this man's name. He is already forgotten."

Queen Lapita, granddaughter of a wise Ratu, stepped off her rampart. Elder Bati took the torch from her hands and lit the kindling piled at the feet of Ghazi who never felt the fire that consumed him. Dust to ashes.

CHAPTER SIXTY EIGHT

Bahram

Cocooned by the dense forest surrounding Na Koro, Bahram could not see the execution blaze on the headland. He did notice when the drums ceased, and it became quieter in the village, all the better to concentrate on his current plan of action. Should he flee or fight? He decided he would persevere like all true conquerors, like Caesar, to better impress the Emperor of Srivijaya. A victory was sweeter when the obstacles were high. His ideas for the future took on a light of their own and burned brightly in his mind. His anger subsided, and he drifted off to sleep. Until first light when Elder Dau awakened him.

"The *Bete* wants to see you."

The memory of last night's fire-walking ceremony intruded once again, and he determined to discuss it with Lapita. Never would he call her 'Bete.' He was still appalled that she had shaven her head. He remembered her fragrant hair, its silky touch, an essential part of her womanly beauty. He dressed and hurried to their meeting, an unusual request so personal that Bahram hoped for some apology.

Shortly after dawn, it seemed like Vahilele's normal early morning. When he crossed the common grounds where the usual number of islanders chatted, he saw Matai Malolo heading toward the shore with tools that indicated he might work on the cliff painting they had discussed. The chubby elder would probably paint for an hour, then sit and talk the rest of the day. Now that the sailors were gone, Bahram would have to address the lazy attitudes of the tribe.

Dau had directed him to take a path that wound through the forested headland on the northwestern side of the island. Alert for spider webs strung between trees, Bahram walked steadily up the rocky incline. He was aware of the dangers hidden within the lush foliage of this island paradise, and he kept a vigilant eye on this unfamiliar fork in the trail as it curved ahead. He could not imagine why Dau sent him this way. It was a primitive narrow path although he saw signs of recent use. Perhaps the Princess was luring him to her secret love nest. The thought was energizing. Her submission was paramount, but he had many items on his agenda.

Elder Dau told him Ghazi and Lalai had investigated Bati's rumor of a clandestine gathering on the cliff last night, but Bahram had not heard their report. He would look into it later.

He needed to choose replacements for Abu and Nawfal. Gold coins and an elevated position would bind loyalty. *Rangi might be receptive to new ideas. I don't trust Vunde Moto. The expression on his face is always hateful, no doubt relating to Abu's treatment of his daughter, but I can't chance a mutiny.*

When he was crowned King, or Kisra, Bahram would arrange for guards to protect members of the council. Too many villagers had spears, and anger might lead to violence. The multiple-pronged sticks were needed to fish, but each hut should have a spear limit.

He still considered using an individual poll tax for domination as the Arabs had done in his country, and the Romans before that. His neck bent, eyes on the path, he pondered the repercussions of another regulation on people already restless over the current laws. If he could distract them with a slight increase in their share of trade profit, they would not grumble about a higher tax that he would explain paid for food for the less fortunate.

His brain churned with his largest problem of exporting vesi and sandalwood off the island. He would have a monopoly on the industry if he could contract with a merchant ship to make regular stops at Vahilele. No other country in Srivijaya offered these exports. Then he recalled today's new venture! Captain Safwan's ship would be coming back for prawns on a regular schedule. He already had the problem solved! Bahram's feet barely grazed the earth as he pranced up the hill.

The ocean breeze grew stronger as he climbed. Below him he saw palm-thatched roofs of dwellings nestled in the dense vegetation. Beyond the crystal blue lagoon, the lateen mainsail on the Arab ship was made ready to unfurl at open sea. They weighed anchor and glided through the waves, sailors with long oars prepared to push off the coral that earlier this year destroyed the *Nabataea*. He would have to enlarge the channel through the reef to allow passage of larger merchant ships into the lagoon. And he must consider that entertaining Safwan too often might be detrimental to his relationship with Lapita. It was time to marry the woman. She needed a King to control her, and she needed the distraction of children, the King's offspring. Bahram was eager to embrace his destiny.

Through crowded shrubs, he emerged atop a cliff in a clearing of trampled grass. He abruptly halted. Near an ancient altar of red rocks, a blackened skull perched on a tall post amid warm ashes. Bahram quickly strode to the sacrifice and without hesitation plucked the hot skull from the pole and threw it off the cliff, into the wind. He was prepared to destroy every pagan altar on the island. This worship of *Kalou-vu* would end when he became King. The Persian watched the abomination fall soundlessly into the crash of the waves a hundred feet below, past the petroglyph ledge where he glimpsed Matai Malolo at work. Bahram could teach his people a softer religion. He would outlaw violence and make laws promoting good thoughts, good words and good deeds.

He moved more slowly up the steeper rocks, but his mind raced with his list of plans for a new agenda. Over the shifting wind that was picking up momentum, Bahram heard the warbling of perfect notes. He rounded the trailhead, his feet scrambling up the sandy soil to behold the magnificent cerulean union of sea and sky. His breath came ragged and sharp. Below him four herons took flight, headed east. His attention was drawn to the right, up natural rock risers layered to the pinnacle. There he found Lapita, arms upraised, caroling like a songbird with magical notes of ancient lyrics. Her regal stature took away what breath he had left after the steep climb.

Her back was toward him. If Lapita heard his footsteps, she did not acknowledge them. Aware she balanced precariously upon the edge of eternity, he scuffed the toe of his dusty sandal in the loose stones to give her warning. *She must be treated carefully when submerged in a trance.* He moved slowly. He did not want to startle his queen into falling from her rampart. He was certain that when she had children, she would have less inclination to indulge her preoccupation with spirits and ritual. Sons and daughters belong to the present.

He admired his choice with pride. Adorned with multiple bracelets of scarlet feathers, her hands were upraised to the azure canopy, her silhouette accentuated by the golden silk worn tightly around her waist. Feathers crested a headdress constructed with her own shiny black tresses streaming over her bare back down to her firm rounded hips. Lush curves increased his appetite. Although he anticipated no resistance, he was prepared to give a lesson in submission, right here. Right now. He had been faithful on this island, and she had an unspoken contract with her debt to him. Last night's humiliation in front of his people had a price. After she acknowledged their proper relationship, he would gift her a ruby and emerald bracelet as a promise of a secure future. Later today he would tame the elders.

Bahram was annoyed that Lapita did not immediately turn to welcome his presence. Beyond her, black clouds amassed on the horizon and rolled toward them, blocking out the sun.

The ethereal solo drew to a close. Lapita slowly lowered her arms and stepped back from the ledge, head bowed, motionless except for her skirt whipping around her bare legs. Bahram confidently ascended toward her, his passion escalating in the presence of the storm bearing down upon them.

As she turned, he did not take heed that glassy eyes hid a portal to her soul. He saw only her full red lips, her long sweet neck above her silky breasts. He purposefully advanced with words of tenderness to culminate his intention to subdue this island. This was the perfect time, the perfect place to begin his supremacy. They were alone. This would be a productive meeting.

CHAPTER SIXTY NINE

Siga

Siga had waited for hours, huddled with the Tanoa in her hands as her mistress had instructed. Her eyes had witnessed unspeakable justice meted out to the accused who had no defense but their own selfishness. She had spent the night here on the rampart with the Bete who insisted Melane rest for the benefit of the child she carried. Elder Bati had escorted the widow to her home.

At dawn Melane returned for the vigil, with a jug of wai and tapioca for Siga.

"Kana, little one. This will be a longer day than the long night passed. Our Bete needs you kaukaua."

"Where is Dedan? We might need his sharp teeth."

"He is out of harm's way, with Savu." Melane's hand went to the pouch tied at her waist. "But I am prepared to protect the Bete from evil."

Siga regarded her mistress's rigid back and doubted a lowly servant such as herself could help a goddess. She hoped Melane would be able. The Bete, the High Priestess, perched on the edge of a cliff, and Siga was too far away to rescue her if she lost her footing. But Siga knew how to follow instructions, even those she did not understand.

She had learned that wisdom came with patience.

And so she waited.

For patience.
For wisdom.
For the unknown.

Siga heard Bahram yell from the path, "Lapita! Where are you?"

And she watched her mistress stand firm, chanting into the cagi. Over the cliff edge, Siga saw the Moors' ship sailing west past the northern tip of the yanuyanu, headed to Viti Levu and beyond to a world she would never see. Siga was not moved. Everything worthwhile to her was in Vahilele. Immediately after the fire-walking ceremony, the yalewa felt an intense force rolling in waves from the Bete. Throughout the following darkness, Siga had reflected in wonderment about the honor she had, to carry the spiritual vestments of the Priestess, to prepare her food, to care for her personally. Siga did not doubt she would dedicate her life to serving Queen Lapita, the wisest of women. Her nana would be proud of her.

Yet Siga trembled occasionally, and Melane stilled her fear with a pat on the arm and a gracious smile. "It is difficult to wait for the unknown." The intensifying cagi whipped Melane's words, but not her fierce countenance.

"Lapita!" Bahram was closer.

Siga heard footsteps on the trail nearby. Once she had been in awe of the Persian, but now she knew he elevated himself by stepping on others. He accused everyone else of being selfish while he himself was molded by greed. His spirit was hollow.

She was pulled to the back of their shelter by Melane where they crouched, leaving the Bete alone to confront this powerful man. Siga thought to wriggle away, but Melane held her tightly and shook her head. "Wait," she whispered.

Siga wondered what magic Melane possessed to give her such calmness in the face of danger. In this shelter clawed into rock under the roots of scrub brush, Melane and Siga were protected from the wind of the approaching storm. But her mistress was out in the open.

Then Bahram was in sight. They saw him reach out to Queen Lapita, his back to the cave. When Siga tried to crawl forward again, Melane restrained her with a firm hand on her shoulder. *Why is she holding me back? I know my duty.*

The Bete turned to face Bahram who had locked his grasp on her elbow.

Siga could not wait any longer. Her Priestess needed assistance. She jerked away from Melane and stepped out on the ledge, feeling the tempest of the cagi swirl her hair and pepper her face with grit. From the face of her mistress, the fearsome eyes of the Phoenix blazed like torches of fire. Siga gasped. Her blood ran cold with this otherworldly emotion. Bahram hesitated. He called out, "Lapita! It's me." He reached out to pull the Phoenix closer.

"Sega! Sega!" The Bete's devoted servant shouted and rushed toward the edge of the cliff to grab this man who was twice her size. Siga's fingers seized his tunic, and she tugged. The Persian's swift blow knocked her to the ground. All she held was his sash. When she scrambled up again, she was jostled by Melane who was right behind her.

Bahram turned his back to Siga and shook the Phoenix whose feathered arms did not resist. He ignored Melane pulling at his shoulder. Too late, Bahram recoiled from the glint of the obsidian blade she held. Her right hand swung across his chest to punch his abdomen and rip upward to pierce his heart. He bellowed.

"Ignorant savage! You will be punished for this!" He thrust Melane away and clutched the flow of blood that dripped from his chest. He crumpled as his vitality drained away. "Lapita," he whimpered. "Find Ghazi!" He fell to his knees, stunned.

Hearing Melane's wounded spirit howl, "Yaca, Yaca," Siga inhaled her heartache. Momentarily, she was rooted to the spot. Melane jerked the coin necklace from Bahram's neck, her scarred face twisted in hatred. From the waistband of her sulu she pulled another coin still on its cord and waved them before his face. Siga could not move. Never before had she felt so strongly the emotions of another.

Bahram's eyes widened. He looked into Melane's fury, without defense. "The skull. Ghazi." He moaned in recognition of the ultimate Truth, his own impending death.

He tried to stand but staggered backwards into Siga. She faltered and sank to the rock edge, grasping at air.

On her knees behind Bahram, Siga wavered on the precipice, looking straight down, releasing the sash to be carried off by the wind like a trophy. She scrabbled in the thin dirt to secure a desperate hold on a solitary shrub. Melane shoved the Persian. Siga felt his weight roll over her when his feet lost touch with rock, but she held fast to the roots deeply anchored for many storms. A curse was torn from Bahram's black soul and snatched by the wind. His shriek lingered until it was overpowered in the foam bubbling over the white rocks below.

Siga the child wailed for herself, for her father, for all those who were lost forever. Siga the cupbearer shuddered and prayed until she felt kaukaua. Her aching fingers held tight to the shrub. She was afraid to attempt a climb to safety. Queen Lapita and Melane stood above her, their attention riveted out to sea. It was not over yet.

The Bete approached her rampart again, still controlled by the Phoenix. With chest heaving, Melane watched her new Priestess silently. Then she raised the bloody knife, and threw it out over the wasa. As the wailing storm approached, Siga hunkered down on the ledge, at the feet of these great women.

The Phoenix raised her wings toward the sea to chant over the roar of thunder. "*Uradamudamu. Na Ura. Na Ura. Liwa.*" The sound of the words came like a voice of a multitude. "*Calevu ni yalo. Liwa.*" A mighty wind blew. Lightning struck. The trader ship fleeing the island foundered and splintered upon the distant coral reef, spilling Captain Owen Safwan and his comrades into the angry waves. Siga watched the ship break apart. No doubt the island's red prawns would roll under the sea billows to remain the secret treasure of Vahilele. No doubt Dakawaqua was there as well.

Then Melane's hand was in front of her, offering assistance to higher ground. As soon as Siga's feet were firmly on the rock, she reached out to grab Queen Lapita's skirt. The Phoenix backed away from the precipice onto rocks stained in blood, but it was the Bete who stared into the rain that commenced with huge intermittent drops. Siga guided her into the shelter. The transformation had weakened the High Priestess, and her body convulsed in response. Siga was kaukaua. She held her mistress, absorbed her pain and crooned to her spirit.

Over the Bete's head, Siga saw Melane brave the wind and the rain to offer her own pronouncement. "Vahilele! Vanua!" Two Sassanian coins followed the flight of their owners. Melane screamed into the east wind. "Mana! The power of the Phoenix is True and has come to pass! Forever mana!" Her shriek could be heard over the roar of the storm. Then she fell to her knees and sobbed. Siga went out to lead her, too, into the ganilau, the dry cave of an eagle. Through sheets of rain, she could see they were not alone on the headland. The makawa closely surrounded them in spirit. And beyond them were the flesh and blood mataqali who now turned to make their way down the slippery trail to their old way of life. *Mana Vahilele.*

In their somber shelter on the rampart, royalty waited out the downpour. Siga served them Yaqona to commemorate the rebirth of a legend. The Bete's limp arm with feather bracelets embraced her brother's wife wherein hope nurtured infant royal blood. "We will make a new story out of old for an eternal bond is fused between us." Her voice was raspy, her spirit spent. But the heart of Vahilele's new Priestess had triumphed in this war of cultures.

Melane and Lapita slept soundly that night, with Siga on guard. And in the morning, she brushed their hair and fetched water for them. She was honored to assist a renewed royal family.

The sun chased the storm from the sky, and the colors of a new day drenched them in the harmony of the yanuyanu. Against the golden glow from the east, the Bete of Vahilele stood kaukaua and raised her arms. She hoarsely decreed: "As one moon eases into another, our people loose the evil influence of those who transgressed against Vahilele. We shall live in peace."

Siga looked forward to telling her friends they could all have new hope in a peaceful future. But how could she explain to them the intense emotions rolling off Queen Lapita when she was in a trance? They would not understand that Siga actually shared what the Bete felt. And she experienced Melane's heartache as though it were her own. These trusts might be too large to reveal.

CHAPTER SEVENTY

Lapita: The Legend

The next day Lapita was still wobbly on her feet, still deeply saddened, her soul still bruised by the loss of men she once respected, but she was on the beach with her morning greeting to the Tiki god. Her lagoon did not have the remnants of the shipwreck, but Rangi had reported several barrels had washed upon the northern shore.

When Lapita returned to the Bure Kalou, Siga had papaya juice and eggs ready to serve her mistress.

"You take good care of me, dear one."

Praise from the Bete was always special. Siga beamed.

"Let us seek your grandfather to share vosa. He is surely concerned about your sorrow. We can comfort each other."

"Grandfather is at the cliff paintings already. He is anxious to remove any trace of the foreigners."

"Will you walk with me? I am unsure of my footing on that slippery ledge."

"We will go together."

Lapita's heartbeat quickened when she saw the pride flash in Siga's face. Her little one must learn that a fine line hovers between self worth and pride.

When they reached the rocks that elevated the path to the paintings, Lapita stepped aside to give her lead to Siga.

Spray from the surf spewed high on the rocks, and Siga led the way holding Lapita's hand over the most narrow passage. The Bete briefly stopped and looked down at the rocky coast where Vunde Moto directed the salvage from the shipwreck. No lives had been spared.

Deliberately directing her thoughts to a new day, Lapita continued to the petroglyphs where Matai Malolo was indeed busy. The design that Bahram had instructed him to add was chipped away entirely, and the elder was diligently deepening the rust color of the tribal history.

Queen Lapita's nod and smile approved his labors, more visible as the sun climbed higher to dispel shadows. Later in the day, the westerly glare would make work on the cliff paintings impossible. "Manumanu vuka, your grandfather undertakes an important challenge."

"Why do you say that, Bete?"

"These paintings are our past and the light to our future."

Matai Malolo nodded. He held aloft the paint jug with a narrow top and damudamu flame design and pointed at the petroglyphs with his brush. "As they fade, they are forgotten. We must preserve them."

"Generations ago," said Lapita, "Someone fulfilled his destiny by drawing out the description of the lives of his kai. He did not know who would see these cliffs. All he knew was that it was important to tell people not yet born about the stewards of Vahilele in his time. We do not know who did this, and we do not know when, but we do know that long ago there was somebody like you and me who felt the sun, and heard the waves, and enjoyed their families. No doubt he lived, and loved, and lost like we do. Maybe it was more than one artist, and they reached forward to show us all that we experience is not new on this island."

"Then we are not special," said Siga.

"We are indeed special. Everyone who looks at these paintings can see behind them through the tunnel of the past and know, like this artist, they have a purpose. Like I had when our culture was weak, and too many of our people were willing to ignore evil. I was here to stand kaukaua."

"It is good that you did," Matai Malolo said. "I am glad that my wife and daughter were not here to see how our decision to influence a bloodline was pride not wisdom."

"It is true that your interference did not justify the outcome, but Siga is the last Golden, and we must go forward from here."

"My purpose is to stay with you," interrupted Siga. "I know that I know."

Matai Malolo chuckled.

"Indeed, without your vigilance I might have fallen off the cliff in my trance." Lapita gazed fondly at her young helper who had become wiser in the past six months. Her destiny was yet to be revealed. A young woman with many moons ahead. "Our journey is not yet behind us. We will go one day at a time and help each other."

"Melane's baby will need my care," said Siga.

"He will. A strong king needs a kaukaua beginning. You will be there."

"And you also?" Siga's face showed concern.

I must be truthful with her. "As you get stronger, I will get weaker. That is the way," whispered Lapita.

"And I am getting weaker as you distract me." Matai Malolo's voice was gruff. "Will you maramas leave me to my purpose?"

Siga's laughter sparkled in the glimmer of ocean spray against the rocks at their feet.

As Siga led Lapita back over the ledge, she inquired, "Are there not many questions that have no answer, Bete?"

"What do you think about, little one?"

"When we first walked here, you answered my question but I did not know it. Then you showed me how wisdom does not depend on an opinion."

Lapita paused. "It is important to ask questions." She did not understand the direction of Siga's vosa.

Siga pulled something out of the pouch around her waist and offered it to Lapita.

When Lapita saw the button in her palm, she inhaled sharply. She recognized Bahram's souvenir from his

Captain's shirt. "There is a story here. Tell me, manumanu vuka."

"I found this in the basket of marama cloths that Maca Matanitu had in her vale. I think it is Saca's button, but I forgot to tell you. Is it important, Bete?"

"No longer. You are right to show it to me. This was the knowledge I wanted the council to investigate. If we had asked questions, you would have brought this to me earlier, but knowledge is not wisdom. Evidence that Bahram was in the widow's hut confirms the guilt I suspected, but it would not have changed the minds of the elders. Wisdom surrounds us, but it takes an open mind to receive it." Lapita touched the cheek of the earnest face before her. "Dear one, I have faith that you will grow in wisdom."

On the way back to the village, Siga and Lapita had to cross the freshwater brook that streamed from the mouth of a cave entrance. Savu Vatu and Dede Nikua sat on opposite sides. While Dede silently watched, Savu skipped stones across the top of the water, and Dedan chased them.

Siga paused on the path.

"Go. Join your friends," said Lapita. "It is time to live your youth."

Siga blinked several times. "Bete, can you see that Dede is surrounded by a gray smoke?"

Lapita looked across the stream at the young woman whose innocence had been disrupted by abuse, but the Bete did not see a manifestation of grief. "Manumanu vuka, you have the special vision that your grandmother had. I pray you use it wisely."

Savu waved.

Siga waved back but hestitated. "Bete, do you remember your promise to take me to the headland?"

"Yes, dear one, but your first visit there was much different than I had proposed."

"Savu and Dede have never climbed that high. Can we take them now? In daylight?"

"An excellent idea. Ask them to join us."

Siga ran forward a few steps and paused again. "Are you able?"

"A good question. Today I am. I shall start now, and your young legs can overtake me along the way." Lapita's joy in her island home carried her across the beach and into the forest where the serenade of island birds perfected the harmony she savored.

Soon she heard the rapid footsteps and hushed excitement of the children, soon to be leaders of ni mataka.

Near the top of the promontory, the path split. One fork wound around the face of the cliff to enter the largest cave, the burial place of Vahilele royalty.

Her father wanted to gather a tribe of peacekeepers, but he couldn't see they were useless without power. Lapita took the fork that climbed higher, leading to the rampart touching wind and sky. The children's laughter stilled.

My grandfather, Tui Waitu, came here for inspiration, a fearsome place. I rejected its responsibility as long as I could. Now I embrace the wisdom of strength for I have learned the bond to Truth is only as powerful as the belief in it.

Without vosa, Lapita and the children walked the flat rock where hundreds of voices had shouted for justice, where hundreds of stones had enforced tribal laws, where judgment was finalized by the entire tribe, together. The Bete's thoughts drew the conclusion that the next generation must learn the true past so failures are not repeated.

The foolish route must be marked so a wise route can be followed.

All that remained of the execution was a pile of ashes in line with two empty stakes. Lapita would let Siga choose what she wanted to tell her friends. Solemnly, they walked past the judgment site and up to the rampart on the cliff above.

Siga lifted her chin into the breeze, her dark hair flowing behind her, eyes on the horizon. Savu picked up a red feather caught in a crevice and gave it to Dede. They exchanged glances and joined hands. Witnessing that moment, the Bete knew the loneliness that Siga would experience. Her friends were bound to each other. Siga had moved out of their orbit like a special star with her own destiny. A fearsome place to be.

"Look to the east, young ones. Every morning Tiki rises over the water, bringing light and warmth to his children on Vahilele. Every sunrise is a new beginning."

1950: The Storyteller

I end The Story in Lapita's role as Bete, with arms raised. "We shall live in peace!" Then I lower my arms. "And all the children of Vahilele say 'Amen'."

The children shout, "Amen."

The crowd which has gradually swelled to listen to this historic ending applauds vigorously. Some of the teenagers wear the T-shirts of western influence. There are many who wear the tapa sheaths that still have a world-wide renown. We are gathered on the slope of a Vahilele village near the ruins of a pottery kiln in the shadows of a Methodist Church.

In this twentieth century, a full moon rises as it always has, a beacon mocking man's eternal quest for power. Queen Lapita's people are gone, the Golden race moved on. To keep man's peace, our tribe long ago accepted the religion of a different culture. But our hearts are bound to eternal Truth.

Amen. May it be so.

GLOSSARY OF FIJIAN WORDS

adi	honorific prefix (woman)
balavu	tall
baravi	shore
bilo	cup
bokola	prisoner of war
boso	boss
buka	fire
bula; bula!	life, healthy; hello
bulikula	deep golden cowry pendant
bure	sleeping area
ca	bad, evil
cagi	wind (n), air
cakacaka	work
calevu ni yalo	path of the spirit
cauravou	youth, bachelor
cola	hello/good morning/life
Dakuwaqa	sea monster/godlike shark
dalo	taro, edible root
damudamu	red
Davui	rare Triton Trumpet Shell
Degei	god in form of snake who lived in Fiji mtns

ganilau	eagle cave
gata	snake, sharp
ika	fish (n)
kai	people
kakana	food
kalou	Spirit
Kalou-vu	deified ancestor, #1 god spoke to Bete, priest
kaukaua	strong
kaukaumata	omen
kerekere	please
koli	dog
koro	village
kura	juice from Noni fruit
kuro	pot
lailai	small
levu	big, great
lialia	stupid, crazy
liwa	blow (wind)
lovo	earth oven
lululu	handshake
maca	dry, empty (in ceremony)
madua	ashamed, bashful, shy
makawa	ancient
mana	power
manumanu vuka	bird (literally animal that flies)
marama	lady
marau	happy, satisfied
masi	tapa (bark cloth)
mataqali	clan of more than one family
meke	ceremonial dance
moce	goodnight/goodbye
moto	spear

mua	sailor
nana	mother
nanoa	yesterday
na ura	prawns
Ni bula	good day
Ni mataka	tomorrow
Nokonoko	ironwood
nuku	sand
nui taka	hope
peipei	baby
Ratu	title of nobility
rarawa	unhappiness, sorrow
reguregu	ceremony leading up to burial
saka	sir, madam
salusalu	necklace of parts of banana tree or single white shell
sega	no
sevusevu	formal presentation (usually kava)
sulu	skirt of varying lengths for men and women
tabu	forbidden
tabua	sperm whale's tooth
tagane	male
Tanoa	kava bowl
tapaka	tobacco
taro-va!	Stop!
tatau	tatoo
tavioka	tapioca, cassava
tik hai gone	fine child
tokatoka	family unit, sub clan
totoka	pretty, handsome
tovolea mada	go ahead and try
tu	stand

Tui	title when prefixed to a name
turaga	chief, gentleman
turaga ni vanua	chief of the land
uvi	yam
uradamudamu	red prawn
vaka malua	go slowly
vale	house, building
vanua	land, place
veiwali	laugh
vinaka	thank you
vohosia	sorry
vosa	speak, talk, word, language
vuka	fly (v)
vulo-vulo	ceremonial phrase
wai	freshwater
wai donu	ceremonial phrase
walu	like a spanish mackeral
wasa	ocean, sea
yalewa	young woman
yalo	soul
yanuyanu	island
Yaqona	kava beverage

ABOUT THE AUTHOR

Georgia Ruth Wilson lives in the storied gold-mining foothills of North Carolina where she records and shares the folklore of neighbors, many of whom can trace their roots back to England, Wales, Scotland and Ireland. Published fiction and nonfiction references are available on her website georgiaruthwrites.us along with a special page regarding the development of this historical fiction tale in the faraway Fiji Islands.